THE SOUTHERN DEVIL

THE SOUTHERN DEVIL

DIANE WHITESIDE

BRAVA

KENSINGTON PUBLISHING CORP.
http://www.kensingtonbooks.com

For Elaine, Julie, and Katherine—
Thank you for your patience and wisdom.

Prologue

Memphis, June 1872

Jessamyn Tyler Evans stared out of the carriage windows eagerly, drinking in every precious sight of Somerset Hall, starting with the high turrets of the private racetrack her father had built as a wedding present for his wife, Sophia. The stream rippled past, marking Somerset Hall's boundary. Then the tall oak tree appeared, whose branches she'd climbed so often to look for the Evans family, her parents' best friends and her two childhood playmates, Morgan and Cyrus Evans. No matter what joys and pains were associated with those men as adults, including marriage and widowhood, her childhood memories were only of innocent fun.

Jessamyn leaned out farther, almost rocking Richard Burke's carriage in her eagerness. It was ten years since she'd lived here and nine years since her father had sold it, but it still looked much the same as she remembered.

The great paddocks, the core of Somerset Hall's fame, were green and lush and blessed with dozens of beautiful horses. Colts tossed up their heads as she drove past, then raced, showing they were faster than the sedate carriage. One fine yearling was a chestnut, running with the wind for pure joy. She craned her neck to see him as the road turned, then sat back, tears filling her eyes. He was the image of old Aldebaran, her father's favorite stallion.

Yellow roses still covered the small chapel. She'd woven a garland of them and cast them into the stream with a prayer for forgiveness, when she'd learned of her mother's death.

The large main house was built of red brick, with white columns and porticos, in a comfortable Palladian style. Shutters were open onto the east loggia, showing a glimpse of the library where Cyrus had studied for West Point, while a bronze statue of Hermes was still slightly askew amid a fountain. She and Morgan had knocked him sideways during a particularly lively game of bat and ball.

Dear God, how happy they'd all been.

The carriage drew up in front and Aristotle, her family's old houseman, handed her down. Behind him, Richard Burke— Somerset Hall's present owner—smiled warmly at her from the top of the stairs, where he stood next to his sister.

The hair on the back of her neck promptly stood up. She'd thought Eliza Burke, Richard's spinster sister, had invited her here for answers about Somerset Hall's origins. Why the devil would Richard Burke, who had little use for women, be charming to her, a penniless widow?

Setting aside her suspicions for the moment, she smiled at her old friend. "Thank you, Aristotle. How are you doing now?"

His face split into a grin. "Very well, Miss Jessamyn. Very well indeed." He patted her hand and rolled his eyes toward his current employer, silently warning her as he had so many times before.

She squeezed his hand briefly in thanks and turned to her host and hostess, who'd come down the stairs to greet her.

"Mrs. Evans, what a great honor to have you here," Mr. Burke rumbled.

"Please take a drink with us," his sister added.

"Thank you." She curtsied slightly and followed them to the side porch, her father's favorite place for entertaining in hot weather. The rose garden reached the house here, curved around a delicate fountain that her parents had brought back from Italy on their honeymoon. Her bedroom had over-looked this part of the garden, with its path to the family's stables.

Cassiopeia, Aristotle's wife and her old family cook, brought out the serving tray, which offered lemonade and an array of treats that would have tempted even the Widow of Windsor. Jessamyn managed a private smile for Cassiopeia, with a silent promise of a later meeting as old friends. Cassiopeia silently retreated to a servant's correct distance beside her husband and Jessamyn was left with the Burkes' unfamiliar company.

She sighed softly and sipped her lemonade. Richard Burke was talking about a rich miner from Colorado, a topic that interested Jessamyn very little. Was that Socrates, her old groom and Aristotle's brother, coming down the path from the sta-bles? His uncle had been Somerset Hall's chief groom for decades and Father had brought Socrates here when she was six.

Why was Socrates so concerned to see her now? Didn't he realize she'd meet all of them later, as befitted their friend-ship?

"So you see what a good deal it is," Burke finished.

She frowned internally and reviewed his last few sen-tences. Something about a land deal in Denver? "Excuse me, sir, but I'm afraid I don't quite understand."

"Charlie Jones . . ."

Charlie Jones? Her cousin Charlie? Every nerve inside Jessamyn came screaming to life. If her Sharps carbine had been handy, she'd have loaded, cocked, and aimed it.

"Will trade me a thousand acres of prime Colorado rail-road right-of-way for Somerset Hall. He plans to remove the top two or three stallions, plus a handful of mares, before fever season starts and send the rest of the horses to the knackers."

Kill the horses? Kill her beloved horses, the fabled gold of Somerset Hall? Take just enough horses to be able to re-create

Somerset Hall's fabled stud farm and do it before yellow jack struck again at high summer, as it had for the past five years, turning Memphis into a panicked, dying city. That way, a few grooms could handle the horses and the knackers would take the risk of entering Memphis during a time of year when half of the population dropped dead of high fever, yellow skin, and screaming insanity.

Damn Charlie to hell. The cheap bastard wanted Somerset Hall and its stud book enough that he'd actually made an excellent offer for it. Her father had done whatever it took during the War to keep the horses alive—smuggled feed in from St. Louis, hidden the horses, even paid bribes to both sides of the conflict. Jessamyn pressed her lips firmly together and waited for her host to finish speaking.

"All you have to do is sign here. I'll give you five hundred dollars for your right of first refusal." He produced a traveling desk and opened the leather portfolio within, revealing a sheaf of papers.

No wonder Burke hadn't sold many of the horses since the War if this was how he conducted business. She'd also heard rumors that he'd overpriced them, even for their legendary quality.

Jessamyn's decision had been made the instant she'd heard who wanted to buy the land. She would crawl through hell on broken glass before she let Cousin Charlie set foot on Somerset Hall. "No."

Burke straightened, papers in hand. His sister stared at Jessamyn from just behind him, with a bottle of ink in her hand. "What do you mean—no?"

She folded her hands in her lap, lifted her chin, and straightened her spine even further. Her former governess, Miss Ramsay, the daughter of a British naval officer, would have been proud, especially since Jessamyn's heart was leaping inside her chest like a rabbit trying to escape a fox. Aristotle, Cassiopeia, and Socrates were lined up on the brick walkway like an honor guard, hopeful and desperate.

"According to the terms of sale when you bought Somerset Hall, I have six months to match the sum you paid my father. Until then, you cannot accept any other offer."

Burke's jaw dropped and he slammed his fist down on the table, making it shake. "You're only a penniless Army widow! Where the devil will you obtain enough money?"

Jessamyn tilted her chin slightly higher, thinking of the lawyer's letter inside her purse. "In Colorado, sir."

By way of Kansas City, if I can just find a husband first.

And claim the gold in Colorado without seeing Morgan again . . .

Chapter One

Tennessee, December 1863

Twenty-one-year-old Lieutenant Morgan Evans stepped inside the tiny, ice-cold room in the small farmhouse and waited, his weary eyes running affectionately over General Nathan Bedford Forrest. He'd just returned from a week in the river bottoms and knew he looked it; not that clothing mattered much when his weapons were ready to fight. By the other window, the few tattered, starving staff members worked hard at a dinner table. His old friend Rafe was sitting at a lady's dressing table before a glass mirror, scratching diligently in a ledger.

The scene was a very far cry from the comforts of a few months ago, when they'd been part of a major Confederate army. But the self-taught Forrest had whipped too many enemies too easily, then told the truth once too often about his superiors' lack of fighting ability. He'd finally gained an independent command only by going to a place long overrun by the Federals, with only three hundred of his handpicked men and no supplies whatsoever, told to enlist whatever men he could find.

Morgan tried to think up a joke to tell on Rafe about sitting at a lady's dressing table. After two years with these men, there was very little they hadn't shared and jokes they hadn't played on each other.

He'd followed Forrest for almost two years, ever since the icy night in February 1862 when only Forrest had the courage to find a way out of Fort Donelson before it surrendered to U. S. Grant. Forrest had been given permission to take command of every man willing to ride with him that night, no matter who their original units and commanders were.

Morgan and his father, John, had simply glanced at each other, then gathered their horses when they heard the offer to follow Forrest. They hadn't needed to talk to know that escape was more honorable—and more militarily useful—than surrender. Three years in the Arizona Territory, after Morgan's mother and brothers had died of yellow jack, had stripped them of sentimentality about warfare, even as it had honed their skills as cavalrymen. Later the same night, they'd happily realized they followed a genius when Forrest forded a river running chest deep in ice, without disaster. Two months later, John Evans died at the Hornet's Nest during the Battle of Shiloh, leaving Morgan an orphan. He'd had little time to mourn, since Forrest had a way of keeping his picked men more than busy.

Morgan's stomach rumbled and tried to glue itself to his backbone, an occurrence of such frequency over the past year that he ignored it. He'd eaten far better when he'd ridden with Cochise as a teenager.

Forrest dismissed the fellow he'd been talking to and Morgan quickly snapped a salute. "Evans, sir, reporting as ordered."

"Evening, Evans. How many were you able to bring in?" At the moment, Forrest looked and acted like a mild-mannered country farmer. But in battle, he became an incendiary fiend, the image of how he fought.

"Forty-eight, sir. Three of them had rifles, one with some ammunition." He'd spent a week gathering those recruits at various hidden rendezvous, all in dense thickets along river bottoms during the cold, wet December. Still, it was easier work than hunting with the Apaches.

"Very good." Forrest considered him, and Morgan straightened further, frowning slightly. He could do nothing about his muddy, threadbare, much-darned clothing. But he could keep his carriage erect, as befitted an Evans of Longacres, as his father had taught him.

"I understand you have some connections in Memphis, Evans," Forrest observed.

Inside, Morgan came on alert. Forrest had made a fortune in Memphis and his family lived there. Why was he asking Morgan, whose ties were much thinner? "Heyward Tyler, my father's Harvard roommate, lives there with his family. Our families visited regularly throughout my childhood. Also, my father and I visited him for a few days in '61 during our return from Arizona, before we enlisted."

"Would he welcome you again?"

"I'm sure he would, sir." Morgan's eyes narrowed as he watched the general. "He served on General Albert Sidney Johnston's staff but was invalided out just before Shiloh."

"Ah!" Forrest pounced on the tidbit. "So if you arrived on his doorstep, he would shelter you."

What the hell? If Uncle Heyward sheltered a spy and the Federals caught him, he'd be sent to prison, which would be very dangerous to his health. But Uncle Heyward was a patriot so he should still be willing to serve the Confederacy, no matter what the risks.

"Why, sir?" He'd have to take Uncle Heyward into his confidence and negotiating Jessamyn's high standards of honor could be tricky. He had no notion of how she'd regard spying, even though she must support the Confederacy as her father's daughter.

"You're no doubt aware that the Federals are hunting us."

Morgan snorted and answered just as laconically. "Occasionally, sir." Their eyes met—half-smiling, half-weary, a look born of too many years spent riding into battle together.

Then Forrest bent over a map and beckoned Morgan to join him. "They've sent many hounds after us." His finger stabbed at far too many roads. "But the most important is Grierson."

Grierson, the bastard who diverted us from relieving Vicksburg? He'd be the devil to fool and he's a veritable bull-dog in a fight. With only three hundred trained men and no real weaponry to protect two thousand raw recruits, Forrest's new command could be trampled by Grierson in an afternoon.

Faces flashed before Morgan's eyes, of the men and boys he'd just brought in, who'd come to protect their homes from the Federals, who trusted what he'd told them of Forrest. Faces of the men he'd fought beside for almost two years, the few remaining of those who'd slipped past Federals and swum icy rivers to escape Fort Donelson. His hands clenched and unclenched.

Forrest nodded, watching Morgan. "Lucky for us, they're keeping him close to Memphis. I need someone who isn't known as mine, but can find out where and when Grierson will move. As soon as you learn, bring me word."

Morgan snapped to attention. He'd do his damnedest to keep his friends alive. "Yes, sir!"

"Good." Forrest continued more slowly. "There's a paid informant in Memphis, whom Richmond is mighty fond of. But most of his material tastes more like sugar water to me than military information. If you think his findings are useful, then they may be worth listening to."

The younger man nodded, smiling grimly. A double agent? Or someone selling worthless information for as much gold as he could find? In either case, better men had died because of such Judases. His lip curled.

"If you think he's trying to set traps for better men, then kill the rat."

Morgan smiled unpleasantly, remembering the lessons he'd learned from the Apaches. Some of those tricks would be a fitting punishment for such a traitor. "It would be a pleasure, sir."

He saluted and was excused, plans churning in his head. Most of them centered on talking to Heyward and Jessamyn as quickly as possibly, especially his old friend. Jessamyn would know exactly how to discover the information he needed. She'd always been the thinker in the trio of friends he'd grown up with: Jessamyn Tyler, his cousin Cyrus Evans, and himself. He'd had the inspirations and Cyrus had been the rock, who'd planned and carried things through.

But he had to be careful of Jessamyn's sense of honor and trust, which her damn mother had ripped apart ten years ago. The old growl boiled up in his chest, as it always did when he remembered those two days.

He'd been eleven years old and Cyrus was sixteen, but Jessamyn was only seven when they sailed north from New Orleans on that fancy riverboat in 1853. Everyone aboard was listening to Matthias Forsythe, a California millionaire, talk about how he'd made his fortune. Heyward and Sophia Tyler, John and Rosalie Evans, and all the other first-class passengers had been transfixed by the bastard's stories. But as befitted children, Morgan, Cyrus, and Jessamyn sat in chairs against the walls and simply watched the grown-ups.

"You see, gentlemen, it was easy. I picked up that miner's claim as payment for an unpaid bill at my general store. They struck gold there a week later and matters have gone very well since!" He had laughed and held up his hands, covered with flashing rings. *"I have an instinct for succeeding in get-rich-quick schemes!"*

"What's Aunt Sophia looking at?" Morgan had whispered, *referring to Jessamyn's mother.* Both families considered each other kissing kin: not blood relatives, but dear enough to be kissed on both cheeks and treated in all ways like blood kin. *"He's not talking about any fun stuff, like fighting Indians."*

"She's looking at his jewelry," Jessamyn had said, terror and cynicism creeping into her voice, a note Morgan had never heard from her before. "It's the same look Uncle James gets when he sees a pigeon at the racetrack, ripe for the plucking."

He'd swung around to stare at her and met Cyrus's eyes. His elder cousin had looked equally appalled.

The next day there'd been a great uproar when Heyward Tyler found his wife's bed empty just before dawn, upon his return after an all-night poker game. A search of the entire riverboat established that she and Forsythe had disembarked, just in time to catch a riverboat bound for New Orleans.

Jessamyn's face had turned gray when she'd heard and yet seemed alarmingly unsurprised. Morgan and Cyrus had drawn together on each side of her in a silent vow of protection.

After that, she'd quietly accepted only those with the highest standards of personal honor and duty into her circle of friends.

He hadn't seen Heyward or Jessamyn since '61. He'd barely spoken to her the two days he'd visited here in '61, since most of that time had been spent talking politics with her father. She'd been a fifteen-year-old girl then, still looking more like the tomboy he'd grown up with than a Southern belle.

If he'd been looking for her now, he'd have sought the scrawny eleven-year-old tomboy he'd ridden with, fished with, and laughed with. She also had one of the cleverest minds he'd ever had the pleasure of dueling with. The three of them—himself, Jessamyn, and ever-reliable Cyrus, his orphaned cousin—had been inseparable whenever they'd been in the same town. None of them had ever been able to lie to each other.

They'd parted only when Morgan's father obtained an appointment for Cyrus to West Point, as the simplest way to provide for him. Cyrus's rigid sense of honor had been honed there to an almost ridiculous edge. Why, he'd refused to resign his commission when Mississippi seceded. Instead he'd stayed in the Federal army and was now fighting for the Union in the East.

But Jessamyn was Southern born and bred. She'd understand and help him.

Morgan rode quietly into Memphis just before sundown, his worn clothing and tired mare confirming him as the country bumpkin his forged pass proclaimed. He dodged clumps of suspicious, well-armed Federals, saying he was looking for a midwife for his pregnant wife—and tried not to think about how recently they'd eaten and he hadn't.

He eventually eased his way into the expensive old residential district above the river, where bankers and cotton brokers had once strutted and preened as they watched fortunes pass up and down the Mississippi. Here, the Tyler mansion glimmered in the brief December twilight, its white columns shining like a beacon above the street. A green wreath hung on the front door. Smoke rose from a back chimney, carrying the delicious scents of pork and other culinary delights.

Morgan's heart shifted and his breath caught. It looked exactly as Longacres had at Christmas, while his mother was still alive before dying of yellow jack.

A riverboat's whistle sounded, snapping his head up and around toward the Mississippi River, less than a mile away. There a troopship headed north, full of convalescent Federal soldiers.

Morgan cast a last, wary glance around from under his wide-brimmed hat. A soft cluck to his patient mare set her into motion again and they headed for the kitchen door, not the front door which he'd always used before. He tied the mare's reins to a hitching post, promising her treats soon. If he knew anything about the Tyler household—and Jessamyn in particular—there'd be delicacies for visiting horses. After all, they were famous for "the gold of Somerset Hall," their famous horses that Heyward had somehow managed to keep together despite every calamity and thieving hand that war could bring.

After a wry glance at himself in the window—he certainly didn't look like an Evans of Longacres anymore—he knocked politely on the door, straw hat in hand.

The tiny cook opened the door, immaculately clean from her crisp white apron to the brilliant scarlet turban atop her head.

He sniffed deeply, unable to help himself. Heaven on earth rolled through his nose in the glorious aromas of baking bread and roast chicken.

She started to give him a commonplace greeting but her golden eyes narrowed, looking even more feline in her petite face. He recognized her immediately from his visit in '61: Cassiopeia, the houseman's wife.

Horror crossed her face but she quickly wiped it clean. What the hell was wrong?

Then she pursed her lips, looking him over like a particularly scrawny turkey. That was more what he'd expected—a grudging acceptance, as befitted a country bumpkin begging a meal in the city.

She held the door open and stepped back, her voice as neutral as if she were announcing the time of day. "Best come in, Mr. Evans."

Morgan scraped the mud off his boots and stepped inside. A slender young woman was silhouetted against the hallway leading into the main rooms.

His heart thumped and his body came alert at the sight of those curves. He blinked, quickly adjusting to the dimmer light indoors.

"Morgan?" It was Jessamyn's lilting voice but grown almost husky for a woman. She came all the way into the warm kitchen, holding out her hands to him. "What on earth are you doing here? Is anything wrong?"

For a moment he stopped breathing but her looks were as burned into his brain as her form was stamped on his eyes.

Good God, what a beauty she'd become at seventeen. She looked like the goddess Diana, slender and curved, lithe enough to leap into the saddle and ride all day. Her face was a pure oval, with great green eyes, a straight little nose, and curving red lips, surrounded by raven black hair that he longed to thread his fingers through. Or better still, cup her face in his hands and kiss her until her heart was pounding as hard as his was now.

For the first time, his father's endless lectures on the duty to sire sons, as the Evans of Longacres, sounded like an enjoyable task.

He'd never had many opportunities to be around women. He'd left for Arizona before he'd investigated the opportunities in the slave quarters. There, his father had made him swear not to sire a half-breed as the price for riding with Cochise, which his fifteen-year-old self had thought an easy price to pay. Oh, he had some experience with the gentler sex—he'd tumbled two since the War started, both of whom had made it more than clear they were available. But Jessamyn was different. Their fathers had been classmates at Harvard and their marriage was first planned above Jessamyn's cradle. All he had to do now was name the day and she'd be his.

"Jessamyn," he began and looked at her more closely. She was thin, too thin even for her. Her mouth was drawn tightly and her eyes were red. She seemed to be on a knife edge of control and physical strain.

He started again. "Jessamyn, honey. It's good to see you but . . ." He tried to think of a polite question.

Her green eyes were enormous, as they roamed over him. "Are you well? Are you wounded? Have you eaten? Did you ride here? How is your horse?"

Morgan chuckled, a little hoarsely, but mightily glad to see some return to normalcy. Trust Jessamyn to be concerned about his mount. "I'm well and my horse is well enough. There's nothing wrong with Honey that a few days' rest won't cure." He didn't add he'd stolen her on his way into town from a man who'd been mistreating her.

Jessamyn pulled herself together with a visible effort. "I'll dish you up a big bowl of soup and some fresh bread, plus some milk, since you must be very hungry."

Morgan's stomach rumbled an enthusiastic assent and he seated himself on a bench at the battered table, while she prepared the simple meal with the ease of someone who'd spent a great deal of time in this room. The house was oddly quiet, too, as if it lacked the dozen or more house servants it had always known before.

As promised, his bowl was filled to nearly overflowing, while an entire loaf of bread was placed on the table beside a crock of butter and a pitcher of milk. He swallowed hard and rubbed his hands on his legs, trying not to grab anything on the table. He said a simple prayer, and a moment later, his mouth was too fully occupied to form words.

"You're probably wondering why I'm here," he offered when his first rush had slowed.

She smiled slightly but didn't deny it.

"I knew Uncle Heyward had been invalided out. But Great-Aunt Eulalia's latest letter strongly suggested I visit him soon. So I begged leave to visit." Morgan crossed his fingers under the table that Jessamyn wouldn't suspect he wasn't telling her the whole truth.

Her face turned white and shuttered. "Great-Aunt Eulalia is, as always, entirely correct. Would you like some honey with your bread?"

He glanced at her sideways. But if Uncle Heyward's health was a difficult topic, there'd be time enough later to discuss it when he'd gained the courage to broach it. He nodded agreement and she rose to fetch the sweet.

He hesitated when the bread was three-quarters gone.

Jessamyn simply set another loaf from the pantry down in front of him and refilled the milk pitcher.

"Please eat as much as you like," Jessamyn said gently, her Tennessee drawl flowing through the simple words, as she sat back down across from him. "We've plenty of food at least."

His eyes shot to hers. "What do you mean?"

She shrugged as if there were some things too painful to discuss fully. The afternoon sunlight showed lines on her face, of experience and grief, which made her look far older than her seventeen years. "We sold the town house to a cotton broker from St. Louis, who'll take possession on January first. As part of the arrangement, he's sending us food."

He froze, before setting his bread down unbuttered. But the Tylers had always been extremely rich and very careful with their money. He knew how much others had lost, including his own family. But he'd always thought the Tylers' homes would survive, especially Somerset Hall, their great stud farm. "How bad is it?"

Her eyes met his, dark green and decades older than her years. "Dollar-wise? Father lost his business to the War."

And when it broke out, you'd been raised as his heir, with your beautiful horses and your ambition to become the finest female sharpshooter of all time . . .

"But we still had all the knickknacks here and at Somerset Hall, plus hope that the War would be over soon. So I sold a piece here and a piece there. After Father was invalided out . . ." She stopped, swallowing hard.

Morgan rose and cleared the table, then sat back down cautiously, respecting her courage and her ability to keep the household and stud farm together. Heartsick himself about whatever Uncle Heyward's illness was, he wouldn't add to her burdens by asking her to describe it now.

Jessamyn blinked back tears. "Father seemed—adrift for months afterward. Then his cancer began to grow faster and faster, sucking away his life and what remained of the business. We've sold everything possible, trying to find a cure for him."

His heart stopped. "Uncle Heyward has cancer?"

She nodded. "His mouth and jaw. Please be cheerful when you see him. There's a New York doctor who might help but he's very expensive. We're selling Somerset Hall in two days to cover the cost."

"The gold of Somerset Hall?" he groaned. The great cool barns with the beautiful, friendly horses and the green paddocks? The marshes where he'd shot ducks with Uncle Heyward and his father and Cyrus—and Jessamyn? The house of a thousand happy memories—sold?

"Everything's being sold for Father," Jessamyn repeated, a catch in her voice. "There is no other way. Father leaves tomorrow to complete the sale and Cyrus will be here within the week to escort us to New York."

"Good God," Morgan said harshly, his throat tightening. Longacres had been burned by Sherman's army earlier that summer. He'd wept with rage and grief when he'd heard, as he'd mourned other casualties of war. But he'd rejoiced when Somerset Hall escaped the same fate, thanks to its Tennessee location. Losing Somerset Hall for cold, hard cash was a sickening fate, like watching a mentor begin work in a gambling den.

Then the rest of Jessamyn's words sank in. She and her father would leave for New York within the week, escorted by Cyrus. If Cyrus caught him here, that pillar of rectitude would probably arrest him as a Rebel, despite being his cousin. Still, if he didn't return to Forrest with Grierson's orders within a few days, his friends would die.

His jaw tightened and he brought himself back to the present. He had to find those orders quickly.

Cassiopeia surged back into the room, her apron strings crackling behind her. As soon as she saw Jessamyn's tear-stained face, her eyes snapped to Morgan's with a ferocity that would have bored holes into a brass cannon. "Mr.

Heyward is awake now and asking for Mr. Morgan." Her glance at Morgan said she wasn't sure why.

Jessamyn nodded and stood up. "We'd best go immediately."

He followed her down the hall, trying not to look too closely at those gently swaying hips. Her scent, lavender water and roses, mixed with a trace of the horses she loved and something ineffably Jessamyn herself, was more than enough distraction. He'd rehearsed this meeting a hundred times on the ride here but now all he could think of was one lissome female.

Still, his experienced eye managed to grieve over the darkened spots on the rooms' walls where paintings had once hung, the empty corners where furniture had stood and Ming vases had offered bouquets of fresh flowers, the spots on the floor where oriental carpets had rippled like jewels. Only the kitchen had a full complement of furniture and warmth, however homely; everywhere else was a barren shadow of its former glory. He couldn't find the Sheraton table that he'd knocked over and chipped; even it must have been sold. He shivered and walked faster after Jessamyn.

She paused outside the library and looked up at him. "I'm so glad you're here, Morgan, no matter how long you can stay, just to have someone I can talk to again. It's been so difficult these past months."

He patted her shoulder, quelling the hair rising on the nape of his neck. Of course, she trusted him. If she didn't, given her high standards after her mother's betrayal . . . "You can rely on me, Jessamyn."

She leaned her head against his chest for a moment, her hands trembling slightly. He kissed her forehead gently, telling himself the chill running down his spine was the normal nerves before the start of a spying mission. They stayed like that for a moment before she pulled away.

Jessamyn knocked briskly on the door, calling out, "Father, Morgan is here to see you."

A dim voice answered, not the stentorian call that he was used to.

Here in the library, at least, all was as it had been—a sanctuary for masculine minds. Books lined the walls, from the floor to the ceiling. Large, leather chairs invited tired men to take their ease from a long day's work, with tables close at hand for their refreshments. A bar stood in one corner ready to provide those drinks, whose key a five-year-old Morgan and ten-year-old Cyrus had stolen but been forced to return before they could investigate the bar's contents. The air was heavy with the scent of pipe tobacco, and the old cabinet was still full of beautiful pipes. At least that hadn't been sold.

In the center of the room, Heyward Tyler had thrown his blanket aside and was trying to stand, fiercely gripping his immense armchair. A large bandage was wrapped around his head, supporting his chin. But it couldn't disguise the ugly bulge protruding from his cheek the size of Morgan's fist, like a foul beast destroying the great man. The flesh hung loosely now on his once hearty frame. But his green eyes, so like his daughter's, were still warm and welcoming despite their faded color. "Morgan, my boy!"

He held out his hand, wavering slightly.

All the air flew out of Morgan's lungs. He felt as if his horse had thrown him, sending him somersaulting onto the ground before an artillery battery. He could have received a thousand letters from Great-Aunt Eulalia, rather than a handful, but they wouldn't have prepared him for seeing one of his childhood idols at death's door.

Three years of near-constant combat gave him the reflexes to cover his reaction. He took a few quick steps across the room and supported his godfather, under the pretext of an embrace, and blinked quickly, forcing back his tears. He'd been prepared to see his father shot down in battle but seeing Uncle Heyward like this wrenched his gut worse than a midnight raid on a munitions dump. "Uncle Heyward," he choked out, using the old affectionate greeting, despite their lack of any blood kinship.

Uncle Heyward patted him on the back, in a weak echo of his famous thumps. "You'll have a glass of port with me, of course."

Morgan's eyes met Jessamyn's over her father's head, asking her silently if alcohol was approved.

She nodded slightly, with a faint shrug. The same knowledge lit her eyes that he knew walked in his: Her father's death was so close that indulging him in a glass of port made no difference. "The glasses are in the cabinet, Morgan. I'll leave you two alone, while I see to dinner." She kissed her father's cheek and left, closing the door very quietly.

Morgan carefully lowered the older man back into the chair and tucked his blanket around him, then went for the wine. When he visited friends under the Dying Tree, the place where surgeons placed battlefield wounded destined to die, he always gave them anything they asked for and spoke as quietly as possible.

Uncle Heyward covered his mouth with a handkerchief, a cough racking his chest, then accepted his glass with much of his old spirit. "Tell me about Longacres, Morgan. I heard you freed the slaves when your father died."

Morgan shrugged. "I've never owned a slave and saw no reason to start. Father would have said you corrupted me."

Uncle Heyward chuckled proudly. The old devil had never owned a slave in his life either. "Have any of them stayed?"

Morgan chuckled, thinking back to the latest triumphant letter he'd received. "Quite a few. Cousin Sophonisba and Great-Aunt Eulalia are my managers—"

"That should terrify any malefactors into obedience," Uncle Heyward remarked with a flash of his old spirit.

Morgan heartily agreed. "Sherman's men burned Longacres when they passed through last summer. Even so, very few of the freedmen left. According to Great-Aunt Eulalia's letters, there's still enough food to eat and cotton for a little spending money."

"I'll wager those two terrors are even trading vegetables— or labor—with the other planters, and lecturing them on how to behave," Uncle Heyward wheezed. He closed his eyes, his chest rising and falling rapidly under the heavy velvet dressing gown.

Morgan watched him, heartsick and building up memories. He'd learned all too well to do so whenever he had the chance.

"Why are you here, son?" his host asked, rousing himself to sit up.

Morgan studied the ruby lights burning in the wine's depths. Morgan's father had always said to tell his old friend the truth, no matter how bitter. But how could he lay this burden on a dying man?

"Out with it, Lieutenant!" Uncle Heyward snapped.

Morgan raised an eyebrow. "Sir?"

"As a major, I outrank you."

He arched an eyebrow but his mouth quirked affectionately. "You were invalided out, sir," he reminded his godfather gently.

"You're here on military business, aren't you?"

"My father always said he never could fool you, sir."

Uncle Heyward grinned and took a tiny sip of his port. "Nothing else you'd try to keep quiet."

Morgan bit the bullet but kept his voice down. While he trusted Jessamyn, he didn't know Cassiopeia well, although she was related by marriage to Somerset Hall's chief groom. She'd only arrived in 1859, after he'd left for Arizona. "Forrest sent me to town. I'd like your permission to stay here and do some investigating."

Uncle Heyward stared at him. His wineglass started to rock in his hand and he set it down shakily. The lines on his face deepened, adding decades to his age, and he closed his eyes, hiding their agony. He was silent for a time, leaving the clock to fill the silence.

What the hell was wrong? His father had always said he could trust Uncle Heyward with anything and treated the Tylers like the other half of their own family. Morgan started to wonder if he'd misjudged his old friends. He was reminding himself of the old escape routes from this room, when his godfather spoke again.

"I was a soldier of the Confederacy and I will keep that vow. So you have my permission. Should the worst befall you and me, Cyrus Evans will ensure that no harm comes to Jessamyn," he finished more softly.

Morgan blew out the breath he'd been barely aware he was holding. He started to frame his first question about the best place to hunt.

Uncle Heyward's eyes flashed open, suddenly, unexpectedly green again. Their ferocity speared Morgan to the heart. "But stay as far away from Jessamyn as possible. She has Unionist sympathies, although she never speaks of them, in deference to me."

Morgan rocked back in his seat, nearly spilling his port. "Jessamyn, a Unionist? Doesn't she understand the need to stand with her state, as a Secessionist?"

Her father shrugged, his eyes full of pity for the younger man and the knowledge of pain to come. "I raised Jessamyn to be my heir and taught her to think for herself. I can't be too surprised when she disagrees with me."

Morgan flinched, physically sick at the prospect of using Jessamyn in this fashion. *Independent, intelligent,* and *loyal* were the three terms that best described Jessamyn. If she'd decided she was Unionist, no man could change her mind. How the hell could he pull this off without her knowledge? How could he fool her?

Then he remembered those green recruits, their faces shining with trust and enthusiasm at that icy river bottom rendezvous, when they heard how Forrest routed the Yankees. He couldn't let them be destroyed by Grierson. This was war and one girl's feelings meant nothing in comparison to saving the lives of two thousand men.

"You'll need to watch for Jessamyn's cousin, Charlie Jones, a nasty viper if there ever was one."

Morgan nodded, thinking back to a few old meetings. Charlie was Sophia Tyler's nephew. Like the other Joneses, his family had cut off all contact with Heyward Tyler when he divorced Sophia shortly after she ran off with Forsythe.

"Worse, Cyrus will be here in a few days to escort Jessamyn and me to New York."

Morgan's heart twisted again. Damn, he'd never grow accustomed to thinking of Uncle Heyward as ill. "Jessamyn mentioned that. I'll have to work quickly."

"You'll also need to watch for the servants," Uncle Heyward added. "There's only four here now, all completely loyal to Jessamyn. Cassiopeia the cook, her husband Aristotle who's the houseman, his brother Socrates the groom, and his twin Plato who's my valet."

"If Cassiopeia has family further downriver," Morgan protested, "then I may be able to gain a hold on her."

Uncle Heyward brushed that notion aside. "Unacceptable. All the men are related to Galileo, Somerset Hall's chief groom. I won't have him disturbed."

Damn. No accomplices in this house except Uncle Heyward? He hated doing this. Still, he'd been successful before when he'd acted on his own and he could do so again. But he needed to hurry.

Uncle Heyward's gaze fixed on him, sharp as a surgeon's lancet. "You're posing as a deserter, of course."

"Yes, sir."

"Hmmm, that should work. It's Christmastime. Even with a war, there are still many functions that a Tyler needs to attend. Jessamyn does what she can, of course, but I can't escort her as I should," Uncle Heyward mused with a conspiratorial air.

Morgan cocked his head, a wild hope beginning to build. The Tylers' social connections had always been superb, even better than his own family's. By escorting Jessamyn, he might be able to discover exactly who knew Grierson's orders, thus saving a great deal of time.

"You'd be around soldiers, of course," Uncle Heyward drawled. "They're as common as boll weevils, since there's a Federal garrison in town."

Morgan shrugged, well aware his smile had turned wicked. "I believe I can manage to be polite to Federals, sir."

"Well, of course you can. You're an Evans of Longacres," Uncle Heyward agreed. "We'll give you Andrew Dorr's clothes, my old clerk's, so you'll look like a civilian."

Morgan bowed. "Thank you, sir."

He'd manage somehow around Jessamyn. Maybe by telling her a minimum of the truth.

Jessamyn settled herself into her seat and smiled up at Morgan, who held it for her—perfectly, of course. "Thank you."

He nodded and sat down next to her, looking precise in Andrew's old clothes.

On the other side of the table, their hostess's daughter shot her a viciously triumphant glance. Jessamyn nodded slightly, still wary at being seated next to Morgan at a dinner party, even though he was using an assumed name. But Clarabelle Hutchinson had stopped by the house that afternoon to borrow some greens for the party's decorations and spotted Morgan. Ever on the alert to remove possible competitors for the bachelors' attention, she'd immediately assumed Morgan was Jessamyn's impoverished suitor and invited him to the party. She'd been both insistent and loud, threatening to cry and summon her father to support her stated desire to see the numbers even. Jessamyn suspected that Morgan had only accepted out of his old childhood protectiveness toward her.

Now she sat beside him, praying nothing would go wrong.

Certainly her old friend had changed. He'd struck her dumb when she saw him in '61, eighteen years old, tanned and lithe as a mountain lion after three years of life on the frontier. He and his father had stayed for only two days and a night, most of that spent closeted with her father. She respected him for enlisting in a cause he believed in, even if she didn't give allegiance to the same cause. She was extremely proud of Cyrus, who'd honored his oath and stayed in the Federal army, despite the agonies it cost him to lead troops against men from his native state.

She glanced around the room, looking for possible threats. A Rebel soldier at a dinner party with Federal officers. Mercifully, no military secrets would be discussed tonight. She hoped.

The chaplain on the other side of her rose to give the blessing and Jessamyn obediently bowed her head.

Memphis's position as a major cotton port in a border state had kept its upper echelons mixed, both Unionist and Confederate. Both sides still socialized together cautiously, especially at Christmastime. Jessamyn had kept her mouth shut over the past few years about her Unionist sympathies, given her father's service as a Confederate officer.

Tonight's dinner party was designed to aid Confederate POWs in Northern prisons. The hostess was Lorena Hutchinson, a Confederate sympathizer whose son was a prisoner of war. She was an expert at using her formidable social skills to aid him and other POWs as best she could, which included drawing on her contacts in the local Federal garrison.

Mrs. Hutchinson smiled sweetly at her small dinner party, composed of equal numbers of local Federal troops and families related to POWs. Tomorrow they'd be taking a shipment to the garrison, for delivery directly to the POWs, who were hungry and cold in the Northern prisons.

Jessamyn shuddered at the thought. Like every other woman

at the table, she was here to charm the Federals into helping those supplies through.

"Thank you for the lovely blessing, Reverend Getty," Mrs. Hutchinson purred and the dinner began. Morgan silently passed a dish of creamed peas to the matron beyond him and Jessamyn smiled at the lieutenant on her other side. Thank God nobody seemed to have recognized Morgan, which wasn't very surprising since he hadn't walked the town's streets for six or seven years.

Conversation became general, enlivened by Clarabelle's flirtations with every bachelor and superior looks at Jessamyn—which Jessamyn found easy to ignore. Morgan was eating quietly and steadily, not with the speed and diligence he'd used when he'd first arrived. His wrists were so thin and strong; how long had it been since he'd eaten regularly?

She glanced at his face, then looked quickly back at her own place setting. Studying his mouth—his lips, his teeth, his *tongue*—was too intimate, almost frightening. What would it feel like if he pressed it to hers?

The ham arrived, followed by a lull in the conversation as the party enjoyed the very good food. It was broken by the officers around Clarabelle Hutchinson.

Jessamyn cocked her head to listen as she buttered her roll; her dinner companion was shoveling ham down his throat, relieving her of paying any attention to him. Morgan was calmly passing chutney to the matron on his left.

"I will personally oversee the loading, Miss Hutchinson," the skinny, red-headed lieutenant pledged, gazing earnestly at Clarabelle. "You need have no fear for your precious jars of honey."

"But I will see them to St. Louis," the dark-haired lieutenant on her other side vowed, slapping the table. Flatware rattled briefly then settled back into place.

The red-haired lieutenant leaned forward to glare at him. "You can't do that, Wyeth. You're on staff duty tomorrow, ensuring that the orders of movement are done properly."

Morgan's hands stilled and he shot a hard look at Wyeth.

Jessamyn glanced rapidly between the two men, wondering why her skin was prickling. What was going on here? Why would Morgan be interested in who was a staff officer? She pushed the concern aside as nonsensical; thinking about that would be the hallmark of a spy, which Morgan was far too honorable for.

Clarabelle Hutchinson giggled and patted both officers' arms. "Gentlemen, gentlemen, you are so magnificent! I'm sure both of you can help this charity."

Morgan went back to eating his dinner as if nothing had happened.

Jessamyn looked at him uneasily, her stomach heaving. She refused another helping of ham and confined herself to sipping spring water. Her nerves were jangling as badly as when a prank was about to go bad. She began to shred her dinner roll, while she made polite conversation.

During the after-dinner musicale, she convinced herself she'd imagined her nervous upset, probably because she wasn't used to staying out for an entire evening with a gentleman of her own age. Especially one as handsome as Morgan, who had the look of a young cavalier with his clear-cut profile and high cheekbones. He could have been all too pretty but somehow he had a harshly masculine face, probably because his cheekbones were so very sharp and his eyes so very alert and his jaw so very strong. But his mouth certainly did look very capable of kissing a girl thoroughly.

That thought led her to another—what Morgan might do on the return home, activities she wasn't at all sure she'd reject.

Sitting next to him in the small buggy made her insides purr and melt, while she wondered what it would be like when they were married. She watched him drive, sensing the rippling muscles under his skin, enjoying how easily he controlled the high-spirited bay gelding.

Morgan brought her into the house, lit by only a few isolated gas lamps. Everything was very quiet, wrapping them in a cloak of intimate silence, so that they tiptoed across the wooden floors and the grandfather clock sounded like a drum.

He stopped at the foot of the stairs and she looked back at him, still holding hands. "Aren't you coming up?"

"No." His thumb rubbed over her knuckles. "Your father gave me the room next to yours. It would be more proper if I wait an hour, until you're asleep."

"Oh." His reasoning sounded solid but she didn't want to release him. This was the first time she'd ever spent an evening with a young man, and his company had been everything a gentleman's should be. She blinked up at him and tried to find something logical, or ladylike, or welcoming, to say.

"Jessamyn." Was he groaning?

She opened her mouth to ask—and his lips covered hers.

Their teeth banged against each other's. Her lips caught his lips, then felt his tongue. His breath touched her lightly, making her shiver. She sighed and instinctively opened her mouth wider for him.

He tilted her head to meet his and she yielded, closing her eyes with a little moan.

A whirlwind rose through her body as his tongue danced and played with hers. She arched against him, wrapping her arms around his neck and rubbing her suddenly aching body against him. He kissed her thoroughly, exploring her mouth deeply and completely, bruising her. She moaned into his mouth and pushed against him, silently begging for more. He tightened his hold on her.

The big grandfather clock started to strike. Boom!

Morgan released her immediately and sprang away. She stared at him, her hand covering her mouth. Her heart pounded against her chest, like a terrified bird.

Boom!

He was tense, vibrating with it, as if he wanted to mount her. Her future husband.

Jessamyn licked her lips. Boom!

Morgan jerkily bowed to her. "Good night, Jessamyn. Now take yourself upstairs—fast."

She picked up her skirts and ran, frightened by her response to him. Boom!

She heard the front door close behind him before the clock finished striking midnight. Her dreams that night were of being his wife.

Morgan sat in the waterfront dive, nursing his gin, while he waited for Richmond's pet informant to appear. He'd carefully mixed his drink with water, of course, as he'd been taught the first time he'd spied for Forrest. It was a very easy way to look as if he was drinking, while remaining sober. But it did nothing to improve the taste of either the water or the gin.

He lifted the tankard for another sip and stiffened briefly. Then he deliberately swallowed the foul-smelling swill and waited for Charlie Jones, Jessamyn's scapegrace cousin, to join him in this dark corner.

Charlie paused in front of the table, the same age but better fed than Morgan, flaunting his money in gaudy clothes. His passage across the room had been noted by other patrons but Charlie paid them no heed. "Well, well, if it isn't Uncle Heyward's godson. What are you doing on this dung heap?"

Morgan spoke very deliberately and as softly as possible. " 'Comrades, leave me here a little, while as yet 'tis early morn.' "

Charlie's eyebrows flew up at the password's beginning. " 'Leave me here, and when you want me, sound upon the bugle-horn.' " He swung around a chair and sat down. "Ridiculous to have to chant idiot phrases to begin a piece of business."

"The first couplet of Tennyson's 'Locksley Hall ' is a set of idiot phrases?" Morgan pushed a glass and a bottle of good brandy over, as he'd been instructed.

Charlie glared at him and sniffed the brandy suspiciously. Then he poured himself a full glass, crossed his arms on the chair back, and tapped his fingers on the wood. "How much do you have for me?"

Why Charlie still had his scalp was beyond Morgan's comprehension. "What do *you* have for me?"

Charlie frowned but lowered his voice. "Grant's order of battle at Chickamauga."

The other patrons were surreptitiously eyeing Charlie's clothes.

"Old news, Charlie, and the other side of the state. What else?"

Charlie's voice dropped further. "Sherman's orders to Grierson."

Morgan immediately turned calm, as if he were riding into an ambush. "How much?"

Charlie deliberately drank some brandy before answering, all the while surveying Morgan. "Five thousand dollars."

"You're crazy."

Their watchers were moving closer.

Charlie shrugged. "Just sharp business practices, to charge what people will pay."

"Fifty."

"Two thousand."

"Charlie, I can discover those orders for myself."

"But I have them now."

"Show them to me."

"Show me your money first."

Did Charlie have a copy of the orders? Probably not, if he wasn't willing to show them.

The audience was two paces behind Charlie, hidden in the shadows behind the posts. He seemed barely aware of them.

"Is the gold all that matters to you?" Morgan's Bowie knife thumped eagerly against his thigh, with his dirk up his sleeve. But if he killed Charlie, the city watch would throw him into jail and he couldn't fulfill his mission. Perhaps there was another way to teach Charlie a lesson and still let Richmond keep its pet for another day . . .

Charlie yawned, finished his glass, and poured himself another.

"You're a buzzard, feeding off the carcasses of better men, Charlie. You should be shot, just like that buzzard."

"Stop preaching, Morgan, and pay up. If you won't be that businesslike, then get the hell out of my life and leave me to make a fortune in my own fashion."

Morgan pushed the table up into Charlie's face, knocking him over into the human buzzards behind him. They jumped on him immediately and Morgan leaped for the closest window, leaving behind all the sounds of a spectacular fracas.

Jessamyn followed Mrs. Hutchinson and Mrs. Leggett into the Union Army's Memphis headquarters, barely listening as they graciously thanked the young lieutenant for forwarding the Christmas packages to the Confederate prisoners of war. Her attention was split between the difficulties of carrying a heavy basket full of jellies and jams, while simultaneously trying to decide on the most fetching attire for her afternoon tea with Morgan. But when a sergeant nearly knocked her over as he ran a message down the hallway, she was forced to pay attention to her surroundings.

The big brick building, once a hub of commerce, now buzzed with all the frantic chaos of an aroused wasps' nest. Riders galloped up and barely paused long enough to toss the reins to anyone close at hand before they disappeared inside, shouting someone's name. Men sprinted down the crowded hallways, elbowing their way through, barely pausing to salute. Mud splattered dandies' once-immaculate uniforms and dark circles ringed everyone's eyes. Jessamyn would wager that all of them, every officer and enlisted man, had no thought in their heads but to capture General Bedford Forrest.

The small party, every woman laden with gifts to succor

their relatives languishing in Northern POW camps, headed down the long corridor to the chaplains' offices. Jessamyn glanced casually down the narrow corridor toward the telegraphers' office and paused, caught by an odd sense of familiarity.

A broad-shouldered man was striding toward it, his form so very different from the usual young messenger boys that went there. He moved gracefully, with the easy, fluid glide of someone who'd spent years in the saddle. He held his head proudly under that big slouch hat, too, the attitude striking a note that hummed through her.

Someone slammed a door and the man's head snapped around, showing his profile for the first time. It was Morgan— here in Union Army headquarters and wearing a Union Army uniform, to which he had no right.

Jessamyn's knees buckled as her breath whooshed out of her lungs. Her vision grayed. Morgan, *a spy?* He wasn't just visiting her father?

"Are you all right, Miss Tyler?" Mrs. Hutchinson asked, catching her elbow. The telegraphers' office door shut, cutting off any sight of Morgan. "I knew you were carrying far too heavy a box."

Jessamyn fought for breath, determined not to cause a scene—not here, not now. *Dear God in heaven, how could she have been so blind?*

The lieutenant frowned at her. "You can sit down in Captain Townsend's office. It's just around the corner."

The telegraphers' office? "No!"

Everyone looked at her in surprise.

She tried again more temperately. At least she was breathing again, probably because she was terrified of letting them see Morgan. "No, thank you. I must have simply caught my foot on a rough spot. Please, let's deliver these to the chaplains so they can be sped on their way as quickly as possible."

"If you're certain you're quite well," Mrs. Hutchinson said slowly.

"Just a momentary weakness," Jessamyn assured her, praying that any attachment to Morgan was exactly that.

How could she have trusted him, that dishonorable rat?

She was silent throughout the rest of the trip, her heart choking her throat.

Morgan was in Memphis dressed as a Union officer. He must have come to Memphis as a spy. If he was caught, they'd surely put her father in prison for harboring him and her father would die in one of those foul, freezing cells. Whether within a few days from pneumonia or a few weeks of starvation, her father would die—thanks to his dishonorable godson, Morgan Evans.

It was an absolutely unnecessary thing to do. Totally selfish and lazy since he could have found out the information he needed in other ways.

He was a lying dog, who was using her and her family's connections, for his spying.

He was worse than her mother. At least her mother's betrayal hadn't risked anyone else's life.

She wished bitterly that she could cry.

At home, she refused Cassiopeia's offer of tea and went straight up to her room. She rocked in her grandmother's old chair, clutching herself lest the stabbing pain in her chest tear her apart.

Morgan knew, thanks to her, exactly which staff officer would transcribe the orders for Grierson.

Given that, he could walk into the telegraphers' office and simply look for all messages sent by that staff officer. He'd know exactly where and when Grierson, the Union general with the best chance of catching that devil, would move against Forrest.

Damn and double damn. It would be her fault if Morgan's news reached Forrest and anything happened to those Union soldiers.

But if she turned Morgan in, they'd execute him as a spy. Or worse, send him north to a prisoner-of-war camp. Mrs.

Hutchinson had lost one son at Shiloh. Another had died of typhus in a camp. The third was starving in yet another camp—one could see it in his handwriting. Could she condemn Morgan, with all his proud, vivid alertness like a bird of prey, to such a living death?

Jessamyn yanked herself out of the chair so hard that it banged the wall, and she began to pace, her hoops thudding against the furniture as she snapped through the turns. Tears dripped silently down her face but she ignored them.

She couldn't deliver Morgan up to certain death. On the other hand, she couldn't just stand by while Union soldiers galloped into the ambush that devil Forrest would prepare, thanks to Morgan's information. What was she going to do?

A riverboat's whistle sang in the distance, before being answered by another. Two riverboats traveling on the Mississippi this afternoon, both gunboats—a very strong display of force.

Jessamyn stopped in her tracks. Grierson must be moving against Forrest very soon. He'd need every bit of support he could get. It would also explain all the chaos at the Union Army headquarters that afternoon.

Today. Grierson must be leaving later today, since Chaplain Palmer had been wearing his second-best uniform, something he hadn't done since he'd come back from the fighting at Vicksburg earlier that year. He'd been temporarily assigned to Grierson's staff.

But Morgan would have to wait until dark to leave town, to slip past the sentries. If she could delay him for only a day or two, then Grierson and Forrest would fight things out their own way. Morgan wouldn't be arrested as a spy and Union soldiers wouldn't be mowed down in certain ambush.

How? She stared at herself in the mirror, her fingers tapping urgently on the dresser. A bottle danced, rattling against the wood, and she steadied it automatically.

Her eyes lit. A Paris perfume bottle, only slightly different in shape from some of the laudanum bottles that allowed Father escape from his cancer long enough to sleep at night.

Sleep.

Cassiopeia could make Father sleep through anything. Or just make him a little drowsy. She was able to do similar miracles with Jessamyn and others in the neighborhood, who came to her for help.

If Cassiopeia could somehow drug Morgan into sleep and her husband carried him up, they could keep him confined for the next two days. Father and Plato would be gone to Somerset Hall, almost three hours distant, and wouldn't return until Christmas Eve. Mrs. Hutchinson would be at her home next door; she'd stop by from time to time but it should be possible to keep Morgan's imprisonment a secret from her and the Army.

Two days. With Cassiopeia and Aristotle's help, she'd drug and hold Morgan captive for two days. After that, she'd release him outside town, to return to his duties as a Confederate lieutenant, before Cyrus arrived.

And pray Charlie didn't do anything obnoxious before they left.

Then she'd be free to start rebuilding her life.

Chapter Two

"Cake?" Jessamyn offered, extending the plate toward Morgan.

He eyed the gilded, curved bit of porcelain and the lumps of sugary bread covering it. "Thank you, no." Five years of almost continual warfare had taught him to value simpler pleasures: sleep, good whiskey, a full stomach more than sugar.

He sipped his sherry cautiously, then more deeply when the rich, dry taste rolled over his tongue and down his throat. He purred softly and relaxed into the armchair. Irritated though he was at having to wait until dark to leave, at least he was doing so in comfort.

The information he'd gained was priceless and he'd already memorized it. He'd leave at sunset, in time to save his friends—and protect those who'd sheltered him here.

Jessamyn smiled at him over her own, smaller glass of sherry. The entire scene was everything his father had promised him for a happy home: the approving female, the fire crackling on the hearth, good wine, plenty of food, the distant storm beyond the windows. He swirled the pale golden liquid in its delicate glass, admiring how the lamplight glowed in its depths.

A few minutes and a few swallows later, he laid his head back against the chair, eyelids drooping. "What time is it, Jessamyn?"

"Past three, I believe." Her voice was a little hoarse.

Morgan frowned and forced his eyes open. He'd returned after three. "I need to leave at five for an engagement."

"As you please." Her intense watchfulness didn't match her words' carelessness. Aristotle, her big houseman, entered silently and stood behind her, studying Morgan like a dispassionate sphinx.

Something was very wrong. Morgan set his glass down but missed the table. It fell to the hand-knotted rug and rolled under the bench. What the hell was going on?

He tried to stand up, holding on to the chair desperately. The room blurred and spun around him.

Morgan collapsed onto the rug, still groping for something, anything, to pull himself up by. The last thing he saw before all went dark was the hem of Jessamyn's skirt as she stood over him, as ardent as a Greek fury.

Dreams crossed his mind after that but nothing he could ever clearly recall. He returned to sanity slowly, slipping in and out of consciousness several times.

He didn't open his eyes immediately, of course. He'd spent too long with Cochise and the Apaches to let his enemy know he was awake again. So he tested himself privately first.

He was wearing only a nightshirt, with no sign of his guns or knives, dammit. He shifted his hands and arms a fraction. Nothing holding *them* down, at least.

He tried to move his legs. Hell and damnation, an iron shackle was locked around one of his legs, with the cuff probably fastened to the bed.

Morgan opened an eye cautiously, found no one directly in sight, and checked what he was lying on. The bed itself was an iron affair, so solidly built that Hercules would have thought twice before attempting to shift it, and bolted to the wall, dammit. He had as much hope of moving the contraption as he did of shifting the moon. He'd need to find some other way to leave this prison.

A riverboat's whistle blew three times, with the same volume as how it sounded at the Tylers' home. A muscle twitched in Morgan's jaw. Jessamyn might have drugged him, damn her pretty little head, but she hadn't taken him far. As soon as he figured out how to escape, he could leave Memphis quickly and tell Fórrest when Grierson was coming. He had to save the general and the rest of the men.

And one day, he'd take revenge on Jessamyn for stripping his manhood like this. He'd have held his head high if Sherman's men had captured him. But to be drugged and chained by a seventeen-year-old chit was intolerable!

Morgan opened his eyes a little more and found himself in a large attic room, well lit by oil lamps. Two locked, large dormer windows showed leafless trees, with a crescent moon shining faint and far away. A few mismatched side chairs and a half-dozen steamer trunks were scattered through the room. A cozy Franklin stove and painted canvas mat made for a comfortable, if simple, atmosphere compared to the Tylers' principal living quarters. He must be at the back of the house, near the kitchen garden and the stables.

"Evenin', Mr. Evans," Aristotle rumbled from behind Morgan, the harsh rattle of a man whose larynx has been ruined.

Damn, not Cassiopeia's husband and Socrates's brother, the former dockside brawler who worshipped Jessamyn. That devil had probably known the instant he'd woken up. Tricking him would take both luck and considerable effort.

Morgan controlled his disappointment and sat up slowly, his shackle catching on the linen sheets. If Aristotle intended to handle this politely, then he would do likewise as long as it suited him. "Good evening, Aristotle."

The big man eyed him impassively from an armchair near the door. Aristotle and Cassiopeia had come to the Tylers from Memphis's underworld, although Morgan had never heard the full story, and Aristotle's face displayed a hard past. He'd lost one ear and the lobe of the other, while his nose had been broken many times. But his eyes shone with intelligence above his branded cheek and his immaculate livery. He steepled his fingers and began speaking. "Miss Jessamyn asked me to explain the rules to you as soon as you woke up. First, either I or my brother Socrates will watch you at all times."

Damn and blast, he had little chance to get past either of them. He might be able to pick the lock on the shackle, given some tools. But fighting his way past one of them would take considerable luck. He quelled the flash of anger and tried to talk his way out. "Aristotle, I'm a guest in this house. It's ridiculous for me to be locked up in the attic like a present for next year's Christmas."

Aristotle chuckled deep and low in his chest. "That's right, Mr. Evans, you're a guest here so you'd better get used to this room. You're shackled to the bed but you can walk ten feet or so in each direction, enough for exercise."

Morgan gauged the distance. Exercise, yes, but he couldn't reach Aristotle's chair, let alone the stairs. "Thank you but let's talk about the shackle . . ."

Aristotle inspected his immaculate fingernails. His hands looked more than capable of wringing a buffalo's neck. "Don't bother thinking about shouting. Mr. Tyler's mother used to shout sermons about hellfire up here but she never bothered nobody. They won't hear you either."

Morgan nodded grimly, his mouth tightening as he remembered the vehement old lady. Thunderstorms had frightened her more and more with age, triggering days of prayers and shouts to prepare for the end of the world. Finally, Jessamyn's father had built her an attic room over the ballroom so none of his neighbors would be disturbed by her loud denunciations of modern morals. Morgan knew exactly where he was—and he reluctantly believed no one would hear him call for help.

Aristotle tossed a two-finger salute to Morgan's comprehension. "Your dinner's on the table next to the bed. Chamber pot's in the cabinet just beyond. It'll be emptied when Socrates and I are both here."

"Of course." The two men exchanged glances of reluctant respect. An obviously experienced jailer like Aristotle wouldn't come near Morgan without his brother to provide backup.

"There's books in the cabinet on t'other side," his warden continued calmly. "Also a chess set and some other game pieces."

No weapons visible, nor anything he could pick the lock with. They'd only given him a spoon to eat dinner with.

"Aristotle," Morgan began, gentling his voice as if he were trying to coax a skittish mustang into accepting a bridle for the first time. "Miss Tyler is just a woman, a young unmarried lady at that. Surely the two of us, as men who've seen the world, know better how matters should be handled. Talk to me, man to man."

Aristotle's expression chilled. His eyes hardened into black granite. "Five years ago, when my wife and I were owned by a Memphis brothel," he began, every syllable clipped and precise, "my eight-year-old daughter was sold to Mr. Henry Chalmers for the performance of unnatural acts."

Morgan froze. An eight-year-old and unnatural acts? Why that . . .

"Before she could arrive at Chalmers' plantation, my friends rescued her and passed her to the Underground Railway. Miss Jessamyn hid her at Somerset Hall, where my uncle was head groom, which Chalmers and the sheriff's bloodhounds searched from basement to attic without finding her. Today she lives safely with my sister's family in Canada."

Morgan nodded, not trusting himself to speak. In truth, he was glad, once again, that he'd freed all the slaves at Long-acres.

"In return, my wife and I promised Miss Jessamyn that we'd give her our lives as long as there's slavery. Whatever she wants, we'll do."

"I would never dream of asking you to turn against your mistress," Morgan assured him, a trifle mendaciously.

Aristotle raised a disbelieving eyebrow. "I told Miss Jessamyn it'd be tricky hidin' you up here in the attic like this. Still, she was dead set on doin' this. But should you cause any trouble for her, any trouble a'tall—"

Morgan met his gaze directly, braced for the attack.

"There's enough lye in the washhouse to melt your dismembered corpse before we dump you into the swamp. Even rats wouldn't recognize you as a man after that."

Morgan's mouth curled in a mirthless smile as he acknowledged the warning. Jessamyn might seem like any other innocent Southern belle but she'd managed to attract and hold the loyalty of competent, deadly predators.

Aristotle snorted softly at Morgan's expression. Then he settled into his chair, eyes half-shut, allowing Morgan a small semblance of privacy.

Not being fool enough to take that posture as anything other than pretense, Morgan shook his head and headed for the chamber pot. Five years of almost constant fighting, first with the Apaches then with Forrest's cavalry, had taught him to take advantage of whatever he could, when he could. A few minutes later, he was gnawing on a chicken leg, savoring the complexities of Cassiopeia's cooking—and calculating distances and angles.

He needed to be out of here before Cyrus arrived. Cyrus was extraordinarily precise on points of honor, especially when it touched family. His father had been a Texas land promoter turned swindler. One of his victims had called him out and killed him in a duel. Every penny had gone to paying off those he'd fleeced. Although he never spoke of it, Cyrus seemed determined to prove that his sense of honor was far better than his father's. Morgan knew damn well what Cyrus would do if faced with a choice between honor and family: arrest him immediately.

By the time Morgan had finished the fried chicken, his

headache had faded and he'd returned to devising ways to wring Jessamyn's pretty neck. He was trapped in this room for as long as she chose to keep him here, until Judgment Day perhaps, dammit. He spat a curse in Apache and tried to think of a different way to wriggle out of the shackle, just as a light tap sounded on the door.

Aristotle came alert immediately and rose to his feet. An instant later, he had the door open and was bowing greetings. "Miss Jessamyn, I didn't expect you so early. Socrates."

Socrates, Aristotle's brother and Jessamyn's personal groom, nodded a silent greeting from behind her shoulder. He was loyal to her unto death, as Morgan had used more than once to his advantage during a childhood prank.

Jessamyn stepped forward to study Morgan critically. "He looks rumpled and half-asleep," she observed.

"We weren't expecting you so early," Aristotle offered, rapidly clearing the table beside him.

"Father just left for Somerset Hall with Plato," Jessamyn answered, tearstains visible on her face. "He'll stay with the Burkes for a few days after it's sold before returning in time to meet Cyrus." Her voice sharpened. "How's our prisoner doing?"

Morgan was immediately wary at the look in her eyes. Despite his rage, he'd hoped his captivity was only a temporary sojourn, a small contretemps between friends. But Jessamyn didn't lose her temper very often—and she didn't cool quickly at all, once it happened.

He adopted his best manners. "Quite well but a little stiff." He started to swing his feet over the side of the bed.

Jessamyn studied him, clearly seething with anger, her skirts and petticoats swirling around her legs, before turning to Aristotle. "I want to speak to him alone."

The big man stirred out of his impassivity. "That's not safe for you, Miss Jessamyn. Either I or my brother should stay here with you."

"What I have to say to him needs to be said in private."

Wry amusement colored her voice. "If I know you, Aristotle, you have more than one way prepared to tie him up. Is one of those methods something that will hold him while I'm alone with him?"

Aristotle blew out a breath, looking both embarrassed and guilty at the same time. "Well, now, one of them might be. But it's something I learned in a house of ill repute on the dockside and no decent woman should see it."

"That should do then. Can you and Socrates manage him or should I summon Cassiopeia to assist?"

"Two of us will manage him jes' fine," Aristotle rumbled, with a swift glance at his brother. The ever-silent Socrates nodded and came forward.

"Lie down on the bed, on top of the quilt, Mr. Evans, and this will go easy on you," Aristotle said calmly, standing in front of Morgan.

"Like hell," Morgan spat and sprang. He fought hard, using every dirty wrestling trick he'd learned from the Apaches. Aristotle and Socrates knew counters for most of them; besides, there were two of them and only one of him. Still, he had the satisfaction of once hearing Aristotle huff in surprise.

But in the end, Aristotle caught Morgan's free leg in one ham-sized fist and shoved it—with the rest of Morgan—back toward the bed. Socrates grabbed Morgan's shoulder and snapped another cuff on Morgan's wrist.

A minute later, he was spread-eagled across the bed, every limb firmly chained to a separate bedpost. His nightshirt was hiked well up on his thighs. He could wriggle a bit on the quilt, or arch his back, but he couldn't leave the bed.

Disliking his helplessness and disarray intensely—especially in front of Jessamyn—Morgan glared at Aristotle. The big man simply shook his head before bowing to his mistress, genuine respect filling his attitude. "Is there anything else, Miss Jessamyn?"

"No, that will be all, Aristotle. I'll call you when I leave so you can return to sentry duty."

"Yes, ma'am." He glanced back at Morgan. "Just be very careful how you behave around him. A polecat still has sharp teeth, even when you've got him in a trap."

She patted his arm reassuringly. "Thank you for warning me, Aristotle. I'll be very cautious."

He disappeared slowly down the stairs, lamplight glinting on his shaven skull. She closed the door behind him and made her way to the center of the room. She surveyed Morgan from there, emerald eyes traveling over him slowly. She seemed an innocent girl in her simple gray dress with the starched white apron and collar.

Morgan fought the temptation to yell at her. No innocent miss could have drugged and kidnapped him so successfully. The only thing he could use against her was his voice. "Jessamyn, we've known each other for years. Our families planned our marriage in your cradle. Let me go."

Her green eyes drilled him, filled with a cold anger he'd never seen before. But he didn't dwell long on that, given his own fury at her treatment of him.

"Like hell," she snapped back. "You're a Rebel spy and Union soldiers will die if you walk out of here with that information."

How had she found out? He shrugged the disquieting discovery off and tried to cozen her. Unfortunately, his voice roughened. "Jessamyn, we played together as children. You know me."

"I don't believe I do, especially since you dragged me into your spying. You used me to find out the fastest way to learn Grierson's orders, didn't you?"

Morgan's eyes widened in shock. He controlled himself instantly but the damage was done.

"Damn your lying, thieving ways!" Jessamyn cried, bright spots of color on her cheeks. "I always thought that you were an honorable man—not a lazy, skulking spy who'd take advantage of a dying old man's kindness! You knew your own army considered him too ill to fight, didn't you? Didn't you?"

"Yes, but—"

"You could have gone to a tavern, or stayed in a shed, and found your own sources of information about Grierson. But no, you had to stay with your dying godfather because he might be able to find the news faster for you!"

Dammit, why could Jessamyn always see the truth? Morgan's rage boiled to the surface. "Dammit, Jessamyn, I'm a soldier, fighting for my country. I have to use every weapon—"

"What sort of weapon is an old man being eaten alive by cancer? You have no honor when you don't protect the helpless! Was spying for the *rebellion* all you could think of?"

Morgan yanked against the chains, clenching his fists. There was just enough truth in her accusation to cut him to the quick. "If you feel so strongly about loyalty to the Union," he snarled, attacking the least of her accusations, "then why haven't you married Cousin Cyrus, that West Point graduate, and started rearing a brood of Yankee troopers?"

"Because I," she gritted between clenched teeth as she stood over him, "unlike some men I could name, have a sense of duty toward those who trust me. I will care for my invalid father first, before I seek my own satisfaction in the marriage bed."

Morgan flinched and opened his hands, acknowledging a hit. He was too fond of her father to overlook the older man's need for Jessamyn, as death approached.

"You're a Rebel spy, Mr. Evans," she snarled at him, "who should be handed over to the authorities immediately, before you can cause any more harm. However, because of our families' long friendship . . ."

Why didn't that sound like the complete truth?

"You'll only be held here a few days. Then you'll be released outside the city to join the rest of your miserable, lying, Rebel friends."

Morgan frowned slightly, sifting rapidly through what she had and hadn't said. "I'll still have the information I stole from the Union Army."

Jessamyn laughed at him. "Grierson will already have marched and met Forrest in battle. Any other information you might have gained will be of little consequence."

He gaped at her, stunned by her accurate and succinct opinion. Hell and damnation, Forrest himself couldn't have summed up the situation more neatly than this seventeen-year-old gentlewoman, who'd never done anything riskier than shoot a few deer and birds.

"If you love the Union so strongly," he asked, slowly feeling his way through the web of her loyalties, "then why haven't you simply reported me to the local authorities?"

She glared at him, before she answered. "They'd shoot you as a spy or send you north to a prison, where you'd die of starvation or disease. We—our families—have been friends for too long. For my father's sake, I can't let that happen."

He frowned, considering her options. "And?" he probed.

Her chin came up as she met his eyes defiantly. A pulse beat hard in her throat, above her simple pearl brooch. "Holding you captive, privately, until your information becomes worthless is the only way to ensure that my duties both to the Union and to my family are satisfied. If the Union Army comes here searching for you, they will find me but not my father. They are welcome to imprison me, if they don't take him."

Morgan stared at her, startled out of his anger into assessing her situation. Devil take it, she had struck a difficult balance and she'd pulled the wool over his eyes to do it. Respect sprang up hard but he tamped it down ruthlessly. Forrest and his command could be wiped out if he didn't return with the news.

"Jessamyn, I'm working to help my friends in Forrest's army."

She pulled a face. "Traitors to the Union."

"Soldiers fighting for their cause who know the odds against them," he corrected as gently as possible, despite his anger. "My friends George and Nathan—we've fought and bled together for years. Huddled together against the cold and wept over our friends' graves. I can't let them die, Jessamyn."

Her mouth tightened.

"The new men have no weapons. If Grierson catches them, they'll be butchered like baby rabbits caught by a fox."

She flung up her hand. "Enough, Morgan. You have your loyalties and I have mine. We can agree that both are valid— but I will not release you from this room a minute earlier."

He accepted the small concession. "Very well. Your Union boys are good fighters, after all."

He eyed her expression and read her pacing's slower tempo as signs of hot temper, albeit slightly more under control. He'd have to tease her out of it, when both of them were calmer. He relapsed into silence, thinking hard. He needed to pick the locks on his shackles but with what? Something sharp, slender, flexible, and quite strong.

"You should not be alone with him, Miss Jessamyn," Aristotle repeated vehemently much later that night. Thanks to the lamplight, she could clearly see him shoot a livid glance at Morgan. "He's a fighter and a spy. You'd be better off trusting a water moccasin, which can also kill you with one bite."

"I know that, Aristotle." She patted him reassuringly on the shoulder. "Since Socrates has to help the Hutchinsons' mare give birth and Cassiopeia has already started boiling sugar for candy, I'm the only one who can watch Morgan. You're the only one here who can lift the kettle for her. Otherwise, she could drop it and burn herself with those five pounds of sugar, maybe even kill herself."

Aristotle grunted furiously and eyed his captive, clearly unappeased. Morgan didn't blame him.

"What can he do to me?" Jessamyn argued, in the clear tones of someone who relied on logic rather than instinct. "You and Socrates have already spreadeagled and shackled him to the bed. He's wearing his nightshirt so you're sure he doesn't have any weapons. Where's the danger?"

No damn danger at all, agreed Morgan unhappily. He'd be more than happy to provide some, if he could think of a way. But his only weapon was his voice and his one hope to escape was to use her hairpin as a lock pick on his shackles. Very thin odds—but not quite impossible. Time was passing, dammit; he needed to escape soon before Grierson destroyed his friends or the Yankees found him here.

"Do you want to search him again?" Jessamyn offered.

Morgan stiffened, appalled. *Please, God, no!* Aristotle's idea of a search was extremely thorough.

Aristotle blew out his breath, clearly unhappy, and drummed his fingers on the bedrail. "No, not again, Miss Jessamyn. But I won't be gone long. If he causes you any trouble"— he glared at Morgan, who glared back—"I'll see that he deeply regrets it when I return."

Jessamyn smiled. "Agreed."

Morgan grumbled internally.

Aristotle left with one more warning look at Morgan, who barely managed not to sneer. She settled herself in the chair across from the bed, out of reach but able to see him clearly, and began to flip through a book.

Morgan watched her broodingly. He needed to start her talking, move her closer so he could obtain that hairpin. But how? She had a great deal of glossy ebony hair, all neatly done up with a multitude of hairpins. Some of those Federal officers had watched her hair very closely. In fact, they'd ogled her.

"You're looking very well tonight in that dark green dress, Jessamyn," Morgan offered, wishing he knew more about flirting. But two liaisons, totaling less than four hours—and less than one hour of preparatory chatter—weren't much to go by. He'd have to make it up as he went along, judging by how she responded.

She arched an eyebrow. "Thank you, Morgan. Why the sudden interest in my clothes?"

"They're far more interesting than the décor in this room," he answered, which was at least somewhat truthful.

She snickered and his heart leapt hopefully. Maybe she could relax with him and come closer. Maybe.

"Almost anything would be more interesting than walls covered with fat yellow roses," she agreed. "But don't think I'll release you from those shackles, just because you have a golden tongue."

"I wouldn't dream of it," he agreed mendaciously. "But I would like to remind you of all the admiring glances sent your way at last night's dinner party."

She blinked and a trace of color crept into her cheeks. For the first time, she looked like a young girl. "Morgan . . ."

"That young lieutenant across from me could hardly keep his eyes from you," he continued, forcing his voice to stay gentle and teasing. Why the devil did he want to growl and change the subject? Then storm out and tell those Federal fools to stay the hell away from her? "In fact, I believe he said something about how beautiful your eyes were, like a forest glade in springtime."

She blushed and looked away, her eyelashes sweeping down to veil her expression. "Morgan, please. I rarely attend dinner parties with bachelors. You must be mistaken."

His voice deepened, despite his strong wish to retain a light touch. "Perhaps I did misunderstand his reaction. If I'd seen a beautiful girl, I wouldn't have stayed on the other side of the room from her. For a start, my body would have driven me closer to her."

She blinked at him, those long, long eyelashes fluttering over her deep green eyes. "What do you mean?"

Hell, could Jessamyn truly be so ignorant of a man's response to her attractions? But Uncle Heyward had always guarded her closely, which was understandable given how his wife had gallivanted off.

"When a man sees a lovely woman, he starts imagining what he'd like to do with her. Kiss her, touch her, fondle her, take her clothes off . . ."

"Morgan!" She stared at him, her eyes wide and her breathing very fast. Her expression was shocked and quite fascinated.

At least she hadn't slapped his face or run away, and his body liked this train of thought. "Look at me, Jessamyn. Do you see anything different below my waist?"

Her gaze roamed over him before dipping slowly, shyly down to his hips. His cock promptly surged upward.

"You—you're lumpy down there," she breathed, staring at him.

Hell, yes, he was lumpy. In fact, he was half-hard and becoming rapidly firmer. "Would you like to look, Jessamyn?"

"Look?" she squeaked, giving him a look of shock—and intense curiosity. "Oh, I couldn't."

He recognized her expression immediately. She'd worn it when he'd dared her to ride her horse through the swamp near Somerset Hall. "Scared, Jessamyn?" he drawled, in exactly the same tone he used then.

"Don't be absurd!"

He laid his head back and started whistling, determinedly ignoring his aching cock. "Of course you are."

"Am not!"

Morgan did his best to look innocent. "Prove it: touch me."

She went completely still.

Her pulse speeded up.

Touch him? But what harm could that do? The key was by the door, not on her. Surely he couldn't hurt her.

She eyed his iron shackles warily. Hercules couldn't have broken free of them. "Of course I'm not scared," she said proudly and stepped up to the bed.

At that moment, his cock swelled quietly, proudly between

his legs, lifting his nightshirt into the air. The hem—oh, goodness gracious, the hem barely reached his thighs. Below that, between his legs, a fat crimson pouch peeped out.

Jessamyn squeaked but didn't jump away. Her pulse skittered and she crammed her fist in her mouth, as heat built between her legs.

Dear heavens, he was becoming aroused. She'd seen a stallion service a mare a few times before but she'd never seen a man's private parts. Morgan—this was Morgan, beautiful, dangerous, and available for exploration.

He groaned, the sound somehow making her breasts ache until she wanted to play with herself. She twisted restlessly, rubbing her legs together. Why on earth was looking at him having this effect?

She slowly pulled the cloth up to his waist. Her breath caught in her throat at the sight that met her eyes.

Now she was definitely staring at his cock, which responded to her attention by swelling even more strongly. Had she ever seen a man's private parts? Surely not, as well bred as she was.

Morgan closed his eyes, enjoying the distraction from being chained—and the sensations that danced through his veins when her eyes roamed over him. Now if he could just persuade her to touch it, give him a chance of escaping this place . . .

There'd been that one girl in Jackson, who'd petted it like a kitten, before he'd ridden her; that had been very enjoyable. The other fellows told stories of women who liked to fondle men's cocks or even excite them with their tongues. But he'd never had time to try any of that. His two encounters with a female had always been focused more on getting the deed over with. He'd treated them politely, of course, but there'd never seemed to be much need for dawdling.

Perhaps he could somehow persuade Jessamyn to touch

him. And if her head ever came within reach of his fingers, and she should happen to lose a hairpin in the sheets—he'd gain his lock pick and a way out of here.

"Jessamyn," Morgan said as gently as he could. "My right ankle, the one that's had the shackle on it for the longest time, is cramping. Would you consider—could you possibly rub it, just a little bit, please?" He tried to make himself sound as inoffensive as possible. If she could touch his body in one distant spot, then he could slowly persuade her to come closer and closer. It had to work.

"Uh, your ankle?" She jerked her eyes away from his ribs and stared at the chain on the limb in question, which he couldn't lift more than a few inches. Obviously judging that it was no threat to her, she lightly rubbed her finger over the big toe. To his considerable shock, sharp pricks of heat ran up his legs and into his groin and chest when she did, very similar to how he'd felt with the Jackson lady. Did it have a direct connection with his cock?

He moaned softly, involuntarily.

Her eyes flashed to his. "Oh, poor Morgan, you must truly have a cramp." She stroked his big toe again and the delicious sensations were stronger this time, centering strongly in his balls.

He opened and quickly closed his mouth. How could he object? And when she paid similar attention to his other toes, tremors raced up his legs into his balls and cock. He hung his head back against the pillow, trying hard not to groan in delight. After all, dammit, this woman held him prisoner, even if her hands could drive him crazy. "Again, Jessamyn," he gritted, "please do that again."

"Perhaps rubbing your leg would help?"

Her husky whisper brought his eyes up to meet hers. That would bring her hands close to his very aroused private parts. How long could he survive without erupting? When handling himself, he usually lasted only a minute or two.

Her eyes were dark and dilated, her cheeks flushed, as she licked her lips nervously. She seemed a mite excited, given how her nostrils had flared.

"Certainly, you should rub my leg," he agreed, infusing more confidence into his voice than he truly felt. "Keep moving your hands upward so you also give my thigh a good rub. Knead, then release. Knead and release."

She nodded jerkily and obeyed, her movements in perfect rhythm with his voice. His chest and nipples were so tight, the fine cambric nightshirt rubbed them as sharply as the coarsest homespun. And lordy, lordy, he was hard enough that his cock was flush against his stomach.

But she needed to be more excited so she'd toss her head, shaking her hair free and losing a hairpin, to give him his chance at escape.

Her free hand rubbed her breast quickly before falling guiltily away. Did she perhaps play with herself? Maybe another time, he could persuade her to do that for him.

Her slender fingers, uncommonly strong for a woman, slid up the inside of his leg. Morgan caught his breath as the deep pulses ripped through his body. Pre-come slipped over his cock, warning of his imminent eruption.

"Have you ever seen a man's pleasure?"

Her eyes widened. "Never." She glanced nervously over her shoulder, gauging the distance to the door. "Surely I should go now."

"You can't go, not now!" Genuine desperation rang through his voice. "I'll explode if I don't climax and I can't do it for myself."

She half rose from the chair, staring at his privates. He could feel the drafts of cold air tickling his balls, where they were tucked up hard against his cock, ready to launch his seed. She could probably see them very well from her location beside the bed. Somehow, despite his already fierce excitement, his cock found the ability to harden even more. He gave himself far less than a minute before he exploded, regardless of whether or not anyone was touching him.

"Aristotle should be here, if I'm to handle you so much," she protested.

"I can't finish if another man's watching me," Morgan growled. In truth, he had no idea if he could or not—but he wasn't about to waste time finding out. His cock needed her to be excited and so did his escape plans. "Dammit, Jessamyn, have mercy on me! I'll explode in another minute, if you don't help me."

She swallowed hard, her tongue sliding over her lips. Then she stepped closer to him. "What do you want me to do?"

"Just put your hands around my privates and start rubbing. Up and down, up and down." His eyes slid shut as his seed began to rise from his balls. "Hold me firmly—yes, like that."

"It's almost like milking you."

"Yes," he gritted. "Faster, faster."

"You're dripping, Morgan."

"I'm coming, dammit! Ah, yes, now!" he roared as the climax blasted through him like a freight train. Stars burned behind his eyes as his muscles locked and he shot jet after jet through her hands. Glorious, shattering ecstasy—far stronger than he'd ever had by his own hand or with another woman.

Morgan stirred slowly afterward and considered opening his eyes. Someday his father's words would come true: he'd be old enough not to fall asleep immediately after carnal encounters.

Something had changed since Jessamyn had left, though: now he was chained to the bed by only one ankle.

"There's a pitcher and washbasin on the table for you, Mr. Evans, plus a washcloth and towel." Aristotle's voice was completely neutral.

Morgan's eyes sprang open and he glared at the impassive Negro. Dammit to hell, he hated being a captive, where anyone could watch. Especially since he hadn't gained a hairpin to use for a lock pick.

Someday the tables would be turned and his fair jailor would be the one begging for ecstasy at his hands.

On the other hand, he had successfully talked her into carnal pleasures. So he should be able to convince her to sample more of those, until she finally lost a hairpin.

He smiled, not nicely, and rose to clean himself, ignoring his audience.

Chapter Three

Morgan paced the attic room, ignoring the impassive Socrates. Outside, a cloud brushed over the sun, darkening the room further. He clenched his fists, cursing his jailers silently, and resumed his prowling.

By now, Grierson would probably be close to Forrest, who was burdened by so many raw troops—six times as many as his seasoned men. Besides, Forrest had neither artillery, horses, nor supplies. He wouldn't be able to make his usual vicious, lightning attacks upon the enemy and he'd also need every man.

Yet Morgan, a lieutenant who'd fought for the Confederacy since Mississippi seceded, had been locked up in Memphis by a gently bred young lady and was of no use to his general in this crisis. It was time to put aside his wounded pride and face the truth.

Jessamyn had won. Even if he escaped within the next hour, he would not be able to warn Forrest of Grierson's coming. However, if he escaped that night, he'd still be able to rejoin the army at the planned rendezvous—and join the coming battle. It was his duty to fight, no matter what he had to do to reach the battlefield. Even if he had to obey some nonsensical order Jessamyn gave him and pretend to be a willing follower in carnal matters.

Dammit, he'd learned far too well over the past hours just

how much he enjoyed his own sensuality, especially when laced with bondage, demanding orders, and the contrasting sharpness of a heavy shackle.

But he didn't want to be the one wearing the bonds. No, his excitement always built when he imagined himself giving Jessamyn the orders, watching her writhe as he handled her, made her climb the pinnacle to carnal frenzy, made her wait until he gave her permission to climax.

He was now bitterly aware that he would never be happy until he had a willing woman in his bed, passionately eager to wear his bonds and follow his orders to carnal ecstasy. The sweetest revenge of all for these miserable hours would be to have Jessamyn as that woman.

But he had to walk away from that revenge. Fighting beside General Forrest was more important.

Jessamyn covered her yawn and wished there were a Christmas hymn that Clarabelle Hutchinson could play faster than a dirge. Still, the rest of the performances at the musicale, here at the military hospital, had been well received, and Clarabelle's was the next to last. She adjusted her attentive smile and shifted her thoughts elsewhere.

Father would return day after tomorrow, from selling Somerset Hall to Richard Burke, just in time for Christmas. He and Mr. Burke were concerned that Somerset Hall remain in family hands, given Burke's lack of children. So they'd agreed that should Burke or his heirs ever wish to sell the house and its grounds outside of their immediate family, Jessamyn and her heirs would be given six months to buy Somerset Hall at the price Burke had paid for it.

She considered that clause, a "right of first refusal," something she was very unlikely to ever use, given her poverty. Selling the shell of Somerset Hall would barely provide enough money to take them north, in hopes of finding a surgeon who could save Father's life.

She and Father would leave Memphis next week for New

York. Now it was time to say good-bye to Morgan and her childhood dreams of marriage to him, time to start building a future with someone else. A man she could always trust. A man who would tell her the truth, whether it was pleasant or distasteful, unlike Morgan.

Her mouth tightened as she clapped politely for Clarabelle.

But she was enjoying touching Morgan, tasting him, seeing his eyes darken in passion. Hearing him groan as she took him over the edge of control.

Such sweet payback for how he'd treated her family. She'd forgiven him easily when he'd enlisted in the Rebel cavalry, seeing it as his duty to fight for his own beliefs, no matter how misguided they were. But when he'd risked her father's life, in his spying—that was, that was . . . She ground her teeth, unable to utter in these environs the stableyard words that best described his foul arrogance.

She had to release him soon, so he could leave town tomorrow night before Father returned and Cyrus arrived. But she couldn't let him leave without seeing him one more time . . .

The weak winter sunlight was fading as Morgan flipped through *Ivanhoe*. Jessamyn stretched high on her toes to look out the dormer window, trying yet again to see what was happening at Army headquarters—and to ignore the fact that she was alone with Morgan. From this high on the bluff, sound carried quite well from the town below and the river beyond. Also, it was winter, when the leaves had fallen from the trees, so even the slightest noise from blocks away could be heard quite clearly.

So many men had left over the past week to chase Forrest that she'd grown accustomed to the Memphis garrison being quiet. But an hour ago, she'd heard cavalry saddling up with a great martial clatter and jangling. The hubbub had grown so great that Socrates had gone to move Morgan's horse out of their barn and into the much more inconspicuous garden shed. Then Mrs. Hutchinson had abruptly requested Aristotle's help to hide her family's valuables from what she saw as impending looting by the Federal troops. Unable to spreadeagle Morgan to the bed without Socrates's help, Aristotle had given Jessamyn a blistering lecture on keeping her guard up against Morgan and reluctantly left them alone.

Jessamyn rolled her eyes again at that unnecessary warning and strained a little farther to see around the mansard roof's corner. Every young lady should be wary of Morgan, especially his tempting looks and voice. His broad shoulders or those strong arms. And the way the muscles in his thighs bunched when he neared climax . . . She blushed.

At any rate, she'd had Aristotle dress Morgan in street clothes, which should greatly reduce his attractiveness.

Metal rattled and horses' hooves drummed, echoing across the pavement and the brick houses.

Despite all the noise, she couldn't tell where the cavalry were going. She tried to tell herself they were just a small party, planning to join the others in pursuit of Forrest, but her tumbling stomach didn't quite believe her brain. Cyrus would be here within a few days and he'd know exactly how to interpret the commotion. His strong sense of duty would also command him to put Morgan into prison.

"Do you plan to touch me again?" Morgan asked suddenly, his voice a honeyed drawl against the growing shadows.

Jessamyn glanced over her shoulder at him, trying to read his expression in the weak winter sunlight. She was dressed less formally today, in a blue house dress with petticoats but no hoops, given the narrowness of the attic stairs. "Why?"

"Do you really think you need to tie my hands to the bed? I swear I won't kill you, Jessamyn, if you run your fingers over me."

She spun around to face him at that and considered him warily. He'd closed his book and his expression seemed honest.

Why was he flirting with her again? Boredom? Were young men truly so fixated on carnal matters that they'd think of nothing else when isolated? Miss Ramsay, her old governess, had warned her of that masculine tendency but she'd never before had the opportunity to observe it.

Still, he hadn't tried to hurt her the night before when she'd handled him. She couldn't believe he'd injure her physically, no matter what he'd done to her family in the service of his precious Confederacy.

And she truly wanted to put her hands on him again, to do more than just run her fingers up and down his hard cock. Why, she'd lain awake last night in bed playing with herself, as she'd dreamed of doing so. She'd even brought herself to ecstasy while fantasizing about kissing the hard muscles of his body.

She gulped at the memory, her limbs softening.

If she was to be cautious, she'd have to summon Aristotle and Socrates back to chain him down. She scowled at the thought of letting them handle Morgan's naked body again and made up her mind. "Would you do anything I ask?"

A muscle throbbed in his cheek. "You have my word."

If she agreed, she could touch him and finally learn everything about what a man's body was like and what pleasured it, after so many years and so many books. Dispassionately, of course. After all, Morgan was a splendid male specimen: healthy, strong, and virile. Her only interest was in learning what potential mates were like. There was no chance now that they'd ever marry.

Her mouth went suddenly quite dry. "Agreed."

He bowed briefly, then stood up beside the bed to face her, his head held just as arrogantly high as ever. Broad-shouldered, slim-hipped, long-legged. Jessamyn's hands tensed at her sides as she fought against simply lunging at him. "Take your shirt off," she ordered, "and your suspenders."

He did so, far too slowly for her taste, revealing a military

Adonis clothed in beautiful muscles, even when marked with so many scars. Some looked old and ragged, possibly from before the War when he'd ridden with the Indians.

Her breathing was far too fast when she walked over to him from the window. Jessamyn ran her fingernail down one particularly ragged scar on his forearm before dropping it to his hip. He grunted softly when her hand moved toward his stomach but never moved, his eyes slitting with pleasure like a wild animal. She tried a similar caress elsewhere, scratching his forearm again—and he purred. His eyelids drooped, veiling his expression.

She circled his neck lightly with her fingers, the strong cords throbbing against her palms. Groaning something, he arched his head back, sending his thick, chestnut hair sliding over the back of her hands. She shivered, transfixed by an unexpected stab of lust. She hadn't known that the feeling of someone's *hair* could have that effect on her.

She ran her fingers very lightly down his shoulders, exploring the differences between neck muscles and collarbone and shoulder sockets and biceps. Then back across his chest, finding the great sweep of his—pectoral?—muscles, under the neat mat of dark hair. Her thumbs met in the middle and traced the center line back up to his collarbone. He groaned her name, leaning forward to meet her touch.

He was such a pleasure to her eyes, if not to her heart. Even her bones seemed to melt in appreciation.

She swirled her fingers back over his chest muscles, around and around until she centered on his small male nipple. It was hard and pointed, a small taut nubbin, like a little dagger demanding attention. She caught it between her fingers.

He growled, his head falling back, and his body rocked in rhythm with her touch. Her pulse leaped, as hunger pooled fire-bright deep within her. She tightened her legs, muscles throbbing deep within her and liquid heat gliding onto her thigh. Dear God in heaven, she needed to protect herself somehow from completely acting out her animal desires.

"Turn around and grip the bedpost," she gasped.

He hesitated for a long, long moment until she thought she might have to speak to him again. But with a great shuddering breath, as if he argued with himself, he spun around to straddle the bedpost.

She gulped, caught by the play of muscles in his hard thighs, and moved closer. Would he straddle her the same way, if he knelt over her to let her taste his cock?

His head swiveled to watch her. Were his eyes just a little too intent, rather than dazed with passion?

She stroked herself against his back, letting her skirts and petticoats rasp his legs. She was warm, so warm, as if it were an August day, not late December. He rocked against her, groaning her name softly, his hands tight around the iron bedpost as she'd ordered.

Lord above, how she wanted to unbutton her bodice, open her corset and chemise, and press her aching breasts against him. Surely it wouldn't hurt if she undid the top few buttons. Not enough to show anything but enough to give herself some air?

She forced herself to step away, her breathing ragged. "Unfasten your trousers. But don't touch your intimate flesh."

He choked off something, probably impolite, before she could understand the words, but obeyed. She fumbled over undoing her two buttons, her tongue flickering over her lip as she watched him. She needed to touch him, see him, taste him . . . Dear heaven, where had that thought come from?

Outside, the hoofbeats were louder but not worthy of attention, especially not when compared to being able to openly examine his—cock?

She circled him, nibbling a fingernail nervously, and closely surveyed her prize. It was definitely thicker than her wrist, of a remarkable length—what woman could possibly conceive of taking such a fiery brand inside her?—flushed crimson and brushed with throbbing blue veins, standing proud and tall, gilded by liquid gliding from the top. So utterly unlike the cold marble statues she'd seen in size and color, so much more interesting—and so very much more inviting and delicious. She wanted more of it, more of him. She wanted to touch it, measure it, rub it, rub herself against it, fill herself with it . . .

Fill herself with Morgan . . .

She delicately touched the very tip, where it was shaped rather like a mushroom. It was hot, velvety soft, yet hard underneath—and it jerked violently, all the way down to its base.

She yanked her hand back and her eyes flashed up to his face.

He was biting his lip so hard he'd drawn blood. His jaw was clenched so tightly she couldn't tell if he felt pleasure or pain. Involuntarily, she stepped away from him.

His hands tightened on the bedpost, a fine tremor running all the way through his body. A narrow crimson line trailed down his chin, and his gray eyes were hooded like an eagle's. "Don't you want to handle me, Jessamyn?" he crooned.

She hesitated, panting, her stomach heaving and her pulse racing. Every instinct warned her that he was both dangerous and irresistible.

"Do you think I'm interesting? Attractive? All you have to do is reach out, Jessamyn."

Caught by the lure in those soft words, she finally nodded. She might be doomed for this but she had to do more. "Lie down on the bed," she whispered, "and hold on to the posts."

He obeyed her, his eyes on her the entire time, as if challenging her to fondle him. He made a shameless display, while centering himself on the bed: He wiggled his hips and bucked and bent his knees. His cock bobbed and curved harder toward his belly, while his trousers slid farther down.

Her breath stopped at the sight. She was shockingly conscious of the aching heat between her thighs. She wanted, more than she'd longed for the sweetest Christmas present, to slide her tongue over him. To run her teeth over him, just to test his firmness. And feast her mouth for hours on the rich delicacy of his engorged flesh. Heaven knows how she'd wrap her lips around him but such challenges were the spice of life.

The first slow smile of pure carnal heedlessness slowly awoke on Jessamyn's mouth. She licked her lips slowly, sat down on the bed beside him, and reached for him.

Morgan grabbed her hands and tumbled her onto the bed under him, settling his full weight between her legs and covering her mouth with his other hand. His gray eyes were wide open and completely focused on her, while his iron-hard cock rubbed against her thighs. He meant to have his way with her and he was much, much stronger and deadlier than she was. He was entirely masculine, entirely dangerous—and her body was still hot and eager for him, him alone. Morgan, who was beautiful and dangerous and forbidden.

She was breathless with shock—or was it anticipation?

He smiled down at her, in a curve of dark masculine intent. He imprinted himself on every inch of her, the hard planes of his chest flattening her nipples' hard points, which brought them up faster. His scent stealing into her nostrils, the sound of his breathing seducing hers into matching its steadiness. The narrowness of his hips demanding that hers widen to cradle his. The hard strength of his legs ready to thrust hers open.

Something feminine deep inside Jessamyn recognized him and melted in welcome. Her eyes widened, and her hands flexed to hold him—not to push him away.

"And now, Jessamyn *mine*," Morgan growled, his eyes blazing with assurance as they roamed over her, "you will learn what a *man* does with *his* captive. I will plunder your mouth until your lips are bruised—yet your voice will cry out for more. I will knead and plump and suckle your breasts until you ache, but you will arch under me in anticipation and desperation for another touch." His gaze swept over her, lingering insultingly on the top of her chemise where it peeped out of her dress.

Good God in heaven, what was happening to her? How could Morgan's voice sink into her blood like the richest of aphrodisiacs, until all she wanted was to grab his head and pull him down? "Morgan, no! Don't speak like that."

But her protests sounded all too much like sighs of maidenly virtue, rather than true outrage.

"I will lift your skirts, Jessamyn, up to your waist. Your skirts and your petticoats. I will rip off your drawers—"

"Please, Morgan . . ." Could that be cream gliding hotly down her thigh?

"And my cock, Jessamyn, which your hands have pleasured so well?"

Her body clenched, her thighs tightening as if riding him. Her blood sang, starting the rise to ecstasy.

"You will welcome me into your body and then beg me for more, as you have made me ache for your hands."

The world narrowed to Morgan's gray eyes and his body pressing into hers. Her heart surged into her throat at his look's fierceness.

Silence lay between them for an instant as he stared into her eyes. She knew with complete and utter certainty that he would do everything he had said and more—and that she would respond as he had foretold. Her body began to open and heat in welcome for him.

Sound beat against the windows: horses were gathering less than a mile away.

Morgan's head jerked up to listen. The hoofbeats turned, fading slightly. Was the cavalry going elsewhere or simply winding around the hill in order to cover both entrances?

The sound of steel-shod horses and heavy military tack drummed through the closed windows, louder and louder. Cavalry horses and their riders were moving up the hill, at a trot, coming with purpose toward the Tyler house.

Dear God, someone must have definitely told the Federal army that Morgan was staying here.

Morgan sprang off the bed, but the shackle brought him

up short. He spat a string of curses and began to rapidly fasten his trousers.

Jessamyn shuddered. She should be glad they'd been interrupted but all her body wanted to do was pull him back down on top of her and demand that he satisfy her immediately.

Pulling her sleeves down over the telltale bruises on her wrists, she forced herself to leave the bed and fetch the key to Morgan's shackles. She tossed it to him and yanked open the door. "Go out through the window. Your horse is in the Hutchinson's gardener's shed."

His eyes flashed as he caught the key. "You really didn't intend to keep me."

"Of course not," she spat. Damn, that was a stupid comment. "God knows what they'll do to Father if they catch you here. Go!"

Aristotle burst in and began to strip the bed, always keeping an eye on Morgan.

"We have unfinished business, Jessamyn," Morgan snarled, pulling on his boots as fast as she threw them to him. "I still mean to take my revenge. One day, you'll be the one lying in a bed under me, begging for more of my touch."

Her heart stopped beating. She'd enjoyed sharing a bed with him far too well.

Aristotle came swiftly erect, a long thin knife in his hand, snarling like a waterfront dog.

Jessamyn reached for her tattered pride and tossed her head up. "I wouldn't marry you now if you crawled."

Morgan laughed. "Who mentioned marriage?" He disappeared without a trace, silently shutting the window behind him.

Jessamyn buried her face in her hands for a moment, praying her stomach would drop out of her throat. She couldn't follow Morgan out that window, no matter how much her blood heated at the thought. He was a reckless, dishonorable rogue who made her behave far too much like her mother.

"Are you all right, Miss Jessamyn?" Aristotle asked gently. "Cassiopeia will stall those soldiers as long as she can and you know Socrates has made sure there's no trace of that man's horse. In another minute, I'll have this place looking as it did when old Mrs. Tyler was here. You'll be safe."

She nodded blindly, tears prickling behind her eyelids, and released her childhood dreams. "I'll go down to see them now."

She went down the stairs heedlessly at first. The rooms' emptiness tore at her heart, reminding her of just how much had been lost. Everything that spoke of family was gone—pictures, trinkets, even heavy pieces of furniture like her mother's piano. All that remained was some gold in a St. Louis bank and the cash from Somerset Hall, scarcely enough to give Father a chance at living.

But she still had to protect Father and the servants. If the Federals suspected she was lying, they'd arrest them all and even a single night in jail might kill Father.

She stopped on the second floor, at her bedroom, and quickly changed her dress into an equally simple black one that lacked any telltale reminders of Morgan's lust. She pinned a simple mourning brooch at her throat, a memento of her grandmother and family duty. Then she held her head high as she went to deal with the cavalry. She came down the final flight of stairs like a queen, her lip curling at how vehemently the Yankees were telling Cassiopeia it was her duty to allow them to search.

Of course, the remarkable fact was that they hadn't already burst into the house, sabers drawn, and burst every door in their eagerness to find anything remotely smacking of a Rebel spy.

She glanced out the windows on the landing. Silhouetted against the blood-red sunset, all the sentries were still trampling the lawns and the gardens, circling the house in search of evidence. At least they weren't baying like bloodhounds searching for an escaped prisoner.

They'd been there almost ten minutes and Morgan must be well away by now. Why on earth were they being so restrained?

She tilted her chin a little higher and came down the stairs into the foyer. The first things she saw were the headgear—those small, flat hats called kepis, so popular with the infantry. A handful of broad-brimmed hats, with curling plumes, marking cavalrymen. A glimpse of Cassiopeia's turban, bobbing vigorously, as she insisted that the gentlemen sit down and have a nice cup of tea while they waited.

Then she stopped, her hand resting on the banister. A top hat? What the devil was a civilian doing in this company?

Its owner turned around and Charlie Jones, Mother's disreputable nephew who'd been forbidden entry to this house years ago, looked up at her. His lips curled, like a cobra scenting the air. "Good evening, cousin."

Her body went cold. No explanation for his presence was pleasant. Her brain turned calm, working at twice its normal speed. He was obviously a friend of the troops so she didn't want to start by antagonizing him. *Very well, try the gracious hostess tactic first.* She pasted a warm smile on her lips and hoped it extended to her eyes. "How do you do, cousin? Would you care for some tea?"

She glided farther down the stairs, grateful Miss Ramsay, her English governess, had drilled her so long and hard. Ladylike manners were Miss Ramsay's counterweight to Father's encouragement of Jessamyn's sharpshooting and horsemanship skills. Here good manners were a mask for fighting a deadly game, while the military watched them. What the devil was going on?

"I need to talk to you." He grabbed her elbow, his fingers biting deep.

She drew herself up in a ladylike demand to be freed. "Charlie!"

Several of the officers growled and clapped their hands to

their sabers. "Mr. Jones! She may be a Rebel but she's still a lady," one of them snapped. "You will treat her as such."

Charlie gave her a look she remembered all too well from her earliest years, the promise of dire retribution once they were alone, and released her slowly. His voice was business-like for the Federals, though. "My apologies, cousin. I moved too quickly in my enthusiasm to see you again."

She managed not to rub her elbow. Damn, Charlie had hurt her worse in that single instant than Morgan had, when he'd held her while she struggled. "I understand, Charlie." *And I'll never be alone with you, if I have any choice.*

"Would you care to speak in the front drawing room?" she offered. It was the only room downstairs, other than the library, that still retained much of its furniture. Its huge double doors couldn't be as easily closed as a single door. So he'd probably have to leave them open, thereby letting the officers watch—and keep offering her some form of protection.

He agreed without any argument, which made her very uneasy. What was Charlie's game? Did he have some idea Morgan had been here? But she kept her expression serene when she faced him, despite how hard she locked her knees under her skirts. "Yes, cousin?"

He drew closer to her and spoke softly in a tone that the others couldn't hear. If they were his friends, why was he keeping this secret? The hair on the back of her neck prickled.

"I know you're harboring a Rebel spy."

She spat the answer back at him, glad it was the truth. "No, we're not."

His eyes narrowed. He was a young man who promised to be very handsome. But when he did that, he looked more like a pig. "I know Morgan Evans was in town."

She shrugged, praying her hammering pulse wouldn't betray her. "Morgan Evans rides with General Forrest according to Aunt Sophonisba."

He slammed his fist against the marble fireplace. "Doesn't

matter if he's here or not. If I swear out evidence against you and have my friends do the same, you and your father will spend time in jail."

"You know Father would never survive even one night in prison. How can you suggest doing something like that to him?"

He smiled, happiness leaping into his eyes.

Oh damn, she'd just given him a path to what he wanted, which was always money. But everyone knew Father was penniless.

"Your father just sold Somerset Hall," he whispered, coming even closer.

She fought the urge to step back. Showing weakness to Charlie was never wise. "So?"

"Give me the money and there'll be nothing said about Rebel spies."

All the air whooshed out of her lungs, as if she'd been struck. How could he even suggest taking that money? "Pay you blackmail? With the gold for the surgeon who might save Father's life?"

He nodded. "If you don't pay me, he won't live another week," he pointed out callously.

Jessamyn saw red, entirely forgetting to think matters through. "Why, you dirty rat! You make a rattlesnake look upright!"

She slapped him hard and he immediately hit her back, sending her staggering against a sofa. The cavalrymen started forward in a clatter of belts and spurs, as Cassiopeia shrieked a Creole imprecation.

Charlie reached for Jessamyn, clearly intending to land at least one more blow before he was stopped. She tried to scramble to her feet, tasting blood from a split lip.

Suddenly a deep, harsh voice cut through the clamor. "What the devil is going on here?"

Silence fell as everyone turned to stare at the man standing in the doorway. He was tall, a few inches shorter than Morgan but slightly stockier, with dark red hair, albeit brighter than Morgan's. He wore a Union Army's lieutenant colonel's uniform, a saber hanging ready at his side. A black eye patch covered one eye with a white bandage underneath, while the red streaks of healing wounds distorted the cheek underneath. Jessamyn hadn't seen him since the fall of 1860, before the War broke out, but she recognized him immediately. All in all, he looked like heaven on earth to her.

"Cyrus!" she cried and bolted for him. "Oh, Cyrus!" She buried her face against his chest and his arms promptly wrapped around her. She gulped for air, taking comfort from the one man—other than her father—who'd always been totally trustworthy.

"Cousin Jessamyn," Charlie began silkily.

She shuddered. "He thinks we're harboring spies."

Cyrus snorted, the sound neatly expressing a very low opinion of Charlie. "Gentlemen, I'm very sorry you've had a long ride up here today for nothing. I can assure you that my cousin and her family will no longer do anything to weaken the Union. In fact, I've come to take them back to New York with me."

Jessamyn could have wept for joy to hear him claim her as kissing kin.

One of the soldiers muttered under his breath before speaking up, loud and clear. "My deepest apologies, sir, for distressing your family. Please believe that if I'd known they were related to you, I would never have ordered a patrol to come here." He cast a furious look at Charlie. "We'll leave now, sir."

"And the men outside?" Cyrus drawled, steel threaded through his quiet Mississippi tones.

The cavalry officer managed an excuse of a smile. "We'll return tomorrow at first light to repair the grounds, sir. Your family's home will receive every consideration, as if it were mine, sir."

"Thank you, Lieutenant. Good-bye."

The cavalrymen tumbled over themselves to find the door,

dragging Charlie with them. "Dammit, Jessamyn, the next time you won't get off so easily!" he shouted.

Jessamyn shivered, gripping Cyrus's arm for support. Dear God, if she ever had money and Charlie wanted it, he'd have no hesitation in using the most brutal tactics to seize it.

"Are you well, Jessamyn?" Cyrus asked, tilting his head forward to see her more clearly. His voice was softer now, almost coaxing. He must have used the same tones when he and his troop of dragoons rescued the wagon train from a blizzard on the Great Plains. He'd been fresh out of West Point and the emigrants had been nearly hysterical, but he'd managed to steady them. They'd written a marvelous letter of recommendation afterward, which the Memphis and Jackson newspapers had proudly printed. "Come, sit down and catch your breath. I'm sure Cassiopeia is making fresh tea for all of us."

She settled on the velvet-covered sofa and drew Cyrus down with her, reluctant to lose contact with the one constant from her past that would carry into her future.

In a few days, after her father returned and had recovered from his journey, they'd journey to New York, a place she'd never seen and where she knew no one. They would have little money, once the surgery was paid for. If the surgeon refused to operate, then the money would be spent on making her father's final days comfortable. After that, she'd have to make her own way, as best she could.

She also knew, with a bone-deep finality, that thinking about Morgan excited her, and terrified her, beyond her ability to be rational. What would happen when she faced him again? Would he tumble her across a bed and laugh as she begged to be mounted, as eager as any broodmare in heat? She desperately slammed the door shut on that nightmare.

She shivered, chills running down her spine, and leaned against Cyrus. He was here; he was warm and safe and reliable and strong. She didn't have to worry about Morgan anymore.

Cyrus wrapped his arm around her and hugged her close. "Ah, Jessamyn," he whispered, a bit huskily.

Something in his voice sounded different from how he'd addressed her when they'd last met. Her bruised femininity stirred deep within her. She laid her head back against his shoulder and looked up at him, sliding her hand along his shoulder.

He was watching her, admiring her as if she were the most wondrous being on earth, eager to memorize her. His eyes traveled over her face and lingered on her mouth. His cock stirred against her hip, but he made no move to satisfy it, nor did he try to touch her.

His hunger for her, tightly leashed as it was, brought a spark of warmth back to her heart. There would be a future and she could find joy in it, even passion with a man.

She smiled at him, a little shyly, not quite sure what to do or how much she wanted. Just that she was willing to try, with Cyrus.

Chapter Four

West Point, New York, April 1864

Heyward Tyler's breathing rattled, fell silent, then resumed with a faint wheeze. Jessamyn stroked his hair back from his forehead, her other hand resting lightly on her small bouquet of roses. She had no more tears left to cry, at least not today. As he'd requested, time and again while his voice was still clear, she would fight to think only of the future. She would be a good wife to Cyrus and she would somehow pray that Morgan came safely home from the War.

Their cottage's principal bedroom was sparsely furnished but the few pieces were solidly built and very comfortable. Patriotic mottoes hung on the walls, exhorting soldiers to do their duty, and lace curtains allowed the day's last light to filter in. Plato stood silently on the bed's other side, ready to do anything needed for his beloved master. Tears tracked slowly down his face, but as ever, he said nothing. Cassiopeia, Aristotle, and Socrates stood beside Jessamyn, clean beyond anything she'd seen before. Cassiopeia was clutching a smaller bouquet of roses, which matched Jessamyn's, as if it might fly away. She'd even changed her favorite scarlet turban for an indigo one, on this glorious day.

The doctor was continually amazed that Heyward Tyler had lasted this long; Jessamyn wasn't. He'd promised her that he'd live to see her married and he'd kept every vow he'd ever made to her.

When they'd come to New York, the surgeon had quickly operated, shocked that Father had survived with a tumor so large. He'd done well at first, all the while strongly encouraging her budding relationship with Cyrus. Jessamyn still blushed to think of how he'd more than once "accidentally" locked her out of their little cottage, thus ensuring that she'd spend more time with Cyrus. There were also the times when he'd left Jessamyn and Cyrus alone in the front parlor. Oh, Cyrus knew very well how to bring her to ecstasy!

She could only guess why he'd supported Cyrus's courtship so strongly, despite his attachment to the Southern cause. Cyrus was the best of men, despite his occasional bouts of temper, and they'd known each other since childhood. Or perhaps it was because her father knew how little time he had left. In any event, less than a month ago, the tumor had returned and was growing far faster than before.

Cyrus had been a first lieutenant before the War, although one with an excellent record. Most Southern-born officers who chose to stay in the Union Army had a difficult time, but thanks to Cyrus's old friends, whom he'd saved from the blizzard, he'd been brevetted to major and sent to a Northern state's cavalry regiment, rather than a regular army regiment. Brevetting was a form of temporary rank that lasted only during wartime; when peace returned and the army shrank to its smaller size, an officer would go back to his former rank. Cyrus had fought brilliantly and been brevetted to lieutenant-colonel, before his wound at Gettysburg had sent him to West Point as a professor.

Yesterday Cyrus received orders to report to Washington and take command of a cavalry regiment, an unbelievable honor for a Mississippi-born officer. He'd leave tomorrow for the front, where he'd barely survived the last battle.

Her throat tightened at the thought of Cyrus dead or dying.

She closed her eyes, fighting for composure. She had to learn how to survive this fear, had to go on even when it felt as if her gut were being ripped out through her backbone . . .

When he received the orders, Cyrus had called on Father immediately and they were closeted for well over an hour. Then Cyrus had sought her out, gone down on his knee—she smiled, tears welling up at the memory of that proud man down before her—and begged her to consider his suit. He hadn't planned to ask her so quickly but her father's illness and the War's dangers had forced his hand. If he died, she'd at least have his pension and his friends to protect her.

The silly man had then apologized for not giving her time to fall in love with him and she'd laughed. She'd known to the roots of her being that she wanted to spend the rest of her life with him. She'd hurled herself at him, knocking him over, and oh, dear Lord, how they'd kissed. It was truly amazing that she was still a virgin. Only Cyrus's self-control could account for it, not hers.

She smiled reminiscently, curling her fingers around her father's paper-dry hand.

So here she sat, in a made-over wedding dress and veil, with a chaplet of flowers on her head, waiting for Cyrus by her father's side. The bedroom was decked in roses and orange blossoms, with netting and white ribbons everywhere possible, until it resembled a wedding bower. Colonel (Bvt.) Michael Spencer, Cyrus's West Point roommate and best friend, would be the best man. Michael's wife, Elizabeth Anne, was waiting in the front parlor with the chaplain, while his two daughters were playing outside, delighted at the opportunity to be attendants.

If she had been marrying Cyrus in Mississippi or Tennessee, Morgan would probably have been Cyrus's best man. Jessamyn flinched at the thought of standing close to him again. Would she still be as incredibly conscious of every breath he took?

Then horses' hooves and the crunch of steel wheels over

gravel announced a small carriage rolling up the driveway. Cyrus was here, safe for the moment. Joy blazed through her, until she felt she could have floated to the ceiling.

"Daddy! Daddy!" exclaimed the two Spencer girls, their affection for their father carrying even into the bedchamber.

The front parlor windows squeaked, probably because Elizabeth Anne and the chaplain were looking out. "How very thoughtful of them," the chaplain's booming voice observed.

"What?" Jessamyn whispered. She started to rise, trying to shake out the pins and needles in her hands from staying in such a cramped position for so long.

"Sit, sit!" Cassiopeia shooed her back into position. Jessamyn rolled her eyes but obediently turned back to the bed.

Her father stirred. "Jessamyn?" he croaked.

Her throat tightened at how weak his voice was and how faded his eyes were. "Yes, Father, they're here," she said gently, leaning over him. "Can you sit up now?"

"Yes." He coughed and tried to lift himself. Plato immediately gathered him in his arms, while Aristotle came to his aid but was hardly needed. Jessamyn quickly shifted her flowers to the table, her heart shattering once again at how easily the much smaller manservant could maneuver him. Socrates shouldered in to plump up a pillow, an odd sight in those big hands.

With the ease of long practice, they soon had her father settled against the pillows and whisked away the bloodied handkerchiefs from his resulting coughing fit. The cancer was breaking down the inside of his mouth and throat faster and faster. Cassiopeia carefully gave a different elixir to him, one with a sharp scent that startled Jessamyn. She shot a hard look at Cassiopeia.

Her father's eyes suddenly brightened and he almost had all of his old alertness, as he reclined against the pillows.

Cassiopeia slipped the spoon and small bottle into her pocket, her mouth grim.

Jessamyn closed her mouth reluctantly, her throat tight. Cassiopeia must have given him the special tonic he'd asked for, the one that would enable him to witness all of the wedding, even if it ripped away much of his little remaining strength.

For a moment, tears threatened Jessamyn. She'd rather have as many days as possible with him.

But he grabbed her hand and squeezed it in a shadow of his old strength. "You make a lovely bride, my dear. John and Rosalie Evans would be very happy for you."

The tears receded, allowing her to live in the moment. "Thank you, Father." She leaned down and kissed his forehead. He kissed her hand, only briefly fumbling for her fingers.

A brief spurt of excited voices, quickly hushed, announced the men's arrival. The chaplain came into the bedroom, smoothing his vestments, and Elizabeth Anne began to play Handel's "Largo" on the piano in the front parlor.

Jessamyn gathered up her flowers, while Cassiopeia stood beside her. Her heart was beating so fast, she thought her father must be able to hear it. For a few hours today, she would have her entire family together.

The two Spencer girls, one blond and one brunette, came solemnly through the door, their eyes enormous, and lined up alongside the wall.

Then Michael Spencer appeared—in a black frock coat and charcoal gray trousers, not a uniform. *Civilian clothes?*

He paced forward, clearing the way for her to see dearest Cyrus.

And Cyrus, too, was wearing a black frock coat and charcoal gray trousers, the clothing of peacetime. On this day of days, there would be no reminder of brother against brother, cousin against cousin, or bloody death.

She wanted to run to him, hurl herself at him, tell him he was the best of men for being so kind.

His mouth quirked and he winked at her very deliberately. She beamed at him and Cassiopeia gave a great, heaving sob of joy.

In deference to her father's fragile health—and Cyrus's limited time here—the chaplain kept the service very simple. A brief prayer, a simple yet graceful reminder of the joys and duties of marriage, then he led them through their vows. Jessamyn swore with a clear heart, gazing into Cyrus's loving face, and at the end she impulsively kissed his hand. He caught her cheek then and rubbed his thumb across her mouth in a foretaste of the night to come. She could hardly wait.

Cyrus's voice was deep and solemn, very steady like the man himself. But when the chaplain pronounced them married, Cyrus swept her up, off her feet, and kissed her until the world spun around her in a cascade of stars. Fires raced through her veins and her breasts ached to be free of her corset. *More, oh more, please,* she moaned into his mouth, twining her arms around his neck . . .

Jessamyn blinked at him when he lifted his head. "Hmmm?" she mumbled. Applause filtered into her dazed brain. She blushed but didn't try to move away.

He caressed her cheek, his good eye desperately hungry but leashed. "We have the rest of our lives, love, as long as God grants us. Let us spend this time with your father."

As long as God grants us. A shiver ran down her spine but she cloaked it, tossing her curls back. "Let us rejoice together, dearest husband."

Memphis, June 1865

Morgan eyed the bustling docks and considered the fruits of war, while gnawing on a chicken wing—his first meal all day.

Up here on a tin roof above a saloon, the air was comparatively quiet even if odiferous.

Down there, Federal troops, fat and happy in their blue uniforms, trotted back and forth unloading barrels and crates from riverboats. Wagons and drays rushed along the bluff while dogs scampered, hunting for scraps of food. There was even a very professional outfit, led by a tall black-haired man, loading gunpowder into a heavy Conestoga wagon with its canvas cover folded back.

The winning side, in other words.

After four years of war, Morgan was twenty-three years old and still half-starved. He was the lucky possessor of a very good, and equally half-starved, horse as well as Longacres, a few thousand acres of prime cotton-growing land in Mississippi.

He was also the Evans of Longacres and, as such, the head of the family. Cousin George, for one, looked to him for advice and assistance. Cousin David, whose arm had been shattered at Chickamauga, needed a place for his family of seven to stay, as well as an income. He was the best damn farmer in Mississippi, too, and if anyone could rebuild Longacres, it was him. Morgan had pointed him in that direction, told him where the last of Father's English gold pieces were and how to pay off the taxes, and promised he'd tell him later where to send reports. He'd also asked him to send Cousin George to read law, a profession where a windbag like him should do well.

Morgan broke the wing apart and began to suck the bones clean. When he finished, he'd have to beg some work so he could buy the gelding some feed. Then he'd have to figure out how to get them both across the river.

After that he'd head west, as he'd always dreamed. Once he'd seen Texas when he was fifteen, he'd known the wide-open spaces beyond the Mississippi River were where he belonged, although he'd never believed in the Great Southern Empire that Jefferson Davis had preached and his father had followed. His father had gone beyond Texas and settled in Arizona, where the Southern imperial dream said there'd be a railroad, cattle, and a golden empire.

But Morgan had found his own pleasures instead. Riding with Cochise had seemed like paradise, while the Apaches had treated an Anglo teenager as a man and taught him how to be a damn good cavalryman. Those times in Arizona before the War seemed like a dream now, when the Apaches fought Hispanics, not Anglos, before Cochise had been bitterly insulted and attacked by that stupid Army lieutenant and turned forever against Anglos.

There was too much open warfare now in Arizona for Morgan to make anything of his father's old holdings. But perhaps in a few years . . .

After he'd surrendered at Franklin—Morgan reflexively snarled at the memory—he'd thought briefly of crossing the Mississippi at St. Louis.

But Cyrus was stationed there, at the big Army depot. Cyrus with his beautiful wife, Jessamyn. The happiest man in the world, as Great-Aunt Eulalia reiterated in letter after letter.

Cyrus, the one man in the whole damn world whom Morgan would never try to cuckold.

So he'd have to give up the idea of revenge on Jessamyn. Shit.

Morgan thought of all the things he'd planned to do to her, how he'd have kissed until her mouth was red and pouting, teased her until she was pleading for more, and seen her legs widen in eagerness . . .

His cock swelled yet again inside his threadbare gray trousers. He cursed viciously and hurled the chicken bones away.

They caught a cat on the rump. It sprang into the air, yowling like a demon evicted from hell and alarming every horse for two blocks. Anxious neighs filled the air. A dozen horses reared, while a previously placid saddle horse bucked. Someone ran to calm it—and tossed his cigar toward a bucket.

Unfortunately, it caught a flag flying below a third-floor window.

Equally upset by the ruckus, the lead mules hitched to the powder wagon brayed and reared. Unfortunately, their driver had been watching the barrels being loaded, not his animals, and lost control of the reins. The team bolted, swerving into the main street, and sending the driver off the seat.

Morgan's heart leaped into his throat.

The smoldering flag and flagpole were now a merry little blaze. The team was aiming to pass directly underneath it, unable to see the flames. If the flagpole fell into the wagon and those kegs of powder caught fire, the entire block—if not the neighborhood or even the town—would be blown up. Men ran for their lives in all directions.

"Shit!" The mules were coming toward him and he might be able to jump into the wagon, if the mules came closer to his side of the street. The tall, dark-haired man was running behind the wagon, trying to catch it.

Calm swept over Morgan, the familiar coolness of the battlefield. Time stretched and slowed until the mules seemed to be barely trotting.

He crouched, knowing he'd only have the one chance. The normally calm mules' eyes were rolling, flecks of foam falling from their mouths. They brayed again, swerving, and brought the wagon closer to him.

He ran across the roof and leaped, pushing himself as far as possible into the air. He landed, thudding into the back of the wagon between barrels and half knocking the wind out of himself. He gasped but there wasn't time to completely refill his lungs.

He vaulted into the front seat, found the reins, and hauled back on them, shouting at the mules to stop. He didn't curse them; in his four years of stealing Union Army mules, patience and sweet talk were more useful.

He slowed them, even got them to curve away from the blaze, but couldn't make them stop.

But the black-haired man had caught up. Fearlessly, he ran to the leaders and grabbed the near-side mule's head, the one Morgan had already noted as the true ringleader. "Whoa, Chicago, whoa," he shouted in a clear Irish brogue.

The mule tried to keep running but less enthusiastically. The Irishman began to croon to him, catching the bridle and using his full weight to slow him down. The mules' ears flickered, obviously knowing and liking this man. The flaming flag and flagpole were only a few yards away. The fellow was either insane or the bravest man Morgan had ever met.

Morgan eased up on the reins slightly, no longer sawing at the mules' mouths to force them to obey but rather coaxing them. The team slowed.

Someone finally had the courage to throw water over the burning flag from the window. Morgan took his first deep breath.

The Irishman sang a verse of a very sentimental Stephen Foster air. The mules shook themselves out, their harnesses jingling, and did something approaching a prance.

Eyebrows climbing, Morgan coughed, clucked his tongue, and loosened the reins into a normal driving tension. The mules responded by adopting an extremely sedate air and fell into perfect driving rhythm.

The Irishman stepped away from the lead mules and swung himself up beside Morgan. "Good afternoon, boyo."

"Afternoon, sir." Morgan neatly turned the team around, avoiding several buggies, and headed back for the docks before he spoke again. "That was an amazing job of calming down those mules."

"You took quite a leap yourself."

Morgan shrugged, keeping a wary eye on the near-side leader. He wasn't sure the mule was truly tired enough to be reliable again. "It was the least I could do. I startled the cat, which began the whole affair."

Blue eyes flicked over him, evaluating every inch, then returned to his hands. Morgan stayed relaxed, the reins loose between his fingers but ready to instantly take command. He'd driven a great many teams of Army mules over the past four years, in good weather and bad, over bad roads and foul, when his superiors were yelling at him, and when Yankees were shooting at him. He had no concerns on how to handle either an Irishman's opinion of his driving or powder barrels as cargo.

"Not many men would admit that," the Irishman commented, his voice returning to a Western drawl. He was an uncommonly handsome fellow, but he carried himself with the quiet steadiness of a deadly fighter. "Can I buy you lunch?"

Morgan opened his mouth to proudly decline but his damn stomach chose that instant to express its own opinion, very loudly. He flushed.

The fellow never blinked. "I'm William Donovan, of Donovan & Sons, and I'd like to talk to you. I'm looking to expand and I'll need some good men."

Old memories flickered, from when he'd journeyed back to Mississippi from Arizona. "Fremont's contractor, from California? The one who hauled silver ore across the Sierra Nevada in the winter, when everyone said it couldn't be done?"

Donovan bowed, a slight quirk to his mouth. "Some overstatement there—but yes."

"I'm Morgan Evans and I'd be glad to talk to you."

The embarrassed driver came limping up at that moment with two other men, to take the wagon. Donovan sprang down and spoke quickly to one of them, who nodded, his hard eyes running over Morgan.

A moment later, Donovan was escorting Morgan up the street to a surprisingly clean little restaurant, where they settled into a private booth in the back.

"Afternoon, Mr. Donovan. Lemonade again?" asked the white-aproned waiter. "Fresh-made and ice-cold."

"Yes, thank you, Joseph."

"Beer for you, sir?"

"I'll have lemonade, too." *Lemonade? Since when did a teamster drink lemonade?*

"The lunch special or order off the menu?"

"The special will be fine, thank you."

Morgan nodded bemused agreement, all the while considering his host, who had the manners of an English nobleman and the attire of a dockyard porter. The attire was necessary for a teamster, but where had the manners come from?

"I don't drink spirituous liquors," Donovan said quietly.

Morgan flushed again, embarrassed at being caught staring. "Sorry. It's none of my business."

"That's quite all right." Donovan turned the conversation into a variety of unexceptionable topics. Morgan ate his lunch, mostly vast quantities of a superb soup and fresh bread, and easily kept up his side of the discussion. He also had a damn good time with a companion who was courageous, intelligent, and charming.

Finally Morgan sat, shredding the last piece of bread, too full to move fast. His only regret was that he couldn't take back some of it to his horse.

"Are you still interested in talking about employment?" Donovan asked.

Morgan's eyes sharpened. "Certainly. What do you want?" He wouldn't murder or rob, which many men were being hired for.

Donovan leaned forward, speaking more softly although no one was listening. The lunchtime crowd was gone now and the staff was cleaning up, leaving the tables around them empty. "Donovan & Sons carries high-risk freight into high-risk areas—items like silver ore, gold, payroll, military supplies. We typically travel through areas full of Indians and highwaymen."

Morgan blinked, his mind automatically falling into the same ways of thinking he'd have used under Forrest. "Do you want to send men in ahead and clear them out?"

Donovan shook his head emphatically. "No. That costs

time and money, both of which cuts into the profit. We want the client to trust us, which means we must arrive on time or earlier, if possible."

Morgan's eyebrows climbed, thinking back to sneaking dozens of mules past alarmed Yankees. "That's harder."

Donovan shrugged. "We don't try to hide wagon trains. We travel like a military convoy, with such force that villains don't attack us. Smaller, more precious cargo is carried so stealthily thieves can't find us."

Morgan was extremely fascinated. "In either case, you'd need excellent fighting men in case you're attacked."

"Exactly. I'm looking for honest, hardworking men who also know how to handle themselves in a fight. I pay very well, including a pension to the family should the worst befall."

He named a sum that made Morgan gape. If they'd offered Union teamsters that much, those boys would have broken ranks to come south.

"I believe Rebel veterans might fit in. Are you interested?"

Morgan nodded eagerly. The opportunity to travel the West and make money to build a future? He could start building the dynasty that Father had always demanded and try to stop thinking about Jessamyn so much. "Hell, yes!"

Arkansas River, western Kansas, June 1866

William Donovan's wagon train, bound for Santa Fe, was making camp in late afternoon, deep in Indian country. The big Murphy wagons' wheels had been chained together, creating a stout fortress, while all the mules had just been groomed and fed. The double layer of sentries was in position, with the next shift of drivers sleeping in the wagons. Rifle close at hand, the cook had dinner almost ready to serve. Donovan & Sons prided itself on having the best cooks available; in fact, Donovan had been known to pay cooks a bonus.

Despite the apparent peace on the bluff overlooking the river, William and Morgan were scrutinizing the territory ahead through field glasses as they considered their chances of dodging a Comanche attack. Morgan's field glasses were a bonus for a nasty expedition through the Mojave Desert.

Then a sharp whistle went up from the sentries to the northeast, the distinctive warble a signal of cavalry coming.

William and Morgan spun to look and glimpsed three cavalrymen approaching between the low hills. But given the broad-brimmed hats and the bandannas over their mouths to keep out the dust, they might as well have been anonymous.

"Good horses," Morgan commented.

William chuckled. "Tuck your Rebel prejudices away and give the Yankee horseflesh some credit. Those are damn fine horses and they've been well tended, too. What do you think of their military skills?"

Morgan grunted. "Never said Yankees couldn't fight. They're well disciplined and experienced, and especially good at not exposing themselves needlessly to any Indians hereabouts." He left unsaid what they both knew. The wagon train was too heavily armed and fortified to suffer Indian trouble but three lone riders, especially cavalry, would be an easy target. They'd have to offer them hospitality.

"You talk to them," William said, closing his pair of field glasses. "I'll tell Cook there's company coming."

Morgan shot his friend a mock glare, well aware he'd have to do all the wagon train's public conversing for the next month, given the bet he'd lost in their last trip to a brothel. Money would have been easier to lose, given the amount he'd made on that half-baked, get-rich-quick railroad scheme.

William clapped him on the shoulder and went off whistling.

When the cavalrymen cantered up, Morgan stepped out to greet them, a little wary of meeting Federal soldiers even with friends at his back. Every man but one in this wagon train was a Rebel veteran, as were most of those working for

Donovan & Sons in these lawless plains. But some cavalrymen were still fighting the last war, even if their ranks were
also swelled by Rebel veterans.

The lead rider swept off his broad-brimmed hat and pulled
down his bandanna. His face was tanned as dark as Morgan's,
his hair a brighter shade of red than Morgan's. A black patch
covered his right eye, although a jagged white scar led to it
across his cheek. His good eye was the same clear gray as
Morgan's. He bowed low in the saddle, a Mississippi drawl
rolling richly through his hoarse voice. "Good evening—Mr.
Evans."

Morgan's jaw dropped. By all that was holy—Cyrus? Here,
miles from anywhere? He hadn't heard that the head wound,
which had taken his cousin's eye, had also been bad enough
to carve up his cheek. With an expertise born of four years as
a guerrilla, Morgan visualized the saber blow that had caused
it—and was astounded his foster brother had survived.

In an instant, the years rolled away and he remembered
their old friendship. "Good evening, Captain Evans. You'll
stay the night, of course."

Cyrus nodded acceptance and signaled to his men with a
quick flick of his fingers. "Thank you on my men's behalf.
But I actually came to talk to you. You may not want me
close by afterward."

Morgan stilled, his face hardening. "We can speak privately
over here."

One of the troopers took Cyrus's mount, giving Morgan a
look that promised bloody vengeance. But discipline held, as
Morgan would have expected from Cyrus's men, and the fellow
took both horses away to be tended with the wagon train's
animals.

They found a small dip, still within sight of camp and its
sentries, but out of earshot if they kept their voices down.
Morgan turned to face his cousin, the man who had successfully wooed and won Jessamyn.

Cyrus folded his gauntlets together and tucked them into his belt. "This is our first chance to speak together since the War ended. We need to reach some sort of agreement."

Morgan nodded, acutely conscious that he'd never seen Cyrus quite this angry before. Cyrus was cold and deadly with it, his eyes fixed on Morgan as if they could bore through him like an auger. He came alert, ready to fight.

"I acknowledge my debt to your father, who reared me as his own child, after my parents' death," Cyrus continued in clipped tones. "He provided for my education, including my appointment to West Point. I have always felt a full member of your family, a brother in love and in blood. But . . ." He paused, his throat working and his fists clenched.

What the hell kind of lecture was this? From the man who'd married the woman intended for Morgan? Morgan barely managed to restrain himself from launching a blow.

"As your elder, I feel it my duty to say that your conduct was outrageous."

"*My* conduct?"

"To endanger Jessamyn and Heyward Tyler—when he was on his deathbed!—by taking your spying games into their house. You could have used a common tavern or a low boardinghouse instead. Spying is an acceptable part of war but endangering innocents is not."

The truth in that ripped deeper the guilt Morgan still felt, especially when he reread Great-Aunt Eulalia's letter about Uncle Heyward's death. He still felt guilty that he might have speeded Uncle Heyward's death by making him worry about Jessamyn's safety for a few days. Reflexively, Morgan lashed out in return, attacking the man he'd hero-worshipped since childhood. "Who are you to counsel me on acceptable behavior, when you are married to the woman promised to me from her cradle?"

"Are you calling me a thief?" Cyrus bellowed and charged. They came together in the middle of the small hollow, landing blows whose ferocity matched their speed. They were surprisingly well matched, fighting toe to toe and usually—although not always—politely. Soon Cyrus had a bruised jaw and Morgan a bloody nose, while the sun was sinking in the west.

Still they fought stubbornly on. Morgan's shirt was a bloody, dirty mess and Cyrus's uniform was ruined. But neither of them had showed any evidence of weakness, although Morgan was holding back slightly, still somehow protective of his cousin.

"Five minutes until dinner, gentlemen," came William's Irish brogue.

Morgan didn't take his eyes off Cyrus.

"After that, if you're still fighting, Carson the blacksmith and I will wash both of you. We don't want Cook's efforts wasted on two heathens."

Cyrus landed another punch to Morgan's jaw, rocking his head back. Morgan thudded a fist into Cyrus's ribs, making the other back off.

When the dinner bell rang five minutes later, however, they both stopped and looked at each other. Morgan began to smile at having matched his idol in a fight for the first time. Then he rubbed his cheek, wondering if Cook had made any stew. Venison might be difficult tonight.

Cyrus was shaking out his hands, eyeing the split and battered knuckles. His head came up and their eyes met.

Perfect understanding blossomed, as it had so many times during childhood.

They met in the middle and embraced, hands gripping forearms in the Roman salute and free arms around shoulders, grinning with joy over a good fight. When they walked back to camp, it was side to side with their Colts thumping quietly at their hips.

Morgan was acutely conscious of how much alike they looked now. Cyrus had always been the steadier element of their childhood triumvirate, with Jessamyn as the intelligence and himself as the prankster. Now Morgan stood a few inches taller, although Cyrus was slightly stockier. He was a captain now, owing to the smaller peacetime army, although he'd been brevetted to colonel during the War.

"I'm glad you survived that wound," Morgan said suddenly. Standing in Cyrus's presence now was like being close to the embodiment of manliness: battered but still deadly. Damn, he hoped he could one day do as well.

Cyrus didn't pretend not to understand. He touched the eye patch. "Your boys gave it to me the first day at Gettysburg, where I served with Buford. Losing an eye was worth seeing Lee run, if you'll forgive me saying so."

Morgan snorted. "I'd probably have given both arms to have seen Grant surrender."

They laughed together in perfect harmony.

Natchez, Mississippi, December 1869

Jessamyn caressed Cyrus's shoulder, the slightest of movements and one almost improper during a waltz. But here, late in the evening at Cousin George's wedding celebration, a happily married couple could be forgiven anything. And she did so enjoy touching Cyrus every chance she had, even if it was through his uniform.

The Natchez ballroom was huge and lavishly decorated, as befitted a Christmas wedding involving two of Mississippi's greatest families. Flowers and greens garlanded every conceivable surface and projection, while gaily dressed men and women were crammed into every corner, chatting as if society depended on the latest gossip.

Her husband winked at her and she grinned back. Dearest, dearest Cyrus. Five years of marriage and she was still the happiest of women. If only she could spend every day with him, but that was not always possible when one was married to an Army officer stationed on the bloody Kansas frontier. So she polished her old tomboy skills of horsemanship and sharpshooting, which forced her to concentrate enough that

she couldn't dwell on possible dangers to him. The typical female pursuits of needlework and watercolors, on the other
hand, left all too much time for her fertile brain to create a
million terrors to threaten him. Seeing her contentment with
the more unusual skills, Cyrus had strongly encouraged her
to improve them, even if it had made her—and him, for his
approval—known as a free spirit.

She chuckled to herself. Dearest Cyrus was passionate beyond belief and superbly skilled with his lips and tongue. She
was a lucky, lucky woman to share his bed, even if he did
tend to repeat the pattern of his attentions. Even if she sometimes wondered what marriage to Morgan would have been
like, since he'd made her so hot so quickly that last afternoon
in Memphis . . .

Sitting across from Morgan at the wedding dinner had
been awkward. She'd known every time he'd picked up a
knife or fork, turned his head to speak to the lady next to
him. She'd even watched in helpless fascination as his Adam's
apple moved in his throat when he drank.

"Have you seen Morgan?" Cyrus asked, looking over her
head.

Dear God, was he reading her mind? She had to wet her
lips before she could answer. "Morgan?"

"After two days here, the fellow is still three deep in chaps
wanting him to 'invest' in their old plantations." Cyrus chuckled, deep and soft. "What they really mean is an interest-free
loan to pay the taxes. If he'd just be rude to one of them, the
rest would scatter to the hills."

Cyrus twirled her for the fun of it, sending her flounce up
and over the steps to the musicians' platform. Jessamyn giggled as he had expected her to.

"Little cousin has the best manners in Mississippi and the
best stories of any Westerner. Pity this is the first time we've
both seen him since our marriage; I'd like to spend more time
with him."

Jessamyn sniffed, reminded of Morgan's numerous sins.

"He's probably inviting them to join in another one of his Western ventures, whose address is undetermined, reports few and far between, and the rewards unknown but potentially great."

"Those damn get-rich-quick schemes," Cyrus commented.

Jessamyn came alert at the worried note in his voice, realizing he'd just described both his father and Morgan. She closed her eyes and leaned her head against Cyrus's shoulder. She would not mention her own concern that Morgan was shirking his responsibility to the family, since David was managing Longacres, not Morgan.

The man was shady and untrustworthy a dozen times over, from everything she'd heard in the past six years. Nothing at all like reliable, adorable Cyrus.

Her beloved husband immediately pulled her closer, possessively, wrapping his arm tighter around her waist. He nuzzled her cheek and she shivered, recognizing the preliminary to a bedroom romp. Her pulse immediately speeded up and she tilted her neck in invitation, just a little.

"It's very late. Does my darling feel a little tired?" he whispered, his tongue flickering against her skin. The wicked man had perfected this so that almost no one could see exactly what he was doing.

Jessamyn gripped his shoulder desperately, her skin flushing under her respectable blue silk ball gown. "Your darling feels the overwhelming need to take her husband someplace private for a lecture," she retorted.

He chuckled, added an extra twirl to their dance pattern, and somehow spun them both off the dance floor. Jessamyn found herself in front of the great double doors leading to the staircase up to their room. She laughed up at Cyrus, recognizing how neatly he'd maneuvered her, and slipped out with him.

Morgan's mouth tightened as he watched the doors close behind Cyrus and Jessamyn. Somewhere below his chin,

Thomas Maley, one of his father's old business partners, was pontificating about the merits of modern agricultural methods. Modern meaning anything invented after 1790 but before 1820.

The hell of it was that Thomas Maley's gibberish was less distressing than meeting Jessamyn again, and far less painful than watching Cyrus and Jessamyn together.

He'd known seeing Jessamyn again, for the first time in six years, would be concentrated agony. He'd anticipated the hard-edged carnal suffering of his flesh's reaction to her voice, her scent—the overwhelming urge to leap upon her and have his revenge for ripping away his very definition of himself as a man. He was desperate to have her under him, begging him for more even as he thrust into her—but she belonged to Cyrus.

What he hadn't expected was that Cyrus and Jessamyn together were one of the happiest married couples he'd ever seen, fully as content as his parents had been. They shared both laughter and silences together, while seeking excuses to talk to each other. Dammit, he'd memorized every smile on her face when Cyrus was teasing her out there.

As for their evident physical joy in each other . . . Morgan had nearly stormed onto the dance floor and torn them apart when Cyrus had twirled her, displaying her ankles to the world. And when Cyrus had nuzzled her cheek and she'd laughed up at him with that look of eager anticipation, then slipped outside with him—Hell, what a fellow wouldn't do to have the same joy in his life?

Now that he was becoming established in the world, he'd planned to find himself a biddable wife while he was here in Mississippi. He hadn't wanted anyone too complicated, just someone to keep his house and bear his children. But who could think of convenience once they saw Cyrus and Jessamyn's delight in each other, blazing like a beacon before them?

Morgan slammed down his glass of Madeira onto the

table. "You'll forgive me, gentlemen, but I have another engagement I must attend to. Good evening."

He nodded curtly and shouldered past them to the door. He needed a bottle of whiskey and at least one willing woman if he was to forget Jessamyn tonight.

Chapter Five

Kansas City, June 1872

Morgan Evans pushed the signed bank draft across the desk to Halpern and sat back, taking a deep puff on his cigar. The stout man didn't quite snatch the paper up but it seemed to leap into his hands all the same. No man would let the payment for one hundred custom-made ammunition chests slip by.

Morgan hid a smile and stood up, stretching as he strolled over to the window. Once he, too, would have been just as impressed by a sum that large. Now it was just another purchase for Donovan & Sons, one of the most prominent freighting houses west of the Mississippi.

He was almost as accustomed to buying for Donovan & Sons as he was to the two Colts that he'd worn since he was fourteen, or the Bowie knife against his thigh. He flexed his fingers automatically and rolled his shoulders back, the habitual motions of a *pistolero* keeping his muscles ready for the next quick draw.

Paper crackled sharply in his breast pocket, rasping against his vest's silk lining and making him stiffen. The telegram's words burned in front of his eyes, as alarming as when he'd first read them this morning.

AUNT EULALIA BROKE LEG STOP NEED HELP STOP CAN YOU FIND JESSAMYN STOP GONE TO VISIT ARMY FRIENDS STOP UNKNOWN DESTINATION AND DURATION STOP MAY BE IN KANSAS CITY STOP GEORGE

Morgan's mouth tightened and he drummed his fingers on the window frame, ignoring the busy street below. Here, men came for a quick taste of civilization before returning to the wilds of Texas or Kansas, or parts even farther west. Cattle bellowed from the dockyards a few blocks west, their rich stench reminding all comers of this town's foundation. Gunshots cracked in the distance, while a train whistled sharply. Brilliantly colored posters touted the dubious delights to be found inside local establishments, while gaudily dressed women paraded up and down in a vivid display of their personal wares. Barkers shouted encouragement and drunks staggered out of the saloons found on every block. The wild vitality normally would have made him grin.

But now he focused on personal affairs. Cousin George could deal with Great-Aunt Eulalia very well on his own, as he had many times before. But where the hell could the nearly penniless Jessamyn have disappeared to? She was barely surviving on her pension as an Army widow, the only one of his relatives—however shirttail—not to ask money from him, and had been living in Jackson, Mississippi, with Great-Aunt Eulalia. He'd seen her briefly in Omaha a week ago but she'd vanished before he could locate her. After receiving George's cable, he'd cabled the Donovan & Sons' office there but they couldn't find her in any of the hotels or lodging houses.

Logically, he should ask Pinkerton's to find her; they had the resources to do so quickly.

Despite intellectual certainties, now he found himself staring out the window, looking for a slender, black-clad female with a lissome glide. Folly to think George's suggestion made it likely she'd be here. Jessamyn with the green eyes like a forest glade and the red mouth made to drive a man insane. Jessamyn, who deserved to be throttled—or locked in his bedroom—as repayment for what she'd done to him.

"It's certainly been a pleasure doing business with a genuine Southern gentleman like yourself, Evans," Halpern said sincerely, as he finished locking up the draft. "Would you care to join my family for dinner again this evening? Just a simple meal, which my daughter Millicent prepared with her own hands. She's an excellent cook, as you know."

He glanced significantly at the pictures behind him. They'd been rearranged since Morgan's first visit, so Millicent's image now held pride of place. Blond, pretty, amiable—any sane man would be glad of a wife like her. On the frontier where Morgan spent most of his time, and where men outnumbered women by twenty to one, she'd have been married within a week of her arrival.

God knows he should be married by now, with a brood of youngsters. Familial duty required it, society expected it, his wealth anticipated it. Even satisfying his strong carnal desires could be done most discreetly within his marriage vows.

So why the hell didn't Millicent Halpern make his cock twitch at all? Or was she another one of the females he was polite to, simply because he didn't give a damn?

Hell, he needed to be married, with or without passion.

Perhaps if he had dinner with the Halperns again, he'd find something in her that would interest him enough him to make an offer. He didn't have to stay too long, since he was meeting the Donovans and Lindsays later for drinks. Morgan hesitated.

Halpern, a very sharp man, read him accurately. "No need to give me an immediate answer, Evans. Millicent will always be glad to set another place at the table for you. But it's a hot day and I'm feeling rather parched. Larrimore's Hotel across the street makes an excellent mint julep. Would you care to join me?"

"That would be a pleasure, sir," Morgan accepted, his Mississippi drawl sliding across the other's flat Bostonian accent.

Outside, the late afternoon traffic rushed up and down the street in clouds of dust, and pedestrians bustled along the boardwalk. No sign here of a gliding black-clad female on whom he'd sworn vengeance. He could not imagine her lingering amid this wild tumult, since Kansas City held few attractions other than as a place to change trains for places west. As an Army officer's widow, Jessamyn had friends aplenty at Fort Leavenworth or Fort Riley, or farther west in Kansas, Colorado, or New Mexico.

So why did Cousin George think she was here now, when Morgan had seen her in Omaha a week ago? For a woman to shuttle first north along the Missouri River from Memphis, then back south again to Kansas City, implied almost a distracted state of mind. Such a frenzied journey would be so uncharacteristic of the disciplined female he'd known all his life that Morgan dismissed the possibility out of hand. Jessamyn Tyler Evans would not be found in this town.

Having reached that conclusion, he was able to anticipate an iced mint julep with a sense of relief and rubbed out his cigar in the street.

Larrimore's Hotel was a luxurious establishment catering to the area's wealthy businessmen, complete with marble columns and steps at its entrance, Brussels carpets and brass spittoons throughout its lobby, velvet-covered furniture and flocked wallpaper, and crystal chandeliers and gas lamps. It also rented rooms by the hour, with complete discretion, for any activity a gentleman wanted to perform, as Morgan knew very well.

Halpern headed for the bar with the ease of long habit. Crossing the lobby behind him, Morgan automatically searched his surroundings for threats, as his years of fighting on the frontier and during the War had taught him.

Little to worry about from the fat burghers scattered among the chairs and sofas on the first floor.

A great staircase led up to the second floor and the private parlors there. A man was taking those stairs gracefully, with the ease of an animal in perfect health.

Morgan grinned as he recognized the fellow. Jeremy Saunders, a Consortium switch and an excellent street fighter, as well. Simply put, he was an extremely well-trained and well-paid gigolo, able to play the predator or the recipient in the carnal fantasies popular among Consortium members. Why, only two nights ago, Morgan had seen him excite at least two women into ecstatic paroxysms with his hands and mouth.

Years ago, William Donovan had sponsored Morgan into the Consortium, a highly secretive network of private clubs for wealthy men and women. Morgan had enjoyed the training and the companionship he'd found there. But he'd also never forgotten that experience nine years ago which made him seek out the formal discipline offered by the Consortium.

Smiling slightly as he recalled some of the wilder sessions at Consortium parties, Morgan quickly scanned the balcony above the lobby but saw no one suspicious.

By now Saunders had reached the second floor. Morgan started to rejoin Halpern, envying Saunders his late afternoon diversion.

A flutter of black silk next to a white marble balustrade caught his attention. A chill raced up Morgan's spine and he spun around.

The woman raised her hand to Saunders before stepping back from the balcony. For that instant, Morgan could see her face clearly in the gaslight. Dark eyes in a pure cameo face, red mouth created to drive men insane . . .

Jessamyn was meeting Saunders here in a private parlor? Everything primal in Morgan roared in denial.

He said something to Halpern, he never knew what. It

must have made some sense because the man didn't raise an objection. At least, not one loud enough to force Morgan's attention.

A second later, he was taking the stairs two at a time, a growl vibrating in his throat. Dammit, why did Jessamyn always have to rattle his concentration?

Jessamyn Sophia Tyler Evans stood with one hand on the sofa in the parlor, uncertain what to do next. This was not, after all, a situation covered in any etiquette manual. She had to explain what she wanted and how long it would take.

She wished to God, yet again, that Cyrus were still alive. Not dead and buried, leaving her to fight for those trapped in a desperate, plague-ridden city, after a terrified Richard Burke and his sister abandoned Plato, Aristotle, Cassiopeia, Socrates, and the horses. Dear God, they'd told her they would stay to guard the horses, no matter what happened, no matter who tried to steal them in the grips of yellow jack's madness. Until she could return and take them all to safety.

When they were children, Morgan would have called this rendezvous a wild prank. He'd have known exactly how to help her, without a word of explanation from her. But she wouldn't trust him now with a plugged nickel, let alone information about a fabulous treasure.

So she'd have to hope that this stranger's honor would prove as strong as Cousin Sophonisba had promised.

Cousin Sophonisba—technically Cyrus and Morgan's cousin—had spent decades investing in real estate located in riverfront boom towns. She was also an incredible miser and Great-Aunt Eulalia's best friend. Jessamyn had spent three days with her in Omaha, trying to obtain a loan. This hotel and the stranger facing her were the result.

The hotel's private parlor was as snobbishly respectable as Cousin Sophonisba had described, with lace-edged cloth on every well-polished surface and hand-stitched Biblical mottoes on the walls. But Cousin Sophonisba's miserliness had provided barely enough money and recommendations for this lodging and the gentleman escort to admit Jessamyn into the reading of Uncle Edgar's will. She'd emphatically refused to loan Jessamyn any larger sums, nor details on exactly how she'd learned of the gentleman escort.

The highly polished mantel clock ticked imperatively. Fifteen minutes before three in the afternoon. They had to reach Abercrombie's office by three or else all of this was for naught.

Jessamyn fell back on the most basic conventions of polite society as a bridge. "Would you care for a cup of tea, Mr. Saunders, while we talk?"

"Certainly, Mrs. Evans." Mr. Saunders, a very well-mannered and well-dressed gentleman, moved toward the chair beside her.

The door burst inward with a single splintering crash and Morgan Evans sprang into the room. He was elegantly dressed in a formal black frock coat and gray trousers, neatly tied black cravat, crisp white linen, with the gaslight glinting on his chestnut hair. He might have looked every inch the handsome, wealthy cavalier, except for the naked Bowie knife in his hand and his expression of completely murderous intent.

Morgan? Here in Kansas City? Dear God, why did he have to be so much more attractive than the very well-mannered Mr. Saunders? Jessamyn snarled, wishing she could once again sneak cod liver oil into Morgan's maple syrup.

Saunders spun to face him. His fingers twitched, as if reaching for a weapon, then stilled.

Was Morgan about to ruin something else for her? "Gentlemen!"

They both ignored her, deadly fighters very ready to come to blows.

Jessamyn sprang to her feet, trying not to shriek curses at Morgan. As a frontier soldier's wife, she'd seen too much violence on the Kansas plains. Bloodshed was only a hairsbreadth away here.

Morgan lifted his left hand slightly. His fingers flashed

briefly and he tilted his head, in the barest excuse for a nod Jessamyn had ever seen.

Something like surprise washed over Saunders's face. He lifted his right hand in a similar gesture and also nodded, a trifle more deeply.

Was this some strange new form of game?

"If you weren't Consortium, you'd be dead, Saunders," Morgan announced, his gray eyes like chips of ice as he watched the other. "Since you are, we'll play this by Consortium rules. I claim first rights to her."

"First rights? Who the hell are you, Morgan Evans, to talk about first rights?" Jessamyn demanded, wishing she could hurl lemonade into Morgan's face as she had when she was six and he was ten.

Morgan's eyes ran over her briefly before returning to Saunders. Dammit, he was still as deadly as a mountain lion and handsome as a dream of sin.

Why was she thinking about that now?

"Are you denying that I was the first man to have a taste of you, before you married my cousin?"

Jessamyn flushed but squared her shoulders. "What does that matter? I'm a widow now and responsible for myself."

His voice deepened. A darker note crept into it, full of carnal remembrances. "Do you deny that I taught you the power of the darkness to focus your senses on pleasure? The delights of chains?"

Memories that she'd hoped to forget, that she'd fought to wipe out, flooded back in. Her lungs tightened as shards of lust raced through her veins. She flushed scarlet.

Saunders didn't, quite, whistle.

Morgan growled and tossed the big knife between his hands, before gripping it more firmly. He could gut the other in an instant, given that hold.

Saunders stiffened at the primal, wordless warning and bowed deeply, lowering his eyes. "Please forgive me, sir, I had no idea of your relationship. You must believe I wouldn't have agreed to meet her without your permission, if I'd known."

Morgan relaxed subtly, although he continued to watch the other. "Understood. Given the circumstances, you will understand if I ask you to leave immediately."

Jessamyn bristled, furious at being treated like a piece of property. She'd arranged this meeting, not Morgan—the scapegrace who called himself head of the family! "Now wait a minute, gentlemen . . ."

They both ignored her.

"Of course." Saunders bowed again and turned for the door.

Morgan sheathed his knife. "Saunders," he murmured and shook hands with the other. Jessamyn could have sworn money exchanged hands.

But where did that leave her? She still needed a man to accompany her to the lawyer's office.

Morgan ceremonially closed the door's remains behind Saunders, blocking the gaping hotel management and guests. He turned back to her. "Now, cousin . . ."

Too furious to think straight, she slapped him. "How dare you throw him out! What am I to do now for a man?"

His eyes flared and he grabbed her by the shoulders, his fingers biting into her. "If you want a man, then by God, I'll be that man! Nine years I've waited, Jessamyn, and no two-bit gigolo can handle you."

She tried to hit him again but all she could do was pummel his arms. Trying to kick his shins only ruffled her skirts, without affecting him in the slightest. "Damn you, Morgan, let me go!"

His grip was remorseless but his voice held all of whiskey's secret fires. "Like hell. Remember what I said nine years ago? The next time we were alone together, I'd be the one handling you. This is the first time we've been alone together since then, Jessamyn."

Her jaw dropped. "What? You can't mean to hold that over my head now."

"Why not?" He watched her narrowly, iron determination in his gray eyes. He was immovable, both his intent and his form.

She stared at him, appalled to think he still carried a grudge that old when both of them had changed so much.

Morgan was stronger, broader of shoulder, deeper of chest, his arms and legs more heavily roped with muscle. The gray eyes were sharper now, not those of a wary young man. His nose had been broken more than once in the intervening years, giving him a piratical cast. He'd shaved off his mustache since she'd glimpsed him a week ago in Omaha, which allowed the hard lines of experience bracketing his mouth to be clearly seen.

He wore a subtle hint of menace, well hidden under finely tailored broadcloth and immaculate linens. He'd looked and acted the perfect gentleman at the very few family gatherings she and Cyrus had encountered him at, since the War.

But the man who held her so implacably was no gentleman. The guerrilla of nine years ago hadn't been, either, but he'd lacked the power to carry out his threats. This man would, and could, carry out those threats. Or were they promises?

Held this close to him, she knew the strength in his arms and shoulders. Knew that he would brook no nonsense from any woman he chose. His legs were solid against hers, even through the layers of her skirt, as if he needed to take only one step to press her against the wall and have his way with her . . .

She'd always known he was a shady character, who performed deeds no decent fellow would know of.

Her breasts tightened, as fireflies darted over her from his hands. Dammit, the old fire was starting to burn, as it had the last afternoon in the attic.

The mantel clock began to chime.

Her head flashed around to stare at it before she looked back at Morgan.

She fought back her body's awareness of him. "I needed him as my husband, you fool! For two hours, starting now."

"Husband?" Jealousy swept over his face.

"In a lawyer's office," she snarled back. "I have to be there with a husband, or all is lost. Damn you, let me go!"

The clock chimed again.

His eyes narrowed before he pulled her up to him. His grip was less painful but just as inescapable as before. "A bargain then, Jessamyn. I'll play your husband for a few hours—if you'll join me in a private parlor for the same span of time afterward."

She gasped. A devil's bargain, indeed.

"Nine years ago, I promised you revenge for what you did. Two hours won't see that accomplished but it's a start," he purred, his drawl knife-edged and laced with carnal promise.

She wanted to accept the bargain, lose herself in his arms—but then she'd be a loose woman like her mother, consorting with a dishonorable man. He was the only man she'd ever wanted to be disgraceful with and he could destroy her.

Her fears stirred, honed by seven years as an Army wife on the bloody Kansas prairies. She reined them in sternly: No matter how angry he'd been, surely Morgan would never harm a woman, no matter what preposterous demands he'd hurled nine years ago when she'd held him captive.

Her fingers bit into his arms as she desperately tried to think of another option, something respectable.

If she took him with her, he could steal the map and she'd lose everything she'd come here to gain.

But if she didn't appear with a husband, she'd lose her only chance of regaining Somerset Hall . . .

She was an adult woman now. Surely her nerves would not be overset by two hours in his arms. Surely . . .

The mantel clock sounded the third, and last, note.

She agreed to his bargain, the words like ashes in her throat. "Very well, Morgan. Now will you take me to the lawyer's?"

Morgan escorted Jessamyn across the street with all the haughtiness his father would have displayed escorting his mother aboard a riverboat. It was a bit of manners ingrained in him so early that he didn't need to think about it, something he'd first practiced with Jessamyn when she was five and their parents first openly spoke of a wedding between them. Such an inbred habit was very useful when his brain seemed to have dived somewhere south of his belt buckle as soon as she'd agreed to slake his lust for revenge.

What would he do first once he had her alone? There were so many activities he'd learned in Consortium houses, of how to drive a woman insane with desire. How to leave her sated and panting, willing to do anything to repeat the experience. More than anything else, he needed to see Jessamyn aching to be touched by him again and again.

A black curl stroked her cheek in just the way he intended to later. He smiled, planning his first move, and reached for the office door.

Ebenezer Abercrombie & Sons, Attys. At Law, announced the sturdy letters on its surface.

Jessamyn leaned closer to Morgan and squeezed his arm, with all the assurance of a long-married woman. God knows he'd seen her do it with Cyrus before. Morgan shifted himself so she could fit comfortably, as he'd seen his cousin do. She settled easily within a hand's breadth of him and tilted her head at Abercrombie expectantly. The entire byplay took only a few seconds.

Morgan smiled with all the smooth charm he'd polished as one of Bedford Forrest's spies. "Good afternoon, Abercrombie, is it? I'm Morgan Evans and this is my wife, Jessamyn Tyler Evans, who has business here."

An all too well-tailored man, Abercrombie bowed over her

hand with an almost visible air of relief. "My dear lady, I'm so glad you were able to bring your husband. Your cousin Charles and his wife are seated in my office, waiting for the reading of the will to begin."

Charlie Jones here? Hell, if he'd known that, he'd have escorted Jessamyn just to infuriate Jones.

Abercrombie offered his arm to Jessamyn and escorted her into that inner sanctum. Morgan followed them across the clerk's office, his eyes caught by the sway of Jessamyn's hips and the ripple of her black skirts along the floor. Her dress was faded, almost tattered, as if only long custom kept it in one piece. Still, the form underneath was so magnificent as to make distinctions of dress unimportant: slim and lithe, long-necked, tiny waist, with a gently curving bosom and hips. She'd been an enchanting girl but she was an eye-catching woman. His gut tightened at all the carnal possibilities implicit in her body.

He wondered idly what kind of devil's brew he'd gotten himself into. Whatever it was, he'd likely jump into it again, if it meant finally slaking his lust for her.

Angry voices could be heard coming from within Abercrombie's office.

Jessamyn steadied herself for the coming confrontation as they passed through the clerk's office. For now, she was glad she had Morgan at her side: His manners, in public at least, were unexceptionable—unlike the people they were about to meet.

Abercrombie cleared his throat hesitantly and opened his office door.

Jessamyn quickly glanced over the room as they entered, looking for any potential weapons Charlie might grab. It was a typical lawyer's throne room, full of heavy wood, leather, and thick carpeting. Books and ornate certificates competed for space with velvet drapes, while a very modern chandelier shed bright gaslight over the scene. An enormous desk, big enough to shelter two women from an Indian attack, held pride of place, with an equally massive leather chair rising behind it. Faint sounds of conversation could be heard from another room, through a closed door flanked by two heavy bookcases. Four chairs faced the big desk, arranged in two groups of two.

Abercrombie cleared his throat and offered an introduction, effectively defusing any previous argument. "Mr. and Mrs. Jones, may I present Mr. and Mrs. Morgan Evans. Mr. Evans is the husband of your cousin Jessamyn, the late Mr. Jones's niece."

Morgan came to attention beside her. "Good afternoon, Jones. Mrs. Jones." He was formal, his normally slurred Mississippi vowels now clear and precise.

Her cousin Charlie and his wife, Maggie, spun to face them. She slowly relaxed her hands from feline claws and pasted an insincere, seductive smirk on her face.

"Evans." More open hostility echoed in Charlie Jones's voice than Jessamyn could remember hearing aimed at Morgan before. He hadn't changed much since that December afternoon in 1863, except for fancier clothes and jewelry. Now she could see the grips of two fine Colt revolvers nudging his fancy waistcoat and the thickness of a Bowie knife along his hip, backed up by cold eyes and a humorless mouth.

"Mrs. Evans."

He flashed a hard look at Morgan. "Your husband?"

She raised her head coolly, unwilling to let him see she was bluffing. "We were married last week in Kansas."

"Finally fulfilling our parents' fondest wish," Morgan drawled. He dropped his hand to his Bowie knife's hilt and caressed it, silently challenging Charlie to a knife fight.

Sometimes there were advantages to being escorted by a man who knew how to test society's limits. Jessamyn preened and stood straighter, a pose she'd once seen a dance hall girl adopt to display confidence in her gambler escort.

Charlie's eyes narrowed and he started to rise.

Abercrombie squeaked and clutched a massive law tome to his chest.

Maggie Jones crooned, "Ooh, Mr. Evans, you're so heroic."

Her husband slammed a hand down onto her shoulder and she subsided with a sniff. The move cost him any chance of a timely grab for a knife, taking him out of the potential fight. His glare promised retribution to her as he muttered, "Congratulations on your marriage."

Morgan smoothed his lapel and moved forward. Jessamyn looked down her nose at the others, an attitude both her governess and the dance hall girl would have understood, and went with him, her brain rapidly sorting through her observations.

Great-Aunt Eulalia had warned her that Charlie had made a fortune in Colorado but she'd hoped she'd been wrong. To reach the treasure before he did, she would need more than a little cash, some luck, and her old Army friends. Where could she find the wherewithal to defeat Charlie and his new wife?

Then that female made advances to Morgan as they passed.

"What a pleasure to be with you again, Morgan," Mrs. Jones cooed and rose to greet him, her perfume as predatory as her voice, utterly ignoring her husband's presence. Her bronze day dress clung to her magnificently curved figure and her hair was dressed in rich curls, spilling down her back. Her perfect features could have served as a model for Cleopatra, while her enormous dark eyes devoured Morgan as if she wished to drag him off into another room.

Morgan drew himself up to his full height and tucked Jessamyn's arm closer to his side. Icy disgust shone briefly in his eyes before he veiled them.

How fitting that Charlie, whose appetite for other men's gold was unlimited, should be married to a woman with strong appetites for other women's men.

"Congratulations, Charlie," Jessamyn cooed, "on marrying a woman who's truly worthy of you."

He flushed angrily. "Maggie." His command was harsh and laden with undercurrents of anger and jealousy.

His wife stopped in her tracks. A wild mélange of expressions raced across her face—lust, frustration, anger—before her features settled into deceptively meek obedience. "Mrs. Evans."

"Mrs. Jones." Jessamyn gave the barest nod consonant with polite society and twitched her skirts aside, ensuring they wouldn't touch the other female's. She'd ask Morgan about Mrs. Jones later, assuming the two of them were still talking.

Abercrombie ostentatiously rustled papers from behind the desk. "Please sit down, ladies and gentlemen, so we can begin."

They silently took their seats and settled in. Morgan's eyes flickered around the room one last time when he sat down, the warmth of his body seeping into Jessamyn through her threadbare dress. He clearly hadn't missed a single detail of Charlie, Abercrombie, or their surroundings. That kind of skill probably came in handy during all his shady doings.

For the first time in years, Jessamyn clearly remembered how he'd lain sprawled across that iron bed in the attic, sated after her hands and mouth had brought him to completion . . .

Her mouth went dry as heat lanced through her.

Maggie Jones gave a long, languishing look at Morgan before Charlie's hand clamped down hard on her wrist. She choked and sat erect, facing Abercrombie and tapping her toe.

Abercrombie settled into his chair, opened a leather portfolio, and became all business. "As I have mentioned before, Mr. Jones left strict instructions about the disposition of his estate." He unfolded a long piece of paper and began to read. "I, Edgar George Charles Jones, being of sound mind and body—"

"Get on with it, Abercrombie!" Charlie snapped. "Just tell us where to find the gold."

Morgan studied his fingernails. Very well kept hands, too, despite the calluses and scars. What would they feel like on her skin in an hour or two? What would he want to do? Dear God, how could she be so aware of him?

Abercrombie looked at them over the top of the paper, one eyebrow raised, every inch the first-rank lawyer. "Mr. Jones predicted his family would say that. Do you feel the same way, Mrs. Evans?"

Jessamyn shrugged. "I would prefer to listen to the heart of the matter, rather than the legal words it's wrapped in," she agreed cautiously, keeping a wary eye on Morgan's all too well-controlled reactions.

"Very well. Mr. Jones wrote much of his will in an informal, almost epistolary style. Here we are." He began to read, tracing the words with his finger.

"Forty years ago, I had an itch to go west and see the shining mountains and the great desert. I saw those marvels and more, and I had great adventures among the Indians and the Mexicans."

Jessamyn nodded, remembering the stories told so often among the Jones family about those adventures. She'd heard the tales very young, before her mother ran off, while they still visited Uncle Edgar and his family. Charlie had probably heard more stories since his father was Uncle Edgar's brother and they visited more regularly.

"One day, I came upon a Mexican beset by Indians amidst the mountains northwest of Santa Fe. I aided him, for no civilized man deserves to be injured by those savages, and at length we drove them off. Alas, it was too late for the gallant fellow, for he had taken his death wound. Before he breathed his last, he insisted on giving me a map, saying it would lead me to great fortune. He was the last descendant of the one who had drawn it—Teniente Diego Ortiz."

Beside Jessamyn, Morgan gave a very soft snort of disbelief. She glanced sharply at him but his expression remained politely interested in Abercrombie's reading.

Why wouldn't he accept Uncle Edgar's account? Were such tales so common in Santa Fe as to be discounted? Of course, he'd always laughed at them when they were children.

"I followed the map deep into the mountains and found Ortiz's gold, a great hoard that had been hidden there for centuries."

"Oooooh," breathed Maggie and pressed her hand to her throat, the ruffles at her bosom quivering. Charlie's eyes blazed with greed, his mouth white and set. Surely they both had gold fever, the same obsession Jessamyn had seen drive men frantic—or kill them—while prospecting in the Rockies.

Morgan appeared merely attentive to Uncle Edgar's account, no more or less than if he'd been listening to a retelling of a Shakespearean story. Not the reaction of someone bitten by the gold bug.

Or perhaps he was simply better at hiding his interest. It was difficult to believe he wouldn't catch gold fever as Mother's lover had, given Morgan's fondness for get-rich-quick schemes.

"With great difficulty, I brought much of the gold back to civilization. But there remains more gold than a man can put his arms around. I settled here in Kansas City, where I could retain close ties with my friends in Santa Fe."

Much of the gold? Hallelujah, there was still more out there to be found. If she could find it, she could rescue her friends and the horses and save Somerset Hall, while keeping Charlie out of it. She simply needed money and time to fetch the gold. A great deal of money.

"The War Between the States was unkind to my family and my fortunes. I lost my beloved wife and our children, as well as most of my property."

Abercrombie paused to sip his coffee. Charlie leaned forward impatiently and Maggie looked frustrated. Morgan crossed and uncrossed his ankles, like a gentleman whose greatest concern was whether he'd be late for dinner.

Jessamyn frowned. Surely Uncle Edgar could not have lost the map in the decades since he left Santa Fe.

"But I still retained the map, my home, and most of its contents. After much thought, I decided upon the following disposition of my estate. My home will be sold and the proceeds divided among my loyal servants. The contents will be divided among my friends and my servants."

"The map! Dammit, who gets the map?" snarled Charlie.

"Patience, Jones, there's more to hear," Morgan drawled, his eyes sharply assessing Charlie.

Charlie's face turned ugly, reminding Jessamyn of a man she'd seen during an Indian fight, who'd been frustrated and furious when his captain had ordered an end to the shooting. Only the sergeant's quick action in pointing a loaded rifle at him had stopped the fellow from shooting his captain then and there. Charlie had the same fixed stare, the same absolute willingness to do violence to get his way.

Her heart sank as the true difficulties of the task ahead seeped in.

Abercrombie speeded up his pace. Maggie patted her husband sympathetically on the knee and they smiled at each other warmly. Jessamyn shivered at their bloodthirsty understanding of each other.

"The map represents the greater part of my estate and therefore passes to my blood kin. I had two siblings, both of whom have passed on before me: my sister Sophia and brother James. It was my earnest hope that both branches would combine and share the gold. However, after a lifetime in this family, I cannot believe in that future. Therefore, in the interest of fairness, I have made the best copy possible of the map, without the marks or fading caused by time."

A copy? Despite any marks or fading of it, she'd still prefer to have the original map.

Morgan tilted his head slightly and regarded Abercrombie quizzically. It was his first true sign of interest in the proceedings.

"One version shall pass to Sophia's children and the other to James's children. Since the journey is long and arduous, beset by many dangers from both man and nature, I insist that only men may undertake it. Therefore, each branch of the family must have at least one adult male member or else both versions of the map will pass to the other branch."

Jessamyn's mouth tightened. Hidebound old man. Uncle Edgar had made his point, but she'd have her copy, even if she had needed Morgan's help to be here. Just what, or how much, she'd have to pay for that help was something best not yet thought about.

"I have placed each copy in identical brass tubes. The eldest descendant of my eldest sibling, Sophia—."

Abercrombie nodded toward Jessamyn before continuing.

"Shall have the opportunity to choose one tube. James's eldest descendant shall receive the other tube. Both branches of the family will then have an equal opportunity to find the remaining treasure. Whichever branch finds the treasure shall divide it equally among themselves."

"Do you have any questions, Mrs. Evans? Mr. Jones?"

Jessamyn shook her head. "None, thank you." First choice? How would she know which was the original?

Maggie looked as if she wanted to say something cutting, but Charlie's hand clamped down on her arm. Morgan shifted, ready to stand up quickly.

Abercrombie swallowed. "Very well then."

He reached into his desk's center drawer and pulled out two long, slender, brass tubes approximately the size of a telescope. Each was tied up with a scarlet cord, knotted and bound with crimson sealing wax at every intersection, creating a completely tamper-proof package. As promised, they were completely alike except for a few, almost imperceptible dents. "Mrs. Evans, which one do you want?"

Jessamyn stood up and came over to the desk, Morgan rising behind her. Her corset was a steel band clamping down on her ribs, a surprising sensation since she'd worn one every day of her adult life.

She took a deep breath, reached, and her hand closed around a brass tube. Charlie's hand shot out and snatched the other tube off the desk. Jessamyn hesitated but handed her tube to Morgan, who produced a knife as easily as any magician. She'd known he'd have a penknife, which she didn't, and she could observe him closely, in case he had ambitions for the map.

"Please open your bequests now," Abercrombie ordered, "to ensure you each received a satisfactory map."

Morgan and Charlie quickly attacked the cords. Charlie was absolutely silent as he worked but Maggie hovered over him, urging him to hurry.

Jessamyn closely watched Morgan expertly slice the red cords and fought to retain an appropriately dignified demeanor. He wrenched open one end and an old, brittle piece of parchment, wrapped in fine silk, dropped out.

The map was stained in very odd patterns and its edges were frayed. But the lettering was still crisp, while the lines were sharp and clear. Morgan suddenly lifted an eyebrow but said nothing, his finger poised above the parchment.

Jessamyn gulped. She'd chosen the original.

Maggie hissed like an angry spitting toad as Charlie carefully pulled fresh white parchment out of his tube. "Well, at least it's a readable copy, unlike the other. Open it, Charlie dearest," she urged. "Let me see the map that'll bring us a fortune." She leaned closer to him, fondling his hip.

Morgan briskly slipped Jessamyn's map back into the tube. He twitched his coat back, revealing his Colt, all the while watching Charlie closely. Grateful for his protection, Jessamyn shifted closer to him, leaving him a clear line of fire to her treacherous cousin.

Charlie kissed Maggie, looking very pleased for the first time that day, and cooed over their map's bold black inks and crisp details. From her few glimpses, Jessamyn thought that the original was more precise but she couldn't be sure.

Jessamyn started to plan. She needed to find someone who could take her to the gold, despite Charlie's treacheries. Someone with resources, who was as nasty and shady as Charlie. Someone, dammit, like Morgan.

She had friends in Denver, who'd offered to help her. But they couldn't provide enough aid to stand up against Charlie in a race for gold.

"If that's the end of it, we'll be going now," Charlie announced and began to roll up his version.

"Next train to Denver isn't until tomorrow morning," Morgan observed coldly.

Charlie gave Morgan a look that would have gutted and filleted a catfish, as he slid his copy back into the tube. "Maybe we're heading east. Or south."

"Or maybe Timbuktu. Don't try to cozen me, Jones."

"Now, now, gentlemen," Abercrombie reproved. "Won't you sit down for the remainder of the will? It includes bequests made to family members."

Charlie was so busy glaring at Morgan that he barely glanced at Abercrombie. "Send them to us in Denver. We're too busy to sit through more idle chatter." He grabbed his wife's arm. "Come along, Maggie."

They were gone a moment later, escorted out by Abercrombie, who wore the air of an unwilling lion tamer. Maggie Jones managed to give Morgan one last glance offering an infinity of carnal possibilities before the door closed. Jessamyn's hackles rose as her hands curled into claws. The greedy, smelly slut.

She frowned an instant later, wondering at her own reaction. What did she care whom Morgan cuckolded? Lord knows Charlie undoubtedly deserved every nasty trick he received.

"Do you think he might have a special train waiting?" She rolled the brass tube over and over, wondering how to reseal it, a far more profitable thought than considering Morgan's plans for the evening.

Her head was spinning. Charlie, the gold, Morgan's designs on the gold, a night with Morgan—she was at a loss to say which was more alarming.

Her mouth was dry, yet her skin was tight and hot.

Morgan tweaked the curtains aside and looked out the window. "No, not here. Jones would need a Denver & Rio Grande train for that, which would be hard to come by in Kansas City. He'll be on the morning train to Denver instead."

He dropped the curtains into place and came back to her. "I'll buy you a train ticket back to Jackson tomorrow, though."

Chapter Six

Jessamyn stared at Morgan in absolute shock. "Tomorrow? But I can't go to Jackson—I have to find the gold!"

He shook his head, his expression uncompromising. "Jessamyn, there's no treasure. Ortiz's gold is one of New Mexico's oldest legends and no one's ever found it."

Rage blurred her vision. Did he want to get her out of the way and claim the gold for himself? She shook her head, refusing to accept the emotional distraction. The gold was her only chance to regain Somerset Hall and she needed all her wits to defeat Charlie. "What about the map? You've seen and handled it. Don't you believe in it?"

"I swear to you on my mother's grave, Jessamyn, if you give me five minutes on the Plaza in Santa Fe, I can buy you a dozen such maps."

"No!"

"Twenty minutes and I'll have ten men, all swearing to be Ortiz's grandsons and ready to lead me to the gold."

"That's impossible! I heard stories as a child, whenever I visited Uncle Edgar, especially from Aunt Serafina, about the gold. How Ortiz had found it, how Uncle Edgar had carried it out, how heavy it was."

Morgan hesitated then set his jaw. "Legends told often enough frequently become truth. Your Uncle Edgar probably found a smaller vein and decided to become famous by saying he'd found Ortiz's gold. Come, let's go have a drink before we return to the hotel."

"No!" She yanked her arm away from him. "Then loan me some money and let me go after the gold alone."

"You don't know what you're asking, Jessamyn. You'd be racing against Charlie Jones, who knows more about double dealing than a convention of faro dealers. Treasure or no, you won't survive without a top trail boss *and* a dozen teamsters."

"You could lead them. You're a top trail boss."

He shrugged impatiently. "Why should I? Jessamyn, Ortiz's gold doesn't exist."

"I'd give you a bonus," she offered desperately.

"Jessamyn!" he bellowed and shook her by the shoulders. "How many times do I have to repeat myself? Ortiz's gold does not exist. You cannot bribe me with it. There, does that satisfy you?"

She was forced to believe he meant it. After all, he'd been traveling to Santa Fe, in the New Mexico Territory, for years. She frowned, her mind whirling through possibilities. If not a golden fortune, then what else did he want?

Revenge.

She could offer her body to Morgan unreservedly—except for protection against pregnancy, of course.

The air suddenly seemed hot and stifling in Abercrombie's spacious office.

She must be mad to even think of bargaining with Morgan, especially a bargain that would put her in his intimate power for weeks on end. The man who'd carelessly, selfishly risked her father's life. Who was so devoid of family feeling as to pursue easy money in faraway places, while his crippled cousin labored to rebuild the family heritage in his stead? And God help her, the one man who'd heated her blood to where she'd have forgotten all claims of duty and honor to follow him.

But if it was her only chance to save Somerset Hall, with her beloved friends and the horses . . .

She would rescue her beloved friends and horses from that plague-ravaged town, no matter what devil's bargain she had to make.

Abercrombie opened the door.

"Get out!" Morgan shouted.

The door slammed shut.

"What's that brain of yours spinning now?" Morgan asked suspiciously.

The only card she had to play was that he still wanted her in his bed. All the promises he'd made nine years ago seemed still fresh in his mind, hot for action.

Her treacherous body trembled, remembering how his chest had rubbed against hers.

Years of marriage to another Evans had taught her something of how to handle these men. She deepened her voice, trying to make it seductive. "When you were tied to my bed, you told me one day I'd be moaning for more."

His eyes narrowed. "So I did. What of it?"

Locking her knees, she carefully spelled out her bargain. "If you help me find the gold, I'll share your bed for the entire trip, not just for the two hours we spent in Abercrombie's office today."

"Are you trying to bribe me with your body?"

She spread her hands. "Morgan, you won't take gold so what else can I offer you? Why not accept my body as a reward for traveling through Colorado?"

"You're a decent woman! No gentleman would ever accept your offer."

She sighed, adopting her most ladylike expression. Miss Ramsay would have been very proud. She'd always said men needed ladies to give them guidance. But that guiding men was like training horses: it was best done with a light hand on the reins. "You're quite right: you're entirely too much of a gentleman to accept such a bargain. I'll simply have to find someone else. It would be far safer for me than spending so much time with you."

He frowned, his eyes glinting like silver daggers. "What are you talking about?"

She shrugged, trying to look both impoverished and upright. "I'm not sure you're entirely trustworthy."

"Explain yourself, Jessamyn." His tone would have terrified anyone who wasn't his cousin's widow and therefore safe from murder, at least.

"What trappings do you show of a steady, God-fearing man? You travel the West for a living with no fixed address. You brag of your ability to make money by smelling out get-rich-quick schemes and swindlers."

"Dammit, Jessamyn, I am trustworthy," he snapped.

"Of course *you* are, Morgan." Pleased she'd come up with an argument he couldn't counter, she continued. "But you have acquired property by investing in fly-by-night characters and chance-met businesses, not by diligently attending to your own business."

"I've made a fortune that way and I've never broken the law," he growled, white grooves bracketing his mouth. "My word is my bond, no matter how much I must pay to satisfy it."

"But you agree those are your friends, don't you? So how could I feel safe traveling with you through Colorado?"

Her heart in her mouth, she took the risk of approaching him. Deliberately, she stepped close enough to almost brush his chest, enticing him with what he could have if he agreed. Reminding her of how a few minutes had seared him into her memories. "Since you're telling me that you don't want me, that weeks spent sharing my bed would be unpleasant for you? Since you object that strenuously, then I'll have to go to Denver and find someone else to take me to the mountains."

She sighed for effect and lowered her eyes, guarding her

expression—and wishing to God she wasn't so incredibly aware of every bone in his body, every muscle. Dammit, even the way his Adam's apple bobbed.

He roared in the back of his throat like a frustrated lion. "You won't find a better expedition than I can mount, thanks to Donovan & Sons. I can bring you all the way through the San Juan Mountains, following that goddamn map, better than anyone else in the world." He pulled her up to him, stroking her back, and lowered his voice. "And the nights, Jessamyn, will be better with me than with anyone else."

She slid her hands up his shoulders, praying that sleeping with Morgan wouldn't be worse than traveling with another trail boss. That weeks of sharing Morgan's bed wouldn't leave her half-insane with heated memories.

His gray eyes flared with primal hunger. Her foolish heart skipped a beat.

"Any limits on those nights, Jessamyn?"

Her breasts were suddenly heavy, aching for his touch. "Anything that won't cause pregnancy."

He gave a harsh snort of laughter and wrapped his arm around her waist, pulling her suddenly, brutally close. "I don't want a child from this either, Jessamyn. I just want to hear your voice begging me for more of my touch."

He cupped her chin in his hand, his calloused fingers rough against her skin. "I must be insane," he muttered.

"Then we have a bargain?" she queried, unsure if her leaping stomach was due to appalled propriety or carnal anticipation.

His gray eyes seemed to have become flames as he nodded. "Of course. Now start thinking about all the ways you're going to please me."

He trailed his fingers slowly down her cheek, leaving tendrils of heat behind. How could he have this effect on her with just his voice and a teasing touch?

He smiled down at her, all hot eyes and white teeth. "I told you the next time we were alone, after the War, that I would do what I wanted to do with you. That you would be the one crying out in hunger and ecstasy. Correct?"

Jessamyn nodded slowly. "You did say that."

He tucked a strand of hair behind her ear. She shivered, eyes fixed on his.

He kissed her forehead and nuzzled her cheek. His voice hardened subtly as he whispered in her ear. "That you'd be the one promising anything, in exchange for another touch, not me. True?"

Jessamyn swallowed hard but told the truth. "Yes."

He lifted her chin with a single finger, his other hand lightly clasping her waist, and let her clearly see his determination. "You're mine now. I've spent years studying, practicing ways to drive you insane with lust."

Jessamyn closed her eyes, shaking, and strongly wished she knew someone else who could take her into those mountains.

He touched his tongue to her lips, teased them open. Breathed lightly into her mouth until she sighed and relaxed slightly. Sucked gently on her lips until her whole mouth was open and yearning for him. Then his tongue entered her, swirling over her teeth, teasing her tongue, twining and dancing with it.

She moaned softly and stretched up to meet his kiss, utterly absorbed. He kissed as if they had all the time in the world, as if days and weeks and months could go by while he learned the taste and shape and feel of her mouth.

Her eyes drifted shut and her hands clasped his shoulders, pulling him closer. She rubbed herself against him shamelessly, sighing his name. Her breasts firmed inside her corset, her nipples stabbed against the plain linen, as her blood began to race.

A soft tap on the door shattered her absorption in Morgan. She tried to pull herself away, blushing furiously.

Morgan simply surveyed her, smiled with a very satisfied air, and tucked her into the crook of his arm. They were both facing the door when Abercrombie entered. She tried to look nonchalant, but she knew her mouth was bruised and her hair almost certainly mussed.

Abercrombie gaped—and Morgan growled. Abercrombie promptly wiped his face clear of all expression, except a vacuous politeness. "You inherited a few personal items from Mr. Jones's wife, Serafina, which are in this small chest." He tapped a stoutly made, locked wooden chest, slightly smaller than a carpetbag.

"We'll take it with us," Morgan answered casually.

"Would you care to join my wife and myself for dinner, Mr. and Mrs. Evans?" the lawyer asked nervously, his eyes darting to the knife at Morgan's hip. "We always enjoy hearing the news from the West."

"We are honored by your invitation, sir," Morgan said politely, standing so close to her that she could smell his brand of soap. "But we're scheduled to dine with my employer, William Donovan, and his family tonight. We must leave in a few minutes."

At least she'd have a brief reprieve before she'd be alone again with Morgan. Perhaps she could regain some of her composure.

Morgan hailed a cab as soon as they were outside. She settled against the seat, trying not to lean against him. "Where are we going?"

"Back to my hotel." His tone held more of a growl than a civilized comment.

"I thought we were to dine with Mr. Donovan?"

He snorted and began to play with her fingers. "We'll meet with him and his wife later. There's time enough for a taste of you now."

She stared at him. His voice was slow, soft, and heavily laden with lust. His face was silhouetted against the window, masked by the flickering late afternoon shadows. She had no idea what he meant to do and a thousand fantasies leaped to mind, every one setting her pulse racing.

He lifted her hand and started to kiss her fingers one by one. When he finished with the little finger, he returned to her index finger, licked it, and sucked it into his mouth.

Lust speared through her to her loins. She gasped and sank against the seat, her core softening. Hot cream pulsed between her legs and she groaned softly, half in anticipation and half in denial.

Dear God, was this how her mother had felt when she'd looked at Forsythe's jewelry?

Upon arrival at the hotel, Morgan registered her as his wife with all the arrogance of his aristocratic ancestry, then took her upstairs, waving off any offers of champagne. She was certain everyone watched them depart, with lascivious smiles. At least she had the right to be called Mrs. Evans.

At every step, she was acutely conscious of the man beside her. Of Morgan's leg brushing against her skirts, as he prowled beside her in the stride that had always captured her attention. Of his fingers burning through the thin silk of her best day dress. Of his coat catching briefly on her bustle, or dress improver as polite society called it. Of the rise and fall of his chest under his sober black vest and white shirt. The dawning stubble on his chin. The pulse beating in his throat, above the starched white collar and black string tie. And his gray eyes, sharply scrutinizing everything, as they moved through the corridors' hissing gaslight.

His room was small, although of the finest quality. She stood between his bed and the door, near a long mirror, shaking slightly as she tried to study the inanimate objects. Rosewood bed, marble-topped table, Brussels carpet, crystal lamps . . . But all she was really aware of was the man closing the heavy velvet curtains.

Now the chamber was lit only by the two lamps shining directly onto the bed. At this hour of the day, the neighboring rooms and hallways were empty, wrapping them in privacy.

A single bead of sweat ran down Jessamyn's back as her breasts seemed to grow heavier and her nipples tighter, as the seams of her old corset's silk brushed against them through her chemise. She didn't know if she wanted to run from him or hurl herself at him.

Morgan's hands came to rest lightly on her upper arms. Her head came up, startled, and she met his eyes in the long mirror opposite. She looked dark and mysterious, with her black hair and black dress against his black clothing and the room's shadows. But the lamplight struck fiery sparks from his chestnut hair, glints from his gray eyes, as if he were a torch ready to be set alight. She stared at him, all of the past forgotten for the first time.

"Your dress is very soft, my dear," Morgan purred, his voice as enticing as a whiff of the finest French brandy. He caressed her lightly, every fingertip evident through the thin cloth. His voice deepened and slowed, his Mississippi origins coming to the forefront. "But I do believe your skin will be even softer, and finer, than this silk."

Every word uttered in that deep, rich drawl settled into her bones. Heat coiled deep, reached up her spine. Desperate to regain some sanity, Jessamyn tried to return the situation to one of logic. "Morgan, we need to talk about how to deal with my cousin's—"

He stroked her shoulders and lightly ran his hands down her sides to her waist and over her hips. Involuntarily, she quivered as tiny lances of ecstasy skittered across her skin in the wake of his touch.

His drawl was even darker and more enticing as he undid the top buttons of her dress. "And I do believe the goddess Venus herself would be jealous of your figure. The womanly breasts and hips, the narrow waist, the firmness of your flesh thanks to your delight in horsemanship and dancing . . ."

His hand trembled slightly as he pushed aside a curl to kiss her neck. She tilted her head to give him access, but to her surprise, he nuzzled her gently first, then a delicate lick, a very light scrape of his teeth against one of her most sensitive, erotic points. Her knees buckled. Her wits frayed and she moaned, trembling at his dark, explicit promises of exactly what he planned to do to the rest of her body once he had bared it.

Eager for more, she reached back and slid one of his hands forward, until his fingertips grazed the underside of her breast.

"Do you wish a more direct touch, my dear? Or could certain portions of your anatomy be aching, perhaps?" His clever fingers caught her nipples between them, while lifting her breasts out of her corset. His wicked, all-too-knowledgeable eyes were heavy-lidded as he watched her in the mirror. "Is this how you play with yourself when you're alone, Jessamyn?" he whispered in her ear. "Lifting and squeezing your breasts? Gently? Or a little more firmly?"

She gasped sharply, thrusting her hips back against him. Her hands fluttered, not quite certain how boldly to encourage him. Her bustle tilted up and collapsed against the small of her back so that only her thin dress and petticoats lay between her and Morgan. But her dress was so old and thin, her petticoats so fragile and limp, that neither formed much barrier to feeling her companion's body. And this time when she rotated her hips in a woman's first invitation to a man, her derrière encountered the heat of his cock—standing hard behind his fine linen trousers. Her tongue swept across her lower lip in anticipation.

"Firmly then." Morgan's voice ensnared her again, pulling her attention back to his luminous eyes watching her in the mirror. "Do you prefer your nipples plucked, my dear lady? Or simply held while the rest of your skin receives attention?"

She choked, tossed her head back against his shoulder, and found herself writhing under his hands. "More often plucked, if you please," she managed to gasp. Dear heavens, even her best summer corset was no protection from Morgan, who obviously knew far too much about how to reduce a woman to a morass of quivering lust. It would have been easier to control herself if he hadn't continued to ask naughty questions or comment on her responses, while he fondled her breasts.

She was barely able to form a complete sentence, lances of heat pricking her flesh as her core clenched and melted for him. Then he lifted her skirts in back, leaving her completely respectable in front. His big hands stroked her flanks, the callused fingers sending answering ripples up her veins.

Jessamyn wriggled against him, almost dancing under his hands. If—when!—his expert fingers moved to the inside of her thighs and started to explore her, she could hardly be expected to remain calm.

"Your breasts are crying out for more attention, my dear," he crooned in her ear, his eyes heavy-lidded with lust. "Place your hands on them as you do in private—"

"What?" she whispered, startled that he'd speak openly of such intimate activities.

"You're a very passionate woman, Jessamyn." His wicked voice was honeyed brandy, an invitation to sin in the warm lamplight. His sensual mouth curved in a half-smile, as if he, too, remembered private delights. "Pleasure yourself now."

She was helpless to resist the rasp of an order beneath his voice's wicked invitation. Her hands lifted, tentatively at first, then with more certainty as she lost herself in the familiar movements.

"Ah, just as I wished to see you. Preparing yourself for my possession," Morgan whispered in her ear, as his callused hands shaped and stroked her derrière.

She moaned her willingness, stretching up on her toes when he lifted her—and sighing in ecstasy when his fingers finally, finally found her through the slit in her drawers.

A deeper flame burned in her veins when she saw the image of lust they made in the mirror, both outwardly the image of propriety from the waist down at least in their street clothes. But both their faces showed carnal hungers—hers the desperation of a woman eager to find satisfaction, his the delight of a man enjoying the slow climb to fulfillment. She writhed against him restlessly, while he was steady except for the continual movements of his hands against her and the magic of his voice drawing her deeper and deeper into a world where nothing existed but the pleasures of their bodies.

She deliberately rocked against his hand, savoring how his eyes widened and her movement drove his fingers deeper into her dripping cleft. Waves of lust tightened her belly and breasts until she fought to breathe, ached for the climax so very near, that he was keeping just beyond her reach. She arched against him and pushed down harder, her eyes slitting like a cat's as she heard his breath suddenly catch.

"Are you hot for me, little Jessamyn?" Morgan whispered, as he nibbled that sensitive point on her neck again, matching the tempo to the movements of his fingers inside her. She moaned, her hips falling into the same primal rhythm.

"Do you hunger for completion? Will you ask me this time, as you didn't nine years ago?"

The soft words were heard but not by her brain. Her body, desperate for fulfillment and well accustomed to a man's loving, understood. "Please." She forced her eyes to open, thereby meeting his in the mirror. "Please take me, Morgan."

His face blazed with passion and triumph. At another time, she'd have flinched to put herself at his mercy. But now she was simply desperate for relief.

"Put your hands on the mirror," he growled.

She obeyed promptly, eager to be finally possessed by him.

He tossed her skirts up over her rump and she braced herself instinctively, watching eagerly. They were both almost fully dressed, yet about to indulge in the most carnal pleasure of all. How very, very hedonistic of them. Her body blazed its approval, gushing a torrent of cream down her thighs.

"Good girl," he rumbled approvingly and turned away briefly, only to return rolling a thin sheath over his cock.

A condom? She blinked in surprise. She'd heard of them, even seen a few, but never used one before.

Morgan unbuttoned his fly, baring himself very little. She whimpered in frustration as her hips wriggled imploringly.

He stroked her hips, shaping them for an instant. His leg slipped between hers. Jessamyn gasped and arched against him, tremors rising through her at the touch of his trousers' linen against her highly sensitized flesh.

Morgan lifted her off her feet then pulled her down hard onto his cock. It barreled into her, driving through her core, propelling all the air out of her lungs. She gasped her pleasure at finally being filled by a man again. Climax hung just out of reach.

He started to withdraw for another stroke. She clamped her internal muscles down hard on him but he slowly drew inexorably out, his cock's crest rippling along her tight muscles in both promise and temptation. He shuttled into her again and again, working his way into her as hard as she tried to hold him in her, until finally he was seated to the hilt.

Everything in her was one giant knot of desperation, screaming for release.

Morgan's eyes met hers in the mirror. They were both breathing harshly and sweating hard. For the first time, she saw carnal hunger as desperate as her own in his eyes.

"This time, dammit," he gritted out. "This time, you'll be the one gasping in ecstasy."

"Then do it, damn you!"

His eyes flashed sparks of light. He braced his arms under hers, supporting her. He began to move, drawing out until only his very tip remained inside her. She fought to hold him, losing herself in the bliss of a man's possession. Then he drove back in and her deep inner muscles flexed to welcome him, their flesh hot and wet against each other.

He pistoned in and out of her, harder and faster, the mirror slamming against the wall. Shattering all the memories of the long lonely nights of widowhood.

Rapture built higher and higher, tightened every muscle until she was ready to explode.

He growled and nipped her neck just behind her ear. She shrieked in surprise and climaxed immediately, shuddering and gasping his name as long, rolling blasts of pleasure roared through her body.

Deep inside her, he pumped rich jets of himself into her core, the heat muted by the condom.

Her eyes almost closed as she lost herself in sheer, ecstatic bliss, with his arms locked around her. She'd consider his unreliability another time.

Chapter Seven

A ftershocks still pounding his spine, Morgan dragged air into his lungs as if he'd just staggered to the top of Pike's Peak and let Jessamyn down gently. She sighed, shuddered, turned, and hid her face against his chest.

He twined her raven ringlet around his finger one more time, savoring its silkiness, before lifting his hand from the nape of her neck. She shivered slightly at that last, faint caress to a very sensitive spot—and his gut tightened. Playing with her hair was almost more intimate than the carnal possession he'd just had of her.

His tongue ran out over his dry lips and he threw his head back, staring at the carved plaster moldings overhead as he fought for control. He'd never before been at liberty to play with her hair, not when he was a fifteen-year-old boy helping an eleven-year-old tomboy clean up after an escapade. Certainly not when he'd escorted her so briefly that Christmas nine years ago. But now, now he could do anything he liked with her, as long as he chased after Ortiz's illusory gold.

Christ, what a mess he was in. Jessamyn believed that he was a rogue and a scoundrel because he had benefited from get-rich-quick schemes and lacked a stable home life. He'd been a spy, when every other man of her acquaintance—Cyrus, David, George, and the others—had fought in a regular unit.

By any comparison to Cyrus, he looked like an untrustworthy rolling stone.

He still wished he hadn't risked Uncle Heyward. If that stupid neighbor chit, Clarabelle Hutchinson, hadn't invited him to that dinner, he'd probably have left and matters would have proceeded differently. But he'd taken the easy way out— the reckless, lazy way, as Jessamyn so accurately expressed it—and heedlessly endangered Uncle Heyward. He was damn lucky it had worked out. But Jesus, he'd sweated until he'd heard Uncle Heyward had left Memphis safely!

But that wouldn't help today's mess. He should have refused her offer this afternoon, just to prove he was a gentleman now. But if he had, she'd have made her way to Denver and God knows what offer she'd have made there or what scoundrel she would have made it to.

No, he was doing this to protect her.

Morgan softly snorted in derision, well aware his cock had been doing most of the thinking—and would likely continue to do so, every time he was around her.

But how the hell could he convince her he was a gentleman if he kept behaving like a scoundrel, taking her along on the damn fool expedition she was so crazy for and sleeping with her?

Visions of her, naked and flushed with passion, begging for more of his touch, swept into his head. He'd spent nine years learning the discipline he'd lacked the last time they'd been alone together. This time, she'd be the one whose self-control shattered and he'd have the self-control to walk away at the end. Somehow.

In his letters, Cyrus had spoken proudly of her as a wife and helpmeet, able to follow him anywhere the Army sent him. But with him, she was always escorted by multitudes of soldiers. On this trip, only a dozen rough teamsters would protect her on a dangerous race against Jones and his wife, a pair who made Apaches seem like pillars of the community.

He touched her lightly on the shoulder. "We need to leave, Jessamyn. There's just enough time to clean up before we have dinner."

She blushed. "Certainly." She straightened and stepped back, her hands immediately working to settle her clothing. Though her mouth was bruised from his kisses, her eyes were as reserved and thoughtful as they'd been nine years ago.

Morgan reminded himself sternly not to preen and strut like a rooster when he escorted her down the street, if for no other reason than she'd be gone in a few months. He gritted his teeth at the reminder and briskly disposed of the used condom.

Then he stealthily sorted through his chest of carnal toys for some trinkets to distract her with, should a private occasion arise.

The restaurant was, of course, the best Kansas City had to offer, given that William Donovan was dining there. French cuisine prepared by genuine French chefs, not someone flourishing an acquired accent, and served in an atmosphere of eye-catching opulence. Gold and green marble covered the walls and floors, framed by heavily carved wood. Gaslight hissed and danced on hundreds of crystals dangling from chandeliers and sconces, casting a surprisingly warm light across the central room and its assembled diners with their formal clothing.

The maître d', who obviously considered himself a superior being, raised an inquiring eyebrow as Morgan and Jessamyn approached.

"The Donovan party, if you please. They're expecting us."

The maître d' unbent immediately with a gracious smile. "Mr. Evans, what a pleasure to see you! Mr. Donovan told us you'd be joining him. This way, please."

He stepped away from his desk and swept past another waiting couple without a glance. Morgan and Jessamyn followed him up the stairs to the private dining rooms on the second floor. Here the corridors were just as opulent as the great room below but hushed, as if to encourage the exchange of secrets in the rooms beyond. Skillful waiters moved quickly, silently stepping aside to let the newcomers pass and averting their eyes as if even the guests' identity was a private matter.

The maître d' tapped on a door at the end of the hallway. William's deep voice answered quickly and the man opened the door with a slight bow. Morgan followed, acutely aware of how cold his hands had suddenly become. William was his closest friend and his mentor in so many ways, and the bond between them ran deeper than blood kin.

Still, before his marriage, William's appetite for the fairer sex had been legendary. If Jessamyn was the first woman whose attractions incited him to adultery and he turned his charms on her . . . Morgan's fists clenched before he told himself he was being a fool. William was besotted with his darling wife, whom he'd married little more than a year ago. He'd stopped spending time in brothels the day she moved in with him.

Inside the elegant little room, William and his wife, Viola, rose to their feet. Their surprise at Jessamyn's presence was quickly covered by smiles of welcome, although William's glances at Jessamyn seemed particularly warm.

Morgan stiffened, tightening his grip on Jessamyn's arm, and forced himself to make introductions. "My dear, allow me to introduce you to my employer and good friends, William and Viola Donovan. William and Viola, may I present you to my cousin, Mrs. Jessamyn Evans, who's traveling with me?"

Jessamyn nodded politely, every inch the perfect Southern lady. She'd stiffened slightly when he introduced her as "cousin," but at least she hadn't openly objected. "Mrs. Donovan, Mr. Donovan, it's a pleasure to meet you."

Morgan didn't drop his guard, barely managing not to snap out a challenge to a fight. William's eyes swept over

Morgan, amusement in their depths. Thankfully, Viola provided a distraction.

"You're introducing us to family members at last? Lovely!" She rushed around the table to kiss them both on the cheek.

Only Morgan felt Jessamyn's reflexive flinch—and his own. William followed his wife's example and greeted them, polite toward Jessamyn but still searching Morgan's expression.

Morgan settled into his chair, pasting a smile on his face as he watched William out of the corner of his eye. The party, led by Viola's laughing energy and Jessamyn's Southern graciousness, soon ordered the restaurant's specialties for supper.

His jealousy of William faded, replaced by a wry laughter at himself. As if the man ever noticed a woman other than Viola now!

"Where are Hal and Rosalind Lindsay?" Morgan asked, more as a way to postpone the inevitable discussion of why he wanted to take leave. "I thought they would join us tonight."

Viola's eyes danced and William smiled, lounging back in his chair like a cougar. "Captain Lindsay," he answered formally, "was unavoidably called away on business. His wife—"

"Of five days," Viola inserted with a smile.

"Insisted on accompanying him, to ensure that he accomplished all matters in a satisfactory manner. Said business needing to be conducted—"

"At their house. We may see my brother and his wife again sometime tomorrow," Viola finished and chuckled. "Maybe. Or maybe not."

"More likely not," her husband agreed, without heat, and patted her hand. She turned it over to clasp his and smiled at him, their confidence in each other as radiantly clear as it had always been.

Morgan shifted uncomfortably before reaching for his champagne. His parents had cherished each other like that once and he'd always hoped to find something similar in his own marriage.

William's brilliant blue gaze came back to him, with all the clear-eyed watchfulness he wore in the private clubs as a master of women's fantasies. There were damn few masks, if any, capable of standing against it.

Morgan squared his chin and looked back at his old friend and mentor. Beside him, Jessamyn was silent, studying every word and move the others made. He began his report.

"I completed the deal with Halpern this afternoon and was able to get an excellent price on those ammunition chests."

"Congratulations," William murmured. His eyes never wavered from Morgan's face.

"I'd like to take a few weeks' leave now, maybe a couple of months. Jessamyn's uncle left her a map showing where there might be—"

"Is!" she inserted fiercely.

William and Viola's heads swiveled sideways to look at her. Her jaw was set mulishly as she glared at Morgan. "I know Ortiz's gold is buried exactly where Uncle Edgar said."

Viola's eyebrows shot up. "Ortiz's gold?"

William let out a long, soft whistle before rising to lock the door. He sat back down with a very thoughtful expression. "Where do you plan to hunt?"

"The San Juan Mountains," Morgan answered. "She has a well-made Spanish map, starting from the Three Needles on the Rio Grande's headwaters. After that, the trail leads a little west but mostly south into the mountains."

"Anyone else know about this?"

"Her cousin has a copy of the same map. You know him and his wife: Charlie and Maggie Jones."

William's eyes flashed and he slapped the table angrily, as if it was a poor substitute for the real scoundrel.

Viola sighed, her soft mouth drooping. "Maggie was so distraught after her baby died. I tried so hard to be a friend and help her every way I could."

William put his arm around her and she leaned against his shoulder, her face half-hidden. "You can't save people from themselves, sweetheart."

"True. But perhaps if I'd set a better example as a Christian, she'd have changed."

"Viola, darling, she stole everything you had and sold it." And no one else will ever take advantage of you again, promised his pitiless expression.

"But if she hadn't done that, I wouldn't have marched into your office and we wouldn't be married," Viola countered and tipped her head back to bat her eyelashes at him meaningfully.

William choked.

Morgan bit his lip, trying not to laugh, and Jessamyn spluttered behind her napkin.

William patted his wife's arm. "You are, as ever, perfectly correct. But I believe you'll agree with me that Morgan and his lady will need to make every effort, if they are to survive and reach their destination before Charlie Jones."

"Certainly," Viola agreed promptly. "Jones is a very dangerous man." She kissed him on the cheek.

William smiled at her fondly then cocked an eyebrow at Morgan. "How well funded is Jones?"

Morgan snorted, his jealousy finally completely erased. "Extremely. After you refused to haul freight from his Rosabelle Mine, in retribution for stealing all of Mrs. Donovan's possessions, Jones traded the Rosabelle for Nelson's Firelight Mine."

"How did he persuade Nelson?" Viola asked, fascinated. Jessamyn put down her fork, ignoring an excellent roast chicken, to listen.

"Officially, Jones said that his new bride wanted a home closer to the comforts of civilization. In truth, a large number of thugs nearly destroyed Nelson's hoisting shaft. Taking the warning, Nelson cut his losses and accepted the trade. Whereupon Donovan & Sons promptly signed a contract with Nelson at lower rates, albeit still very profitable, than with Jones."

"But the Firelight had never been a major producer," William observed.

"Up until then, no. But shortly after Jones took possession, he sunk a new shaft, turned lucky, and struck a very rich vein of gold. He's now the second or third richest man in the Colorado Territory."

"I'll wager Maggie spends it as quickly as he can bring it out of the ground," Viola said tartly.

Morgan spread his hands in agreement. "Or faster. She's his only weakness. But he's still extremely rich."

"I assume Cousin Charlie still controls the same thugs who brought him the Firelight," Jessamyn commented thought-fully, buttering a roll. She looked entirely too civilized, in her proper black dress with her precisely wielded silverware against the crisp white tablecloth, to be discussing such mat-ters.

The others stared at her, startled by her matter-of-fact de-scription of her cousin's viciousness. She looked around at them and shrugged. "It would be very much in his fashion, you know. He always liked to keep other bullies and thieves close at hand to increase his mischief. But if so, where can we find an army to proceed against him?"

"We won't need an army." Morgan infused his voice with more certainty than he felt. He'd seen the nearly ruined Fire-light after Jones's thugs had wrecked the hoisting shaft and he'd prefer to have ten men for every one of Jones's. "His men are mostly miners and bully boys, more accustomed to camps than mountains and trails. I can hire better fellows than that in Denver. War veterans, for example."

William considered him for a long moment, his blue eyes hooded and nearly unreadable. He glanced down at Viola, who nodded silently, before he spoke. "Take whatever you need from Donovan & Sons—men, horses and mules, supplies."

Morgan frowned at him, knowing exactly what the offer would cost the firm. After all, he'd spent most of the previous year acting as William's general manager, while William and Viola honeymooned abroad. "It's the middle of summer, the busiest season. You'd be stretched too thin."

William shrugged, his blue eyes as implacable as a broadsword's steel. "I want my best friend to return alive."

Morgan knew damn well how poor his chances were of directly defeating any edict delivered in that tone. "I'll repay you."

"Don't be absurd!" Viola cried.

Morgan barely glanced at her. "It's business, Viola. I ran Donovan & Sons for the past year while you were in Europe. You can't afford to lose a dozen men at the height of the season."

"You're our best friend and we want you back. William, tell him not to be silly!"

Her husband pursed his lips, considering his general manager. "You can repay me at cost." He put his hand over his wife's.

"Cost plus—"

"Cost," William said flatly.

Morgan laughed. "Deal. I should have known better than to try to outwit you."

Viola snickered, a remarkably unladylike sound that she covered with a sip of lemonade.

"Thank you," Jessamyn said softly. "You're very generous."

"You'll take Grainger as your second-in-command," William added in tones that were as implacable as they were silky.

Morgan nearly spewed his wine across the table. "The fellow who is your best trail boss between Trinidad, the Denver & Rio Grande's railhead, and Santa Fe?"

Jessamyn gasped softly but didn't speak.

"I know exactly how important he is. But he's an ex-cavalry officer, no pilgrim, and our best organizer for a trip into far

THE SOUTHERN DEVIL   143

country. You need someone like him at your back, since I can't accompany you."

Morgan nodded gratefully. When no other comments came, he brought up the company's *enfant terrible*. "May I have Lowell too?"

William's eyebrows went up. "Now you want the Kentucky lad, too, who's an excellent marksman and a near-genius in any wilderness, despite his difficulties around civilization." He drummed his fingers on the table, staring into the distance. Morgan watched him silently, barely conscious of holding his breath. Finally, William spoke. "Very well, you can have them both. I recommend you also find yourself a good guide."

"Have you been into the San Juans?"

"Just once, five years ago. And you?"

"Saw them from the south with Cochise, before the War. We didn't enter them."

William grunted his sympathy with Cochise's decision. "The San Juans are high mountains, many over fourteen thousand feet, as if giants stacked blocks end over end. Also, the Ute Indians there are very good fighters, even if they've recently signed a peace treaty. You may have a map but local experience will count for as much, or more."

Morgan nodded. "I'll ask Grainger to find someone."

"How do you plan to travel there?"

"Train to Denver, then south to the Sangre de Cristo Pass. After that, travel by horseback." He turned to look at Jessamyn. "Do you want to ride astride?"

She stiffened, clearly affronted, and very precisely set down her fork to glare at him. "As a lady, I always ride aside, of course. I have an English hunt saddle, which Cyrus ordered made for me in London. It's waiting for me, with the rest of my gear, at the boardinghouse."

"Excellent," Viola approved. "How many riding habits do you have?"

"One, thank you, cut from cavalry blue."

Morgan's fingers tapped briefly on the table, at the reminder of her years with Cyrus.

Jessamyn continued, her eyes barely flickering toward him. "Plus an American Lady's mountain dress, which will also do for riding in a pinch."

"Very good. Those full trousers are quite comfortable, aren't they?"

"Indeed they are, even hidden under the skirt."

The two ladies smiled at each other in perfect harmony and went back to eating.

William drummed his fingers on the table. "You'll use our private car as far as Denver, since it's standard gauge, with Abraham and Sarah Chang to look after you. I'll have it hitched to the U.P.'s morning train to Denver."

"There's only narrow-gauge railways after that." Morgan considered his options, given how fast railroads were being built in Colorado.

"Yes, you'll have to switch to the Denver & Rio Grande. I'll ask Rosalind to arrange a special train with them to the foot of the Sangre de Cristo Pass. Some of your horses and supplies will meet you in Denver, of course, and the rest at the Plaza de los Leones." He unlocked the door and tugged the bell cord, summoning the waiter.

"Thank you," Morgan said with feeling.

William barely bothered to glance up from the coded telegram he was writing. "My pleasure. Just remember Jones will probably be doing the same thing."

Morgan shrugged and produced his own pad of telegram blanks from an inside pocket. "I'll take my chances. I've had fair warning and I can defeat him."

"Of course," William agreed, his expression harsh. "But watch your back on that trail. You're heading into the roughest of territories."

Maggie preened, admiring herself in the hand mirror her maid held. Her peignoir was in the latest Paris fashion, so or-

namented with pleats and ribbons that the underlying white
silk was barely visible. It was cut low in front to display her
superb décolletage, which was also framed by her flowing
locks.

She arched her neck and smirked. Just like a swan, as that
Italian what's-his-name had bleated before Charlie killed
him.

She snapped her fingers. "Jewelry box!" Her maid flipped
the lid open and Maggie began to select the finishing touches.
They wouldn't be enough to keep Charlie's interest, let alone
make him any use to a woman. But they'd certainly keep a
smile on her face.

Her fingers petted her darlings as she debated. The gold
nugget earrings? Too common, even if they were enormous.
Rubies? No, too heavy. Sapphire earrings, with that delicious
pendant that nestled between her breasts to remind her of why
she'd really married the fool?

The box dropped out from under her hand as her idiot
maid bobbed a curtsy. "Mr. Jones."

Maggie barely refrained from boxing the fool's ears. She
managed a smile as she grabbed the precious chest and set it
on the table. "Have you finished making arrangements?"

"All done." He settled onto the bed, watching her mood-
ily. She'd thought him a fine enough fellow once, even if no
match for Morgan Evans's bold elegance. She flicked her fingers at her maid, who departed hastily.

"Rail travel arranged, plus surprises for our competition."

"Lovely." She started sorting through her pretties. She'd
need inspiration, if she was to rouse Charlie's male member
to any sort of upright stance tonight. "I'll wait for you in
Newport."

A long golden rope, set with rubies and diamonds, dropped
around her neck. Maggie squeaked and grabbed at it, holding it out so she could see it better. "Oh, how beautiful! Lovely,
lovely! Pigeon's blood rubies, cabochon cut . . ." She scram-

bled in her drawer for her jeweler's loupe, not taking her eyes away from the jewelry.

Charlie suddenly tugged the necklace against her throat, hard and tight, until only her hand kept the metal links from cutting into her skin.

"What are you doing, Charlie?" Maggie squeaked, startled and scared.

His head came around to look at her from only a few inches away, his hot eyes fixed on hers. "Do you like it?"

She sensed a trap but lust, hot and bright, ran through her veins. Her tongue ran out over her lips and she couldn't help a sideways, languishing look at the gold. "It's marvelous."

"You'll have to come to Colorado with me to keep it."

"What?" Her brain scrambled for a reason. He'd never acted like this before. "Why?"

"You gave Morgan Evans a clear offer this afternoon. Or was it two offers?"

She flushed guiltily then tried to recover her place in his good graces. "I was only flirting." She simpered up at him.

The necklace tightened and she gasped.

"Don't lie to me again, Maggie." Weariness infused Charlie's voice. "I know you only married me after he refused you. But he will never gain your favors, not while you're alive. Do you understand?"

She nodded, fighting to breathe. "Yes, Charlie."

The jeweled rope loosened and fell away. For the first time in her life, she didn't grab for a piece of gold.

"Good girl. Now, you're coming to Colorado with me on this race."

"Ride through the mountains? I haven't done that since . . ."

"You married me."

She nodded, too appalled to speak. A month in the mountains, riding every day? It would be far too much like her miserable childhood.

"You'll sleep with me every night, too, for a change. Do you understand?"

Worst of all, she'd spend her nights with a man whose male member lay limp as a codfish whenever he approached his wife—and who hadn't the decency to let her find satisfaction elsewhere. She grumbled inside but kept her thoughts from her face. "Yes, Charlie."

Chapter Eight

The railroad depot bustled with activity, even at this late hour. Locomotives belched clouds of steam, laced with cinders, as they bustled back and forth, moving a handful of freight cars or exchanging a pair of passenger cars for a flat car. Cattle bellowed fitfully, underscoring the stench of their discomfort. A bonfire could be glimpsed between the rolling, hard-edged railcars, edged by hulking shapes of men and the red arcs of gesticulating cigars. Far in the distance, a thunderstorm flashed a few last lightning bolts as it moved southeast toward Tennessee and Memphis.

All of Jessamyn's earlier nerves, which she'd pushed aside while they'd planned the journey, rushed back in full force. What would it be like to be Morgan's lover for weeks to come? Would she become addicted to the drugging pleasure of his kisses, the rich sensations his hands brought, the wild delights his cock sent through her? But it was fruitless for a respectable woman to feel that way about a rogue like him.

Jessamyn plastered a smile on her face and greeted Abraham and Sarah Chang, William Donovan's two servants, at his private railway car, parked on a semiprivate siding. A Chinese couple? Their race was unusual here in Missouri but surely more common in San Francisco, where the Donovans lived. Morgan was obviously very familiar with them and greeted them as old friends. A few quick words confirmed that their luggage had already come onboard, including Jessamyn's guns and sidesaddle.

Sarah showed her through the luxuriously appointed car, with its intricate inlays of rare woods, carved crystals, rich velvets, and deep carpets.

Heat rippled over her skin at the thought she'd be locked into this moving jewel box with Morgan for almost thirty-six hours. Jessamyn shook her head at her body's own carnal foolishness.

They passed through an observation lounge, a stateroom, open sections, a dining room—all superbly made and lavishly furnished. She began to wonder what Morgan would do with her in each compartment. Spread her legs across the arms of one of the great chairs in the observation lounge—and feast on her ecstatic intimate flesh? Her breasts tightened, somehow heating her core.

Toss her skirts up in the second stateroom, just to see how well its mattress was made? Her skin heated, until she could feel every detail of her drawers and the cream just starting to bead.

Bend her over a table in the dining room? Her legs trembled at the thought, until she had to lock her knees as her core clenched.

She tried to ignore these distracting carnal fancies and fix her attention on the car's details, like the rare woods used in the marquetry, but couldn't. Every time she touched a table, her thoughts skittered in a thousand directions, everyone a different position for him to spread her across that surface.

She caught a reflection of herself in one of the windows, and remembered how she'd looked earlier that evening—when she'd moaned in ecstasy as Morgan thrust into her. At the memory, her body promptly softened and ached for him, as if he had only to hold out his hand and she'd flip up her skirts then and there for him.

Shaken, she stepped quickly into the last compartment, the main stateroom, whose luxury stopped her in her tracks. It was midnight now and the train wouldn't leave until dawn for the twenty-four-hour run to Denver. How much of that time would she spend here?

The main stateroom was the most lavishly appointed compartment of all, with monogrammed golden silks stretched across the enormous carved rosewood bed. The walls were made of carved mahogany panels, alternating with beautiful marquetry inlays, and lit by elegant crystal lamps. Overhead, a series of clerestory windows, set with elegant leaded glass and designed to exchange air and light for heat, circled the entire compartment.

Her heart stopped as she remembered the completely different, narrow iron bed in her Memphis home's attic. How Morgan's hard body had pressed her into it, his eyes pinning her more completely than his hand had pinioned her wrist.

Sarah Chang said something but Jessamyn silenced her with a raised hand.

Dear God, how that instant was still branded into every inch of her body, even the way his waistband had ridden down his hips and how she'd longed to push it lower . . .

She gulped and pushed her fist into her mouth. Her teeth scraped a knuckle and the small pain brought her back to the present.

Her stained and battered old traveling trunk rested on a bench, waiting for her like an old friend. She rested her hand on it for a moment before starting to untie her bonnet. She said something trivial to Sarah and urgently began the evening ritual of undressing.

By the time she'd changed into her thin cotton nightgown, she was no longer certain of her own mind. If she'd had a chance to leave, she'd probably have taken it. But her own body's hunger for Morgan and her need to rescue her friends kept her where she was.

Sarah left her with a quiet good night, her face impassive. Jessamyn restlessly smoothed a fold in the silk coverlet, following it all the way across the only bed large enough to hold both Morgan and herself. She shivered involuntarily, her tongue darting out to touch her lips. Surely she was cold, despite the summer's heat which lingered in this enclosed space. She could not possibly be flushed with eagerness, have heat building in her core, as she waited for Morgan to share her bed—could she? It was so very ridiculous to be eager for a man who had no notion of steadiness and reliability, of how to support a woman.

The door closed softly and she spun to face him. He wore only light silk trousers, riding low on his hips, whose transparency displayed every detail of his readiness. Her jaw dropped and cream rippled onto her thigh. "You, you're not . . ."

Morgan eyed Jessamyn, shifting from one foot to the other in that fragile nightgown. And well she should be nervous—how dare she call him less than respectable!

Christ, the cloth might as well not have been there, thanks to the beads of sweat disappearing into the valley between her high, superb breasts, highlighting every curve. And her breasts' taut peaks lifted the fabric even farther, their rich rose vividly apparent.

His body tightened, sweat beading on his throat and trickling down over his chest—just the way her tongue would feel when she tasted him.

He growled and banged down the small chest on the dresser. He would not, could not, leap upon her the first chance he had to make her beg for him, dammit! He'd spent nine years learning how to drive women insane with lust, how to leash his own desires. This afternoon, there'd been only enough time at his hotel to blunt his raging hungers, not teach her to plead for him. Surely, he would not behave like the ravening beast she considered him.

Still, he'd never seen her naked body in that attic room. It might be best to keep some barriers between them—to be removed later, of course—so that he wasn't too distracted by the sight of her.

"But anyone could have seen you," she protested.

Still staring at his cock, he noted and all but purred. *That's it, Jessamyn. You were hot for me nine years ago but you denied it. Tonight, hypocrisy won't be allowed: you will plead for a taste.*

"Why should I care? Tonight is for my pleasures, as I told you nine years ago." He circled the bed, coming closer to her.

He deepened his voice to a purr. "Do you remember the attic?"

Her hand clenched but didn't quite touch the bed. He caught his breath, lust spearing down his spine. He took another step, coming close enough to her to scent her musk. "Perhaps you, too, need to be bound in a small bed—and tasted."

She gaped at him. "Morgan, you wouldn't!" But her musk deepened, while her breasts rose and fell more rapidly.

Hunger washed through him in a great ravening, cleansing flood. Jessamyn was excited by the prospect of some bondage. He could give her that and have his revenge at the same time, the great pleasure of hearing her beg for more.

Discipline settled over him, the hard-won control learned from the Consortium. Lust eased back to the edges of his being, reluctantly forced to wait.

He wrapped his hand around her throat in a caress, savoring how her pulse sped up—and she leaned closer to him, rather than fighting to run from the hard fingers so close to her jugular. "You'll do anything I want, remember?"

She nodded, whimpering a little, her green eyes enormous as she stared up at him. Her little red tongue darted out then retreated quickly. "As I agreed. Anything."

He kissed her possessively, sucking her lower lip into his. She responded immediately, leaning into him, and fervently returning the oral caress. As he'd jealously imagined for seven years, she'd had a passionate relationship with Cyrus. Something primal in him growled at the thought of another man. Something else, equally primal, rejoiced at her skill.

He lifted his head, rubbing his thumb over her swollen lip. She blinked up at him, her eyes quickly starting to refocus. That was his Jessamyn, seldom too far from thinking.

He quickly took out two strands of beads from his toy chest. They were both made from dark green jade, perfectly smooth, and extremely rare. They were also the color of her eyes and he'd never used them with another woman. In fact, he'd laughed at himself for buying them, given their expense.

"Give me your hands, Jessamyn."

She blinked at him, her brain definitely turning over. "Why?"

Hell, would he have to turn her over his knee and paddle her to teach her obedience? She couldn't question every order in the mountains or she'd be killed, if not by Charlie's thugs, then by an avalanche or a thunderstorm. He poured steel into his voice. "Obey me, Jessamyn."

She gaped at him, never having heard that tone from him before. Then she held out her hands, her breasts tightening even further behind them, and her eyes turning soft and deep.

Oh yes, Jessamyn was definitely excited by bondage. A wave of heat surged through his veins at the hungry look in her eyes. He gritted his teeth and fought to control his breathing.

A few moments passed—time in which sweat made Jessamyn's nightgown more and more transparent—before he had the discipline to loop one strand of the beads around her wrists in a loose knot. Dear God, the dark green was just as beautiful against her wrists as her eyes looked against her cheeks.

He gave her time to adapt, of course, as a courtesy to her innocence of this style of carnal play.

She twisted her hands and tugged gently, testing the bond. She could free herself but only with a little work. Perfect. Now she'd have to pay attention to what he wanted, rather

than *think* and do what she wanted. Blood pooled in his
groin, heating in readiness.

"Why?" she asked finally.

"Does it matter?"

She blinked and visibly worked to follow his logic. "Since
this is what you want to do, you don't have to provide an explanation?"

He smiled, well aware he was showing his teeth. "Exactly.
As long as I take you to Colorado."

"I should object to being tied up."

He snorted, his earlier anger creeping back. "Don't be a
fool. You called me a rogue and a scoundrel, Jessamyn. If you
object, I'll use force to gain what I want, stopping only if it
threatens to harm you."

Her eyes searched his, assessing his determination. He
stared back at her, absolutely determined—and she yielded,
bowing her head to him. "Very well." She gulped. "Anything
you wish."

He swept her up into his arms and laid her down on the
bed, leaning over her. "Entirely mine, Jessamyn," he growled.

She nodded, her lips slightly parted. Dammit, why couldn't
he resist her? He swooped down for a kiss and somehow his
hand found one of her breasts and played with it. Stroked it,
fondled it, plumped it, kneaded it—and rolled and plucked
her nipples when they hardened urgently.

She gasped and squirmed under him. Suddenly her fingers
delicately teased his cock, circling the tip.

Morgan snarled and slid down between her legs. Hell and
damnation, he would not be the one begging for another touch.

"Morgan?" Bewilderment in her voice; he told himself
that was good. Keep her off balance so he could recover his.
He knelt up between her legs and grabbed the other jade
strand from the night table, before looking back at her.

The hem of her nightgown was tumbled over her thighs,
showing beautiful, long, slender legs, creamy white against
the crimson silk. She tried to close them, which only made

her magnificent long thigh muscles flex, vibrant under the sheen of sweat. What those legs would feel like when they wrapped around him . . .

His breath caught in his throat and his cock all but lunged out of his thin silk trousers.

Dark curls showed clearly at the junction of her thighs. He bent his head to look, lured by the scent of her musk and the trail of her cream hinted at under her nightgown. What man could resist such a delicacy?

"Oh yes, Morgan!" She lifted her hips eagerly, spreading her legs—all the signs of a woman who enjoyed passion.

If she was so eager now, he'd have to bring her higher before he released her.

He slid his fingers under the nightgown, teasing them both with the contrast between his callused fingers and her silken skin. Exploring the gentle curves of her belly, the sweep of her thighs into the strong juncture with her mound. She'd been an adorable schoolgirl in that gray dress but the sight of her like this, moaning in passion and willingness, made tension coil at the base of his spine, aching to claim her.

But not yet—she hadn't begged for him.

He fingered her intimately, growling approval when she moaned his name and her hips rocked. A slow slick of cream glided onto his fingertips, the best delicacy in the world.

Soon, very soon, he promised himself, and slipped the jade beads between her folds.

She shrieked, bucking up against him. *Yes!* Finally he'd broken past her expectations.

Her eyes flashed open. "Good heavens, Morgan!"

He smiled at her, damn sure he looked very pleased with himself, and teased her clit with the beads.

Her eyes rolled back in her head. "Morgan!"

He wondered how the hell he'd manage to undo his trousers' drawstring with only one hand—and decided he could rip the damn things off if he had to. He tucked some beads into her channel and began to work her over in earnest, careful not to let her reach orgasm. No matter how agonizing the wait was for him, he would hear her beg.

He ripped down his trousers and fumbled for a condom, forcing himself to take the time now while she was still distracted with the beads' unusual sensation.

She sobbed for breath when every bead was rippling over her folds, covered in her cream. She moaned when he finally tasted her, fondling her with his tongue. Hell, he loved to run his tongue through a woman's folds, but not quite enough to forget who he was with.

He teased her clit with the beads and she shrieked his name, making his mouth tighten in what wasn't quite a smile. *Yes, dammit, yes.* She was coming closer and closer to orgasm's madness—but so was he.

He pumped his fingers into her, matching the rhythm pounding through both their veins. Two fingers—and she sobbed his name as she adapted, cream gushing over his hand. *That's it, Jessamyn, just a little more desperation.*

"Please, oh please," she moaned.

Say it, Jessamyn, say it before both of us go insane. Every artery and vein seemed to be pumping blood for one purpose only—mounting her.

"Morgan, please finish me," she sobbed.

Yes! He snatched the beads away from her, making her sob in desperation, then wrapped them around the base of his cock. He groaned at the slick delight, binding him closer to the desperation she'd felt and the ecstasy they'd both soon enjoy.

An instant later, he knelt between her legs, his cock poised at her entrance. He gripped her shoulders from underneath, pulling them together. He surged into her, her hot slick sheath clasping him. She flung her arms over her head, arching back in welcome.

He growled in satisfaction and thrust again, more deeply, their bodies slapping wetly against each other and the beads sending fiery sparks up his spine. Hot and savage and fast, he ground against her, savoring every time her strong internal muscles gripped him. But need was pounding stronger and stronger in his bones.

He rubbed her clit with every stroke, his eyes slitted against impending ecstasy. Suddenly orgasm surged through her and she clamped down on his cock, sobbing, demanding everything from him.

Morgan roared his triumph and came, his seed pouring up from the base of his spine and jetting out of his cock. He was blind and deaf, lights blasting behind his eyes, oblivious to anything except the woman under him, as his body shook until his bones rattled.

He couldn't have moved afterward, even if someone had shouted that an ammunition wagon was on fire.

Chapter Nine

Eastern Kansas

The bed heaved under Jessamyn. The railway car creaked, groaned, jerked, and finally rattled into motion. Crystal pendants tinkled against lamps and silver toiletries danced on parquetry shelves. A drawer thudded shut from somewhere forward and someone shouted something unintelligible outside, possibly foul.

Jessamyn kept her eyes shut, refusing to look at—and thereby acknowledge—her surroundings.

Morgan stretched slightly, adapting his long frame to the train's forward motion. A breeze drifted down from above and grew stronger. She shivered involuntarily at the contrast to the previous hothouse atmosphere and tried to pull the sheet more closely around herself. But it was difficult to find, when she seemed to be wrapped in sated male.

He swept an elegant quilted white coverlet up over her back and shoulders. Jessamyn purred and snuggled closer. "Thank you." Hopefully now, she'd be allowed to sleep.

"My pleasure." His hand insinuated itself under the coverlet and began to follow the shape of her derrière, all too accessible to him since she lay on her side.

She regarded him suspiciously from a single open eye. "Again and so soon? Why?"

"Why not? I'm taking you to Colorado, aren't I?"

She flushed but continued to try to dissuade him. Who knew what his true game was? Did he want all of the gold or only her body? Either was an unsettling thought. "Aren't you hungry?"

"For what?" He raised a single eyebrow at her before kissing her cheek. She blinked when his mouth moved lower. He brushed the elegant cotton aside and explored her shoulder, kissing and gently nipping where her collarbone met her neck.

The train bounced, sending Jessamyn flat on her back. Morgan pounced immediately, sliding his leg between hers. The coverlet slid to the floor but part of the sheet still twisted between them. He smiled at her, all glinting eyes and bared teeth, before circling his hips against her. She moaned involuntarily; he'd learned far too much of carnal practices to be easily ignored.

"Anything I want, remember? Anything," he whispered in her ear. "Do you still agree?"

She forced her eyes open, trying to project a cool facade. "We've very little time. A little more than a day on this train until we reach Denver, then a few hours on another train—"

His expression remained feral. "Until we reach the Sangre de Cristo Pass and start riding across Colorado. Even then, there are the nights . . ." He nipped her throat in exactly the spot he'd mapped the night before.

Jessamyn arched as carnal fire speared her. His hand slid between her legs and nestled into her folds, ruffling them delicately like a priceless flower. They were exquisitely sensitive after last night's hard usage, and his light touch sent a shockingly strong stab of lust through her veins. "Morgan," she gasped. "We need to plan . . ."

"Actually, we'd best make the most of what little time we have in a bed with sheets," he contradicted her. He brushed a kiss against her brow, then her temples. His palm cupped her mound possessively under the sheets, warm and all too inviting.

He dropped another kiss on the corner of her mouth just as she opened it to expostulate with him again. His tongue slid inside and played gently with hers. She tried to pull her head back but he wouldn't let her. Instead he continued to kiss her sweetly, as if they had all the time in the world. Below the sheet, his hand remained motionless.

Why were the Evans men so irresistible when they kissed? How many times had she been furious with Cyrus until the touch of his lips on hers scattered her wits? Was there something in the Evans blood that gave Morgan the power to do the same thing?

Slowly Jessamyn relaxed and opened for Morgan. Her lips softened under his and her legs parted. He rumbled soft approval, stroking her tongue in rhythm with his gentle, almost imperceptible movements below.

She sighed in pleasure and pressed closer, caressing his shoulders. It was the first time she'd touched him to explore him, rather than grabbing him for a quick finish. His hot, sleek, satiny skin, the ripple of strong muscles underneath, the strong cords of tendons leading up to his neck, the heavy twists of his biceps leading down to his arms, the deep furrow of his spine—she fondled them all while kissing him and sighing in delight.

His hand played with her more firmly, stretching her folds, plumping and squeezing them, circling her entrance. Her body rippled and melted under his fingertips, until it seemed that his fingers and her cream were one and the same, both spearing her with lust.

He rocked against her and took his mouth away from hers to kiss her neck. She approved heartily of the move and arched her neck. He nibbled the sensitive spot and she writhed under him, her eyes half-closed. "Ah, Morgan."

She stroked the tops of his thighs and up to his rump, all heavily muscled. A horseman's body. She fondled and caressed, her greedy fingers remembering the skills taught by Cyrus.

Morgan groaned something wordless and slid down her body. She blinked open heavy eyes to look at him. "Hmmm?"

"Lift your leg for me, sweetness."

She obeyed, shooting him an inquisitive look. He dropped a line of kisses down the center of her body, between her breasts, over her navel and down her mound. She arched to meet him, heat flaring through her veins as if he was stoking a furnace with the simple caresses.

He slipped a pillow under her hips, stretched her leg up, and kissed her mound. She lifted her head to watch hopefully and purred her satisfaction when his head dropped lower, his chestnut hair feathering over her legs. His hands and arms were so very strong but his fingers were completely gentle, even though his breathing was ragged.

Then she gasped and bucked when he kissed and tongued her intimately. All Evans men must have been born with a passion for doing this, an inbred skill.

Lord have mercy, she did so love being sucked just like, ah, that, when her man was pumping three fingers into her, preparing her to be ridden. Orgasm was coming so close. She could see it behind her eyes, feel it in her blood and the tightness of her skin, the tension in her loins. She tightened her legs around his head, sobbing. "Morgan . . ." Her voice broke in frustration.

Suddenly he pulled away from her and came up on his knees, his eyes narrowed and desperate, his teeth clenched, his cock rampant and dripping in eagerness. He grabbed a condom from the stash on the nightstand and rolled it on rapidly, while she watched like a tigress in heat. Then he pounced on her, lifting her hips to meet his thrust.

She arched, crying out with satisfaction at finally being filled. His cock surged into her, aided by her eager inner muscles. For a moment, they lay immobile, savoring the moment. Then he began to move and he rode her hard, as if he hadn't touched her the night before. She clutched his shoulders and

clawed his back, just as frenzied. She climaxed first, rich and
strong, washing through her like a great river. She closed her
eyes, tightening her inner hold on him. He groaned at that
and climaxed, pulsing deep inside her.

Afterward, he locked his arms around her and rolled over,
his breath ragged against her hair.

"Should we talk about Colorado or the map?" she muttered. She really should investigate the bathroom.

"Or breakfast? Or more kisses?" He wrapped a sweaty leg
possessively around hers, his hair prickling her smoother leg.

She didn't have the energy to move away. "We should
rise."

"Later."

The conductor shouted a farewell to Lawrence, Kansas,
and the train lurched. Another bone-jarring heave finally put
the U.P. train into motion.

Good riddance to one more piece of Kansas, thought
Maggie, and took another lick at her husband's nipple. This
train couldn't reach Denver too soon for her taste.

Charlie's private car was hitched immediately after the
train's main body. He'd borrowed it from a New York banker
wealthy enough to race trotters against Commodore Vanderbilt. The eastern tenderfoot now wished to gamble in a deeper
game, Colorado gold mines, and thought Charlie would guide
him to the best gold veins, if he buttered Charlie up enough.

Maggie rolled her eyes at that folly and dragged her teeth
lightly over Charlie's nipple. He gasped. Good, the sooner he
caught fire, the better for both of them.

At least the idiot's private car was impressive, even if his
judgment of Westerners wasn't. Why, it even had gold han-
dles on the water closet!

In contrast, the U.P. had accurately and quickly assessed
the situation between Charlie and Morgan Evans. They'd
hitched both special cars to the same train, but they'd placed
one of their director's observation cars between the two special

cars. Unless one group of travelers made an extraordinary effort, it was unlikely they'd come in contact with each other—
thus keeping the peace for the U.P.

It was a damn shame. She could spend hours filling her
eyes with Morgan Evans. She'd never done more than that, a
deprivation that still irked her. But Charlie had made his
wishes very clear when he ordered her along. But perhaps if
she kept him very, very happy on the train, he might leave her
behind in Denver . . .

She stroked Charlie's thigh and kissed her way down his
belly. No matter what she thought of his temperament, he
had a remarkably handsome belly: hard as her mother's wash-
board with a narrow trail of golden hair running straight
down its center. But then Charlie was a fine figure of a man,
at least when he wasn't alone in a bedroom with his wife.

She curled her lip at the bitter memories but continued to
kiss and nuzzle her husband. A slow approach, with many
lingering pats and endearments, was the only hope for any
action at all.

His big strong hands kneaded her hair as he enjoyed her
attentions, with gasps and groans marking every new touch
and kiss.

Her hard work started to produce rewards, at least for
him. By the time she reached his cock, it was turning crimson
and its tip was starting to curve upward. A little more work
and there might be something there she could finally gain satisfaction from.

She paused to scrape one of his short, curly hairs from between her teeth. The aftertaste distressed her, causing her to
make a moue of disgust as she spat out the offending hair.

"Goddammit, Maggie," Charlie roared, pulling himself
away from her. His cock withered like a snowman in July to
a size appropriate to a grammar school boy. "Can't you even
try to look like you're enjoying yourself?"

Maggie reared up, affronted by this insult to her skills.

Some excellent men, both wealthy and handsome, had begged her for another taste of her mouth on their privates. Her temper, which she'd never had a tight hold on, went racing out the window. "Why should I, when you're so little to look at? That measly thing you call a cock is hardly bigger than my pinkie and hasn't been for months. Why, Morgan Evans would never fail a woman—"

His hand closed around her throat. "Have you always believed my cock was so small, dear wife?"

She glared at him, ready to spit curses.

His fingers tightened until she could feel every ring he wore.

She saw her death promised in his eyes, despite his conversational tone. An icy knife sliced through her spine and her vision grayed around the edges. "Of course not!" she stammered. "Your cock is large and magnificently thick."

It wasn't entirely a lie. After all, he'd used it very well on those first few occasions.

Some of the tension eased slowly out of the little room. She tried to relax, while watching him warily.

"If you say Evans's name one more time within my hearing," Charlie said very carefully, although his eyes were not sane in the least, "I will kill you immediately. Do you understand?"

Maggie nodded very slowly. She'd have to find her old dirk, or maybe a Bowie knife, and keep it close by.

He took his hand away and the insane light in his eyes dimmed a trifle. He levered himself out of the bed and began to wrench clothes on. "You'll have your gold, for your fancy Denver mansion," he growled. "There'll be more than enough of Ortiz's treasure for that."

She sat in the middle of the bed watching him, careful not to move quickly lest she disturb him. A wise woman didn't startle wild animals.

When he was half-dressed, he bent to kiss her, his starched collar all awry. She answered it politely, pretending a passion she didn't feel.

"I'll bring you mountains of gold to keep you happy, Maggie. I promise," he whispered against her cheek and was gone.

The train lurched, slamming the door shut behind him and pouring cold air over her. Shivering, she pulled the sheet up around her shoulders. Two years ago, she'd been married to a good miner and had had a small baby. No money yet but the promise of it, and she'd thought herself on the top of the world. Then smallpox had taken the baby and a cave-in had killed her husband, all on the same day. Good God Almighty, how she'd wanted to hurl herself into their grave.

After that, all she'd thought about was having enough gold to leave that small mining town behind and never see that grave again. Only Viola Ross, the future Mrs. William Donovan, had understood her determination to depart. Morgan Evans had seemed the perfect answer, with his excellent job and handsome looks. She'd done everything she could to catch him but it hadn't worked. Finally, he'd told her to her face that he'd no interest in her, whether for marriage or anything else.

Charlie had been in Rio Piedras, too, with his pretty face and his talk of his Colorado mine, but she hadn't quite trusted the way he watched her. True, a woman liked to be courted but sometimes a man could pay too much attention. But in the end, he'd been the best choice and she'd said yes.

He'd done well enough in the bedroom at the beginning, too. But once, his cock hadn't risen and she'd compared it disdainfully to Morgan's. The next time Charlie had taken longer to rise, and longer and still longer. And she'd complained more and more, until finally he was as soft as a mackerel. She was frustrated in the bedroom but pampered everywhere else, as if that would increase Charlie's chances of success. Hah!

It was a pity that she'd never had a taste of Morgan Evans, though. The scarlet women in Rio Piedras had gossiped about him something fierce. She'd always wondered if he was half as spectacular in the bedroom as they said.

A minute later, she rang for her very expensive French maid. If her husband refused to be of any use, then she'd visit the observation car and see what the U.P. directors considered luxurious.

Flat Kansas plains sped past the dining room's windows as Jessamyn and Morgan finished their embarrassingly late breakfast. The train jolted again, rattling the chandeliers and sending the pictures slamming against the walls. A top speed of twenty-five miles an hour was amazing and well worth the frequent jolts and rattles. Abraham Chang cleared away their dishes, somehow balancing the fine china as if the train's continual jolting were actually a silken glide. He'd even poured a full cup of tea without spilling a drop.

Jessamyn was wearing a stylish new day dress, in dark green silk, which had magically appeared when she emerged from the small, exquisitely appointed bathroom. "A present from Mrs. Donovan," Sarah Chang had announced, beaming. There'd been no one to object to, or to question how such a perfectly fitting gift—including the new undergarments—was accomplished.

Was Viola Donovan matchmaking? If so, there was little chance of success for her sentimental heart.

Beside Jessamyn, Morgan scanned a leather portfolio full of telegrams and frequently scrawled answers, using the pad at his elbow, in between sips of black coffee. Riley, Donovan & Sons' stolid telegrapher, collected the replies and occasionally answered questions.

The scene was utterly domestic and remarkably similar to the last time she'd traveled west across Kansas. Then she'd journeyed as the wife of Captain Cyrus Evans, the officer responsible for ensuring the safe building of a portion of this railroad. Of her seven happy years of marriage to Cyrus, six had been spent on this prairie. Together, they'd worked to fight Indians, locusts, drought, embezzling Army contractors, and more.

"A cable from the manager of your Silver Queen mine, sir." Riley offered another piece of yellow paper.

Jessamyn froze, teacup in her hand. A headache began to beat in her temples. The Silver Queen mine, based on a once worthless mining claim that Morgan had bought for unpaid freighting bills. A technique all too familiar to how Forsythe, Mother's lover, had gained his gold mine.

She set her cup down very carefully, despite the train's lurches. But she would not behave like Mother and fall at his feet, overwhelmed by his wealth. She also had friends and supporters so she was not entirely helpless in comparison to him.

Cyrus had always been extremely supportive of her interests. When she'd worked to perfect her horsemanship and sharpshooting, he'd cheered her on. He'd regularly wagered on her skills and won, garnering quite a reputation for the two of them among the small Army community. She'd kept many of those friends after Cyrus's death, when she'd returned to Memphis, and they'd pledged their aid in this venture.

Now she cleared her throat, determined to take at least a few steps on her own. "Morgan?"

His head came up politely but his pen remained poised over the paper. "Yes, Jessamyn?"

"May I send some telegrams to my friends in Denver?"

He frowned slightly. "We'll only be there long enough to transfer between stations," he warned. "No time for a visit."

Did he think she was a fool? Of course she knew they'd move through Denver as quickly as possible. Then she realized he saw her as little more than baggage. Cloaking her fury, she smiled at him innocently. "Yes, I know, but I'd like to drop them a line if I may. Perhaps I can visit them when I return."

It wasn't entirely a lie. She did need to tell them of her changed plans.

An expression of startled comprehension, followed by embarrassment, washed over Morgan's face. "Of course." He pushed a telegraph pad over to her. "Riley will send your cables as soon as you draft them."

"Thank you," Jessamyn said sweetly. Excellent; Morgan was about to receive quite a surprise in Denver.

Chapter Ten

Trinidad, Colorado, nightfall

Lucas Grainger rode down the steep, rocky toll road through Raton Pass, glad for just enough daylight to safely see the big Murphy wagons with their hitches of twenty mules each to the depot. One more round-trip to Santa Fe for a Donovan & Sons wagon train, with no losses of men, mules, equipment, or supplies—and a large profit made for William Donovan's pocketbook. It wasn't enough to repay his debt to the man, but surely one day, he'd have the chance to do so.

Tyrell, one of Donovan's excellent California-bred horses, snorted at a particularly large rock as it rolled past. Lucas chuckled, his voice hoarsened by the past month's hard traveling, and patted Tyrell's neck. "Easy, boy, easy. There's a bath waiting for you at the depot, and fresh hay to roll in afterward. And alfalfa," he added, drawing the last syllable out.

Tyrell's ears twitched as he stepped out eagerly for the town ahead. Lucas shook his head and hid a smile. At least the horse found Trinidad's mud-brick village entrancing. Men usually passed through it as quickly as possible on their way to Santa Fe. A year ago, he'd seen working in Rio Piedras as a penance for not preventing Ambrosia's death, but life here came very close to the same misery.

The familiar hubbub, with its almost military complexity and order, quickly gathered him up when he reached the depot. Goods came here from St. Louis, and parts east, over the Santa Fe Trail's Mountain Branch or the railroad and were stored here until they could be shipped west on wagon trains. Donovan & Sons was one of the great Western freighting houses, specializing in the delivery of high-profit freight to high-risk areas. Even when the Denver & Rio Grande or another railroad reached Santa Fe, Donovan & Sons would still be very busy carrying freight to places too difficult to lay track to. The Trinidad depot reflected the firm's prominence, with its large paddocks, thick walls, and high watchtowers.

Quigley, the foreman, was standing at the office door as he watched the mule train come in. "Grainger? See me as soon as you can."

"Yes, sir." Lucas handed Tyrell's reins to a stableman with a quick nod of thanks. Donovan & Sons was big enough, and smart enough, to have extra hands at their depots just to look after the horses and mules, so the men who rode the trails could find extra rest. "Any news?" he asked casually.

"Nope, just some more fights. Railroaders are fighting each other and us."

Lucas chuckled, turning toward the door. "Same old story."

"Pretty much. And there's a new barsweep in town. An old half-breed named Little, who used to be an Army scout. He came in just after you left for Santa Fe and has been working at the Yellow Rose ever since. But he can't hold his liquor and the railroaders have been using him as a punching bag."

Grainger's hands hovered like claws above his guns. Little, here? Hell and damnation, he needed to get him out of that viper pit immediately. He owed his life a dozen times over to the man.

If only he didn't have to talk to Quigley first.

He took the steps up to the office two at a time, slapping the dust off his hat against his trousers before he entered.

"Good evening, sir." He waited politely, never quite able to shake the old military mannerisms.

"Trip go well?" Quigley asked.

"Perfectly, sir. We made a solid profit." His father would not have been impressed by the amount but he was, especially its proportion to the cost. It was also a damn good feeling to make money when there could be no suspicion that his father or grandfather had arranged for him to succeed.

"Good." Quigley handed him a stack of letters and telegrams, his experienced eyes assessing every detail of Lucas's condition. "You've become very popular. The letters arrived on the last two trains from Denver. The telegrams came last night and today."

Lucas shuffled the letters, recognizing his mother's handwriting (probably a recitation of dinner parties and grandchildren, with a demand for him to immediately provide her some of each), his sister's flourishes with a postmark from Prussia (she must be touring the great spas of Central Europe again with that Austrian prince), and an example of very expensive stationery. A more careful scrutiny revealed it to be an invitation to a match race in France, between two very famous stallions. His brother's doing, no doubt; he had the subtlety to offer the most attractive bribes.

Nothing from Father, of course; that last fight had been far too vicious on both sides. It would be a few more years, judging by previous battles, before either of them would chance a meeting on neutral territory.

"I'd start with the telegrams," Quigley commented quietly. "One of them is from Donovan himself, in Kansas City. The others are from Anderson, in Denver."

Inside, Lucas capered with joy. Almost two years of hard work since he'd resigned from the cavalry and he'd finally come to Donovan's personal attention.

He kept his expression composed, as his tutors had encouraged, while he pulled out the slips with their neatly printed gibberish. "Thank you, sir."

"Have you ever used the company cipher before?"

"No, sir." If it was important enough to merit a cipher, it might be enough to repay his debt to Donovan. He repressed his shout of triumph.

"You'd best use my office." Quigley seated Lucas in the private office and quickly instructed him on how to use the cipher, based on extracting words from a particular edition of Shakespeare's plays according to the location given in the telegram.

Quigley returned with a plate heaped high with beef and beans, plus a steaming mug of coffee. Lucas thanked him absently, already halfway through deciphering Donovan's telegram. The sooner he got through these, the sooner he could get over to the Yellow Rose and rescue Little—even though Little would certainly put up a good fight. The combination of Little and alcohol was always bad news.

Quigley snorted. "Don't thank me until you've read all of 'em. Hell, yes, I got one, too," he answered the unspoken question. "Now get that food down you, while you've still got time. We can talk later." He shut the door behind him with what wasn't quite a thud.

Thirty minutes later, Lucas leaned back against the wall and nursed a fresh mug of coffee as he faced Quigley. "Morgan Evans is racing Charlie Jones into the San Juans," he summarized, his mind racing to absorb Donovan's agenda and Evans's plans. "Donovan wants a native guide for Evans but Anderson's having trouble finding one."

The other man rested his boots on the stack of paper, most apparently copies of Anderson's telegrams. Outside, the sun had set and the depot was starting to settle into nighttime lassitude. "Can't blame Anderson. It's peak season for traveling, so most of the good men are busy right now."

"Donovan thinks I might be able to find a guide, supposedly because I'm closer here in Trinidad to the terrain to be covered. He orders me to take said guide to join Evans at

Plaza de los Leones and be personally ready to join the expedition."

Lucas rubbed Donovan's telegram between his fingers, wondering how far he dared stretch his boss's legendary tolerance for men's foibles, as long as they did their job well. Then he put it down and stood up. "Best go fetch that native guide. May I borrow a half-dozen of the boys to help?"

"Certainly. Where do you expect to find him?" Curiosity shone openly on Quigley's face for the first time.

"The Yellow Rose." Lucas double-checked his knives, in preparation for entering that saloon. They might ask for his guns but they'd never take the blades.

"What? The lowest dive in town—and a railroad haunt, to boot? You'll be lucky to escape with your skin intact! Who do you hope to find there?"

All business now, Lucas slid his dirk back into its scabbard and met Quigley's eyes. "John Little."

"The newest town drunk?" Quigley was usually impossible to fluster, but now his mouth was hanging open.

"Ute Indian, former Army scout, and excellent fighter," Lucas corrected. And falling-down drunk, whenever he touched whiskey. "Who can walk backward through the San Juan Mountains."

Quigley shook his head. "Your funeral, my friend. Let's visit the Yellow Rose."

The Yellow Rose Saloon was an enterprise that had been thrown up in a few days to attract railroad crews when tracks first approached Trinidad. Whiskey had headlined the list of its attractions then, as it did now. Everything else came second: other alcoholic spirits, cards, women, comfort. Proving that it had accurately pegged its customers, the railroad crews flooded in, even though every other workingman in this roughest of Colorado frontier towns stayed away. It was a hellhole of vice, to be approached with caution, where a man walking alone counted himself lucky to leave losing only his cash and some skin, not his life.

Lucas entered the Yellow Rose, followed by a half-dozen Donovan & Sons teamsters. The roaring noise of men shouting for more whiskey poured out of the place, along with the stench of alcohol, unwashed inhabitants, blood, and other foulness.

The tumult covered the door's slam against the rough mud-brick wall but it stilled when the assembly noted the new arrivals. The bar was the squalid room's one claim to glory and its original carved woods and mirrors had somehow survived its clientele. Reflected in a series of fractured images in a corner mirror, Lucas could see four men hauling another, still struggling, out the side door. Excellent, they'd arrived early enough in the evening that Little hadn't yet become drunk and been beaten unconscious.

"Good evening, gentlemen," Lucas greeted the assembly, his voice as falsely amiable as if he faced one of his mother's matchmaking friends. "Just here for some friendly conversation."

He headed toward Little, the other teamsters following. Men muttered and stood aside sullenly, giving every sign of hyenas aching to snatch a lion's kill. A few girls, with better clothes than the average to protect, headed for the stairs' safety.

Lucas's stomach tried to heave at the smell coming off Little when he came close enough to see his old friend. What he could see of his clothes seemed fit only for swabbing out a pigsty. But he'd been a great scout and a good friend, when he was sober. A muscle ticked in Lucas's jaw.

"Sir, may I offer you a drink?" Wary and cold, Lucas touched one of the thugs frog-marching Little on the shoulder. With a roar of surprise, the brute dropped his share of the wildly kicking man and threw a punch at Lucas. Lucas ducked easily and responded to the punch in kind. Soon the other thugs were compelled to assist their fellow, the teamsters were fighting any railroad man who came near, and Lucas and Little were brawling side by side, once again, against all comers in a wild melee of fists, kicks, and knives. Drunk or not, five decades old or not, Little was still a damn good fighter.

Lucas laughed in sheer enjoyment of a good fight. "Care to work for Donovan & Sons, John Little?" he shouted, in between blocking a knife fight's slices and parries.

Little stared at him, a man's head twisted under his arm. He'd gained the appelation because his size was anything but small, a factor he was currently using to his advantage. "You joking?"

"No. Looking for a guide." Lucas twisted his opponent's wrist and disarmed him.

"Certainly I will work for Donovan," Little agreed and knocked out his opponent with a swift jab.

"Donovan!" Lucas roared, grinning.

"Donovan, Donovan!" the other teamsters in the Yellow Rose shouted and a dozen more answered from outside. They charged inside behind Quigley in a flying wedge and smashed through the brawl to their fellows. By the time the sheriff cautiously arrived, the fight had spilled into the street. By midnight, Lucas had personally—much to Quigley's surprise— paid the fines and the teamsters were back at the Donovan & Sons depot.

Western Kansas

Jessamyn hugged her arms around herself, leaning against a cabinet for balance, as she stared out the window at the dark landscape, lit only by the crescent moon's faint glow. Too dark to ride over rough territory, too dark to see landmarks she'd first watched with Cyrus. More than dark enough to worry about Charlie's tricks once they reached the Colorado Territory, and that unpleasant wife of his.

But the dining room around her was a well-lit oasis of civilization. The clerestory windows created a breeze but it was still very warm inside. She was sweating in her very elegant summer dinner dress, while Morgan was in his shirtsleeves.

A few minutes earlier, Abraham had cleared away the remains of an excellent dinner, then produced a small selection of desserts and wines, before bowing himself out.

"What arrangements did you make in Denver?" Morgan asked. He was seated at the dining table, carefully cutting into a queen of puddings, one of her favorite desserts, as if racing across North America were an everyday occurrence for him. She loved the combination of rich custard, topped by a thin jelly—preferably wine jelly—and finished off with a golden meringue.

She shrugged and turned to face him. "Very simple ones, I'm afraid. I hadn't planned on two maps, just on the fact that I'm the only descendant of Uncle Edgar's eldest sibling to bring me the map and the gold." She wandered around the room, straightening bric-a-brac and mourning for how naive she'd been. "So I wrote some of my old Army friends, who are stationed in the Colorado Territory. They arranged for horses and a few trustworthy escorts. Not a large enough party, I'm afraid, to bring out the gold."

"There's no buried treasure, Jessamyn, no lost gold." Morgan balanced the pudding's quivering mass on the knife's broad blade then flipped it neatly onto a plate. He offered it to her.

"Morgan!"

His eyes met hers, glinting and implacable in the lamplight, but he didn't say anything.

She reluctantly accepted the pudding and tried to think of an alternate argument. "Surely there must be gold or Charlie wouldn't be working so hard to obtain it," she observed softly as she settled into her chair. "He's not the man to waste his time on false hopes. He probably heard more of Uncle Edgar's stories because he's had more contact than I've had."

Morgan stopped, one eyebrow elevated, before he started to cut himself a serving. "True. Charlie has always known exactly where to find money. Very well, I'll grant you that the gold *might* exist. Is that better?"

She'd prefer certainty or enthusiasm from him but she'd accept what he'd give. "Yes, thank you."

She paused, glaring at the observation car—and Charlie's private car beyond. "I have to regain Somerset Hall."

"Why now? You were calmer during the War about losing it."

"Because Charlie Jones wants to buy it. He's going to take a few of the best stallions and mares out before fever season, then send the rest to the knackers to be slaughtered. Socrates, Aristotle, and Cassiopeia have volunteered to guard the horses until I return, risking their lives if there's another cholera or yellow jack epidemic." Her voice broke.

Morgan's head snapped up and he stared at her. "Christ on a crutch! He wants to steal the gold of Somerset Hall, the legendary horses!"

He slammed his fist to the side, as if hurling a knife. "Son of a bitch. Please excuse my language."

His vulgarity was a minor irritant beside the risk to her friends. "I've heard worse."

"How can you hope to stop him?"

"I and my children have right of first refusal, according to the contract Father negotiated. Ortiz's treasure is my only hope of stopping Charlie."

A muscle ticked in his jaw. "There's no treasure, Jessamyn."

She searched his eyes and believed him. Morgan was speaking the truth as he knew it, not trying to divert her so he could steal Ortiz's gold.

Her mouth firmed. She would not permit that to be true. "There has to be! Morgan, do you remember when your mother died of yellow jack? Do you remember her screaming as the fever mounted until they finally poured enough laudanum into her to silence her?"

He was very white. "Jessamyn . . ."

She hated bringing it up but she'd use any weapon she

needed. "Or how fast your little brothers died? That's what Socrates and Aristotle and Cassiopeia are risking, just to guard the horses. And what if fever season is bad and people panic and run? Then they'll steal any horses they could find, using guns to do so, and Aristotle and Socrates will fight. I have to find the gold to save them, Morgan!"

He slapped the table, jostling the glassware more than the train had. "Jessamyn, dammit, you are the most stubborn woman I have ever met."

She half rose in her chair, glaring back at him. "I will do whatever is necessary to rescue my friends. So will you or will you not take me on the route the map shows? If not, then I'll leave this train in Denver and look for someone else to escort me."

His nostrils flared, above grooves cut deep beside his tight-held mouth. His eyes were chips of ice. "You will risk your life with every step on that trail. You will have to obey every order I give, before you think about it. Can you do that? Immediate, unquestioning obedience—to me?"

She hesitated. Obey Morgan, the master of the hidden agenda?

His lips curled bitterly. "I see how little you trust me. Very well, our expedition ends tomorrow. We've had a day and a half together and I've heard you more than once howling my name as you beg me for more."

She flushed hotly, crushing down the memories.

"I'll say that my revenge is accomplished. Tomorrow I'll see that you're safely returned to your home."

Dear God, he was entirely serious. "No! I—" She nearly gagged on the words. "I'll give you obedience."

He arched an eyebrow. "You'll forgive me if your enthusiasm doesn't overwhelm me."

"Does it need to? Surely all I have to do is act as I have pledged," she retorted. Hopefully, unquestioning obedience wouldn't be something she'd have to prove. She reached for her wine.

THE SOUTHERN DEVIL   179

"Anytime and anyplace?"

She nearly choked. "What?"

He pushed away from the table, leaning back in his chair, the image of indolent masculine sensuality. Her blood promptly heated to a boil, no doubt trained by the past hours in his bed. She cursed silently.

"The only arena we trust each other in is carnal pleasure. So here and now, you'll prove that you'll obey me absolutely—or I'll see that you return to Jackson and Great-Aunt Eulalia."

"Morgan!"

His eyes glittered as his long fingers toyed with his wineglass. "Are you refusing, my dear?"

"I, ah, shouldn't my word be enough?"

"Would mine be?"

She blew out a breath, recognizing the trap, and gave him the truth. "No, yours wouldn't be. Very well, here and now, I'll give you unquestioning obedience."

And pray that her sanity survived it.

"Actually, I'd thought of a game where you sat on the table, rather than beside it," he drawled, his expression entirely too calm.

She drew away from him slightly and scanned his face suspiciously. "*On* the table?"

"Exactly. Either sitting or lying on it."

Involuntarily, she shot a look at the table. It *seemed* long and strong enough for carnal games. "Then what?"

"I excite you. I can place nothing inside you, though, except my hands and mouth."

He sounded as if he were discussing nothing more dangerous than a game of checkers, which made it very risky indeed. "What's the catch?"

"You can't reach ecstasy until I give you permission."

"What?" Her voice squeaked a little.

He smiled at her all too charmingly, like a tiger hiding its claws in its furry paws. "It's a test of my skill—and your obedience, dear Jessamyn."

"Not in the dining room, Morgan. What if the servants come by? Or Riley?"

"If you're disobeying me so quickly, then there's no need to take you past Denver, is there?"

"Morgan!"

He shrugged, arching an arrogant—and implacable—eyebrow.

She gulped, recognizing the temptation he offered and its promised reward. He'd tease and excite her to a rapturous pitch. Deny that for very long—especially given his skills at arousing her—and when her climax came, she could be overwhelmed beyond anything she'd yet encountered with him.

And in the dining room of all places. He was asking her to do this in a public place, not in the privacy of their bedroom. How very scandalous. She'd dreamed of doing something like this for years, even mentioned it to Cyrus, but it had never interested him. Her nerves prickled and her light dress suddenly seemed much too heavy against her sweating skin.

But she did trust him in carnal matters. He hadn't harmed her in any way, nor humiliated her. She didn't trust his judgment entirely, especially about hunting for the treasure. Given the low sorts he'd obtained his money from, he just might want the gold for himself.

But he'd only brought her body pleasure.

Shaking a little, her mouth dry, she stepped away from him and perched on the edge of the table, her bustle and hoops tilting up and out of the way. She braced herself with both hands for whatever came next.

A growl of approval gathered in Morgan's throat as he stared at her. The glasses rattled in their stands, as if applauding her courage, and his chest tightened. *Oh yes, Jessamyn, you will enjoy yourself here.*

Just as much, he needed to be sure he had her obedience when it was inconvenient for her. Reliance upon her body's behaviors was the first confidence likely to be obtained—and the most necessary in the dangerous world awaiting her amid the rough territory ahead. He'd accept sullenness, as long as she'd immediately dive for cover when he shouted the alarm. Establishing it through carnal methods would be enjoyable and something he was well trained for, although he'd never before trained a woman to be taken into danger. His mouth quirked, considering the calculated gasp with which one of those highly perfumed females might react to something as simple as a drawn knife.

But this was Jessamyn, who was more likely to charge into danger than flee. He needed to be sure she'd obey his orders. So he'd have to push her hard and fast, making her prove her trust even when and where she didn't want to.

Hence, the choice of place—the dining car, a public space where they could easily be interrupted. Jessamyn would have to rely on his ability to avoid a scandal.

Now to test her in deed, which meant providing a stronger stimulus than usual. He glanced around and his gaze fell on the ice. He smiled slowly. Perfect.

He stepped to the doors at either end and quickly pulled the shades. Abraham and Sarah were superbly trained servants who were unlikely to disturb him, but this would ensure their privacy. Then he quickly cleared the pudding on its basin of ice, and their dessert plates onto the sideboard with the rest of the table settings.

Jessamyn watched him, rocking from side to side like a nervous schoolgirl.

He retrieved a napkin, twirled it into a quick blindfold, and returned to her. She'd need to focus solely on the sensations he brought.

"For my eyes? Can't I watch?"

"No."

She put one hand up to stop him. "But what if . . ."

His temper reared up slightly. "Jessamyn, are you going to immediately disobey me?"

She sighed and cast down her eyes. "Of course not."

"Good." He tied the napkin around her head. "Can you see anything?"

She sniffed and tugged the blindfold down farther. She turned her head from side to side, her mouth working a bit as if taste would compensate for her lost sight. "Not really."

He relaxed slightly, relieved at how easily she'd accepted it, once it was on. "Good girl."

A moment's work saw the pudding lifted out of its ice-filled basin and onto the sideboard, while the train assisted with a particularly loud set of rattles to cover the noise. He quickly dipped a champagne flute's base and stem into the ice, until the glass dripped.

He lifted her chin with a single finger. She choked and obeyed. He lightly ran the glass's edge along her throat.

Jessamyn gasped and jumped but quickly leaned back, bracing herself on both hands.

He touched his fingers to the ice and brushed them over her collarbones. She arched up to meet him, gasping in shock, and the water slid into her cleavage.

Christ, the move put her breasts on display for him as if they were on a platter, and his mouth went dry. He promptly enjoyed her breasts, nuzzling and running his tongue over them, as if he could transfer his own fiery lust to her skin. South of his braces, his balls hung fat and heavy, unfortunately, more than ready to unload themselves again in tribute to her beauty.

Her head fell back, her body trembling against him, her hips rocking.

More. They both needed more.

"Touch yourself between your legs," he ordered.

She gasped. "Here—in the dining room?"

"Of course," he snapped, not about to tolerate delay.

Thought was dammed difficult, when her breasts were moving up and down in the cradle of her corset. His hands twitched in exactly the pattern needed to mold her for suckling. "Lift your skirt and toy with yourself through the slit in your drawers. You can't deny that you know how to do so."

She blushed furiously. "Will you please touch me with ice water there?" she whispered.

That brought his gaze back up to her face. While he couldn't see her eyes, he'd swear her expression was one of hopeful anticipation. His mouth twitched unwillingly. "Perhaps. If you obey me."

Jessamyn gulped. Then she slowly, clumsily pulled her dress's mercifully simple skirts up to her knees.

Well done! His cock swelled and seeped pre-come. Morgan yanked his coat and tie off, and began to unbutton his shirt. "Higher, Jessamyn," he warned.

She brought the folds up to the middle of her thighs, revealing her new, fine, white cambric drawers. Below her knees, they were beribboned and beruffled, before giving way to her stockings and kid boots. But between her mound and her knee, they were a simple, elegant sweep of delicate white fabric, moistened now with her cream. Her musk beckoned to him, a scented guide to her feminine delights. His pulse was hammering in his cock.

Now where the hell did William keep the condoms in this place? In the sideboard? He shrugged the braces off his shoulders and started to rummage. "Pleasure yourself, Jessamyn."

"Morgan, that's indecent," she whimpered.

He shook his head at her continued hesitations. "Jessamyn, you're being disobedient again. You know how and I want to see you do this. Just slip your hand between your legs and begin. Come on, you can do it."

There was a long silence, broken only by the train's rattles and creaks. He found the condoms and unbuttoned his fly. Then she moaned, deep and low. His head snapped around.

In the mirror, he could plainly see Jessamyn, head arched

back, pleasuring herself with her hand between her legs. Her folds were cinnamon red and glistening with cream. Perfect obedience and beautiful beyond belief. His balls tucked themselves up against his cock with an almost audible thud.

Jessamyn moaned again. The train rattled over a bump, jostling both of them. She fell down on her back but lifted one leg to gain more room for play. Damn, she was skillful and beautiful when her fingers danced with her clit.

The train's drumming beat roared in his pulse, and in his iron-hard cock. Happily, he sheathed himself in the condom and watched her, all the while stroking himself, savoring the dizzying rise toward orgasm and the savage satisfaction of her obedience.

When it was too much to bear, Morgan dipped his hand into the ice water and caught her wrist.

The shock stopped her abruptly, catching her breath in her throat with a harsh groan. She cursed him viciously but he was implacable. "Not yet, remember? Not without permission."

"Morgan, dammit, now!"

He held her back, forcing her to wait for his permission. Pleasure denied was pleasure increased, he reminded himself. The stronger her orgasm when it came, the more she'd associate it with obedience to him. His hand circled her clit lightly, building her excitement—but not letting her go over the precipice.

She snarled. He toyed with her intimately, probing her, pumping her, measuring every protesting gasp and growl. He would finally have full confidence in her—and she would gain a climax she'd remember in her bones.

"Please, Morgan, please. Anything, I'll do anything," she begged. Her muscles spasmed and conscious tenseness left them, as she yielded to him.

He sent up a prayer of thanks, echoed by a chorus of hosannas from his cock and balls. Finally he had her physical obedience. Now he could reinforce it with orgasm—for both of them.

Morgan set his knee between her legs and shoved her farther onto the table. She panted, licking her lips in desperation. He kneeled over her on the table, very nearly dressed except for his trousers pushed down past his hips and his boots. He knew he was dominating her and was damn glad of it.

He dipped his fingertips in the tiny finger bowl on the side table and flicked a single drop onto her mound, just above her clit.

The shock was so great that Jessamyn arched, sobbing in pleasure, and pushed toward him. He grabbed her hips and pulled her onto him, pumping into her hot, wet sheath. His seed surged forward from the base of his spine into his balls.

He rode her strongly, forcing her to concentrate solely on him and the ecstasy he provided. He pistoned in and out of her, while her muscles fought to hold him. He varied his thrusts, never permitting her—or himself—to climax until finally they were both sobbing from impending ecstasy. He desperately fought himself not to come, using every trick he knew to keep her at her peak.

He plunged deep inside her and rubbed her clit. "Now, Jessamyn! Come for me now!"

She screamed and came, clamping down on him. He climaxed immediately, his balls launching their contents through his cock like a volcanic explosion. Rapture roared through him like a tornado, loud and overwhelming.

Afterward, he wondered just what the hell he'd signed up for. A wise man would follow the map and leave Jessamyn safely in a city, whether or not he believed in Ortiz's gold. Now he was committed to following the map and taking her with him, while fighting off Charlie Jones at the same time. In addition, she still thought he was no gentleman because he was sleeping with her—yet those were the only terms on which he could accompany her.

At least, his old obsession at revenging himself for those days in her attic was over and done with. He trusted her body, even if he did find her carnally fascinating in every possible fashion. He could spend hours simply feasting on her pussy, for example . . .

He ground his teeth—and laughed at himself reluctantly. He'd do the same again to hear her beg for more in his bedroom.

Chapter Eleven

Denver

The U.P. train pulled into the Denver depot just before noon, having been slowed by a washed-out trestle bridge in western Kansas. The depot was a noisy hubbub of prospective passengers, freight cars, and horse-drawn wagons, all intent on quickly going somewhere else. Jessamyn heartily agreed with their sentiments with Morgan at her side. Behind them, Abraham and Sarah Chang stood ready to hand down the luggage while Riley, the telegrapher, buckled shut his satchel.

"There's Anderson," Morgan announced. "Wearing a bowler, under the lamppost, beside the blond giants?"

"I see him." Anderson appeared more the type to brawl in saloons than mince words in a lawyer's office, while the men with him looked like bodyguards. Did they expect trouble from Charlie here, in such a public place? A chill whispered down her spine.

Standing next to the trio was a cavalry officer, who Jessamyn recognized immediately. She waved happily, a greeting returned by both Anderson and her friend.

A minute later, the train pulled to a stop with a last jerk and exhalation of steam from the great locomotive. Morgan opened the door of their private car and looked out. They left with Riley, giving quick farewells and thanks to the patient and discreet servants.

Anderson stepped forward, followed by the soldier. "Morning, Evans."

"And to you, Anderson," Morgan greeted his associate. "My dear, may I introduce—"

"Morgan, this is Captain—"

Their voices clashed with a third: Maggie's voice rose above the crowd, complaining about the cinders damaging her Paris gown. Jessamyn glanced quickly around and saw a pair of brutish thugs fall into place around Charlie and Maggie. Together, the foursome began to shove their way through the crowds down the platform.

Jessamyn's hand tightened on the brass tube, with the precious map inside. The last volume of her aunt's diary rested in her purse, together with her pocket Navy Colt; the other volumes she'd scanned were in her trunk.

"Gentlemen, I suggest introductions wait until we're in the carriage," she said briskly and gripped Morgan's arm.

His eyes met Anderson's with an expression she couldn't read. "Certainly," he agreed.

Anderson took the lead, while the cavalry officer fell into step on the other side of her. With one of the giants carrying their luggage, they briskly cut through the approving station-master's office, where Riley peeled off, after a quick farewell, for Donovan & Sons' local offices.

They stepped into a waiting brougham, and an instant later, the driver cracked the whip, sending the carriage surging forward. Morgan introduced Anderson calmly but Jessamyn introduced her old friend carefully, wary of their reaction. Morgan could easily be jealous of any connection to her marriage, while her friends had to suspect she was living in sin.

"Morgan, this is Captain Michael Spencer, who was Cyrus's roommate at West Point." Like Cyrus, Michael had been brevetted to colonel during the War, but peacetime and its smaller army had returned him to the rank of captain.

"Spencer."

"Evans."

The two men shook hands briefly, bracing themselves against the jolting conveyance.

Spencer's eyes searched her face. "I'm glad to see you again, looking so well."

Jessamyn smiled at him, relieved he showed only concern for her well-being. "Thank you, Michael. Please tell Elizabeth Anne and the children I'll be thinking of them."

"It's an honor to protect her, Spencer," Morgan added quietly.

Michael's eyes shot to him just as the carriage leaned to take a corner, throwing her against Morgan. Morgan's arm was hard around her as the two men measured each other. "Mrs. Evans has a good many friends who would take it personally if any harm was done to her," Michael said softly.

"As would I."

Jessamyn blinked. Morgan, warning an Army officer that he, too, would be protective of her?

"Please forgive the discomfort, ma'am," Anderson cut in, breaking the awkward moment. "But we need to make the best speed possible across town. Every minute counts now."

Jessamyn grabbed for a strap as they careened around a corner. "Why?"

"Because of the delay in your arrival, you've barely enough time to get over the Sangre de Cristo Pass before nightfall."

"Is our private train ready?" Morgan asked, gripping a strap with his free hand.

"Of course. Both yours and Jones's private trains are stripped down for the race to the pass. Your supplies have gone on ahead."

"Starshine is with them," Spencer added. "Since you asked to have your supplies combined with Evans's."

Joy bubbled through Jessamyn like champagne. Her long-time mount and bred at Somerset Hall, the gentle mare was also close to a pet. "Starshine? You're loaning her to me for the trip?"

"Of course. How else could we be sure you'd return safely?"

Tears welled up and Jessamyn covered her mouth, fighting for control. If worse came to worse, Starshine could be one of the few Somerset Hall horses to survive. "I thought when I gave her to you after Cyrus died, that I'd never see her again."

"Of course you're riding her. You could ride to China on that dappled bay."

Jessamyn managed a smile at the old joke and sniffled. Morgan's arm tightened around her, bracing her against yet another bounce through a pothole.

"You're well equipped now, with a ladies' mount like the legendary Starshine," Anderson commented. "But I couldn't find a guide so Grainger's bringing one from Trinidad."

Grainger? If he meant Lucas Grainger, she might know him from the cavalry.

"Grainger found one?" Morgan sounded rather perturbed.

"Donovan told him to, remember?"

"Well, Grainger is damn good but still—"

"And Jones borrowed Palmer's personal train," Anderson added, evidently deciding to deliver all the bad news at once.

"The owner of the Denver & Rio Grande?" Jessamyn groaned. Every Colorado railroad man would recognize and give precedence to that train between Denver and the Sangre de Cristo Pass.

"Correct. But your train should arrive in Plaza de los Leones first, if we can beat Jones to the depot." He looked back at Morgan. "I've bribed the Pueblo stationmaster to make sure you go through those switches first."

"Excellent work, Anderson," Morgan approved.

Jessamyn choked at the open acceptance of corruption, which wasn't behavior Cyrus would have ever tolerated. On the other hand, she had thrown in her lot with Morgan because he knew how to turn shady practices to his own advantage.

"We've sent messages ahead to all the posts in Colorado and other points south and west," Spencer added. "You have many friends who'll help you in any way they can."

A particularly hard series of jolts as they bounced over ruts and potholes silenced all conversation. Shouting at the horses, the driver drove recklessly enough to scatter pedestrians like pigeons and trigger curses faster than dust clouds in their wake.

Morgan pulled her against him, the possessiveness surprising her into silence. She readily absorbed his warmth, familiar from the train trip. But more intimate yet was the feel of his woolen jacket, the silk of his cravat, the stiffness of his starched collar—all sensations that only a wife had the right to enjoy publicly. She'd had all too few opportunities for those pleasures in her seven years with Cyrus, since he'd been absent on campaign so often against either the Rebels or the Indians. But in this careening brougham, she allowed her body to settle against Morgan's in a very wifely fashion, all the while wondering at her own desire to do so.

All too soon, the brougham whipped into the depot and pulled up alongside the office. The men piled out of and jumped off the carriage, rocking it violently. Morgan swept Jessamyn onto the paving, while the blond giants retrieved their luggage. They hastened around the corner and onto the platform.

Before her lay the Denver & Rio Grande's Denver station. It was a fairly modest station, basically a single building with a platform circling it. Beyond that lay two lines of track, each one occupied by a single small train, puffing smoke like a racehorse begging to be set free. A series of switches allowed either train to be brought up to the platform for passengers' convenience.

The nearest train was guarded by a single armed sentry atop it and a handful of armed guards pacing watchfully around it. The other train was encircled by a cordon of armed thugs, standing almost shoulder to shoulder.

Every window in the station and surrounding buildings was full of spectators, as were the muddy roadsides and hills beyond. An even more surprising sight was the military band playing lively jigs. It struck up a rollicking march as soon as Jessamyn and Morgan arrived, one that she'd heard many times on the parade ground.

The closest train blew its whistle sharply and moved forward to the platform. The tall young man atop it sprang up out of a crouch and waved his broad-brimmed hat at Morgan, who tossed a two-fingered salute back. Then he slung his rifle over his shoulder and swung himself down, hand over hand like a monkey, so he could grip the handrails and ride up to the platform by the station.

"Lowell," Anderson muttered, sounding resigned.

"Have any trouble finding him?" Morgan asked.

Anderson snorted. "Didn't until late last night, which is why he's up here and not down south with everyone else. Seems he was celebrating some faro winnings and needed to sleep off the effects."

Morgan laughed. "But he's the best sentry you could hope to find."

"Agreed."

The train swept up in a cloud of steam. Lowell jumped down onto the platform and took his hat off. Seen close up, he was a rawboned young man, with the promise of a very handsome man to come once he filled out the potential of his big frame. A shock of black hair fell over his broad forehead, partially concealing intelligent blue-gray eyes. "No trouble, sir."

"Not since you showed up," Anderson corrected.

Lowell flushed, looking as if praise was an appalling thing to be saddled with. "Not since t'other Donovan & Sons boys come up," he corrected.

Spencer turned to Jessamyn. "Good-bye, Jessamyn, and good luck."

"Good-bye, Michael. Please convey my best to Elizabeth Anne and the girls."

"Thank you for all your help," Morgan said stiffly from beside her. She wondered briefly if he was still irritated by the sight of a blue uniform.

Spencer grinned, a bit wickedly. "My pleasure." The blond giants finished loading the luggage aboard and he stepped back.

Morgan swung Jessamyn onto the train and she hastened to find an open window. Lowell followed her a moment later, while Morgan stayed on the steps.

A woman shrieked a curse. Maggie's vocabulary hadn't improved since the other depot.

"Good luck!" shouted Anderson and Spencer. The military band roared into "Garryowen" and the crowd shouted encouragement, caught up in the moment's madness.

With a snort of steam and a rumble of machinery, their special train moved off down the track, heading for the Sangre de Cristo Pass and the road to Ortiz's gold.

Chapter Twelve

South of Pueblo, Colorado

The private train sped south, black smoke and cinders flying overhead, as if it, too, wanted to reach Ortiz's gold
first. To the east stretched the Great Plains, flat as a table,
covered with grasses and etched with deep ravines leading to
the civilizations of Mississippi and the Eastern Seaboard. On
the west, the Rockies rose sharp and angular to the skies,
laden with gold, silver, and dangerous men. The dividing line
between Eastern law and order and Western recklessness had
never seemed quite so clear to Jessamyn before as she stared
out the lounge's window.

Behind her, little Sally, the dressmaker's assistant, mumbled softly as she finished fluffing out the train on Jessamyn's
new sage green promenade dress. On the table beside Jessamyn
rested her purse, containing her pocket Navy Colt and Aunt
Serafina's last diary.

The private car they were riding in was a hunting car, designed to be hired out to foreign aristocrats for long hunting
parties in isolated locations. Jessamyn had seen some spectacular displays of opulence before the War, when cotton mil-
lionaires had been proud to call her father their friend. This
car's lavish decorations of marquetry, crystal, and velvets
would have been warmly welcomed by those connoisseurs of

overindulgence. Why, there were even two closets in the stateroom large enough for a person to stand up in, which was an unbelievable luxury.

The bandboxes holding her startling new wardrobe had overflowed the tables and chairs in the private car's lounge, an assemblage of frills and furbelows immense enough to make Morgan and Lowell beat a hasty retreat to the simpler observation car, located before the hunting car. The observation car also carried the luggage and followed the coal tender, located just behind the steam engine, in their very small private train.

"Magnificent!" approved Mrs. Jennings, the dressmaker. "A perfect fit, as were all the others. Mrs. Donovan has an excellent eye for color and fabric," she cooed, tweaking the shoulders into place. "A wonderful gift for their friend's cousin."

"Indeed she does," Jessamyn agreed, although she personally gave Mr. Donovan credit for estimating her figure so very precisely. She strongly suspected that the new clothes were an attempt to foster a match between herself and Morgan, which was the most ridiculous concept she'd ever heard of. If Viola Donovan had been there, Jessamyn would have politely returned the garments immediately. But there was no one present to complain to except Mrs. Jennings, the dressmaker. Jessamyn was having difficulty imagining how to do so, without explaining the true state of affairs between herself and Morgan, a prospect that made her shudder.

She decided to bite her tongue and repay the Donovans after she found Ortiz's gold.

She twisted from her hips, catching sight of her reflection in the window, and bemusedly admired the tiers caught up with bows on the very fashionable train sweeping behind her. This was the seventh outfit that hadn't needed any alterations and the first one unlikely to go into the mountains.

Before the Donovans' appalling proclivity for matchmaking, she'd had only one riding habit—the bare minimum needed for such a difficult trip but all she'd been able to afford. Her two new riding habits were truly beautiful and both very practical. The undergarments for riding, such as the spare shirts, trousers, and chemises, were exactly what she'd wanted for extra comfort. And the dresses, nightgowns, and other garments were both feminine and remarkably sturdy, offering prospects for attracting masculine attention and surviving camp life. She flushed at the memory of Morgan's attentions last night and turned back to the window, sending the ribbons on her frivolous little hat dancing against her cheek.

Just then the train's whistle blew, signaling an abrupt halt.

"What on earth?" Mrs. Jennings exclaimed and all three women looked out the windows.

The train came to rest in a siding, beside the main line, leaving the only through line of track open. On its other side was a steep, boulder-strewn slope with a scrub forest above, part of the mountains' foothills.

"We must be waiting for the freight train to go through. There's a regular supply train for all those Army forts south of here," Mrs. Jennings opined. "As soon as it's gone past, we'll start again. You'll still beat Mr. and Mrs. Jones to the pass."

Sure enough, a few minutes later the ground beneath the train began to shake. A whistle blew, loud, long, and deep, heralding the advent of the larger train.

"I'm sure you're right." Jessamyn smiled politely at Mrs. Jennings and started folding her new chemises. If that freight train had command of the only track, then Charlie's train couldn't pass them, a comforting thought.

The whistle blew again, much closer, and teacups rattled loudly in their saucers.

Morgan gave another long look at the uphill slope on the other side from the freight train. He could have hidden Forrest's entire escort amid these boulders and scattered pines.

Cochise would have whooped for joy at the chance to set an ambush here.

Then he moved to the downhill side for a quick check of the passing freight train. They were halfway between Pueblo, where the stationmaster had let them through first, and Plaza de los Leones, the jump-off for the Sangre de Cristo Pass. There were very few places for trains to pass each other on this brand-new railway so it wasn't surprising that his train had pulled off here.

Lowell joined him. If there was to be a fight, this young man would be one of his first choices as a gun partner. "Any particular reason why the hair on my neck should be standing up?"

Morgan shot him a look then loosened his two guns in their holsters, already certain his Henry rifle was fully loaded. They'd both strapped their Colts on when they'd entered the observation car. Lowell loosened his gun and shook out the Bowie knife in his boot as well, keeping his rifle handy.

The whistle blew again, long and loud. The first freight car went past, shaking the ground and the floor under their feet.

"How many cars?"

"Didn't see." Morgan shrugged, turning back to look at the mountain.

A shot rang out from ahead, the unmistakable solid boom of a double-barreled shotgun. Their train's engineer carried a shotgun, in case of trouble, as he'd carefully mentioned when they'd visited him without the ladies' presence. The country from here south to Trinidad was particularly rough, one where no man knew who his friend was.

Colts and a rifle barked sharply in response, from the mountainside. Dammit, which of those boulders hid the rifleman?

Jessamyn's head came up at the sound of gunshots and her eyes met Mrs. Jennings's. Little Sally turned absolutely green above her pink muslin dress and clapped her hand over her mouth.

"Robbers," said Mrs. Jennings flatly.

"Or worse," quavered Sally.

Through the window, Jessamyn could glimpse two—no, at least three, dammit—men dodging between boulders and working their way down from the Sangre de Cristo Mountains toward the train. Worse, Morgan and Lowell wouldn't have a good shot at them from the observation car.

"Into the stateroom. We can hide there and barricade the doors," ordered Jessamyn. "Our menfolk will come for us."

"But there're only two of them." Sally gulped.

"As long as they're alive, they'll come. And Mr. Evans is very hard to kill. Shoo!" Jessamyn grabbed up her purse and shoved the precious brass tube with the treasure map into Sally's hand. If there was to be fighting, she was the best one to use the gun. Hopefully, no one would think the tube meant anything in Sally's hands. "Hold on to this, no matter what happens. Understand?"

"Yes, ma'am." Given something concrete to do, the girl's expression steadied and she rushed into the stateroom.

Morgan and Lowell fired one last round then flattened themselves on the observation car's floor as bullets smashed through the walls above them. They were firing for effect, rather than at genuine targets, since the bandits were careful to keep down. Most of the shots had come from the forward side, toward the engine with the train's crew. But the women were in the private car behind them, with heaven knows how many devils coming after them.

Jesus, if anything happened to Jessamyn, he'd about kill himself. He'd always remember her white face on the morning she learned her mother had abandoned her for that flashy Californian.

In either event, he and Lowell would have to go out the downhill side, away from their attackers—and toward the freight train. And Palmer was a cheap bastard who hadn't flattened much land for the siding. There'd be damned little room to walk on, let alone air to breathe, between this train and the freight.

Morgan jerked his head at Lowell, indicating the downhill side. Together they crawled toward it on their bellies. They'd barely opened the rear door a crack when suddenly a volley of shotgun blasts ripped into the observation car. The wooden sides shattered almost completely, letting daylight and the freight train's roar in. A series of heavy coal cars began to go past, shaking the ground like an earthquake.

Thank God there were no screams from the private car. Jessamyn must be safe, at least for now.

Morgan slipped through the door as quickly and silently as he could, with Lowell behind him. The freight train's howling winds battered them, while the ground heaved under their feet. They pressed against the observation car, staying as low as possible.

Two heavy-footed bastards with shotguns were climbing into the observation car. One of them shouted to his buddies, "I've flushed these two. How're you doing up there with the crew?"

Morgan and Lowell looked at each other, murder in both pairs of gray eyes. So far at least, the bandits were focused on the crew, not the womenfolk. Morgan made a shooing motion with his hand, urging Lowell forward. They'd purge the train of the biggest poison first, hoping the smaller lump in the observation car wouldn't harm Jessamyn and the other ladies in the meantime.

Maybe she could help them keep their heads. She was a well-known sharpshooter and had fought Indians beside Cyrus, although he'd never heard of her using a handgun other than on a practice range. Ice flickered through his veins and settled in his stomach. If these bastards harmed her, he'd show them what kinds of vengeance a white man learned among the Apaches . . .

Lowell nodded cold-blooded agreement. They ran forward, occasionally touching the railcars for balance when the wind and noise grew too strong. They reached the engine and hid behind the tender, which was piled high with wood.

Satisfied they hadn't been heard, Morgan glanced at Lowell, who nodded his readiness. As ever in a fight, he'd taken on the look of a man ten years older, who'd seen blood shed far too many times. If William knew the exact number of times, he wasn't telling.

Morgan and Lowell peered around the tender to tally up their remaining enemies.

One was coming down from the hillside, with a rifle in his hand; probably the ringleader since he was definitely the best dressed. Two stood in front of the coal tender, as if about to leave for the private car. One was stepping down from the cab, reloading his gun; likely only God could help the crew now.

A window abruptly shattered in the observation car and one of the bastards there leaned out, waving a bottle of whiskey and shouting a ribald invitation to join him. And one more lay motionless on top of a boulder, a crimson stream falling from his chest onto the green grass below.

Morgan and Lowell jerked their heads back behind the tender. All they had to do now was boot the six living sons of bitches into hell.

Morgan silently asked Lowell how many knives he was carrying. Lowell displayed them—Bowie and dirk, one in his boot and one up his sleeve. Morgan grinned mirthlessly and tapped his in response, announcing similar blades carried in the same places.

Another silent discussion planned their attack. They'd be the prongs of a pincer, going around the engine to trap the bastards between it and the hillside. They needed to be silent lest they spook the two sons of bitches in the observation car, who could harm the womenfolk. But Morgan also wanted to gut these brutes like the beasts they were. Behind them, the freight train's passing still shook the ground like Satan's chariot.

He flicked his fingers, indicating Lowell's direction of attack. The younger man simply nodded and slung his rifle over his shoulder; given his speed on the draw, his Colts would still be very much available to him, as Morgan's were to him.

The bastards' leader shouted a string of obscenities, ordering the fellows in the observation car to stop drinking and *search* the private car. They grudgingly began to do so—and immediately faced a locked door, which triggered a hail of curses and kicks.

Morgan snickered silently. Just another poor fool tripped up by Jessamyn's quick thinking.

He and Lowell went around the engine on opposite sides, Morgan creeping in front and dodging the cowcatcher while Lowell snuck between the tender and the observation car. Morgan slipped onto the mountain's edge and wove through the boulders quickly, begrudging every second not spent rescuing Jessamyn.

They attacked in a silent rush. Morgan stabbed the bastard who'd shot the crew and silently dropped him. Then he jumped on the leader, who was lifting his rifle to shoot Lowell. Lowell had just killed one henchman and was moving on the other.

Morgan put his Bowie knife to the fellow's throat, pulling him back against him, and the man lowered his rifle. "Don't kill me. Jones paid me to do it," he cried, eyes shifting rapidly from side to side.

"Figures," Morgan grunted. He pressed his knife a little deeper, pricking the man's throat. "What else?"

"What'll you pay me?" Ratlike cunning, at odds with his stylish dress, scuttled into his voice.

Lowell dropped the second henchman and faced them, ready to fight again. No sound came from within the engine compartment, dammit. The engineer was probably explaining steam engines to Saint Peter.

"Nothing," Morgan answered honestly, keeping a wary eye past Lowell for goings-on in the rear cars. Bribing a murderer wouldn't tell him anything he hadn't already guessed.

The man's free arm twitched. His fingers closed, ready to hold a derringer. When he swung his arm up, Morgan killed him, sending blood spewing.

Without waiting to see where the bastard's corpse landed, he and Lowell ran for the private car.

The closet was hot and stifling, with no air moving. Jessamyn tried hard to calm her breathing and think about something, anything other than whether or not Morgan was still alive. She hadn't heard any more shots—but that was small comfort to someone who'd lived in frontier Army posts for six years. She could recite a litany of violent ways to die other than by bullets, and all of them were passing in front of her eyes, exemplified on Morgan's lifeless body.

She'd fought Indians before and killed her attackers, but always at a distance. This was the first time she might stare someone in the eye before meting out death.

Her hands clenched involuntarily and her right hand closed around her pocket Navy Colt. Her father had given it to her before the War but Cyrus had made her practice with it until it was like an extension of her own limb. It was a comforting, familiar weight, something she'd carried for years, including into situations where it might liberate her from a fate worse than death.

Her pulse slowed immediately and calmness crept over her. A minute later, she was able to take stock of the situation as she'd been trained to do, as both an aristocrat and an officer's wife.

The other women should be doing fairly well—or at least as well as could be expected under these circumstances. She'd taken the closet on the downhill side, closest to the freight train and its noise, while Mrs. Jennings was in the closet on the uphill side, closer to the mountain. Sally had disappeared under the bed, where luggage was normally kept, clutching the sturdy brass tube against her thin chest like a guardian angel.

They'd locked the doors and shoved chairs in front of them. All the other pieces of furniture were either built in or too heavy to move. Now two bandits were trying to break down the heavy door by pounding the dining table against it. Their previous effort to open it by shooting had failed, since the bullets wouldn't move heavy furniture.

She didn't dare think about what had happened to Morgan. The old saying that the devil always looks after his own was somehow no comfort; she'd have given anything to be wrapped in his sated limbs and listening to his heavy heartbeat once again.

The freight train's vibration began to diminish. Was it finally almost past them?

With a crash of splintering wood, the door gave way. Roaring like beasts, two men wrenched the door open and tossed the chairs aside, as the wooden walls trembled and fragile wood shattered.

"Wimmen mus' be in here somewhere," said one man on the other side of the thin wall from Jessamyn's head.

"No money fer them but there's a thousand fer the map, Davey."

A *thousand* dollars for the map? If Charlie was willing to pay that much, could he afford to leave any witnesses alive? Dear God, where was Morgan?

"But I ain't had me a wuman in months, Billy," whined Davey.

"You kin have all the wimmen ya want with yer share of the money, Davey. Jes fin' the map."

Wood splintered and crashed; they must have been breaking apart the furniture. A door slammed open and Mrs. Jennings screamed.

"Got me a wuman at las'!" Davey shouted triumphantly.

Jessamyn eased her door open a crack. Davey was a small

man, with a big gun at his hip, who was having great difficulty controlling the wiry Mrs. Jennings. Billy was a larger man, also armed, who'd been pulling down drawers from the top of the stateroom. The stink of whiskey coming off both men was astounding.

Billy looked Mrs. Jennings over and smiled, displaying four crooked, yellow teeth. "Mebbe yer right, Davey." He dropped the drawer he'd been holding on the floor and headed toward his cohort.

Mrs. Jennings shrieked again and Sally peeked out from underneath the bed, clutching the tube. If they found the map . . .

Jessamyn cocked her pocket Navy. Could she kill two men fast enough to save Mrs. Jennings? If she didn't, she'd be dead together with Mrs. Jennings—and probably Sally, too.

Oh, Morgan, Morgan . . .

Davey slapped Mrs. Jennings. She punched him in return, square on the nose, triggering a nosebleed. He howled, released her, drew his gun, and pointed it at her.

Billy's eyes met Jessamyn's, and he pulled his gun.

Time slowed to a crawl.

Jessamyn shot Davey through the crack in the door, dropping him in his tracks. She desperately cocked her gun, fighting to get off another shot.

Jessamyn fired, shooting Billy in the chest.

A bullet thudded through the door just above her hat; Billy's shot had gone wild. It had been that close.

"Jessamyn!" Morgan's strong arms grabbed her and pulled her out of the closet, then out of the stateroom. Lowell jumped past them and into the small compartment.

"They're both dead," Lowell announced a moment later. "Drilled one between the eyes and t'other in the heart, neat as you please."

Jessamyn buried her face against Morgan's shoulder and shook, while her stomach knotted and heaved. Even more overwhelming, she was back in Morgan's arms again. He was alive and so was she, thank God.

His arms tightened around her and he crooned wordless, soothing reassurance into her ears. For the first time since the War, there were no underlying notes of anger in his voice. She allowed herself to rest against him.

The freight train's last car went by. After a minute, the ground was steady and she could dimly hear Lowell awkwardly coaxing Mrs. Jennings and Sally out of the stateroom.

Then another steam whistle blew—once, twice, thrice. Four cars roared triumphantly past with a final flip of the whistle. Charlie and Maggie's train had been following the freight train the entire time. They'd reach the Sangre de Cristo Pass first and cross it tonight.

Jessamyn clenched Morgan's lapels and closed her eyes, wishing to God she could cry.

Four hours later, they finally arrived at the Donovan & Sons depot at Plaza de los Leones, the base for the Sangre de Cristo Pass. In the west, the tops of the Sangre de Cristo Mountains were as blood-red in the late afternoon sunshine as their name. Or as red as the blood that victims of yellow jack vomited just before they died. Dear God, would Aristotle and Socrates suffer that fate back in Memphis? Or Cassiopeia?

Jessamyn squared her shoulders. For their sake, she had to carry on.

Only one of the crew, the engineer, had been killed during the attack. The fireman and brakeman had been so badly wounded that the bandits thought them dead. By a lucky chance, the next train was an Army troop train, with a surgeon on board. He'd immediately taken over responsibility for the crew's care and gave them a good chance to live, if they had good nursing. Mrs. Jennings and Sally had promptly agreed to provide it at an excellent wage to be paid by Morgan. He'd also pledged a generous sum to the engineer's widow and family.

The amounts mentioned made Jessamyn's eyes widen but she kept her mouth shut. She'd have expected a man who'd made his money by gambling on fringe businesses to watch every penny.

However, after that, it had taken time to make arrangements for them, and finally—finally!—proceed to the pass with their luggage.

And all the while, Charlie and Maggie Jones were riding ahead, over the Sangre de Cristo Pass, gaining time on them.

Jessamyn's unhappy stomach had emptied itself twice during the intervening hours but had begun to regard tea and crackers as friends. She hoped it would find coffee and beans, those staples of long travel, acceptable again before morning. Not that it mattered; she'd mount up if she had to be tied into the saddle.

Morgan stepped away from the engine and handed her down carefully, treating her as if she were precious. He'd been very careful of her ever since the attack, almost chivalrous, which was the first time she'd ever seen him that way. Dear heavens, the startling flush of relief when his arms had wrapped around her and she'd realized he was alive. And how they'd both held each other after the attack, while Charlie's train roared past, almost comforting each other.

She thanked him courteously for his assistance, the proper response, and found herself wondering what he would be like if he were a gentleman. Impossible.

She said her farewells to the train crew and thanked them for their hospitality, including the ride in the cab. After many protestations of friendship on both sides, leave was finally taken and the train moved out, heading south to the Army forts there.

She glanced up at the mountainside, wondering if she could see any signs of Charlie's party. But the trail was too deeply carved into the mountains for that—or he was too far ahead.

A handful of men had originally waited for them on the small platform but only one remained. He came forward now, holding out his hand. He was a tall man, with a clean-shaven face like most of the others, and brilliant blue-green eyes. "Welcome to Colorado, Mrs. Evans."

Automatically, Jessamyn sorted rapidly through her memories. The eye color was very distinctive but she couldn't quite put a name to that face.

His eyes danced but his expression remained sober. "We hope your recent experiences didn't give you a dislike of our fair territory," he added.

Hearing more of the man's voice allowed her to make a guess. "Lieutenant Grainger?" she questioned.

He bowed courteously. "Lucas Grainger at your service, Mrs. Evans."

Her stomach churned at yet another trial, which she'd hoped to avoid. Dear Lord, the young lieutenant Cyrus had considered so promising, whose only known interests as a cavalry officer had been extremely hard work, fast horses, and scarlet women. What would he think of her now, traveling with a man she wasn't married to? Well, at least he was being polite in public. She offered him her hand in response. "It's a pleasure to see you again, Mr. Grainger."

He kissed it briefly, courteously, before turning to a narrow-eyed Morgan. "Everything's in readiness as you ordered, Evans."

"Good. When did Jones pass through?" They started walking across the small plaza toward the depot, where Lowell and his friends were rapidly transferring the luggage to the depot.

"About three hours ago," Grainger answered. "So they'll make it over the pass tonight but just barely."

"Which gives them a day's head start on us," Morgan growled.

Jessamyn winced, her eyes just catching a dust cloud on the pass.

"We'll have to start at first light," Morgan ground out, drumming his fingers on his belt.

"I've already given the orders."

A brief silence fell and Jessamyn eyed the mountains, wondering where Charlie was now. She snapped her attention back when Grainger spoke. "Mrs. Evans, before we hit the trail, I'd appreciate a woman's opinion."

Jessamyn glanced at him. "Yes?"

"You've met my mother. Do you believe she'd approve of my clean-shaven look?"

Jessamyn nearly stumbled. Mrs. Grainger, that most notoriously fashion-conscious of all society grande dames, approve of her son going against every fashion dictate? How could she politely tell Grainger that his mother would be appalled? For the first time since the attack on the train and the wounded men's departure for the Army hospital, she had to concentrate on something other than Charlie's increasing lead. "I, ah . . ."

She glanced at him and caught the edge of a pleased glance he'd exchanged over her head with Morgan. Silly fellows, they were trying to distract her. She hid a smile and decided to play their game.

"I'm sure your mother will enjoy seeing more of your face. Perhaps if she understood why it was so important to you to lose your imperial, which you'd cultivated so assiduously, she'd tout your new fashion to her friends."

Morgan chuckled. "It's a sign of being employed by William Donovan. You grow your whiskers when you're on the trail but you shave them off when you're in town."

What an amazing custom. "Why?"

Grainger shrugged, his eyes twinkling. "It's how William Donovan has always behaved. More and more of his unmarried employees do likewise."

She stared at them, completely turning away from the mountains. "No whiskers?" In this day and age when every man considered it his social duty to cover his face with hair?

"Don't you receive a certain amount of, ah, teasing, from un-kind personages in town?"

Grainger snorted. "If we do, ma'am, it's our privilege to teach them a lesson in manners. A few Donovan & Sons fel-lows gathered together are usually more than sufficient to provide examples of proper etiquette."

"And pay any fines afterward," Morgan added.

Jessamyn chuckled and patted his arm, feeling in complete harmony with him over the small joke.

She was still smiling—and deliberately not looking at the Sangre de Cristos—when he took her into the Donovan & Sons depot. It was smaller than the great ones she'd seen in St. Louis or Kansas City but the basic form held true. The stout central building was surrounded by paddocks for horses and mules. A small courtyard and a smithy lay inside, with some horse stalls and a garden. At the moment, it was a combination warehouse, stables, and home. But in the event of an Indian attack, the entire complex could become a fortress.

After introducing Jessamyn to the manager, Morgan took her into a tiny bedroom barely large enough for the bed and a single chair. It also had a few hooks on the wall and a tiny mirror, plus a jug of water on a small table. "This is our room, and you can wash up there before eating. There'll be a hot meal tonight, probably roast chicken, so eat up. You need to build your strength for the trail."

Jessamyn nodded and reached up to unpin her hat. She hadn't ridden as much in the past year as she had while Cyrus was alive. The first few days would likely be very uncomfort-able, until her body remembered its old strengths.

"Charlie may have as much as a twelve-hour head start on us." Morgan skimmed his planter's hat onto a hook. "With luck, we can make up four, maybe six, hours of that before we reach the Rio Grande's headwaters. Do you want to use the water closet first?"

"No, you can. I want to visit Starshine." *And reassure myself at least one of Somerset Hall's horses will survive.*

She started to unbutton her jacket. The water closet was a nice touch of privacy for the manager's bedroom, which they were using tonight. "Are you starting to believe in Ortiz's treasure?"

Morgan shook his head, ruffling his hair with one hand. "No, Jessamyn, I don't. Never have and I doubt I ever will." He straightened up and looked straight at her, his gray eyes very steady.

"But if you'd asked me to spike Charlie's guns by chasing across Colorado with a damn fool map—then I'd have said hell yes and jumped for joy at the prospect."

She stared at him, shocked, all her assumptions tumbling around her head. "Why?" she breathed.

"Charlie sold Union secrets for exorbitant prices during the War. If you asked him about it, he'd just laugh and call them just 'sharp' business practices." Morgan stopped, a muscle ticking in his jaw. Murder dwelled, hot and bright, in his eyes. "We could have used all that gold for something useful," he snarled.

"Guns?" Jessamyn queried, trying to remind herself that he was a man who knew the dark edges of the world, where morals changed like fashions.

He shot her a hard look. "Medicines, more likely. Guns we took from the Yankees but quinine and morphine required hard cash. The way I see it, too many of my friends died to line his pocketbook. Medicines such as the ones which kept Uncle Heyward alive."

Jessamyn flinched, remembering the Ming china she'd sold for morphine to dull her father's pain. "Dear God, Morgan."

He faced her, braced like a soldier for judgment. "I asked Uncle Heyward for permission when I arrived and he agreed. He didn't ask anything for himself; his only condition was to keep you as safe as possible. I know I risked his life needlessly and I'll always be sorry for it."

The ground seemed to shake under her feet. "I didn't know, Morgan. He never spoke of it."

His mouth twisted bitterly. "He was a soldier, Jessamyn, even when he was out of uniform. Unless you told him that you'd caught me . . ."

She shook her head, her brain spinning.

"All he knew was that I came to town on a secret mission for his country. He couldn't talk about it, as long as the War continued."

"And he died before it ended," she said slowly. If her father had accepted the risks, then Morgan hadn't been the selfish fool she'd always thought. "No wonder he asked to be buried in his uniform at Somerset Hall. We managed it, of course."

Morgan nodded. "I know. I said good-bye to him there before I headed west."

She looked up at him, tears rising in her eyes. "I'm sorry I misjudged you, Morgan."

He shrugged jerkily. "I should have managed matters better so as not to endanger him. I'll never forgive myself for risking his death in a Yankee prison."

She hugged him, offering him what comfort she could. "But that didn't happen, Morgan. Don't think about that now; think about how we can defeat Charlie."

His arms came around her in a bone-crushing hug. They clung to each other for a few minutes before he looked down at her, his gray eyes glowing with determination.

"Charlie has a great deal to answer for, Jessamyn. We can't bring back the past, much as I'd like to see my friends alive again. Or gut him for trying to blackmail you out of the money to save your father."

"Morgan!" Dear heavens, she'd thought he'd just disappeared into the twilight that evening, and left all responsibility for her behind. Old angers shattered even further.

His big hands rubbed her arms lightly. "But we can follow

the map to the end first and laugh at him. Given how frantic he is about grabbing money, it may be a pretty fine revenge."

She stiffened her spine and threw her head up. "It will be an excellent revenge."

And she'd pray that the family legends were true and Ortiz's gold was still there. No matter what, she had to regain Somerset Hall so that her beloved horses would be safe from Charlie.

Chapter Thirteen

Plaza de los Leones, Colorado

Morgan eyed Jessamyn's glossy head as he carefully tightened the laces on her riding corset, unable to read her expression by the single lamp's light. He'd hoped late yesterday afternoon she was recovering well from killing the two murderous bastards who'd been about to rape her and the other two women.

Now—now he just hoped she'd survive the ride across Colorado and deep into the San Juan Mountains. God knows, Charlie was a bastard and his men were the worst sort of thugs, capable of any murderous mischief.

But the ride would be long and hard, and the high mountains held their own dangers. They'd be traveling at eight thousand feet or higher for most of the trip. At that altitude, the air was thin and cold. Every step would be an effort, while unnecessary talking and exertion would be discouraged. The working days would be shorter, because recovery time would be longer. His and Charlie's men came from the Colorado mountains so they'd have no problems. But Jessamyn? Since she'd been living at near sea level in Jackson for the past year, she would be easily exhausted until she slowly adapted.

They were traveling at high summer and the snow was melting quickly. But a heavy snowstorm could strike at any time, killing the unwary and trapping the well-prepared in their tents for days. They would cross the timberline, over barren rock, and through ever-present snow at altitudes up to eleven or twelve thousand feet—on slopes covered with gravel and so steep that a single breeze could trigger a deadly rockfall.

Thunderstorms would hit regularly, with lightning bolts that sought out and killed anyone foolish enough to stand erect.

Besides the hazards arising from the high elevation, there were also those typical of a remote landscape: cougars, lynx, grizzlies, Utes . . .

He wished, yet again, that he was enough of the rogue she thought he was to tie her up and send her back to Denver, where she'd be safe.

Dammit, if he was to convince her he was a gentleman, he had to take her along.

He held her corset's strings steady, although it was definitely laced looser than for a daytime corset and far looser than he'd see on a woman gussied up for a very fancy evening. He'd never before laced a woman into a riding corset, which needed the extra flexibility so she could respond to the horse's movement. Wearing one, Jessamyn could supposedly ride for ten, even twelve, hours a day. "How does this feel? Too loose?"

She shook her head, sending an ebony curl teasing her neck. He eyed it hopefully; he'd always enjoyed making love to a half-dressed woman. It would delay the moment when he had to see her mounted, ready to risk her life. Perhaps they could stretch this out for another five minutes, slip their clothes off and . . .

"It's perfect, thank you." She glanced over her shoulder at him, her green eyes cheerful. "I can finish dressing myself now. I'm sure you'll want to check all the arrangements, as Cyrus did."

Morgan frowned. *Arrangements?* Cyrus left her bedroom *early* to check on travel preparations? What the devil had the man been thinking of? Why hadn't he simply taken her back to bed?

Then he remembered their old childhood expeditions, when the three of them had worked together and everyone had a role to play, no matter what society dictated. Like the time he'd wanted to see *A Midsummer Night's Dream,* as performed by the theatrical troupe from London, even though the adults said they needed to be in bed early that night. So Jessamyn had plotted a way to manage it. Then Cyrus stole the stepladder she'd noticed in the sewing room, while Morgan and Jessamyn were supposedly napping as befitted dutiful children. Finally Morgan shimmied into Longacres' private playhouse's second story first, then helped Cyrus up, followed by Jessamyn. They'd triumphantly watched the play from the minstrel's gallery, even returning the stepladder without discovery.

Traveling with Cyrus must have been similar, working together to achieve a shared objective.

He kissed her on the top of her head and rose. He was unable, however, to resist a bit of teasing. "At least this morning, I will. But on other mornings, I may want to leave my tent at the same time you do. And the evenings, of course, offer their own possibilities."

She froze, caught in the act of shaking out her chamois trousers preparatory to donning them, and shot him a wary look. He lifted an eyebrow at her, pleased by her response to a bit of flirting. "The only reason would be to ensure a simultaneous departure on our horses at dawn, of course."

Jessamyn chuckled at his small joke and set her foot into the first trouser leg. "Please, go talk to the horses and the other men. Drink your coffee and check the packs. I'll dress, finish my breakfast, and join you."

Her second leg now safely in, she pulled the trousers up and fastened them. Fully clothed, dammit. Temptation was fading rapidly.

"You make escorting you sound very simple." She'd sounded exactly as she had when they were growing up—as eager and ready for adventure as any boy. None of the society ladies he'd squired to Consortium clubs, or the expensive prostitutes he'd purchased, had ever made spending time with them easy. It was almost worth losing the opportunity to tumble her exquisite body back onto the bed.

"Morgan, I want Charlie's lead cut by every possible minute." She reached for her shirt. Her simple breakfast of coffee and oatmeal steamed quietly on the table beside her, a silent reminder that she was in as much of a hurry as he was.

Morgan strapped his weapon belt close to his waist, shrugged into his fringed leather jacket, and dropped a kiss on her cheek. She blinked then smiled at him.

Once out of her sight, he slipped his two Colts into their holsters, butts forward in the cavalry style, and buckled on his spurs. He pulled on his favorite old battered, broad-brimmed slouch hat and opened the door, his leather chaps creaking softly as they softened to his body.

The outside air had the quiet, slightly damp stillness that came just before first light. A few lamps burned, creating fitful reflections in polished metal and still water in horse troughs. Within the sturdy corrals, horses and mules stirred, their ears flickering, then returned to their feed.

A dozen men there glanced up at his arrival, then went back to work, all moving with the speed and dexterity of long experience. Tin clinked against tin once, in the unmistakable sound of a mug being refilled.

As he'd expected, he found Lowell with the mules. That young man was rapidly becoming one of the best packers Donovan & Sons had. At the moment, he and Mitchell, one of Mosby's former guerrillas, were finishing securing a load with a diamond hitch and grunting at the strain. They hauled strongly on the rope, each throwing their full weight against it with a foot braced on the mule, until it was taut. Finally satisfied, they grinned at each other and stood erect, then quickly tied off the rope ends.

Mitchell jerked his thumb at Morgan then started lairing up the next pack, wordlessly giving Lowell a few minutes to chat. On this expedition, Morgan had ordered two-hundred-pound loads for the mules, not the typical two-hundred-fifty pounds, for faster travel and on the slim chance there would be gold.

The younger man picked up his mug and came over to Morgan. "Mornin', sir." He dipped a piece of cornbread into it and ate. Where had he found that much milk? Was it cow's milk?

"Morning. How do the new Main and Winchester *aparejos* look?"

Lowell swallowed quickly. "The new pack saddles? Stock's a little light but Daly says they'll do for this trip. Picked up some new techniques on padding *aparejos* to make the mules more comfortable, too. Heard 'em from Clancy in Sacramento, who says they worked well on Crook's last campaign."

Morgan's ears pricked up eagerly. If the pack masters had solved that old problem . . .

As Napoleon had once said, an army travels on its stomach. Donovan & Sons was a California-based outfit, originally founded to carry mining supplies and ore across the Sierra Nevadas on wagons and pack mules. Any Donovan & Sons expedition into rough country therefore usually preferred pack mules—and the weakest link was the mules' skin. Because of that, Donovan & Sons used *aparejos,* pack saddles with flexible willow ribs interspaced with hay padding, which were the most comfortable available. But fitting the *aparejos* to the individual mules was a difficult art, which few pack masters understood. Most threw up their hands and called unhappy pack mules unsuitable for hard work.

But contented pack mules were animals that could keep up

with a horse's thirty miles a day throughout a long trip, while eating less and staying calmer than their more glamorous cousins. Mules were also more comfortable in extremely rough terrain, such as the San Juan Mountains.

Morgan had bet everything on an old map and his pack mules, even before he'd lost twelve hours to the attack yesterday. But if Clancy's new techniques were good enough to supply the army of a top Indian fighter like Crook, they might give Morgan a few more hours a day of travel time—and help him catch up that much sooner to Charlie Jones.

"You're sure about this?"

Lowell nodded. "See for yourself. Look at Rosie, Daly's bell mare. Not a body bunch or a belly bunch on her. No sore tail, sore withers, sore loins, kidney sores . . ."

Morgan whistled softly. If his head mule skinner's all-important bell mare was happy, then the mules would surely be happy. Plus, those mules would follow her, given every opportunity. The horses would, too, if left to their own devices, since horse herds were naturally led by top mares—and Rosie was definitely one of those.

Lowell nodded agreement and finished his glass of milk, then wiped his milk mustache off his beard shadow, which truly made him look caught between youth and adulthood.

"What's Jones packing in on?"

"Heard they're all horses. Good 'uns and plenty of 'em. Some ex-cavalry but lots of Thoroughbreds, too."

"Morgans?"

Lowell shook his head and glanced back at the other packer, who was just finishing lairing up the next pack for loading. "Some but mostly bigger breeds. Heard he wanted all of 'em to double as riding stock."

"Not many likely to be good in the mountains, in that case."

An unholy gleam of laughter crept into Lowell's eyes. "Not like ours. Especially not like your Chaco."

Morgan grinned back. He'd demanded Morgans, Mexican-bred Barbs, or saddle-broke mustangs. "Yup. I'd best see to him, before he kicks a stall down."

Lowell snorted in disbelief at that prediction.

Morgan chuckled, slapped Lowell on the shoulder, and headed for the barn, whistling softly. He had good men, good horses, and good mules. He had a fair chance to bloody Jones's nose.

Inside he found Grainger saddling up a big iron-gray stallion with a white blaze on the forehead, who was peacefully chewing a wisp of hay instead of nipping at every passerby. A stable cat placidly washed a paw atop a hay bale only a few feet away, an extraordinarily odd sight near that brute. Morgan missed a step before he strolled forward.

"Morning, Evans," Grainger said calmly.

"Morning, Grainger."

Grainger glanced sideways at him. "Captain Evans saved my life more than once, you know."

"He was a very good man," Morgan said warily, wondering what this was leading up to. "We were raised together like brothers."

"So I heard." His voice was very quiet as he went on but deadly serious. "Mrs. Evans is a great lady and I'll be watching for her. I know she's accepted you, but as an unmarried woman, she should have a protector."

What the devil did Grainger think he planned to do with her? Then Morgan started to laugh at their masculine posturing. "You realize, of course, that Mrs. Evans is more than capable of looking after herself."

Grainger coughed. "I certainly do, sir. But I'll still be here as her backup." He tightened the girth and buckled it into place, followed by an affectionate rub for his mount. The big iron-gray stallion swished his tail and whickered contentedly.

Morgan eyed the big stallion, ready to consider the coming expedition again. What the hell had happened to change that horse?

"You're riding Sherman?" Chaco, Morgan's Indian pony, looked out of its stall, ears pricked forward hopefully.

Grainger shrugged. He was probably one of the very few men willing to chance riding that gray devil. "Seems nobody else had taken him out for some time and he was very well rested."

Some people would have called that fresh enough to buck the devil off.

"Sure you don't want to change mounts while you can?" Sherman was a fiend of a horse, who was alive only because he had twice as much stamina as any other horse in the Donovan & Sons string. Some fool had "promised" Sherman he wouldn't be gelded for another year if he brought him safely back from an Apache attack. Sherman had succeeded and Donovan was keeping the fool's promise, although there was a tally kept of how many months remained before he could be gelded.

"I'll manage." Grainger's mouth twitched in the fitful light. "Besides, we spent some time together yesterday and seem to have reached an understanding. Didn't we, Sherman?"

Sherman swung his head around to look at Grainger, happily accepted a good rub on his nose, and went back to chewing hay.

Morgan laughed, reminded of an old mystery. Why the hell was an ex-cavalry officer working for Donovan as an ordinary teamster?

"Did you look at Mrs. Evans's sidesaddle?" He rubbed Chaco's nose as he fed his desert-bred horse maple sugar candy, his favorite treat.

"It had been cleaned before it arrived but the men touched it up."

"How well did it fit the horses?"

Grainger's eyebrows went up. "It was custom-made in London to fit Starshine, you know."

Morgan stared. Cyrus and Jessamyn had been living on an

Army officer's salary. How had they afforded a custom-made sidesaddle, especially one from London, the *ne plus ultra* of saddlemakers?

"Mrs. Evans won a shooting contest against men with her rifle one December," Grainger answered the unspoken question as he brought out the sidesaddle. "Her husband had made some side bets on her prowess and used his winnings to buy the saddle. While Starshine was her favorite horse and the one used as the model, Captain Evans also asked that the saddle fit American horses, such as Morgans, Southwestern-bred Barbs, and mustangs."

"Good Lord." London-made sidesaddles usually fit only Thoroughbreds, making them almost useless for the shorter, stockier mustangs and Morgans found on the American frontier.

"I personally tested its fit on Starshine yesterday, as well as several of our Morgans. It worked well on all of them."

Morgan's eyebrows shot up. He'd hoped Jessamyn could use at least one of his horses as a remount, but that had seemed a faint hope. "*All* of them?"

"Some of the Morgans needed the blanket to be rearranged slightly, to adapt the tree to them. But two of them were calmer under it than under an astride saddle." Grainger began saddling up Starshine with the calm dexterity of someone who'd handled a sidesaddle before.

"It has a better-fitting tree for their backs." Morgan voiced the explanation and Grainger nodded agreement.

Morgan eyed Starshine, automatically noting the proud lines of her head. He remembered saddling up other horses at Somerset Hall, under the same filtered light with the same sweet smells of clean horses and good feed, while Socrates and Galileo talked about the colts and fillies gamboling in the pastures. His fingers stretched, as if reaching for a bridle to slip over the head of a high-spirited stallion.

That was what Jessamyn was fighting for—to take those

horses and rebuild that world somewhere else, someplace safe from plague. Looking around Donovan & Sons' much smaller stable, he could almost feel the reality of her crusade.

Then Chaco nosed his jacket, looking for more maple sugar. Morgan chuckled, rubbed his old friend's neck, and led him out.

"Mrs. Evans may be able to last longer in the sidesaddle than many of us," Grainger added.

Morgan shot him an incredulous look as he began to saddle up Chaco.

"She regularly kept up with experienced cavalry troopers and outlasted greenhorns. Then she danced all night, if there was a ball to be had."

Morgan shook his head as he threw the blanket over Chaco's back. "Well, that is the standard for a horsewoman," he commented, remembering his mother. "She should also be able to ride over even the roughest terrain, given that London-made saddle."

"What about Mrs. Jones? Is she—"

"Maggie Jones was as tough as old rawhide when I first met her and she rode astride then. But carriages are her preferred mode of transport now."

"She might slow them down," Grainger commented hopefully.

"Especially since she greatly dislikes rising before dawn. And she's gained two dozen pounds, perhaps three dozen, in the past year."

Grainger's eyes gained a calculating gleam in the lamp-light. He brought a diagonal strap under the sidesaddle, stabilizing it, and buckled it. "If we cut eight hours off their lead before we're in the San Juans . . ."

Morgan gave him a wolfish grin. "We'd essentially be on an even footing."

"Giving us ways to slow them down, like raiding them," Grainger completed the thought and slid a Sharps carbine into its neat scabbard on the sidesaddle's off-side. There were two similar scabbards, one for a revolver and another clearly for a telescope. "Or them to slow us down."

Morgan shot a sideways glance at Jessamyn's armament. Cyrus had had her sidesaddle customized for rifle and revolver, too? Did he allow her to ride with him into rough territory as well? His jaw set. She'd need it where they were going.

Jessamyn came out of the depot a minute later, her new dark green riding habit showing her superb figure to its fullest advantage, a broad-brimmed Spanish hat atop her ebony braids. "Good morning, gentlemen," she greeted the company at large.

A dozen of Donovan & Sons roughest teamsters promptly shuffled their feet like schoolboys and doffed their hats. Even Little, Grainger's big Indian guide, bowed to her. "Ma'am."

She smiled at all of them impartially, before her gaze exploded with warmth. "Starshine, sweetheart," she crooned, offering the gentle mare a lump of sugar.

Morgan's mouth twisted. One day, dammit, she'd see him as a gentleman and she'd smile at him openly. One day, although he hadn't yet accomplished it on this trip.

Still, there was no time to waste. He lifted Jessamyn into the saddle and waited until she was well settled, with the reins gathered up in her gloved hands. She sat as erect and squarely as a man, the only visible difference being her skirts flowing over Starshine's side. She slipped her pocket Navy into the revolver's scabbard and the map tube into the other empty scabbard, the one designed for a telescope.

Then Morgan swung himself up onto Chaco's back. His old friend pranced a bit, happy to be reunited with his favorite human and back at work, but quickly settled down. Morgan whistled the quick lyrical notes that signaled "saddle up" to Donovan & Sons' men.

Leather creaked, metal jangled, horses neighed as the teamsters obeyed. Rosie's bell sang, marking her eagerness to move out. The mules came into line, their bells tinkling sweetly.

Morgan raised his voice slightly as Forrest had taught him beside a flooded Tennessee River. "Listen up, men!"

Combat veterans all, they immediately came alert. Even the horses seemed to grow quieter.

"Y'all know we're racing Charlie Jones but you don't know where. We're going to Santa Fe . . ."

Some puzzled frowns appeared. There were far too many men, too heavily armed, too well equipped, for a quick race over the Sangre de Cristo Pass. Little, the big scout, dipped another piece of cornbread into his mug and ate it calmly.

"In search of Ortiz's gold!"

Comprehension quickly dawned. Grins broke out. Somebody cursed happily. Morgan glanced at Jessamyn, who took up the thread smoothly. "Specifically, west to the Rio Grande, then northwest along the river to the Three Needles in the San Juans. After that, we turn south over the mountains to the desert and make our way back to Santa Fe.

"Jones made it over the Sangre de Cristo Pass last night, giving him a day's head start," Morgan continued. "Anybody know who's riding with him?"

"His favorite thugs," Lowell answered promptly, his right as the last member of their party to have encountered Jones's cohorts in Denver, pausing in his consumption of a chicken leg. Would that boy never stop eating? "The Easterners who stole the Firelight from Nelson."

"Any of them good horsemen?"

"Experienced with buckboards and buggies. Never heard much talk of any of them as expert horsemen, though," Mitchell, the usually taciturn Virginian, commented thoughtfully.

"Hard men. Damn good with any weapon you care to mention—pardon my language, ma'am—including mining tools, and can clean out two saloons in less than fifteen minutes, Rutledge and Calhoun, the two Alabamians added, finishing each other's sentences as usual.

"That's quite all right, gentlemen."

"But his outfitter's Hazleton," Taylor pointed out, his saddle probably loaded with more ammunition than the others.

"That's only one man," Lowell objected.

"Who's the best packer in the Colorado and Wyoming territories," Dawson, the cook, countered. "As well as his brother, who's the cook."

"Two men, and another six thugs, plus Jones and his wife," Morgan summed up the competition. "All dangerous men— but we're better."

Agreement rumbled through the circle. He looked around his audience, molding them into a unit in the cold dawn. "For the next five days, we have good terrain—after we cross this pass. We can make time over the San Luis Valley's rolling hills, as we move up the Rio Grande to the San Juans."

Nods of understanding went around the circle. Lowell finished his chicken leg and set it aside.

"But we have to arrive at the San Juan Mountains fresh enough to cross those piles of rock. That's the real challenge: what the spare horses are for, why the pack mules are loaded so lightly. We will not tire our animals by recklessly galloping after Jones. We simply want him and his boys in sight when we reach the Three Needles."

He could see their eyes now in the first, faint glimmers of dawn. Hunters' eagerness shone there and the leashed tension of hounds ready to hunt. He'd seen the same look more than once in his fellow Rebels when they heard dawn orders beside the Mississippi or Tennessee rivers. These men were hungry for the chase and the fight to follow, with anticipation blazing in their eyes.

The same fever boiled in his blood and spilled over into his words. "Let those pilgrims think their money can fly them over the rocky peaks. The mountains will separate the men from the boys."

Teeth gleamed as they roared their agreement, their certainty becoming bloodthirsty. Every man here had seen the high mountains in a wicked mood and the San Juans were some of the worst. Donovan & Sons' teamsters were the cream, and Charlie's men, for all their viciousness and expensive gear, were pilgrims, who'd rarely ridden through the wild, high country. If—and that alone would be very difficult—Morgan's men could make up most of Charlie's lead, then they should be on an even footing crossing those mountains.

Jessamyn's eyes gleamed. She held her head high, with her expression stalwart. She looked every inch a warrior's woman, something she undoubtedly learned beside Cyrus.

A muscle ticked in Morgan's cheek. Cyrus had been an uncommonly lucky man. He continued, more briskly than before, "Questions? No? Then let's move out, boys. We need to be on the trail at sunrise."

Five minutes later, they rode out of the depot, a long deadly string of a dozen armed men, with their horses and pack mules. Morgan rode at the head with Jessamyn beside him. Little was just behind him, with Grainger. They wouldn't need his skills until they sighted the San Juans' foothills. The spare horses and pack mules were in clusters toward the rear of the column, moving in short enough strings to be easily guarded. Everyone, both men and animals, knew exactly what they were doing and looked well pleased to be about it.

Sunrise's golden light flashed on bridles and Colt revolvers. Someone began to whistle "Yellow Rose of Texas" in time with the jingle of tack and the steady thud of hoofbeats, the creak of newly tied packs adjusting to frame and mule.

A few minutes later, they began the steep climb up the Sangre de Cristo Pass beside the rushing river. Morgan had timed their departure perfectly: They should have just enough light to manage this, the most difficult portion, and still have a long day afterward for the race.

But how well would Jessamyn manage, riding sidesaddle? She couldn't grip a horse between her legs, as the men did. She had to tighten her thighs on the sidesaddle's leaping horn, which struck him as a much less secure method for traveling difficult terrain. Besides, she couldn't have ridden as much during the past year, while she'd lived in Jackson as a widow.

The trail twisted into the mountains, turning and dropping a bit, where a rainstorm had eaten a chunk, enough to trouble an unwary horseman. Morgan glanced over his shoulder at her, knowing full well he was behaving like a hen with one chick, and opened his mouth to warn her.

As befitted her name, Starshine was moving smoothly and gracefully up the steep wagon road. Jessamyn sat straight and tall on her back, her carriage as erect as any trooper on the parade ground, albeit a trifle higher in the saddle, with the reins comfortably gathered in her hands. She gave no visible cue to Starshine, yet the graceful mare nimbly rounded the corner as easily as if it were a broad Memphis boulevard. Horse and rider moved a few steps closer to the mountainside, avoiding the gap in the road, and returned to pacing calmly up the trail.

Jessamyn glanced up and caught his eye. "Yes, Mr. Evans?" she asked, one eyebrow arched.

Morgan was damn proud of her—but he couldn't let her see that he'd been worried. He quickly thought of another topic. "Did you see the blue grouse?"

Her head came up fast, looking into the forest. "Where?"

"Sitting on the branch of that fir." He pointed.

She swiveled around in her saddle, following his finger. "Amazing," she purred in satisfaction when she caught sight of the bird, almost completely hidden in the shadows. "No way to reach him, though, if we shot him, since he's on the other side of the river."

"True." Take her into the mountains and the famous sharpshooter appeared immediately.

"Do you remember when you shot that mallard and you waded through the mud to fetch him?"

Morgan laughed, remembering the first time he'd ever shot a duck. "How could I forget? My mother scorched my ears about ruining my clothes and trying to catch pneumonia by taking off my boots."

She chuckled with him. "At least we were allowed to take retrievers with us the next time we went shooting, since our parents agreed we might just hit something."

"Did anyone train Charlie?"

She glanced at him. "With long guns? He was thrown out of Memphis at fifteen. I assume he had some practice with long guns by then."

"No talk of it?"

She frowned. "None that I can remember. At least not of him as a hunter. But Father always said Charlie was only interested in hide-out guns. Derringers, revolvers, and so on."

"Why was he thrown out of Memphis?"

Jessamyn was silent for a long time, her face troubled. "I'm not sure," she said finally. "It was just after you went to Arizona. He left the day before his parents' funeral, immediately after my father met with him. His parents died under unusual circumstances."

"What?"

Her voice was very soft, difficult to hear over Starshine's hooves. "Their town house burned and they were found dead, in their bedroom. Everyone was surprised that they could have slept through the fire."

Morgan bit off a string of curses.

"No official action was taken. I believe his parents' estate went to pay Charlie's and his father's gambling debts."

"If Charlie had anything to do with it . . ."

"Which might be why my father, acting in his capacity as one of the executors, ordered him out of town. Yes, it could easily explain why he tried to blackmail me and why he wants Somerset Hall so much now."

"If he tries to attack you now, I'll be glad to gut him and

stake him out on a fire ant mound," Morgan growled, naming the gentlest revenge he could think of.

Jessamyn's head snapped around and she stared at him, green eyes wide under her broad-brimmed hat. He stared back, his jaw set. If she didn't like that penalty, he'd be glad to design another. Perhaps something involving fire and tying Charlie to a bed.

Her eyes widened. Then she nodded an acknowledgment and went back to guiding Starshine through the difficult ride.

It took almost four hours to climb to the top of the Sangre de Cristo Pass beside that steep little stream, first traveling through the heavy mists of a dense stand of Douglas firs. Jessamyn found it a relief to break out into the windswept, rocky slopes where scattered limber pines reached to the sky, the winds keening through their needles. The ground was still icy cold, with deep patches of snow in every shady corner and water trickling from their edges.

At the top, the party paused to rest the animals and enjoy a superb view of the prairies to the east, seen between the cones of the Spanish Peaks. Pacing to stretch her limbs, Jessamyn watched an eagle circling high above, while she restlessly tossed pebbles over the edge.

This was already the longest ride she'd been on in the past year and her muscles were protesting. Yet she still had seven, or more, hours left in the saddle and she was damned if she'd let any of the men think her weak.

She'd never been this far west before, although she'd seen the Rockies, of course, and spent a week in Denver once for a friend's wedding. But this was entirely different. Nearly a dozen Confederate cavalry veterans surrounded her. She was riding into Ute Indian territory, to race Charlie, his slut of a wife, and his thugs for gold. It promised to be the wildest of rides into the roughest territory—and she was taking Morgan at her side, having pledged to spend it with him in her bed.

A treacherous warmth weakened her limbs at the thought—and the memories it evoked from the train trip. She cursed her own weakness for the man. Was a thought of him the only thing necessary to turn her into a swooning, weak-willed female, who'd beg to be tumbled by a fellow with light-filled eyes and hard, skillful hands?

Morgan Evans. How much did she trust him? To race—and strive to defeat—Charlie with every fiber of his being? Certainly, given that he wanted to defeat Charlie to avenge his friends from the War—and that he showed signs of protecting her from Charlie's insults.

An attitude that almost made her reconsider her previous opinion of him.

Of course, she could hand over the map to Morgan and wait for him in Denver. It would be the safest course to take, if she thought he'd bring all of the gold back to her. But what if he kept most of it for himself, following the same sharp practices he'd used to build his fortune? Ortiz's gold was a treasure so great it would sweep most men's sanity away.

She'd never know if she didn't travel with him.

Dear Lord, how she wished she could believe he was a gentleman, as she had when she was a child. She snatched up a larger rock, the size of her fist, and threw it out across the trail. It shattered against the rock beyond and fell, tumbling for hundreds of feet.

"Jessamyn?"

She jumped and spun around. She'd been so absorbed, she hadn't even heard his spurs jingling. "Yes, Morgan?" She stepped back from the verge.

"About the horses at Somerset Hall . . ."

Why was he bringing them up now? "Yes?"

"If Socrates and Aristotle had some money, do you think they could hire extra men to help them guard the horses? It's almost fever season now so thieves may get bolder."

He was concerned about the horses? And his former jailers? She swallowed to force down the lump in her throat. "I'm sure they could."

He nodded decisively. "I'll wire the funds from Fort Garland tonight."

"Morgan—" She automatically started to refuse his charity.

He smiled at her wryly. "Call it a zero-interest loan, Jessamyn, for when you find Ortiz's gold."

Did he really believe in the treasure or was he simply tossing a sop to her pride? Did it matter, when it might save her friends' lives? "Thank you."

"My pleasure."

He strode back toward his men, whistling the same call he'd given that morning, causing men and horses to lift their heads. Coffee was poured over a campfire, sending steam hissing up. Horses' ears pricked forward. Clearly it was time to depart.

Jessamyn tossed the remaining pebbles aside and turned back to Morgan. She was riding west, in search of Ortiz's gold to save Somerset Hall.

She was beginning to wonder if she understood Morgan at all.

Chapter Fourteen

As Jessamyn had expected, the first day seemed particularly long. The scenery was spectacular: first, the barren mountain peak at the top of the pass with the few twisted pine trees. After that, they descended quickly through stands of Douglas fir, dark and misty with little growing on the ground below, before passing through one of the famous aspen forests, its green leaves singing in the summer breezes. Here wildflowers grew thick beyond the trail, almost reaching a mule's belly, while brightly colored birds flitted past or watched them from branches high above. Waterfalls were frequent and the rivers and streams ran deep and fast, racing each other to carry meltwater to the Atlantic.

Jessamyn sighed over a particularly rapid brook. She could have stayed at this meadow longer but she knew she needed to keep moving. Brief rides back in Jackson had not been enough to maintain her stamina as a rider. Now her entire body was starting to complain about its abrupt reintroduction to horsemanship. But as she'd hoped when she gave Starshine to Elizabeth Anne after Cyrus's death, the mare was in superb condition, quite unlike her mistress.

Thankfully, Morgan and his men were all ex-cavalrymen— how had Donovan & Sons found and kept so many?—and they kept to the cavalry ways for traveling long distances. For ten minutes out of every hour, they dismounted and led the horses, a pattern designed to keep their mounts fresh enough for battle. But from Jessamyn's perspective, it had the salutary effect of stretching her limbs and slowing the arrival of cramps.

They usually walked, with occasionally bursts of trotting, which kept the horses—and Jessamyn—refreshed. Through all of this, the patient mules kept up steadily, their silver bells tinkling as they paced along. The lead mare had a deeper bell, which the mules seemed to recognize. Certainly they fell in behind her quickly, with very little urging from the teamsters.

Jessamyn took another drink of water, capped her canteen, and hooked it on her saddle.

A feathery leaf teased her cheek. She jumped and spun around, ready to take to task whoever had startled her.

Morgan held out a bouquet to her, wearing a mischievous expression. Daisies, fluffy white flowers above fernlike leaves, conical purple sunflowers, and yellow sunflowers had been neatly wrapped in a damp kerchief. "For my lady," he said loudly with a bow, and added very softly, "Just consider how I can excite you with any of these tonight."

Her jaw dropped. Shockingly fast, her breasts swelled against her corset and heat gathered between her legs. Over his shoulder, she could see his men smiling at them like fatuous dolts. She accepted the flowers helplessly. "Thank you."

He caught her hand and kissed each finger. "My pleasure, dear lady."

She blushed scarlet. "Thank you for bringing me on this expedition," she added softly. "It's beautiful here."

He glanced up at her, his eyes softening. "No more so than you."

Her pulse speeded up. She was still somewhat flustered when they took the trail again.

Maggie sulked, took another breath laden with stinking sage, and wanted to throw up. Charlie and some of the men were fishing for catfish, while others napped during the noontime break.

To her right, an oxbow of the Rio Grande River meandered past. But everywhere else was miles and miles of nothing but miles and miles of desert. Oh, there were grasses and other shrubs present, too, given last year's wet winter, but this was still a desert with only cottonwoods to be seen. Worst of all, there was no shopping and no one to flirt with except Charlie, he of the vicious temper and shrinking sanity.

If he had left her at Fort Garland like the adoring husband he said he was, she would not be in this wretched place. Then she could have waited for a stagecoach—she shuddered at the contrast to their private railroad car—to carry her back to civilization, while he fetched the precious gold.

She'd been very well behaved last night: she hadn't mentioned her aching muscles, a hot bath, or her French maid. She'd praised Charlie effusively for the successful train attack upon Morgan. She had not said anything derogatory when Charlie's male organ remained wizened despite her attentions. Of course, given her state of extreme discomfort, she'd been grateful for once that he was incapable of satisfying a woman.

This morning she'd even fetched him coffee before he woke up, an easy feat since she hadn't slept a wink. Then she'd delicately suggested to him that he might—might!—consider sending her back to Denver to watch over their empire.

He'd immediately lost his temper and accused her of wanting to remain behind to take Morgan as her lover. Only reflexes sharpened during earliest childhood had enabled her to dodge the boiling hot coffee he threw at her. The only thing that had saved her life was her open-mouthed astonishment at his accusation of a prearranged rendezvous with Morgan. Truly, if she could have managed it, she would have created one—but she hadn't.

Charlie had eventually forgiven her and insisted, once again, that she accompany him to the San Juan Mountains.

She curled her lip and shifted against the tree, adjusting her leather chaps. Charlie's family lore insisted there was so much gold left that a man couldn't put his arms around it. Anything less than that would not be worth this hellacious journey. But maybe tomorrow she could sleep late.

Suddenly Donleavy, one of Charlie's recent recruits, started fighting to bring in a fish. Maggie sprang up to see what he had caught, grateful for any distraction. The other men—except Charlie, who continued to fish on the other side of the oxbow—clustered around him as well.

After a long struggle, Donleavy finally landed a massive catfish well over a foot long, its snout sprouting great long whiskers. He whooped triumphantly and the others joined in, especially the cook. Dinner tonight would be excellent and a pleasant change from the typical train food.

"Oh, you wonderful man," Maggie cooed, thinking about the superb meal to come. "How happy you've made me!"

Charlie suddenly stormed through the stand of cottonwoods. "You bastard! Do you think you're a better fisherman than I am?"

Donleavy gaped, the great catfish hanging from his hand.

Maggie immediately swung around and batted her eyes at her husband. Dammit, was every man in the world a target for Charlie's jealousy? "Charlie sweetheart, you must have the best fishing rig on the Rio Grande River."

She clutched his arm firmly and smiled up at her husband, praying Hazleton or the cook would remove the fish from harm's way. She would be furious if Charlie destroyed her hope of a good meal. "Please show me how you baited it," she cooed as prettily as she could.

A growl vibrated silently in Charlie's throat and his forearm was an iron bar under her hands. His men were watching them, frozen in place.

She trailed her fingers up his sleeve. "Please, Charlie darling, I'd be so excited to see your—pole."

He looked down at her and she managed to lick her lips, adding a lascivious fillip.

He covered her hand with his. "Whatever you wish, darling."

For once, she wasn't pretending to be a lady when she leaned on his arm while they walked through the grove. He'd been very close to killing Donleavy—because she'd complimented his catch. They couldn't bring back the gold and return her to her Denver mansion too quickly.

Jessamyn rode out of Fort Garland beside Morgan, heaving a private sigh of relief. Making conversation with her old friends had been an effort, both because of her exhaustion and because they wanted to ask about her companions. While she could explain a race across Colorado—almost any wild jaunt could be credited to competitive masculine furors—she found it far harder to string together a sentence about Morgan when she was wondering what wickedness he meant to employ in their bed that evening.

At least she'd learned something of the trail ahead and those who'd traveled it, including Charlie and Maggie Jones.

A few minutes later, she and Morgan joined their companions, who were briskly setting up camp just within sight of the fort's walls, in a pleasant grove of cottonwoods close to Trinchera Creek's silver waters. The San Luis Valley was a broad flat stretch of land, full of sagebrush and sand and almost two days' ride across. It was bordered by the Sangre de Cristos's jagged peaks on the east and the San Juan Mountains' massive bulk on the west.

Thanks to last winter's rains and thunderstorms like the one that afternoon, there was grass for the horses and plenty of water. Her friends had warned her to be cautious of storms higher into the mountains.

But here beside the creek, everything was peaceful. Dawson, the cook, and his assistant were busy making dinner. Some of the men were unpacking mules, carefully balancing the heavy packs as they came off. But many of the horses and mules were unpacked and staked out, while the gear tent had already been set up. *Aparejos,* pads, and blankets were spread out to dry, with their ropes and *mantas.* Other men had started grooming horses and mules, removing the sweat and strain of the day's travel.

"Charlie's ten hours ahead of us," Jessamyn commented bitterly. She'd hoped to be closer. "We only made up two hours in the Sangre de Cristos."

She gathered her courage, preparatory to dismounting. Only her pride had kept her from hobbling in front of her friends at the fort.

"He has better horses than I expected, probably because he hired Hazleton." Morgan tied up Chaco with other horses waiting to be unsaddled. "But they're not rising as early as we are, which should aid us."

He clamped his big hands around Jessamyn's waist and lifted her down. She held on to his shoulders for a moment, hoping her legs would magically become stronger. But what she truly wanted was a hot bath and a long sleep, in more or less that order.

He nuzzled her cheek and her damn pulse leaped. She cursed under her breath.

He chuckled softly. "We discussed sleeping arrangements this morning," he whispered into her ear, took the reins out of her hands, and passed them to Lowell. Starshine nickered hopefully at the smell of fresh hay being unpacked. Lowell nodded and took her off.

Jessamyn cocked an eyebrow at Morgan suspiciously, willing her frisson to die away. This was not the time to lust for him, not when she needed every wit about her. "What do you mean?"

"Keep looking around you."

Her head swiveled, taking in the full details of the hubbub around her. Most of it was exactly what she'd seen produced many times before by a small troop of men traveling across country. But surprisingly, a large tent stood on the camp's far side under a pair of cottonwood trees. A lantern glowed inside it, highlighting two cots, a trunk, and a stool. Somehow she'd expected to share a bedroll with him around the fire with his men, in the classic bivouac technique.

Her attention snapped back to Morgan. "You planned that," she accused.

"Yes." His eyes danced with mischief in the twilight.

She tried to glare at him. She also tried to stop thinking of all the wonderful possibilities offered by that private tent. "Won't it require a great deal of time to set up and take down? If it will slow us down . . ."

"Don't be absurd, Jessamyn. For all its fine looks, that tent can be packed up very quickly. It's also sturdy enough to do well against the cold at higher elevations."

He wrapped his arm around her waist. "Come along. You'll feel better after I'm done with you."

She dug in her heels. "Morgan . . ." She knew she'd recover her old campaigner's stamina within another day or so. But at this moment, lusting after Morgan was more a matter for her brain than for her body.

He didn't slow down, giving her the choice between appearing undignified with her feet dragging behind her or walking beside him. She chose to walk, his Bowie knife brushing against her through her skirts.

She nodded politely to two of his men, Rutledge and Calhoun, two gentlemen from Alabama who had greeted her first. They smiled back and returned to grooming mules, their Colts and Bowie knives ready at their hips like everyone else's in this camp. Donovan & Sons had some of the most remarkably deadly—and gentlemanly—employees she'd ever seen, which more than fit the firm's legend.

"Can you wash up by yourself?" Morgan asked when they reached the tent. "I need to speak to some of the men."

She expected to fall asleep the moment she was alone. "Morgan?"

"Yes, Jessamyn?"

She tried to look as alert and energetic as possible. "I will tend Starshine myself tomorrow, as is proper."

He frowned. "Jessamyn . . ."

"Your men have more than enough to do, between tending the other animals and standing sentry duty. I will carry my share of the burden, beginning with Starshine."

Respect flashed over his face, softened by a wry amusement. "Very well, Jessamyn. You may do that, just as you did when the three of us played pirates."

She smiled at the old memory. Cyrus, Morgan, and she had split the watch into three equal parts whenever they stood guard in the tree house, waiting for a valuable craft— such as a branch—to float down the stream. "Thank you."

He held the flap open for her and she stepped inside, only to gasp at the exquisite sight that met her eyes. Clean sheets and blankets were stretched smoothly across two cots, while pillows were plumped up at their heads. A jug full of water and a basin sat on the trunk, beside two clean towels and a lemon.

She should be nervous about what he was planning. But she couldn't bring herself to care, not when she was facing fresh water and clean towels.

An instant later, she'd tossed her hat onto the trunk, blown out the lantern, and was forcing her fingers to unbutton her jacket. Outside, she could hear Morgan talking to Grainger about the trail ahead. How long would it take her to fall asleep in that lovely bed?

Minutes later, the jacket, shirt, skirt, trousers, and socks were neatly stretched over the trunk, with her boots standing squarely beside it. An instant's work unfastened her corset's steel busk, which held it closed in the front, and dropped it onto the trunk.

Using the light from the campfires outside, Jessamyn poured water into the basin and squeezed the lemon into it. Shivering in anticipation, she dipped a towel into it, wrung it out gently, and buried her face in the cloth. Lovely, cool, fresh water caressed her brow and her cheeks. The towel enveloped her nose and awoke her lips, erasing their flaky, dusty shell. A brisk lemony tang teased her nose, while trails of the same life-giving moisture trickled down her throat.

Jessamyn moaned and swirled the towel over her face. She dipped it back into the water and repeated the process, sighing. Heaven on earth.

If only she could go a step further and wash underneath her drawers. They were made of very fine cambric but they'd been trapped between her chamois trousers and her skin for the entire day. If she could wash her bare skin . . . She was, after all, wearing her chemise, which covered her to the knees.

She hesitated and listened, holding the towel clutched to her throat like a shield. Morgan and Grainger were still talking, while the cook was telling the men that dinner would be ready in less than five minutes. Perfect. Surely Morgan would sit down to dinner with Grainger and he wouldn't interrupt her. She slipped off her drawers and went back to washing herself.

This time, she did so thoroughly, with an eye to cleanliness more than sensual pleasure. She started at the top of her head and worked down, using soap as well, so that the clean portions could dry off. But the regular motions exacerbated her stiff limbs and soon she was whimpering softly. The final stages, when she reached her lower limbs, were particularly agonizing and she had no idea how she would wash her feet.

"Give me the cloth, Jessamyn," Morgan said softly.

She gaped at him. If she hadn't been biting her lip, she probably would have screamed. How had he managed to sneak into the tent without being heard?

"The cloth," he repeated, holding out his hand.

Too tired to argue, she handed it over. Morgan pressed her shoulders back gently and she lay down. His hands were very gentle when he washed her feet and she bit her lip in gratitude.

"Do you do this often?" It was all too easy to remember other times on the train when he'd handled her in the dark and made her sob in pleasure. She was too sore and too exhausted now, of course. But lust still somehow sparkled and danced over her skin whenever he came near, dammit.

"Occasionally." He returned to the cot and unbuttoned her chemise's sleeves. Without saying another word, he began to gently rub a light, unscented oil into her hands and arms.

She told herself firmly that it was only kindness which made him give her a massage when she was exhausted. She turned her head to watch him, sighing a bit as she yielded to his touch.

After that, it was easy to let him rub her face and neck, especially because his strong fingers knew exactly where riding had built every knot and kink in her body. She moaned a little and closed her eyes, keeping them shut even when his hands left her head.

Morgan rolled her over onto her stomach and rubbed her back very gently through her chemise without the oil. Jessamyn muttered and stretched. The sensation was nice but not as smooth as a rubdown had felt directly on her skin with the oil. "Oil, please," she mumbled.

"Are you certain?"

Silly question. She felt better after this massage than after any previous one, even when she'd had a maid. "Yes, of course."

He lifted her chemise up and a breath of air touched her skin. She twitched reflexively but two big, warm, magical hands gently settled over her back.

She sighed and closed her eyes. Morgan knew how to make her feel better. And he did. He worked all the aches out of her back, as well.

The fact that her traitorous female body was starting to feel well enough to take interest in his masculine body was ridiculous. She could no more handle being ridden by a man than she could have tolerated riding Starshine for another twelve hours, much as her breasts might ache at the thought of his wicked skill in arousing them.

She barely moved when he went to work on her legs. It was, after all, the natural next step, she reminded her intrigued libido. Moving might also have meant acknowledging that her intimate flesh was warm and wet, ripe with interest in his touch. Oddly enough, her loins weren't frantic to have him.

Still, there were a dozen men outside, close enough to hear almost everything. She shrugged that observation off, too tired to protest. Besides, she'd been an Army wife for years. If she'd objected to Cyrus's attentions while traveling with his hundred or more troopers, she'd have lost many opportunities to enjoy his pleasures.

Morgan kneaded the backs of her calves until every knot created by the day's long ride was gone. Steadily, he worked up her thighs until they, too, lolled open for him, lax and inviting. Orgasm started to gather in her blood, a slow rich swell like a great tide, but not one that needed her muscles' frantic twitching. Cream slowly dripped onto her leg and Morgan swirled oil across it, then rubbed the cream into her skin.

Jessamyn sighed softly, enjoying another touch of hedonism.

He rolled her over and kneaded the front of her legs. Her leg muscles were less stressed here and responded quickly to the oil. Soon he was stroking her legs with a more intensely carnal touch, one that sent shivers of arousal through her body.

She shuddered, recognizing his invitation, and instinctively rubbed her breasts through her chemise. Frustrated by the cloth, she drew it up restlessly until she could fondle her breasts directly.

Morgan growled softly and spread her legs wider. His hands ranged up the insides of her thighs, stroking and kneading.

He worked more oil into his hands and smoothed it over her mound and down between her legs, working it into every inch. She moaned and twisted under him when he plumped and smoothed every fold, bringing them to their fullest glory, teasing every delicate frill into a bouquet.

Her eyes closed, her hands locked on his shoulders, because the only sense that mattered now was touch when she was floating away on a wave of his creation.

His blunt finger teased her gently, finding those last traces of soreness where the muscles ran up the insides of her thighs into her depths. His finger returned, oilier now, and circled her entrance. She sighed, calmed and captivated, and opened farther for him. He circled her again and again, until it seemed a great spiraling wave was sliding inside her on his hand. Two fingers perhaps—or was it three?—eased into her, pumping her slowly, like the mountain creek flowing past the tent.

Jessamyn moaned again, bucking gently against his hand. Orgasm was close but not yet overwhelming.

"Take it now, Jessamyn," Morgan ordered, his voice harsh against her ear.

She sighed and climaxed, clenching around his fingers while her entire body flowed into rapture. Ecstasy, bright and solid, caught her before tension flowed completely out of her.

"Ah, Morgan," she sighed. "Thank you."

An instant later, she slid completely into sleep.

Morgan knelt between her legs, condom in hand, and stared incredulously at her. His cock was throbbing hot and hard, ready to thrust home, but Jessamyn had fallen asleep?

He snatched up the linen towel and began to stroke himself, while imagining what he'd do when he had her where she could howl in pleasure. All too soon, he was pouring his seed into the damned towel and biting his lip lest his men hear him.

Afterward, he sank back onto his haunches and began to laugh softly. At least one thing had improved in the past nine years. This time, Jessamyn was the one snoring peacefully away, not he. Maybe he had learned some self-discipline after all.

He climbed to his feet and slipped her under the covers, protecting her from the cold night air here at eight thousand feet.

Jessamyn eyed Morgan warily over her coffee mug, trying to gauge his temper. She'd woken up, warm and safe and very relaxed, to find a cup of coffee being waved under her nose. Would he still be polite, since she'd fallen asleep before he'd relieved his own excitement last night?

Without a hint of ill temper, Morgan had told her he'd be back in fifteen minutes to help her dress and done exactly that. Now she'd just eaten an excellent breakfast and the men were finishing up breaking camp in the first light of dawn. Morgan was as busy as any of them and helping with any task, even packing the immense two-hundred-pound packs onto the mules.

She shook her head. Lowell had mentioned that the mules were particularly frisky, being more accustomed to two-hundred-fifty-pound packs.

"We'll cross the Rio Grande today," Morgan remarked, coming back to her after the last mule had been loaded. "Jones crossed it yesterday."

She cocked an eye at him. "How difficult do you think it will be?"

"Deadly, if the river's running too high for the ferry. Time-consuming, if the ferry's still running. Around here, the Rio Grande is over two hundred fifty feet wide and more than ten feet deep, even in a dry year."

She nodded, flinching at the thought of swimming all of the mules across. And the big packs of supplies? Please, God, let the ferry be running.

"How much sharpshooting practice were you able to put in back in Jackson?"

Jessamyn's attention snapped back to him. The last time he'd mentioned her sharpshooting, she was eleven and he'd been furious that she brought down more ducks than he had.

During her marriage, horsemanship and sharpshooting had been her defenses against the terror of worrying about Cyrus and he'd strongly encouraged her to improve her skills, despite the disapproval of the closed military society. He'd even worked hard to teach her the best of military customs, including seeking out former snipers to be her tutors.

"Some," she answered slowly. "George took me out hunting regularly."

Morgan snorted. "He probably took credit for the bag."

She chuckled. "Agreed—but he also shared the meat, which was very welcome."

"You'll need to practice." Morgan's eyes searched hers, fierce as an eagle's. "I've heard gossip that you were very good but that was a year ago. Even if you might have been as good as an infantryman then, you've probably lost some of that edge. You'll need to be fast and accurate, as skillful as a Donovan & Sons employee if possible, if you're to stand beside us in a fight."

Deep inside her, a spark caught and burned. Even Cyrus had never mentioned she might stand with men in a line of battle.

"I'd also like," she said slowly and softly, praying her words wouldn't extinguish that spark of hope, "to look at Aunt Serafina's diary more, since she was a descendant of Ortiz."

"Jessamyn . . ." Morgan sighed.

Little rode back into camp and waved at him. Morgan lifted his hand in response and stood up. He looked back down at her. "Are you sure?"

Jessamyn stared into his eyes, which were open and soft, willing him to understand and *believe just this once*. "Aunt Serafina left a note in the diary, saying she hopes its stories will help me on my journey. What else could she mean but searching for Ortiz's gold?"

He hesitated, then lifted her hand and kissed it. "Very well. If you need extra light at night to read the old diary, tell me."

"Thank you." She sprang up and hugged him, surprised and pleased he'd allow even that small a chance for Ortiz's gold to exist.

Chapter Fifteen

San Luis Valley, Colorado

Jessamyn took another look at the Rio Grande's raging torrent, grateful to be on its western side at last. As she watched, an entire ponderosa pine, almost forty feet long, swept past in the brown water.

The day was sunny and hot but that only sent more ice-cold water pouring off those peaks into the river. Thank God the ferry had been running or they'd have spent at least two days here, laboring to cross. Swimming the horses and mules across, unloading the packs and carrying the contents across item by item. Praying nobody was drowned. Even if every man and animal had survived that trial, some of the supplies would still be lost. What survived such a crossing was frequently surprising and occasionally not enough to keep the men and animals alive.

Roaring water was no respecter of what was useful, as she'd painfully learned in the Army. Dangerous items like bullets and dynamite, kept in heavy locked chests, stayed dry and could be washed up by raging rivers, their contents unharmed. Also things that somebody clutched, and would fight for, tended to survive, even if damaged. But the stuff of life—flour, hardtack, beans, and more—would be soaked and pounded into the ground by hooves. Thunderstorms were just as damaging, when horses panicked and trampled wooden packs.

Risks like those were why Morgan traveled with so many mules, to carry extra supplies.

"Ready?" Morgan asked.

Jessamyn's glance tracked the Rio Grande's long sweep up-river, to the snowcapped San Juan Mountains. "Where do you think Charlie is?"

"Probably just coming out of that marsh, where the river bends hard to the west."

She gathered up Starshine's reins. "What are we waiting for?"

Morgan whistled and the cavalcade moved out, with the two of them at its head. The water was so loud here that it was almost impossible to hear the animals' normal travel sounds, even the mules' silvery bells.

Jessamyn eyed the great river once more and decided to think about deserts instead. She did have some questions she'd been saving up for years. "Morgan?"

"Yes?"

"I understood Cochise was always the white man's enemy in the Arizona Territory."

He glanced over at her, his rifle riding easily across his saddle's cantle, ready for immediate use. With his absolute ease as a horseman and the beautiful Indian pony under him, he seemed the embodiment of a primal warrior and a suitable companion in this wild country.

Jessamyn's eyes widened, something feminine deep inside her coming alive in recognition.

But Morgan was speaking, his Mississippi drawl soaking into her bones. "Cochise's tribe sold wood to the local Army fort then and were friendly to Anglos. I think he saw us as potential allies against Mexicans, their traditional enemies. I made friends with some young Apaches, thanks to a horse."

She forced herself to think about Morgan and Cochise. "What happened? Did your father object?"

"My father wanted a piece of the Great Southern Empire, whenever a railroad built a year-round transcontinental route. Peace with local tribes would be very valuable then and he encouraged me to make friends, with only two conditions. My studies had to be good enough for West Point."

She laughed at that, remembering how Morgan could devour books when he chose. He laughed with her, his gray eyes dancing underneath his hat brim.

"And?"

He shrugged, hesitating a little.

"And?" she prodded him.

He lowered his voice. "There could be no risk of a child."

Jessamyn gaped at him. Good heavens, John Tyler had been ruthlessly pragmatic. "He didn't want to risk a claimant to Longacres."

Morgan's mouth twisted. "Probably. To me, it seemed a very small concession. So I agreed and I rode with Cochise's men every chance I could, raiding other Apache tribes."

"What you must have seen. And learned," Jessamyn breathed. Mountains and deserts, the hidden cities . . .

He nodded, gray eyes searching her expression. "Some of those lessons kept me alive during the War."

"Tracking varmints over bare rock."

A smile dawned, edged and anticipatory. "Definitely."

They both looked ahead at the San Juans' foothills, almost two full days' riding ahead. "Tell me more," she urged.

Crack! Jessamyn's last bullet sent the rock's remaining chunk into the little stream below. Ten out of ten shots into the same fist-sized rock on the other side of the stream, two hundred yards away. She was careful to hide her grin, though; Morgan was a hard taskmaster when it came to practicing shooting skills. The setting was utterly peaceful—a hilltop clearing in the San Juans' foothills overlooking the Rio Grande River, with Chaco and Starshine grazing placidly behind them and tea brewing on a small fire—but he was still a merciless instructor.

They'd spent two days riding across the incredibly flat San Luis Valley with its abundance of sage and sand, and infrequent prospectors and ranchers. Three times a day, he'd taken her out with their guns—first, with her pocket Navy Colt, then with her Sharps carbine, the shorter-barreled version of the famous sniper's rifle. It had been manufactured during the War and converted to a repeater afterward. Cyrus had bought it for her as a Christmas present, when the Army decided they wanted more modern weapons. She sniffed disparagingly at Washington's lack of common sense and returned to considering Morgan's practices.

He'd taken her through the basic drills first, such as cleaning and loading, before he'd let her fire either one. Even then she'd had to prove her skills from the standing position and at close range, before he'd let her so much as kneel. She'd considered mentioning the attackers she'd killed on the train, in hopes that would speed her acceptance.

But she'd held her tongue, deciding that she'd rather follow his directions than pester him, at least for now. These shooting practices were the only times he escaped his heavy responsibilities, except in the evening.

Usually at night, there was only a little talking around the campfire. By the time camp was made, the packs taken off the mules, the animals groomed and fed, then the men fed—everyone was exhausted with only enough hours left to sleep before they had to rise again.

Slowly, they carved a half-hour and another half-hour off Charlie's lead.

Morgan drove himself harder than anyone else, always alert to give a hand or provide direction, the first one awake and last one asleep. In the evening, the two of them would chat a little, mostly family gossip or childhood memories, especially old pranks. Once alone in their tent, he was always certain to satisfy their strong carnal appetites, providing the most enjoyable diversions for both of them.

Jessamyn flushed and began to reload, slipping the cartridges in with the absent skill of long practice. He sat behind her now, scanning the hillside across from them in search of targets.

She'd thought more than once of suggesting to him that he slow down, perhaps let her relax him a bit. He was carrying a heavy burden on this trip. Would it destroy him to let her take the lead just once? Why, she could show him some tricks that might just surprise him, dammit!

At least her fingers weren't shaking as she reloaded. There was something to be said for long practice over the years. Her father had first noticed her innate talent and paid the best tutors to foster it. Cyrus had also encouraged her because he noticed how much calmer she was when he was gone, if she'd been practicing those skills. But he'd also taken the astonishing steps of training her to military standards for speed and accuracy, even seeking out infantry veterans to teach her their skills. She'd remonstrated with him for setting society on its ear in that fashion. But he'd laughed, saying he was a cavalry officer, not infantry, and didn't care about others' prejudices.

Morgan was an entirely different style of instructor than any she'd had before. For one thing, he was faster than anyone she'd ever known, even the desperadoes she'd seen in Kansas. For another, he was either quiet or pushing her to do better. She'd made every shot since yesterday morning but he hadn't let her try any long shots until today. And two hundred yards was hardly much of a test of her skills.

"See that rock higher up above the stream, the one shaped like rabbit ears?" he drawled, focusing his field glasses.

She studied it with her first real flash of interest. Clearly visible now that the afternoon breezes had blown the previous shootings' smoke away, it lay over three hundred yards distant with some very interesting breezes in between, according to the aspens. "Of course."

"Put ten consecutive shots into it, from a prone position, and we'll have tea."

Tea at last? Jessamyn promptly dropped onto her stomach, sliding the precious map tube next to her and without considering her riding habit for a moment. She studied the wind then brought the carbine up, centering her sights on the rock.

"You may fire when ready."

She destroyed the rock completely with her seventh shot and spent her last three shots making the dust dance.

"Well done," Morgan praised and lifted her onto her feet.

Chaco tossed up his head, making his tack jingle softly, while Starshine whinnied. Immediately, both of Morgan's hands rested lightly on his Colts, his hands crossed and ready to meet the newcomers in the wickedly fast cross-draw. Jessamyn stiffened, dropping her hand onto her Colt, her heart pounding in her throat.

Grainger and Little strolled around the hillside, leading their mounts. Jessamyn's heart returned to its normal position at the sight of their scouts.

"Excellent shooting, Mrs. Evans," the younger man greeted her. "Does Jones know about your capabilities?"

Her eyebrows flew up and she shook hands with him. "I doubt it. I was a child of ten when he left Memphis and Charlie has never paid much attention to anyone other than himself."

"He cares deeply for his wife," Morgan cautioned. "She's his Achilles' heel. He stayed in Rio Piedras two months to court her, when he could have departed without her in a week."

"Rumor says he killed an Italian count she flirted with," Jessamyn commented.

The men stared at her.

She spread her hands. "Great-Aunt Eulalia hears all the gossip."

Morgan shook his head. "Great-Aunt Eulalia is the most dangerous woman I know. Let's discuss something safer, like this expedition. When do we reach the Three Needles?"

"Tomorrow," Little answered, eyeing his trail boss curiously.

"Please join us for tea," Morgan invited. "We can also discuss the route."

"Glad to, Evans," Grainger accepted.

A few minutes later, they were gathered to one side of the fire with the soft rich smell of tea flavoring the afternoon air. Below them, the sweet sound of the mules' bells still rose from the valley below, marking their friends' progression alongside the river.

"You know we're headed south into the San Juans," Morgan began.

Grainger and Little nodded. Little's eyes touched Jessamyn's face briefly before returning to Morgan.

"Mrs. Evans inherited an old map, marking a trail . . ." He stopped, started again, and stopped. "Jessamyn, just show it to them."

She unscrewed the tube and began to ease the parchment out.

"Do you believe in this trail, Evans?" Little asked, the longest sentence she'd ever heard from him.

"I believe it will take us through the mountains," Morgan equivocated.

"It also shows a destination," Little prodded. Grainger, she noticed, was not interfering between Morgan and Little. Instead he sipped his tea and watched the two calmly, his eyes assessing the interplay between them.

She set the tube down and waited, with the parchment ready for display.

Morgan hesitated before answering. "I believe that the map is a true one and the destination shown exists. But Ortiz's gold is supposed to be there and I cannot believe that is true."

"Yet you continue to take this road."

"I will travel it to the end," Morgan said flatly, "in order to deny it to my enemy."

That was something to hold on to. He'd fight to take her through, which gave her a chance of regaining Somerset Hall with her beloved horses. She had to get Cassiopeia and Aristotle and Socrates out of there. *Dear God, may there not be yellow jack in Memphis this summer . . .*

"Then let us see this trail." Little looked over at Jessamyn.

Morgan and Grainger stretched the picnic cloth over the grass and Jessamyn carefully laid the old map on top of it. For all its stains and tears, most of the markings were still remarkably crisp. Vivid sketches of landmarks embellished it, mostly distinctive mountains and river bends. Mariners' compasses bordered the edges, their rays aligning with those landmarks.

At the southern edge of the San Juan Mountains, a circle with wavy lines surrounding it lay next to a waving line, probably a river. The circle was vividly unique so it had to be the gold's location. Jessamyn's heart stopped.

"Very clear," Grainger commented, tracing a spidery black line with his finger, clearly the Rio Grande River. Little was pacing around the map, studying its pictures.

"The mapmaker was one of the best," Morgan said flatly. "I immediately recognized its quality in Kansas City."

"Do you think the compass headings are accurate then?" Jessamyn asked anxiously. Both men looked at each other and didn't speak.

"The North Star has shifted slightly since this was made, Jessamyn," Morgan said finally.

"But if you found one of these landmarks and checked the bearing, then you could adjust all the others accordingly, correct?"

"How much of a mapmaker are you, Grainger?"

Grainger shot a look sideways at the other man. "Good

enough but I'm no cartographer. I learned my skills on the battlefield, as a dragoon officer."

Jessamyn stayed focused on Morgan, willing him to create a miracle. "What about you, Morgan? Cousin George said you drew maps for Forrest, while you were one of his scouts."

Morgan traced the unmistakable sketch of the Three Needles, the landmark where they'd turn south, away from the known trails.

"Morgan?" she prodded

"Yes, I can update it." He rose to his feet and began to walk around the map, closely perusing every inch. "The greater difficulty is that it's been almost fourty years since anyone followed this trail. Who knows if we can even find these landmarks?"

"But we know the starting point!" she protested.

"True. The map begins where the Rio Grande meets the Three Needles, but it doesn't show the San Luis Valley."

"According to Aunt Serafina's stories, that's where Ortiz and his men lost their pursuers and felt free to turn south," Jessamyn said, trailing behind him, trying to quell her excitement.

Morgan spun to look at her. "Pursuers?"

"According to her family's legends, the trip started when Ortiz and his troop headed north from Santa Fe on patrol but were cut off by Indians. They were forced to keep heading north along the river, while gradually losing members of their party. There was only a handful left of the original party by the time they entered the mountains."

"They were still nervous," Little commented. "This is a bad trail. It will take horses but there are better."

"Are you sure?"

Little touched a mountain peak near the trail's beginning. "I know this stretch is dangerous and I believe there is a better route here." His finger traced a circle.

"We're not sure you'd come out on the right trail," Grainger pointed out.

Little shrugged. "In the end, it would bring you to this river, the Lizard. From there, you could travel upstream to the place marked." He traced the line to the glowing circle, obviously the destination.

"The Lizard?" Jessamyn asked, fascinated.

Little beamed at her like a proud uncle. "See how it disappears without a trace into the desert, never joining another river? Lizards also dive into the sand, never to be seen again."

"Is there any need to leave the Spanish trail?" Grainger asked practically, his fingers walking compass headings. "A mountain can look completely different from a mile away and a different angle. If we lost the drawing's perspective, we might not find our way back, even with a compass."

Jessamyn choked.

Little was nodding agreement with Grainger's logic. "No, we should stay on this trail, no matter how overgrown, but be cautious."

"How much farther ahead of us will Charlie be, given his six-hour lead?" Jessamyn asked anxiously.

"It depends on how respectful he is of the weather," Morgan answered. "Every wise man comes down off an exposed slope before noon."

"Much sooner if the day promises thunderstorms." The three men shared looks of complete understanding.

"Why?" Jessamyn demanded.

"On the plains, you can travel until you see a storm then lie down when it begins. But here in the mountains, it seems that the storm is intent on transforming you into a lightning rod," Morgan said slowly. "So you seek shelter before the storm appears."

Jessamyn shuddered. Torched by a bolt from the sky?

"If nothing else, the sound makes the horses panic and run," Grainger said practically. "We'll have an easier time because our mules are calmer but Jones may have more problems."

Morgan chuckled wickedly. "Indeed he may."

* * *

The next afternoon, Morgan and Jessamyn looked across the Rio Grande Valley at the Three Needles, a trio of smooth black basalt spires rising from the valley's base. They stood on a mountainside and were almost completely hidden from sight, thanks to the aspen and pine trees around them. Bells sang faintly in the distance as the mules made their way alongside the river, underlain by the roar of the river's mighty waters. Waterfalls tumbled into the valley from every notch in the cliffs high above, roaring as they crashed against the rocks. The sharp tang of ponderosa pines was heavy in the air, mixed with the sweet vanilla scent of their sun-warmed bark. Over the past few minutes, a variety of birds had flitted across the clearing, their presence indicating Jones's men weren't using it for spying.

Morgan scanned the rocks methodically, looking for another of those telltale glints. There were far too many possible hiding places for snipers in these cliffs. He might have been dragged into chasing after Ortiz's gold but he didn't have to be a fool about everything else. Lordy, lordy, he'd bet on long odds before. But finding Ortiz's gold was a million-to-one shot—and in the roughest terrain imaginable to boot.

He double-checked a particularly deep shadow before he moved on.

"Are you sure we want to be up here?" Jessamyn asked, studying the landscape. Elk and mule deer were grazing near a fast-running stream, nearly hidden beyond one of the needles. "I thought you planned to take a first look at the Spanish trail."

"Not until Grainger and Little come back," Morgan answered, focusing the glasses on the easternmost Needle. "For now, I want to look at those spires, especially where the waterfall comes down beside our trail."

"Yes, the water could weaken the rock. Besides, the rock face is so sheer, it would take one of those bighorn sheep to examine it in person," Jessamyn agreed.

The Three Needles were almost as smooth as glass, projecting into the sky from the valley floor and rising higher than the mountain immediately behind them. The easternmost spire, just to the left of the Spanish trail, was the smoothest and the blackest except for one spot. Morgan scanned it carefully, looking for what had drawn his eye from below.

There. He focused the glasses and stared. What the hell was a single, fist-sized piece of quartz, sparkling like a diamond in the afternoon sunshine, doing in the black basalt? He'd only noticed it when a chance gust of wind had blown the waterfall's spray to one side. He hadn't had to think long to realize that a chunk of white quartz wouldn't occur naturally in a big mountain of basalt, like the Three Needles.

He considered the rock around the quartz again. The waterfall was running fast and free, given the wet winter and spring. Other than whatever loose rocks lay underneath it, there was no easy way for a man to approach that piece of quartz. Still, a bighorn sheep wouldn't wedge a rock into a mountain.

Maybe one of the few prospectors to pass through here had done so to pay off a drunken bet. In a dry year, the quartz would be more visible, after all.

Or—maybe a desperate Spaniard, traveling in a very dry year, had wanted to mark the point at which he turned off the main trail. So he climbed up the waterfall, which would have been only a trickle if it existed at all. Then he carved out a niche and wedged that chunk of white rock in. Only a rockfall or an extremely determined man could shift that blaze.

A shiver ran down Morgan's spine.

He knew damned well he'd look for similar quartz along the trail ahead, although it would be hell to see a similarly sized chunk of rock, barely larger than a brick, in those gray mountains ahead.

Ignoring the aberrant chunk for the moment, Morgan handed the glasses to Jessamyn and began to pace, considering tomorrow's trail from various angles. It was steep and narrow but the horses and mules would have no problems with it, at least during the beginning stretch. He was glad he'd brought mules and horses who liked mountains, though. Days of traveling over hard rock, especially when canted at an angle suitable for sledding, would make most horses turn fretful.

In addition, this journey was too peaceful by far, with no dirty tricks from Jones or his thugs. He'd feel a damned sight better if they were behaving in their old ways; politely racing to the gold was far too well behaved for that bastard.

Morgan snarled at himself. It was time to stop being distracted by trifles and face his real problem: Jessamyn, who continued to treat him as a useful rogue—but no gentleman. After all these nights of hearing her beg for more of his attentions, he feared he was the one in danger of begging for more of hers.

"Jessamyn?"

She lowered the glasses. She looked the perfect lady in her dark gray riding habit, with those crisp boots, and her broad-brimmed hat cocked jauntily over her braids. "Yes, Morgan?"

"We've been practicing for accuracy but now it's time to work on speed."

Her green eyes widened. Could she have grinned? Surely not. What woman's speed could match a man's, especially given her Sharps carbine's heavy recoil? That rifle was a horse killer, plus she'd have to lever in rounds extremely smoothly. "What did you have in mind?" she asked cautiously.

Something easy to begin with. "See that dead tree branch across from the empty bird's nest? Put ten shots into it in less than a minute."

She considered the target before looking back at him. "May I name my own reward if I succeed?"

His eyes narrowed. What was her fertile brain up to now? "If you do so twice in succession, both times in less than thirty seconds."

She nodded meekly. A chill ran down his spine. "Very well. Do you wish me to fire from a prone or standing position?"

"Prone, of course."

She lay down, taking up position behind a fallen pine near the edge, and emptied out cartridges onto a patch of sand. While Chaco and Starshine grazed contentedly behind them, Morgan sat down a few feet away on the grass with the field glasses and took out his pocket watch, ready to begin timing her first attempt. A moment later, his eyes widened in disbelief.

Jessamyn was slipping cartridges in between the fingers of her left hand, an old cavalry trick. Her gun could be very rapidly reloaded with cartridges held that way, an advantage that could prove critical on a battlefield. But nobody who hadn't frequently fought in combat learned that habit. Or had she been taught by someone with that experience, Cyrus perhaps?

What was he risking if she won? "What did you have in mind for your reward?"

"Pleasuring you with my mouth," she answered simply and lifted her carbine.

His jaw fell open. God help him, all the blood in his body headed south. He scrambled to regain his self-control, certain he couldn't have heard her correctly. "What did you say?"

"I want to pleasure you with my mouth." She brought the stock against her shoulder and nestled her cheek into the comb of the stock, easily settling into the curve so she could sight down the barrel. It was the same confident, graceful motion she'd use if he lay down while she pleasured him and she wanted to rest her head against his leg.

His chest tightened. Fierce spirals radiated from his suddenly all too hard nipples, where they rubbed against his linen shirt. He fought back a groan. His voice, when it came out, was barely recognizable. "You don't need to earn the right to do that, Jessamyn."

She racked the first round into the chamber, her fingers flicking the heavy gun's lever forward and back. She was one of the very rare shooters whose hands and fingers were so shaped that she could do this with just her fingers, without needing to move her entire wrist and arm. But from Morgan's perspective, the movement looked all too similar to how her hand would rapidly travel up and down his aching cock.

His breath stopped in his throat. His cock swelled against his canvas trousers.

"I'd like to do so exactly the way I want to," she said quietly, her soft Tennessee drawl more pronounced than usual. Her finger rested on the trigger. "When can we start?"

He spread his legs to give his cock a little more room and lifted his pocket watch. "Now." He clicked it but watched her.

Crack! Smooth as silk, her fingers swept the Sharps' lever as if they were moving over his cock.

Crack! Another round, another caress—and lust dived into his groin from his chest. Heat pooled at the base of his spine.

Crack! Another round, yet another caress of her fingers to her carbine which also echoed through his aching flesh. A whiff of black smoke from her carbine teased his nose.

Morgan gritted his teeth and brought up the field glasses. He needed to view the target to be sure she was firing accurately, although she'd always done so before. Maybe if he kept his eyes on that old tree, his shuddering body would stop imagining her fingers on . . .

Crack! Another round. In his mind's eye, he could see her strong, supple fingers fondle the big carbine as they'd fondle his aching shaft. His balls swelled and he closed his eyes, resolving not to leap upon a woman with a loaded rifle.

He managed to watch the last two shots enter the dead branch, all ten having clearly entered the same precise little circle. He clicked his pocket watch.

"Is my time satisfactory?" Jessamyn asked as she rapidly

reloaded. A breeze teased the smoke away so he could see her clearly. Dammit, he would be able to watch her hands stroking her gun during the next round.

He glanced down, wondered why his cock hadn't burst out of his trousers, and looked at the watch. "Perfectly acceptable."

It was the truth, too, although he'd have said that no matter what the watch's opinion was.

He reset the pocket watch and waited, praying he'd survive until she finished shooting.

"What's my next target?"

He pulled himself back from a vision of her long black braid teasing his balls. "The fork in the branch just above your previous target."

She brought her Sharps carbine up again and sighted down the barrel. She racked another shot into the chamber, caressing the heavy gun's shaft.

Morgan groaned silently. How would he survive another round of ten shots without any relief? "Ready?"

"Ready."

"Begin." He clicked his pocket watch and prayed she'd shoot quickly. He should pray that firing twenty shots wouldn't hurt her shoulder too badly. Nonsense; her leather jacket's shoulders were heavily padded to protect her.

Crack! Her fingers flicked and every button on his fly seemed stamped on his throbbing cock.

Crack! Her fingers flicked and his cock jerked. His balls were high and tight, desperate to release their contents. He closed his eyes.

Only pure reflex had him click his pocket watch after her tenth shot. "Name it," he groaned, throwing back his head. If he touched himself, he'd come in his pants like a teenager.

"However you want, just do it *now.*"

She smelled of gunpowder and lavender. "Look at me."

He blinked his eyes open, well aware they were frantic. "Yes?" he growled.

She held up a piece of rope yarn, the kind used to hold a gun in its holster lest it fall out with a careless movement. The slightest intentional pressure would snap it in an instant. "I want to tie your hands with this first."

He hesitated. But there was no threat in her eyes, no reminder of the Memphis attic, only tenderness and eagerness. His cock screamed at him to hurry up.

Her tongue swept over her red lips, while her big green eyes watched him.

He shuddered. Oh hell, with his hands bound, he'd be free to focus completely on the exquisite sensations of being skillfully pleasured by a beautiful woman.

He lay down and held up his hands. "Just do it fast."

She twisted the rope yarn around his wrists quickly in a hobble tie. Shit, he wouldn't even have to break it; he could untie it with his teeth if he wanted to be free. But his aching balls weren't interested in logic, just release.

She dropped down onto her knees beside him and undid his trousers, sliding them down his thighs. His hips rocked. "Oh yes, Jessamyn."

She stroked his cock gently. "You're beautiful, Morgan."

Her touch sent jolts of ecstasy racking his body.

But it still wasn't enough. "Dammit, I want more. I want hard and fast, like you gave that damn carbine of yours!"

She stared at him. Then her lips curved in a wicked grin. "Like this, mister?" Her hand closed around him and squeezed hard.

His eyes rolled back in his head in sheer pleasure. He bucked hard, gasping for breath. "Oh hell, yes."

"Or this?" She laid her head down on his belly just as she had against her carbine. He shuddered. Her mouth closed around him and her hand swept over him, just the way she'd loaded rounds into her gun.

He threw back his head and howled her name, his bound hands closing on her hair. He'd needed her to do exactly this.

She sucked him in perfect rhythm with her moving hand.

He couldn't think, couldn't do anything except feel, was simply an animal of pure sensation centered under the touch of her hands and mouth.

Climax gathered, hot and sharp and surprisingly close at the base of his spine. Her tongue lashed the sensitive spot just under his cockhead, then retreated when he growled. He bucked up against her again, his hips circling restlessly, and her fingers slipped inside his trousers.

Why had he ever wanted to fight such rapture? What did distinctions of who held the initiative matter against this, when everything in him was completely focused on the delight boiling inside his balls, ready to burst into every inch of him?

She pressed firmly on the ridge just behind his balls and it was too much. Climax blasted him as completely as a battle's cannonade. The seed clamoring in his balls rocketed out of his cock and into her warm, hot, welcoming mouth. He bucked and arched and howled, giving her every drop of himself as she had demanded.

Chapter Sixteen

San Juan Mountains, Colorado

Jessamyn clenched her chattering teeth and pondered chivalry, while Morgan rapidly laced her into her riding corset.

Yesterday Dawson (bless his heart) had somehow produced enough hot water for a bath, which was a miracle here at nine thousand feet since it took far longer to boil water. The evening had ended with Morgan tumbling her madly in their tent, just to prove how very much of a high-handed male he was.

After that, with a chivalry as unspoken as it was pronounced, he had left her sleeping undisturbed in her tent this morning, while his men tiptoed through their usual preparations to let her sleep. Finally Morgan returned to awaken her, carrying a lantern and food. In fact, all of his men were very polite and protective of her.

She'd also overheard them mention enough mining towns as places they'd seen and ridden away from to understand that they weren't trying to build chance-made fortunes. It was enough to upset many of her ideas about just how much gold fever ran in Morgan's veins.

But she was too cold to do much thinking, when she was dressing in a tent whose temperature was only a few degrees above freezing.

Only the highest peaks must have been showing a hint of sunshine, but outside, the expedition was in a disciplined whirlwind of movement, a dance as quiet as it was efficient, like muffled music underlying Morgan's hands moving behind her back.

She bent her head forward, trying not to think about where Charlie would be. By leaving this early, they would shave precious hours off Charlie's time. It was worth freezing in her tent for that.

The mules' light silver bells barely chimed; they must have been very tightly gathered around Rosie, their leader. The packers' grunts came soft and deep as they rhythmically loaded the heavy packs onto the mules' *aparejos.* Horses only occasionally bothered to whicker or stamp, only the faint clank of bridles and creak of leather announcing that they were being saddled up. Occasionally, metal scraped over metal, probably cutlery from someone bolting down a last quick bite to eat. Once a rifle thudded hard into its scabbard.

She shivered involuntarily.

"Have some more tea," Morgan remarked, handing her a cup while still keeping the laces taut. She was ridiculously grateful for his evident years of experience with women's corsets; it did so speed up the process of dressing, compared to Cyrus's endearing fumbles.

She gulped the hot liquid down. Normally she'd have hated its heavy-handed sweetness but now it tasted like manna from heaven.

"Do you want to return to Denver? I could send Grainger with you and one or two other men," he offered quietly.

Her head shot around and she glared at him. "Morgan, if I don't claim that gold and regain Somerset Hall, Charlie Jones will paint his name over its door and my horses will be dead."

He tied off her corset strings and stepped away, his expression barely visible in the lantern's dim light. "I could buy

Somerset Hall for you." His tone gave little clue to his reasoning.

"Are you offering me charity, Morgan?" She came erect, disregarding her dishabille, and began to pull her trousers on quickly. "No, thank you, Morgan. I'm riding with you."

"Jessamyn!" He gave an exasperated, wordless bellow.

She glared back at him, her head high. Somerset Hall should be saved by family, not charity.

"It's very dangerous, Jessamyn." His voice hardened. "Starshine could break a leg or throw you. You could break your neck or freeze to death in a sudden snowstorm. Those peaks are full of lynx and mountain lions."

She stomped her feet into her boots. "Plus my cousin will try to kill us both." She shoved her plate and mug into his hands. "I've never taken a penny from you, Morgan Evans, and I won't start now. I'll ride into these mountains and I'll bring back enough gold to save my family's home."

"Dammit, Jessamyn, I wasn't offering charity. I was trying to keep you safe," he snapped, his gray eyes blazing at her.

"Save your breath for saddling the horses." She dropped her skirt over her head and began to button it.

Hard, cupped fingers caught her face, forcing her to look at him. "You're a very stubborn woman, Mrs. Evans."

She frowned at him. "I'm speaking sense—you're not."

He kissed her hard upon the mouth, silencing her protests and sending her arms up around his neck to pull his head down. When he finally lifted his head, she was flushed and dazed, with bruised lips. "We'll have to argue more often," he whispered, "if that's your response."

She blinked at him and tried to form a coherent answer. He chuckled and bundled her quickly into her heavy coat.

A moment later, his spurs jingled softly as he left the tent. It was with considerable difficulty that she didn't throw something at his back.

*   *   *

The old Spanish trail past the Three Needles slipped through a crack in the basalt barely wide enough for a loaded mule then climbed almost straight up for the next two miles. All around Morgan, the air was full of the sound of rushing water heading rapidly downhill and waterfalls spilled like living rainbows. Everyone in the expedition walked beside their mounts, carefully guiding them over wet ground. From the distance came the faint sounds of Little and Grainger scouting the trail ahead, as well as the men guarding the flanks lest Jones stage an ambush.

Silent like everyone else, Morgan had time to think about his infuriating lover. Jessamyn was striding beside Starshine, as if climbing steps in a private park. Her head was up, her breathing steady despite the altitude, and she caught every flash of brilliant color when a bird flitted past. She was the perfect companion to go adventuring with, just as she had been when they were children. He grinned, remembering the day they'd crept out to fish for trout with Cyrus, been caught by a thunderstorm, and had to spend the night in a shack with only trout for dinner. She'd never complained; in fact, she'd delighted in telling as many stories as they did to pass the time.

At the top of the climb, the party came out onto a narrow valley, full of grasses and aspens. A small river danced down the center while broken granite rose on both sides.

Morgan raised his hand to signal a brief rest and froze. He finished the movement jerkily out of sheer habit, unwilling to betray his thoughts to anyone there.

Another small bit of white quartz had just flashed on the mountain's shoulder.

That night, Jessamyn burrowed a little deeper into her delectable nest of blankets and tried not to think about Morgan, who was somewhere out there in the dark with the sentries.

It had been a hard climb over the mountains that day, given the narrow trail over unforgiving, broken granite and frequent fording of fast-rushing streams. Some of the stretches were so difficult that Morgan had allowed the mules and remounts to find their own way, trusting that they'd follow Rosie, the bell mare. They'd been very diligent about staying near her—occasionally snorting at a particularly steep piece of rock or fast-moving stream—but always remaining close, both horses and mules.

There'd been beautiful sights—the mountains themselves with the snow disappearing more and more every day, groves of aspens with their green leaves dancing in every breeze, and elk grazing placidly on meadows covered with wildflowers. Once she'd even glimpsed a puma through her field glasses, drowsing in the sun on a rocky ledge high above. But at ten thousand feet, she had little energy to expend on exclaiming over such wonders.

They'd camped beside a meadow that night, with plenty of grazing for the horses and mules. Tents had appeared for all of the men, much to her surprise, since it increased the risk of a successful surprise attack by Charlie's men. They'd always bivouacked under the stars before. But Morgan had quietly explained to her that the tents were a necessary protection against the forest's mists and greater dampness. He'd posted more sentries to make up for the greater danger.

Jessamyn had agreed with his logic, of course. She'd ridden on campaigns with the cavalry, fought Indians—and lost a much-beloved husband to an Indian's bullet. She understood all too well the necessity to keep a keen eye out for danger.

But every one of those campaigns had included at least fifty well-armed, experienced troopers. This expedition was into some of the most difficult country in the United States, chasing a man who made Cochise seem honorable enough to serve in the Queen of England's palace guard. Here they had only a dozen men for protection while Charlie had nearly as many, with almost every one a paid thug.

The wind moaned through the fir trees overhead.

Jessamyn rolled over again and stared sightlessly at the tent's ridge pole. Her bed was extremely comfortable, providing no distractions. Pine and fir boughs had been neatly interwoven to form a very stable mattress, which a duchess would not have faulted. Atop it, Morgan's and her blankets were laid together so they could share each other's warmth against the cold night air.

If he ever came back. An all-too-familiar, roiling agony swept through her, first learned when her father went off to fight and honed to perfection as Cyrus's wife.

He'd left her after dinner, saying he needed to check on the sentries. But that had been—how long ago? It must have been hours. He could have slipped on a patch of wet rock, gone over the edge, and cracked his head, splattering blood and brains. Just the way Cyrus had looked, with the back of his head reduced to red and white pulp by that Indian's bullet.

Jessamyn gulped hard and started to fling her covers aside. She'd go find Morgan herself.

"Coffee, Evans?" Dawson offered from outside. He'd been tending a very small fire, just enough to keep a small pot of coffee warm but not so large as to harm the sentries' night vision.

"No, thank you," Morgan's wonderful voice answered.

Jessamyn's heart leaped and she sank back into the bed dizzily. Morgan was alive and well, thank God. He must have been checking on the sentries. Heaven knows, he watched over his men as if they were his own family.

She'd only been having a ridiculous fancy, born of the dark and loneliness.

"Get some sleep," Morgan continued talking, wrapping her in more reassurance. She slowly slid under the covers. "Your biscuits will be desperately needed in the morning."

Dawson chuckled and moved away, judging by the slight scuffing from his boots. Someone settled beside the fire and poured coffee, clinking his cup against the coffeepot. Hope-fully, not Morgan . . .

The tent flap stirred and Morgan slipped inside. Jessamyn sighed happily and snuggled down a little deeper.

"I thought you'd be asleep by now," he whispered, tossing his hat aside and unbuckling his gun belt. He always slept with one of his Colts and his Bowie knife under his pillow. "You must be exhausted."

"I was waiting for you," Jessamyn answered. Would he make love to her tonight? She was very tired but perhaps not too much so . . .

He was stripping rapidly down to his skin. She watched him greedily, taking in every glimpse of pale, well-muscled body with eyes well adjusted to the tent's gloom. Every rapid movement was testimony to his continued vitality.

"Do you think we made up any time?" she asked softly, not much caring what they discussed so much as the fact that they were talking.

Morgan shrugged, his white skin making the gesture vivid against the tent. "Maybe. Jones is pushing his horses damned hard and he'll pay for that later, when we reach the worst of the mountains."

She made a face, glad he couldn't see her clearly. Aunt Serafina's stories had been nasty enough about mountain travel.

He pulled on a dry shirt and socks, the single sure preven-tive against pneumonia and other ailments from waking up in the clammy damp. An instant later, he'd snatched the blan-kets out of her hand and dived under the covers with her.

Jessamyn squeaked in surprise and he laughed. His limbs were surprisingly cool for such a normally hot-blooded man. "Sorry to be sleeping with me?"

She quickly recovered and clutched him close, twining her legs around his to lend him her warmth. He smelled of horses, leather, and pines, with a trace of wood smoke. Most of all, he smelled exactly like Morgan. "Not at all, Mr. Evans."

He pulled the covers up around them and buried his face against her neck, holding her close. "You're very generous, Mrs. Evans."

She closed her eyes, a single tear leaking out. Morgan was back. All was well.

Their hearts pounded together, the blood racing through their bodies. Their pulses gradually slowed as they relaxed and warmed up. Once again, Morgan became a big, strong furnace.

Jessamyn automatically settled herself more comfortably, as she would have with Cyrus. Her hand slid up his chest and curved over his shoulder, anchoring her to his strength.

Morgan stiffened briefly, the hair on his legs scratching hers.

"What is it?" she asked, rousing herself enough for a conversation.

He blew out a long breath. "Nothing for you to worry about, dear." He stroked her hair, careful to keep the blankets tucked up around them. "Good night, Jessamyn."

She shifted again, sliding to rest her head against his shoulder. "Morgan?"

"Hmm?"

Maybe she should take advantage of his relaxation and ask him some delicate questions. In a very gentle tone of voice, of course. "Why do you let David manage Longacres?"

He yawned. "He loves the place and he's a far better farmer than I'll ever be."

It was that simple, that he'd do the best for his family regardless of appearances? Jessamyn shivered at how she'd misjudged him. "Do you plan to live there? He can't help but set roots."

Morgan settled his arm a little more closely around her. "I'll probably sell it to him if his sons are interested. Longacres was my father's dream, not mine. As long as it stays in the family, I'm content."

As was she. She sighed and snuggled closer. But tangled

this closely to him, she was very conscious of his chest rising and falling against hers. And his cock, warm and half-hard between them—which brought to mind activities *he* was incredibly skilled at. "Morgan?"

"Hmm?"

"Where did you learn to, ah, um, uh . . ."

"What?"

Oh heavens, she'd let her exhaustion steal her tongue away. "Nothing. Go to sleep."

"Jessamyn," he warned, sounding thoroughly awake.

She squirmed. Now she'd have to ask that truly embarrassing question. Thankfully, he couldn't see her face. "You're a very skilled man, Morgan, in carnal matters but also very passionate and disciplined."

"Thank you, Jessamyn." Oh dear, now he was wary.

She bit the bullet. "Where did you learn?"

"Is that your question?" he whispered.

"Yes. Of course, if you don't want to answer, you don't have to," she said hopefully.

He began to chuckle and pulled her close. She buried her face against him, quite content not to look him in the eye, even if she could have seen anything in this darkness.

"There's a network of private clubs called the Consortium, which also provides training to its members."

Just private clubs? "Is that all?"

He kissed the top of her head. "It's very strict and takes years. We can talk about it later."

She sniffed, more impressed by the man than the possible curriculum. "As you wish. Good night, Morgan."

A week later, Morgan's men were traveling just above the timberline. Although Ortiz, the old Spanish officer, had been clearly determined to travel south, he'd also had an excellent eye for terrain. The trail he'd marked echoed the ridgelines, thereby avoiding endless climbs in and out of valleys, but also regularly found good grazing and water. The longer Morgan followed in the old man's footsteps, the more impressed he became with the fellow.

He was also very glad that Jones was breaking trail for him—felling trees, hauling brush, clearing rockfall. It was backbreaking work and those thugs had to be cursing it.

Morgan had his own hands full finding the old quartz markers, which were damn hard to spot against the mountainsides. They seemed to have been planted at every major turn or junction, such as when two large streams came together. Sometimes he couldn't, such as when a rockfall had apparently occurred in the past two centuries. But he found them often enough to be sure he was still on Ortiz's trail.

Thankfully, there'd been no rain since they left the Three Needles, meaning less wet rock and mud than he'd expected. So the footing was good, even if the air—often at more than eleven thousand feet—was damn thin, something he and Jessamyn had difficulties with. On the other hand, his men, horses, and mules, all longtime residents of Colorado's mountains, had adapted very smoothly.

They were also catching up to Jones, who was less than four hours ahead according to Little. Even inexperienced Jessamyn had commented on how their pursuit was flustering her cousin: the disorganized campsites, the unburied trash, and worse, the numbers of horses lost to accidents. Two of those, a pair of fine Thoroughbred mares, had been abandoned for minor injuries, rather than being shot. O'Callahan, an Irishman by way of New Orleans, had doctored and adopted them, announcing they had a better than even chance of survival.

The most enjoyable aspect was traveling with Jessamyn. Throughout the expedition, she'd been a superbly passionate bed partner. But over the past few days, she'd turned into the best of companions, quick-witted and willing to talk about almost anything as they rode along. By the campfire, she'd laughed and joked with the men, even told stories and once started a round of singing. She tended Starshine very well, of course, but she also helped Dawson. She was the boon companion he'd dreamed of as a child but far better, since a boy could never have imagined her nighttime sensuality.

He snorted in derision, well aware he sounded like a besotted fool. But Jessamyn was rapidly becoming dearer to him than his own skin, which was a terrifying thought. She'd leave him in a moment as soon as she had the gold. The gold which those damn quartz blazes hinted at.

His hands tightened on the reins, bringing Chaco rearing up. "There, boy, there," he soothed.

Peace was quickly established between them but Morgan's frown didn't leave his face. In fact, it deepened when he surveyed his surroundings.

Now they rode through a steadily narrowing canyon, below steep walls of crumbling, gray rock. The right-hand side—or southwest—reared up far higher than the left, and was wrapped with a series of ledges as far as the ice-crowned summit. Only a few miserable shrubs tried to make a living in this stony canyon. Water trickled and fell out of the sides to join a brook running through the center. The noise was irregular and continuous, fraying the nerves, as if the rock itself wanted to join the water and go down to the sea. Bighorn sheep displayed themselves on those ledges in a variety of attitudes, from relaxed grazing to wary scanning of all directions, as if they were figurines on a giant's wedding cake. Even the mules' bells seemed muted and duller here.

The skin on Morgan's neck crawled as he studied the place. But no matter how bad this canyon felt, it was still better than the jagged peaks to the northeast, like daggers thrust from the earth by a vengeful god. He understood quite well why Ortiz had chosen this trail instead of exploring that ridge, where the howling winds whipped the last traces of snow from the pinnacles.

A chance breeze sent spray from one of the small waterfalls across the trail. Chaco pranced and tried to buck, laying his ears back against his head. Morgan was the only one still mounted; everyone else, including Jessamyn, was walking now so they could steady their horses.

Morgan automatically brought Chaco back down and soothed him with a few soft words in Apache. When he straightened up, a group of bighorn sheep caught his attention. They were staring fixedly at a single point, just above a large rocky knob at the mountain's far corner—well beyond what he or his scouts could see.

If that knob fell, it would block the old Spanish trail out of this valley. If it did so while anyone was under it, they'd die instantly. Jessamyn—beautiful, nimble, quick-witted Jessamyn—would be snuffed out of existence like a candle.

"Jessamyn, my pet," Morgan said calmly, although his heart was racing like a least chipmunk running from a hawk. Hopefully, the ridiculous endearment would alert her. "I'd like to look at Starshine. Her gait sounds uneven." He swung down from his saddle and handed her Chaco's reins.

Her green eyes widened above the silk scarf shielding her face from the sun. "Huh?"

He tried to signal her with his eyes. If his suspicions were true, there was a very fine pair of field glasses, or possibly a telescope, trained on them at this moment.

Her face cleared, dropping into an expression of such vacuous agreeability that he nearly laughed. "Yes, darling, of course you must do exactly that."

God bless her quick wits: she never looked at the mountain.

Morgan lifted Starshine's near forefoot and pretended to examine it. His men were now fully alert, with most of them watching him and the rest eyeing the mountains. He spoke as quietly as possible, all too aware of how well sound carried in these rocky canyons. "Lowell, call in the scouts. I want them off the mountain as fast as possible."

"Yes, sir."

"The rest of you—be prepared to turn around and ride, on

my signal." Thank heavens the canyon floor was not too uneven, as canyons went.

"Yes, sir," came the murmurs.

Lowell began to loudly whistle "Dixie," with a strong emphasis on the chorus line, "Away, away." Other men stretched, ostensibly casually, but a good many pieces of gear were double-checked in the process.

Morgan put down the last hoof and patted the proud Morgan mare, who accepted it as her due. "My dear lady," he said more loudly, "I believe it's time you rode again. Your mare could use the exercise."

"Whatever you say, dear," Jessamyn replied in ringing dulcet tones.

Morgan barely stopped his eyebrows from flying up. *Whatever* he said?

Recovering himself, he put her back up on Starshine and mounted Chaco. He was pleased to see that only a quarter of his men had also used this opportunity to mount up, reducing the chance of alerting any watchers. Still, the ones who hadn't mounted were either ex-cavalry or his wilder men, all of whom could mount a horse while it was in motion.

He glanced up at the mountainside again, calculating how far into the canyon he could safely take Jessamyn and his men if the knob was to fall, especially if it took out other ledges in a domino effect. The bighorn sheep were still eyeing that one spot, keeping their lambs on the mountain.

So Morgan signaled his expedition forward, albeit at a slower pace than before. Rutledge soon dropped down from the canyon walls and silently mounted up, then Calhoun, which returned his flankers. Now he only had to worry about his point men, who were the farthest away and hidden by a bend.

Then he saw first one man riding toward him, then another. Grainger and Little were coming back, but would they arrive soon enough? That knob could take out enough ledges to fill the whole damn canyon.

Morgan took Chaco farther, showing off his paces to buy time. Jessamyn matched him on Starshine for a perfect display of equestrian idiocy. Daly edged Rosie, the bell mare, back toward the expedition's rear, causing the mules to also retreat.

Suddenly the bighorn sheep flung up their heads and simultaneously sprang off the mountains, leaping from crag to crag like stones skipping across a pond. Little and Grainger broke into a gallop. Daly smacked Rosie on the rump, sending her bolting off with a loud neigh of disapproval, her bell clanging. The mules hastened to follow, their bells pealing in alarm.

A loud boom sounded and a puff of black smoke appeared on the mountain high above. There was a moment's silence as if Nature were holding her breath. Then, with an awful, grinding sound, the rocky knob started to crumble away.

Morgan whistled for an immediate retreat. His men wheeled their horses and galloped toward the remounts, ducked low over their saddles as if dodging bullets. He would be the last one out, of course, since he would not leave Grainger and Little behind.

But Jessamyn—dammit, not Jessamyn!—sat calmly beside him. "Go back, Jessamyn! There's no guarantee of safety here."

"No." Her lovely mouth was set firmly. Starshine shied and whinnied, eyeing the gravel falling like rain, but Jessamyn brought her easily back under control. "Not without you."

She'd risk her life to stay with him, no matter what she thought of him? Something shifted in his heart, leaving him speechless. If he lost her, his world would be obliterated. All the years he'd thought about vengeance—had been because he loved her. She had to live, no matter what happened to him.

Without a moment's hesitation, he slapped Starshine on the flank. The dappled bay startled in shock at her amazing ill treatment, nearly throwing Jessamyn, and bolted toward the rear. He fought to see Jessamyn through the cloud of dust and rocks, aching because he was helpless to protect her. He couldn't take her to safety, as his heart insisted. No, he had to stay behind, as duty demanded. But dammit, duty had never seemed so difficult before.

Overhead, the knob's remains smashed into the first ledge. With a roar, it, too, broke free and began to fall. An instant later, its corner took out another ledge and the pile of debris racing down the mountainside began to rapidly accumulate. Fist-sized chunks of rock started smashing into the canyon.

Stone dust was rising, thick and choking. Chaco bucked, neighing his challenge to the elements that tried to destroy him. Morgan fought to control him, wheeling him so he could watch Jessamyn's flight to safety.

God help him, he was in love with Jessamyn.

A boulder the size of a man's head crashed into the canyon and rolled across, breaking into fragments.

Little and Grainger finally reached him, bent over their horses' necks like jockeys, and they raced for safety. A minute later, the first ledge's remains crashed into the valley, its huge boulders bounding after the men like starving cougars.

By the time the dust settled, the canyon had become a giant gravel pit and the old Spanish trail had vanished.

But Morgan and Jessamyn, with their men and horses, were safe—although completely blocked from following Ortiz's map.

High atop the mountainside, Maggie took another pull on the cigar Charlie had used to light the dynamite, as she counted up the survivors through the field glasses. The heavy metal and leather contraption made her face hurt, which was red as a lobster from sunburn and peeling like a potato. Even her lips were split and bleeding. She'd warned Charlie that she needed to use lotion and wrap her face against the deadly sun at this altitude, where the air was so very thin. But no, he'd wanted to be able to see her face at all times, in order to be sure she wasn't flirting with Donleavy.

Charlie was insane. Ever since that day on the Rio Grande, he'd decided she fancied Donleavy, simply because she'd praised the man for catching a catfish. Why would she be interested in a hired gun, who obviously had no money? Ridiculous. Nonetheless, he watched her continuously—at least when he wasn't standing over Hazleton with some scatter-brained idea for moving faster through these mountains.

She was damn sure that if they'd been near any kind of civilization, Hazleton and his brother would have quit and left. But there was nothing up here, not even ranchers or the occasional prospector. Only Charlie had the all-important map, which he refused to let anyone else see. So they trailed along with him and bit their tongues on open objections, while occasionally subverting some of his more nonsensical ideas. She'd helped them once or twice.

Even his thugs were growing fretful. But Schmidt, their leader, was still completely loyal to Charlie and he kept the others in line.

"Good work." She closed the field glasses and put them away, careful to keep her back pressed to the stone. They were standing on a narrow ledge and it was a very long drop to the canyon floor below, after all. Morgan Evans had survived, thank God. Of course, if he hadn't, there'd always be other men to warm her bed, even if they wouldn't be of his caliber. "Pity you didn't kill the bitch, though."

Charlie shrugged, packing away his explosives into the small chest with the easy dexterity of long experience. "Doing so wouldn't have stopped Evans. He has the map, and as her husband and heir, he has the right to claim the gold."

Maggie sniffed and edged onto more stable ground. "She deserves to die after how she treated me at the lawyer's. She's poor as a church mouse yet she dared to be rude?"

Charlie straightened up. His eyes met hers from less than a foot away, as chillingly cold as the stone around them. "Is that the only reason you want Jessamyn Evans dead—or is it so you can take her place in Morgan Evans's bed?"

Maggie stomped her foot. "Charlie Jones, you're worth a damn sight more money than Morgan Evans is—and you'll have even more when we find that gold. Do you think I'd risk losing you for a few nights' fun?"

Charlie's eyes didn't warm at all. They blinked once, like a snake's, still fixed on hers. "No, you won't be poor again, which is why I'm here. You'll stay with the man who owns Ortiz's gold for as long as you live."

Goose bumps walked up her arms. She managed a shaky smile, as unstable as the canyon floor below. "I love you, Charlie."

One good thing about these mountains: the thin air kept his marital activities down to staying close. She'd started to make her way back to the horses when he spoke again.

"But I'll kill Morgan Evans the first chance I get, just to make sure you don't get any ideas about being a merry widow."

Chapter Seventeen

Jessamyn poured another dollop of condensed milk into Lowell's tea and handed it back to him, glad her hands were only slightly trembling. It was late afternoon and the entire party was gathered around the fire, pretending they didn't know Charlie's gang was miles away.

Her heart had stopped beating while she watched Morgan sit—just sit, dammit!—as rocks thundered down around him. She'd screamed at him to save himself; couldn't he see that his men were coming? But no one could hear her over the mountain's noise. It had seemed like an eternity until Grainger and Little had joined him. Heavens, how she'd loathed them for endangering him. It was the first time she'd ever wished an officer wouldn't do his duty, except Cyrus, whom she always worried about.

She was still shaken by the experience: the shivering limbs, the inability to think, the eagerness to take refuge in simple things like pouring condensed milk. Or how she'd hidden her face against Starshine's neck when she'd dismounted, taking comfort from her old friend.

Was it worth risking Morgan's life to rescue Starshine's kinfolk? Yes, because Socrates and Aristotle and Cassiopeia were risking their lives to guard them. She had to keep faith with them. She had to pray that another trail would open over the mountains, just as Morgan's expedition had come back together after the canyon closed.

The expedition had regrouped remarkably quickly after the avalanche. Even rounding up the animals had been easy, since Rosie never willingly went far from Daly. Once her initial shock wore off, she'd turned around and come looking for him, followed by the other mules and the horses. O'Callahan's two convalescent mares had arrived last, only a few minutes behind the others.

The men had immediately made camp, of course, in a good location downhill from the former canyon, on the edge of an aspen grove. They'd fussed over the animals and Dawson had provided an excellent meal, while everyone pretended they'd always planned to stop here so early in the day.

Now the horses and mules grazed as peacefully as if they'd never bolted across a mountainside, while men drank coffee and tea as if sitting in their grandmother's parlor. The loudest sounds were a woodpecker drilling somewhere in the forest's depths and the brook gurgling happily on its way to the Rio Grande.

Morgan's only words since the avalanche had been the minimum orders needed to make camp. He sat with the others now, whistling and watching some bustling chickadees. Jessamyn shot him yet another sideways glance and decided not to disturb him. She could ask him in private why he'd slapped Starshine.

"Would anyone else care for some milk?" she offered, holding up the small pitcher and glancing around at the others as she tried to match Morgan's savoir faire. Dawson's equipment included a sugar bowl and creamer, surprising since canned milk was the only cream available.

Back in Memphis, there'd be cream. But it was fever season there. She yanked her thoughts away from that danger.

Heads shook. "No, thank you, ma'am," said Mitchell, his Virginia drawl more evident than usual.

"Not unless Evans is goin' to wet his whistle with some," Lowell commented, catching Morgan's attention with the blatant plea to start talking.

He glanced around the circle. Everyone there was watching him, drawn by his blatant confidence. A wicked smile teased his mouth, that of a rogue with a trick up his sleeve. Her heart leapt in anticipation. "Jessamyn, would you please fetch the map?"

When she returned with the precious tube, he'd cleared a level space on the ground, covered it with a blanket, and ringed it with torches. She carefully placed the map there and weighted it down against the breeze, before stepping back to stand beside Morgan. He wrapped his arm around her waist and she smiled up at him a little tremulously. If the quest stopped here, at least she was with friends.

The men surged forward to stare at it. Some squatted down, while others stood tall to peer over their brethren's shoulders. All were very careful to keep their coffee and tea far away from the fragile parchment. Strong fingers traced their past travels, while deep voices rumbled recognition of landmarks. Finally they began to move back, their curiosity appeased.

Lowell looked up at Morgan, from where he alone still knelt beside the map. "What are the penciled lines, sir?"

"The correct compass headings. The pole has moved slightly since the map was drawn almost two hundred years ago."

"Looks like you can predict the headings now," Grainger observed from where he stood beside Little. It was the first time he'd spoken.

"Pretty much," Morgan agreed.

Curiosity hung thick in the air. Jessamyn tried not to give voice to hers.

Morgan glanced around with a devilish twinkle. "We know where we are on the map. If we head east along those peaks there"—he nodded toward the dreadfully jagged mountain ridge—"we should be able to come back onto Ortiz's route by using a compass."

There was still a chance to reach the gold? Joy bubbled up in Jessamyn's heart but she caught it back. Achieving that meant they'd have to pass that crenellated ridge with its dreadful abyss.

"We're about here on the map." Morgan set a pencil down very carefully.

Heads canted and eyes squinted as the teamsters considered this.

"If so, then the far mountains, the ones crowned by the double snowcapped peaks"—he pointed, making heads turn and nod in recognition—"should bring us back on approximately this heading. Eventually we'd emerge here."

He laid a set of toothpicks across the map. The last one pointed to a triangle mountain, just above the wavy circle marking the gold.

Jessamyn's head swam. They could still make it to the gold, despite what Charlie had done? It just might be worth taking that narrow trail.

Morgan glanced up at his scouts. "What do you know about this route?"

Little shrugged, his gaze pensive. "It's almost certainly longer than the Spanish route."

Grainger snorted. "Any road would be. But do you think it will lead to this mountain?"

"Maybe. It will take us to hot springs below a pointed mountain, beside a waterfall."

Joy surged through Jessamyn. "That's the route then. My aunt's diary mentions those hot springs."

"They're not on the map," Morgan pointed out.

"She said the men soaked out their aches there from working the gold, then rinsed off under the waterfall."

Morgan's eyes gleamed and a wave of interest rippled

through the men around them. "That's it then. A gamble—but it *should* work." He grinned like a buccaneer and began to roll up the map in its silk wrapper.

"There's one other way to tell the route," Morgan added. Jessamyn's head came up so fast to stare at him, she nearly dropped her teacup.

"Ortiz marked the trail's junctions with fist-sized chunks of white quartz, about the size of a brick. They're very hard to spot amid the granite, and rockfalls have claimed at least a quarter of them."

The men burst into excited comment, recounting the route and the rock formations they'd seen

"Ortiz made two maps?" Jessamyn whispered, her voice almost inaudible. There was still hope to rescue Somerset Hall?

Morgan nodded, his eyes fixed on hers. "I planned to tell you tonight."

She gripped his hand, exulting as fiercely as any Amazon warrior. "We'll be able to find the route without exactly matching Ortiz's viewpoint of the pyramid?"

"I believe so."

She kissed Morgan on the cheek, making the others cheer. He shrugged their applause off and started planning. "Have you scouted this trail, Grainger?"

"The beginning of it, yes. We did so yesterday."

"Where can we make camp tomorrow?"

Grainger and Little eyed each other in a silent conversation, before Grainger answered. "Nothing before the hanging valley—and we can't hope to reach it until two, maybe three, in the afternoon. It's very exposed to weather, which is why we didn't suggest taking it earlier."

Jessamyn frowned, thinking about thunderbolts bursting amidst nervous horses—with a precipice nearby.

"No caves?" Morgan frowned.

Grainger shook his head. "Only a few that might hold a

mule or two and not even enough of those for all of us. My guess is that a huge section of rock dropped off those peaks into the valley below, cutting them like roast pork. The hanging valley is the only hollow left."

"How's the valley's entrance?"

"Looks dry, as if the stream dives under the trail to make the little waterfall rather than running over the trail."

Morgan nodded, his gray eyes flint hard in his tanned face. "We'll start at first light tomorrow." His gaze swept over the men. "Normally we'd try to be off a slope like that by noon. I don't have to tell you why we want to reach that hanging valley before any thunderstorms hit."

The men rumbled immediate agreement. Jessamyn gulped, having expected more argument from them. Just how bad could a mountain thunderstorm be?

A yellow-bellied marmot basked in a patch of sunshine, utterly content despite the risk of falling into an abyss should he move a few inches in the wrong direction.

Jessamyn loathed him on sight.

The day's travel had been even more difficult than Grainger and Little had warned. Since the trail ran alongside and halfway up the peaks, it provided an excellent view of their steep sides, including the precipitous drop to the valley floor below. Given that abyss and the unstable rock leading to it, she'd have appreciated a broad trail, such as the width of Pennsylvania Avenue, where the Grand Army of the Republic paraded after the War. Instead this was at best only wide enough for two fully loaded mules.

Worse, there were times when only a single horse could pass, and rests meant leaning against barren rock while she prayed that no surprise bit of Mother Nature's malice—a sudden gust of wind, a bird bursting off its nest, or rain—would knock Starshine over the edge. Then she'd praise her beloved mare for being the best horse in the universe for walking so surefootedly on such a wretched trail. All the while keeping her ears open for any echo of Morgan's voice and praying he was still alive.

She hated to imagine the dangers that a thunderstorm could add.

The fat-bellied marmot's vantage point was one of those appalling narrow points. It was also one of the few sunny spots left, given the dark clouds rolling in from the west over the mountains where Charlie traveled. The storm would break over his party first, not hers.

"Almost there, Jessamyn," Morgan's deep voice rumbled comfortingly from ahead.

She swallowed and nodded, determined not to look over the abyss yet again at the coming storm. Starshine nudged her gently and they hastened on, with Jessamyn leading her mare.

The wind suddenly strengthened, announcing itself with a nasty yank at her hat. She ignored it determinedly, as if it were an ill-mannered guest. It would be a fearsome intruder on the western range, where Charlie and his gang were.

Suddenly the footing roughened and Morgan caught her by the hand. He tugged her into a nook beside the trail and she clung to him, still clutching Starshine's reins. "I would prefer not to walk along that ledge again," she stated emphatically, as if referring to a social engagement.

"Nor I, Jessamyn, nor I." His heart was pounding against her cheek. He lifted his head and tilted her chin up with a single finger. "See that cleft in the rock?"

She nearly laughed hysterically. Cleft? It was wider than most of the trail. "Yes, of course."

"The hanging valley is just inside it. I'm going back out to help bring everyone in."

Jessamyn shuddered. For the first time in over an hour, she dared to look directly into the distance. Thunderclouds were scudding across the sky like a giant's navy. Their shadows darkened the abyss and the distant range, where Ortiz's trail lay and Charlie traveled. Light burst from the top of one thunderhead to the next and Starshine whinnied softly. The hair on the back of her neck rose.

Morgan would stay on this death trap of a mountainside until he brought all his men in—or died there, trying to save them. Dear God, was gaining the gold worth risking a man's life?

Once again, she reminded herself of Somerset Hall and the brave people waiting there, for the escape that only Ortiz's gold could bring. But she cursed her own stupid pride for having rejected Morgan's money, which would have at least kept his life safe.

She plastered a brave smile on her face, as she'd learned all too well as an Army wife. "Yes, of course," she said stoutly. "I'll see to Starshine and help with the other horses."

"That's my good girl." He kissed her quickly—too quickly, cried her heart—and slipped past her. Almost immediately, he had to steady a nervous stallion.

The wind blew a pine branch up from the abyss like a warning of oncoming hell.

She kept her chin up and marched through the rocky cleft. Duty did have one great advantage, that of providing work to keep one's hands busy, if not one's mind.

Maggie shivered under the darkening sky. They were in a high-mountain valley, at the timberline's edge, full of fallen trees, rocks, and streams pouring past melting snow. There was nowhere close by to hide from a heavy rainstorm or ground soft enough to pitch a tent.

Hazleton, a wise man about weather at least, was arguing with Charlie. "If we don't take shelter now, sir . . ."

She added her voice to his. "Charlie dearest, perhaps if we turned back for just a few minutes to that cozy little . . ."

Charlie's gaze could have blown them both to smithereens.

"Turn around? Never! There's plenty of time to cross this valley before the storm hits. There's fifty dollars in it for you, Hazleton, if you succeed."

Hazleton hesitated, his eyes sliding toward where they'd come from. It would take far less time to find cover there than to cross the valley.

Charlie's hand dropped to his gun.

Hazleton's eyes narrowed before he managed to smile. "Glad to do whatever you say, sir."

Maggie tried to remember how to pray, gave up, and cursed her husband viciously but silently.

The men and animals streamed past Jessamyn into the little hanging valley, taking shelter in the cave under the western overhang. The horses were quickly herded deep into the mountain, with the mules next to them.

A slow roll of thunder echoed through Jessamyn's bones, like Morgan's voice inciting her to another round of hedonism. Where was he?

Rain began to fall in heavy splats, like bullets pinging on the rock.

She moved out to the valley's entrance, just inside the cleft, and kept watch for Morgan. How could she have asked him to risk his life by coming to this dangerous place? There would be no rest for her until he reached safety.

Lightning cracked across the sky, far too close to the trees on the mountaintop. The rain came faster, adding weight to the wind that carried it.

The last of the mules arrived and were taken to safety. But there was still no sign of Morgan. Rogue or not, she couldn't bear to lose him.

Someone shouted something at her but she ignored him. Another voice answered the first and she slipped past. No one else challenged her departure.

Now that she'd spent time with him, traveled with him, shared his bed, how could she stand to be without Morgan? He was so very handsome, with those gray eyes that gleamed like a dancing waterfall when he was contemplating mischief. Or the way lamplight struck red glints from his chestnut hair, like those in the depths of a wine glass. Those big, callused hands of his that could be so surprisingly gentle on her most intimate flesh. And his tongue. Dear God, the skills his tongue knew! And that beautiful voice of his, with the lovely Mississippi drawl, that could convince her to do anything at all . . .

Dear God, please don't let Morgan fall over the precipice. Let him live through this storm, not have his head trampled into a red ruin by a terrified horse. Let him come home safely into shelter and not be struck by a lightning bolt. Please, Lord, please . . .

Jessamyn edged farther out toward the abyss, the wind lashing her skirts around her legs. The fat marmot was nowhere in sight and the rain fell from the skies like a wash-day barrage under the black sky. Thunder boomed again and again like cannon fire.

O'Callahan burst out of the rain, running along the trail and leading one of his adopted mares. Startled, Jessamyn plastered herself against the mountain to let him pass. Rain blew sideways across the abyss into her face, almost blinding her, as lightning threw green streaks overhead.

Behind him came Morgan with the other mare. He was soaked to the skin and panting. But the mare was moving smoothly, only slightly wild-eyed from the storm. He'd been risking his life all the way back there for a horse that didn't belong to Donovan & Sons?

He yelled something and yanked Jessamyn against him. She gasped in relief and clung to him, scarcely able to stand against the howling gale. He was shouting something, his face distorted, but she couldn't hear him. She didn't much care either, not when she could touch him again. Her heart was pounding louder than the thunder.

He set first one foot, then the other, into motion. She went willingly, now that she was with him. Together they fought their way, along with the mare, into the hanging valley. Once there, O'Callahan took the mare's reins and edged his way through the crowd, taking both of his darlings to safety with the other horses.

Lightning sparked and sizzled. Morgan locked his arms around her, his chest heaving against her. Jessamyn hid her face against him, desperately seeking comfort from his presence. There was no room inside the storm to think, only to feel.

In the distance, she could just see the stone cleft, like a doorway to the trail.

Lightning crashed overhead and the ground shook. The horses stirred restlessly while the mules weighed the situation, still steady thanks to their lead mare's calm presence.

Suddenly a sharper boom sounded from above. Even the mules looked up at that and the horses whinnied. An immense fir tree fell slowly past the cleft, its branches flaming as it tumbled end over end into the abyss. Jessamyn closed her eyes and began to pray.

The sky was absolutely black over Maggie's head and the smell of oncoming rain nearly choked her. A lightning bolt blasted through the sky overhead. Behind her, one of the pack horses neighed in fright. An incredibly loud series of clangs announced that it had thrown off its pack and bolted.

Never mind the horse. She still had to find shelter somewhere.

Thunder rolled, shaking the ground. Lightning flashed again and again. More clangs and bangs, more loud whinnies and neighs that meant pack horses had panicked and disappeared.

One of Charlie's prized Thoroughbreds galloped past, its saddle empty and sliding to one side.

Hazleton's bay tossed him off then ran. He rolled and flattened himself into a small hollow, hiding himself from Nature's fury.

Beyond him, Charlie's big bay stallion reared and screamed, hooves pawing at the sky. Atop him, Charlie waved his hat in defiance.

By now, the lightning was coming so frequently that Maggie was almost blinded. Her horse bucked and reared, again and again, screaming its distress. She fought to stay on it, keeping her hands wrapped in its mane and her legs clamped around its sides. Dammit, she would not be thrown like all the others.

A lightning bolt erupted from the sky and struck a boulder less than fifty feet away. Her horse reared and twisted, bucking her off its back, and raced off. Maggie landed on her rear, forced to take one long look at the storm's fury. She hid her face in the mud as she'd learned on that hardscrabble farm and pretended she was a worm.

Cleaning up after the storm was more time-consuming than sorrowful for Jessamyn. They hadn't lost any men or animals, although it would take some time to dry the goods that had been soaked. Thankfully, they had enough spares to replace the few losses.

Recovering from her reaction to possibly losing Morgan was also something she wasn't ready to think about directly. For so long, he'd shown himself as a rogue and a scoundrel, interested only in pleasing himself. Yet over the past few days, she'd seen him as a decent—even honorable—fellow. Then during today's storm, she'd reacted as if he was her true love, worth risking life and limb for. Surely she had to have been momentarily insane, overset by a great thunderstorm. Surely.

Falling in love with Morgan would be disastrous, since he had no use for her outside the bedroom. Plus, his carnal usage of her would end once this trip finished. She nearly whimpered at the thought—and worked harder to help Dawson.

She'd simply have to make the most of what she had now with Morgan.

Later that night, when all was quiet and she'd gone to bed, Jessamyn was shocked awake by a draft inside her cozy tent. "What?" she grumbled.

A sleepy pair of eyes regarded her. "Aren't you hot?"

"Not my toes." Morgan had the disagreeable habit of assuming she was as hot-blooded as he was, and throwing off the covers to prove it. She stirred the blankets back into position and snuggled down again.

"You're very energetic," he observed softly, lying back against the pillows.

Something feminine inside her came alert at his tone. They hadn't often come together for carnal pleasures since they'd left the Three Needles, given the hard traveling and the altitude.

That evening, Morgan had announced that they could sleep a few extra hours, since the next day's route was much more protected, a decision greeted with many groans of relief. So Jessamyn was now more rested than she'd been on many previous nights, giving her the energy to savor what she'd almost lost that afternoon.

"I've had time to rest," she answered huskily and rolled over so she could be closer to him. A foolish notion, since they were separated by barely an inch.

"Perhaps your fingers are cold as well?" His voice deepened.

Her eyes widened. Her hands were usually tucked around him when they slept. How could they become cold?

He curled her fingers around his and kissed them, his mouth moving over them so softly his lips felt like an angel's wing. She shivered convulsively. "Morgan . . ."

"You're definitely chilly. The altitude must be playing games with your delicate flesh." He stroked her arm and his hand found her breast. His breath caught in his throat. "Or perhaps I'm a fool to be talking when I could be kissing you."

She chuckled at that and leaned forward, wrapping her arm around him. "You're a chatty one tonight."

He kissed her sweetly, lingering over the little details of tongue and teeth. She stroked his back, relearning in the most primal way what she'd nearly lost to the afternoon's storm. Her breasts tightened against him and she moved closer, eager for more.

He slipped one leg between hers and rubbed her gently. To her shock, its hairy, well-muscled length seemed made to excite every nerve on her thigh, with all of them ending directly in her pearl. She moaned involuntarily when her core clenched hungrily, sending a burst of liquid fire through her veins.

He groaned against her and kissed her neck. She arched for him, sighing, and raked her nails down his back. His cock jerked against her, sending lust rippling through her. Such a favorite activity that she might never have done again with Morgan.

In the dark, under the covers, the scent of Morgan intoxicated her—horses and leather, with the faint sharp tang of pine. Every part of his body seemed made to excite her—from the hard edges of his hip bones, to the arcs of his biceps and the great wall of his chest, down to the long sweep of his thighs and calves. Even the knobs of his toes.

His different textures lightly abraded her softer skin, driving her frantic with hunger for the sharp pleasure of his taut little nipples, or the neat mat of hair on his chest. Or the wilder, stronger hairs on his legs that sent shockwaves through her pearl and up her spine when he rubbed her calf. And then there were his intimate hairs when he rubbed himself over her, after sheathing himself in a condom—and she knew she'd feel those hairs exciting her folds as he rode her.

"Morgan," she moaned, half-insane from the heat pounding through her. "Please . . ."

He chuckled a little brokenly and slipped into her easily. She slid her leg up over his hip and clung to him, digging her nails into him. Her precious, precious man.

His cock jerked and he began to thrust rhythmically. She moved with him, her muscles fighting to hold him. Part of her wanted to remain like this but rapture beckoned.

He groaned something and his tempo increased. Hunger for him clawed at her. His shoulders hunched until he was driving in and out of her. She trembled and fought for the orgasm hanging so tantalizingly close. "Morgan, Morgan, Morgan . . ."

His hand slipped between them and pressed her clit. She gasped, bit down on his shoulder, and tumbled into orgasm. Climax was a swirling wave of pleasure that raced through every fiber of her being, cleansing and refreshing. An instant later, she felt him shudder in the grip of the same wave.

She fell asleep in his arms, still tangled together like cats before the fireside.

Morgan smiled ruefully down at his slumbering lady. Poor darling, she had to be exhausted. They'd journeyed twice as far as usual, in order to make it across that precipice. Then there'd been the thunderstorm, plus the cleanup—and now his attentions. He smirked.

But damn, he'd been terrified when he saw her out on the ledge, looking for him. If he'd had any doubts before about being in love with her, they were gone now. He was completely, passionately in love with Jessamyn Sophia Tyler Evans.

The question was how to win her.

To start with, he would stay close and keep other men away. He bared his teeth into the darkness. Like hell he'd let anyone else near her, now that he finally had her!

He'd have to prove that he was nothing like that bastard who stole her mother, of course.

And he'd bind her to him with as much companionship, protectiveness, and sensuality as he could. He grinned.

Starting now.

Chapter Eighteen

Three days later, Jessamyn rode down another mountain-side on Starshine. Eyeing Morgan's back with the broad shoulders and the lean waist so easily adapting to Chaco's movements, she almost wished she didn't have to find the gold. It might be better to travel with Morgan and his brave companions through these timeless mountains and forests for the rest of her life.

On this sunny day, they were riding beside a babbling brook through an aspen forest, whose leaves sounded a gentle welcome after the jagged granite they'd labored to cross during prior days. Birds darted and sang in these woods, while the ground was carpeted with wildflowers. An hour earlier they'd seen an elk herd and Lowell had tickled enough trout to provide an excellent dinner.

She sighed. Her bay mare flicked an ear back inquiringly and Jessamyn rubbed Starshine's neck. At least she'd have one last, long ride with her old friend.

Morgan held up his hand and Jessamyn brought Starshine to a halt beside Chaco. Behind them, the expedition stopped as quietly as such an assemblage of animals decorated with bells could. Morgan whispered without turning his head. "See the sunny clearing, just a little ahead and to the right?"

She reached instinctively for her field glasses.

"Don't move," Morgan hissed. "He's downwind from us and we don't want to spook him."

"Who?"

"He just stepped onto the grass."

She peered into the forest, through the trees, and gasped. A lynx stood like a king in the clearing's shimmering light, his tufted ears cocked. A collective sigh went up from the men behind her.

At that, the lynx vaulted into the air, his great paws seeming to whirl him like a top. He disappeared, leaving only the aspen leaves rustling behind him.

Leather creaked and groaned while metal jingled, marking the men's return to the everyday world. Jessamyn looked over at Morgan, her hand over her chest trying to still her rapid heartbeat. "Thank you, Morgan. I've never seen one before."

Morgan's gray eyes were as soft and reflective as the lynx's cloudy fur when he spoke. "He's the first one I've seen up close. Usually you only see their tracks, since they're nocturnal. Apaches say they're powerful magic."

She smiled at him.

They were still enjoying their shared wonder at the magical surroundings an hour later when someone coughed. "Afternoon, Evans. Care to take a look at the next downhill junction?"

Morgan's head swung around sharply. "What of it, Grainger?"

"You might want to see this river."

Morgan promptly kneed Chaco into motion and Jessamyn quickly followed.

The downhill junction, where the babbling brook met another, slightly larger rippling stream, looked exactly like many other watery confluences she'd seen over the past weeks: two water courses, with grasses, shrubs, trees, and rocky cliffs rising in the background. Its banks had the merit of being relatively flat and broad, offering a good trail for travel.

Little waited for them under a cliff, watching the stream tumble down the mountain. Morgan immediately rode over to him, pulling out his field glasses. Jessamyn followed close behind him, with Grainger a few paces back.

Silently Little pointed at a rocky promontory by the brook they'd emerged beside. A recent flood had undercut the bank, toppling a ponderosa pine across the brook, and exposing the cliff above. A small chunk of white quartz shone like a beacon ten feet above the ground.

Jessamyn whooped for joy. "It's the Lizard!"

Then Little pointed upriver at another rocky cliff, this one closer to the stream. Morgan inspected it through his field glasses. "There's another marker there. Anything else?"

Starshine pranced and caracoled, reflecting Jessamyn's exuberance.

Little turned in his saddle and pointed downstream. In the distance, Jessamyn could see a triangle mountain.

"Holy Moses," Morgan whispered and lowered his glasses. He'd gone white under his tan.

"Is that the mountain, Morgan?" she demanded. "Is it? Has Charlie been through here? The grass looks undisturbed." She wheeled Starshine, unable to contain her excitement.

Morgan shook himself and raised the glasses again. He answered her an instant later. "Yes, that does look like the triangle mountain—and no, Charlie hasn't been through here."

The rest of the expedition had piled into the little meadow now, bells ringing.

"Gentlemen, we're back on Ortiz's trail—and we've beaten Jones to this point!"

"Yahoo!" Hats were thrown into the sky, sending flocks of birds wheeling even higher. Horses neighed as their riders encouraged them to rear. "Hurrah!"

"Gentlemen, please restrain yourselves until we see the gold," Morgan shouted.

There was some slight grumbling but they quieted down. Jessamyn brought Starshine up beside Morgan again, her pulse racing through her veins. Where was Charlie? He'd had a day's lead on them, besides what they'd lost by the detour.

"We don't know where Jones is. So from here on, we travel as if we could fight at any moment. Grainger will command our rear guard."

Nods of acceptance went around. Jessamyn smiled privately. A Union officer to command Southern veterans? The War's wounds were healing.

"Grainger, Taylor served under Cleburne so he's the best infantryman we have. Taylor, you're with Grainger."

"Yes, sir." The quiet Arkansan nodded to Grainger, his scarred cheek all too apparent in the afternoon sunlight.

Jessamyn smiled approvingly. Cleburne had taught his men to shoot extremely rapidly and accurately, unlike most Rebel troops, who hadn't spent their minimal ammunition supplies on demanding, repetitive target practice. Taylor should therefore provide Grainger with excellent firepower.

"Lowell, you ride scout with Little."

"Yes, sir!"

"As for the rest of you, you know the drill. We travel hard but we don't risk the horses or mules. We should reach that mountain day after tomorrow, with luck."

Jessamyn mentally crossed her fingers.

Morgan, Grainger, and Jessamyn now stood well downhill from the triangle mountain, which was undoubtedly the pyramid shown on Ortiz's map. To be more precise, they stood on the edge of a box canyon, beyond rifle range from the pyramid.

Chills were running up and down Jessamyn's spine at how well the scene matched Ortiz's map.

Beside them, the Lizard became a waterfall and landed in the middle of a lake, which was fed by steaming hot springs on its eastern edge. Most of the canyon floor was a verdant paradise of ponderosa pines and grassy meadows. The Lizard emerged from the lake and wandered through the meadows, eventually exiting from the canyon's narrow southern entrance. The map did not show the box canyon, although it accurately portrayed the Lizard's journey as a small river down the mountain.

On their left lay a narrow ledge along the box canyon's lip, in front of a steep hill. This led to a goat's trail into the box canyon's eastern side, which was absolutely impossible to traverse except on foot and with extreme caution. Beyond the hill lay a rocky gully, glimpsed through a notch cut by a tiny brook, filled with a giant's playground of tumbled boulders, rocks, and gravel.

To their right—on the west—a somewhat broader trail led down the mountainside to the box canyon, the only route passable by horses.

The scene's geography was similar to that of an egg timer. The top bulb, in the north, was the triangle mountain. The lower bulb, in the south, was the box canyon. The Lizard was like the sand running through the egg timer—and out the bottom through a narrow hole. The canyon lip was the egg timer's waist. The rocky gully was the egg timer's eastern hip, while the broad trail was the egg timer's western hip.

"Which route should we take?" Grainger asked, keeping his voice low enough not to be overheard by the others. "The mules won't have any trouble with the western trail and the men can lead the horses down."

"Normally I'd agree with you. But this isn't a normal time and place, not with one of those damn fist-sized chunks of white quartz leading through the notch to the gully."

"Why couldn't the marker lead to the right, with the hot springs, and the grassy meadow beside the hot springs . . ." Grainger snarled, swinging his field glasses around to their left.

Morgan grunted agreement and focused his telescope downstream of the hot springs, looking for the Lizard's first major turn. A cliff sprang out at him and another damn piece of white rock laughed at him.

"Did you go into the canyon, Grainger?" Morgan asked, scanning the scene through his field glasses.

"No. We spent more time inspecting the gully, which has enough large boulders to conceal a full infantry corps."

Morgan shot a hard look at the other man over his glasses. "Rounded boulders, water-washed?"

Grainger raised an eyebrow. "How did you know?"

Morgan drummed his fingers on his guns. "The gully looks like an old placer mine, such as California's Forty-Niners worked, but . . ."

Jessamyn flinched at how well her lover knew his way around gold mines.

"But?" Grainger prompted eagerly.

"The cliff below us—where that cave is?—looks like it could be a hard rock mine. Ortiz gave us two maps and we have two possible sites for the treasure."

Jessamyn's stomach plummeted like the waterfall. "But Charlie's just behind us!"

"If I know anything about that greedy bastard, he'll be coming on fast, even if he kills his horses," Morgan agreed grimly.

"We only have time to investigate one of those sites before he gets here," Grainger warned.

"So we need to take our party to someplace defensible as quickly as possible, which means the box canyon. If we hold the eastern ridge, the pyramid's southern slope overlooking the canyon, and the canyon's southern entrance, we'll have a fortress," Jessamyn said decisively, internally smiling at how much she must sound like Cyrus.

The two men stared at her.

Morgan nodded. "Correct, Jessamyn. With luck, we'll have just enough time to investigate that cave before Charlie arrives."

"I can take some of the men onto the mountain and form

a defensive position," Grainger said, surveying the surrounding countryside. "Little and Lowell will move out into the forest, in case we need skirmishers. The other men will make camp, ready to do battle."

"Agreed. Jessamyn, there's only one cave in the canyon where the gold could be hidden. You and I will investigate it as soon as we have the animals safely corralled inside the canyon. If the gold is there, we'll fight Jones if necessary."

She gritted her teeth and nodded assent, despite a heaving stomach. Dear God in heaven, she couldn't bear to lose him. The thought of laying him out for burial, as she'd done for Cyrus, was intolerable.

Morgan smiled, a very nasty gleam in his eye. "If not, we'll let Jones see for himself, which should satisfy him that we're telling the truth."

The box canyon's cave was in its western wall and almost completely blocked by stones. Morgan and Jessamyn immediately started to pull them away.

Suddenly she shrieked softly and dropped one of the stones. Morgan spun to face her, his Colt in his hand.

"I'm well, truly I am," Jessamyn stammered, "but—look at this rock."

He turned it over so the sun struck it, showing the initials "EJ." Their eyes met.

"Edgar Jones. Uncle Edgar's initials. He was here, Morgan, he was here. Oh, the gold has to be in there!" She started scrabbling to pull the rocks away.

Morgan holstered his Colt, his expression shuttered, and started working faster.

As soon as the opening was big enough for her, Jessamyn started to climb inside but Morgan yanked her back. "No! You don't know what's in there."

"But—"

"You'll be lucky if it's only rattlers."

Did he want to lay his hands on the gold first? Perhaps she

was being foolish but so many rich men seemed to be obsessed by becoming richer. "I can use a gun and I'm smaller than you are."

"I'll go first, Jessamyn." His voice softened. "The cave's ceiling could come down on you."

She glared at him but grudgingly yielded. "Very well."

They threw stones aside until the gap was big enough to admit Morgan. He climbed in with his lantern and disappeared, shadows flickering from side to side in the depths. Jessamyn waited, trying hard not to dance in place like an impatient three-year-old. The sound of his boots died away into the chamber.

Finally he came back to the entrance. "Come on. It's a very deep cave and I haven't seen all of it."

She lit her lantern and followed, her heart so high in her throat that breathing was almost impossible.

The cave was quiet, with an entrance chamber large enough for six to dine comfortably in. It had obviously been used by animals although not often. The only sign of human life, beside Morgan's footprints, were old footprints that had been half-obliterated by dust.

"There's a passage through here," Morgan said. "But be careful; it's very narrow."

Jessamyn's throat tightened, almost choking her. She followed Morgan to the back wall, her heart threatening to thump out of her chest.

The ceiling here dropped to just above her height, making Morgan bend as he edged sideways through the passage. Jessamyn followed him and found herself in a room the size of his mother's drawing room. A gentle breeze drifted through it, teasing her hair. She gasped and started to fall to her knees. Morgan's iron-hard fingers gripped her elbow and dragged her upright.

Against the far wall, gleaming in the lantern light, lay a small golden nugget, the size of her little finger. Propped against the wall were a heavily rusted and dented steel helmet and breastplate, such as Spanish soldiers like Ortiz's men would have worn. Nothing else was there except dust.

Jessamyn swallowed hard, shaking a little. They wouldn't have the gold before Charlie arrived. They'd have to gamble it was hidden somewhere in the gully's rocky maze—and that they could find it before her treacherous cousin did.

"Are you well, Jessamyn?"

She nodded, not trusting herself to speak.

Morgan took her gently by the shoulders, his expression haunting in the lantern light. "Jessamyn, as long as Jones rides straight into this camp, he only knows about the written map, not the stone markers. If so, we can fox him. Can you help me persuade Jones that this cave—the one here—is the only one where Ortiz's gold could be?"

She stiffened her spine. "It will be a pleasure."

Ten minutes later, Jessamyn had washed up and was drinking tea beside the campfire. They'd made camp beside the small lake fed by the waterfall and the hot springs, in the center of the box canyon's horseshoe, which also gave them an excellent view of the wide trail into the canyon. Morgan was sitting beside her, also drinking tea, and they were both pretending to be grieving over the lost gold.

She was also trying not to stare at Charlie and Maggie's noisy ride into the box canyon, with gravel sliding into the canyon as they came down the trail. Clearly, Charlie was foolhardy enough to ride down that nasty slope rather than walk it. She prayed he wouldn't injure his mounts in the process.

Her eyebrows rose when the two of them thundered into the small grove, for all the world like a sheriff's posse come to arrest brigands. Good God, they and their equipage certainly looked travel-worn. And their poor animals . . . It was hard to tell who looked more starved, Maggie or the horses.

Charlie sprang down from his big stallion, throwing the reins at Mitchell, who happened to be nearby. Mitchell angrily opened his mouth, looked at the Thoroughbred more closely, and instead muttered, "Thank you, sir."

He collected Maggie's mount and headed for the picket line. Jessamyn would have to thank him later for gracefully taking those two wretched beasts somewhere they could receive food and cosseting.

"Good evening, Cousin Charlie," Jessamyn said as pleasantly as possible, clinging to a hostess's duty. Maggie had settled on a stool by the campfire, as if her legs wouldn't hold her up. "Would you care to join us for tea?"

She politely poured Maggie a cup of tea, which the female accepted eagerly.

"Where's the gold?" Charlie demanded. His eyes shifted from side to side with a rattlesnake's eagerness to kill. "Give me the gold or I'll kill you when you leave this valley."

Jessamyn froze, her cup halfway to her lips. Charlie's words held the ring of truth, not bluff.

"There isn't any gold in that cave, Jones," Morgan said flatly. "Your uncle took it all."

His eyes narrowed. "You're lying."

Morgan watched him narrowly, his hand not quite lingering on his knife. "Go look for yourself. You can follow our tracks in the dust and see what we did. Your uncle's tracks are there as well, but slightly muffled by dust and animal tracks."

"If you're lying, we'll kill you all," Charlie threatened.

Maggie held out her cup for a refill, which Jessamyn shook herself into providing. She also passed a plate of cheese crackers, which were greedily pounced on. If she wasn't mistaken, there was better than a week's worth of bruises on Maggie's face, besides hunger. Much as she hated the slut, she couldn't bring herself to let another woman starve.

Charlie's eyes searched them one more time then he and Maggie raced for the cave. Mitchell and O'Callahan were now walking Charlie and Maggie's horses, with water buckets handy. Daly paced beside them, offering them handfuls of hay.

A howl of rage came from inside the cave, then a woman's scream echoed through the rocks. Morgan was at Jessamyn's side in an instant, his hand on his gun. The rest of his men rose, their hands ready on their weapons.

Charlie and Maggie stormed out of the cave, white-faced and shaken, but the sight of his armed audience seemed to shock him back into sanity. "Evans. Dear Cousin Jessamyn. You were correct about the lack of gold." A bitter smile touched his mouth. "Do forgive us if we must leave immediately."

Morgan nodded coldly. "Certainly."

Charlie and Maggie left without another word. Mitchell and O'Callahan had brought the horses up, now cool and collected with noticeably fatter saddlebags. Their two unwelcome guests followed the Lizard downhill, their men edging down the hill to join them and all of them looking down-at-the-heels.

Jessamyn stood to watch them, with Morgan at her side and the rest of the expedition gathered behind.

"How much grain did you put in the saddlebags?" Morgan asked quietly.

"Two days' ration," Mitchell answered calmly. "We had plenty to spare. But those brutes can look after themselves."

Morgan grunted. "Aye, one way or another they will, either by honest hunting or by robbery." He turned to face his men.

"Double the sentries tonight and tomorrow for when our visitors return, hunting supplies or gold." He glanced around the intent faces. "The horses will be their first target. Corral them and the mules under the canyon's lip so they can't be stampeded. We'll search the gully for Ortiz's gold as soon as we can, to see if we must remain or can leave for Santa Fe."

There was a low growl of agreement, like a pack of wolves. Morgan smiled approvingly. "Don't take Jones lightly: his men are desperate and their guns, at least, are still in good condition. But we have an excellent position and will prevail."

A mile downriver at sunset, Maggie ate yet another trout, while dining with Charlie and the rest of their party. Behind them, the horses happily ate their first good meal in days.

No matter how good a cook Hazleton's younger brother was, he couldn't disguise the fact that, ever since they'd lost most of their supplies to the thunderstorm, their diet had been meat and hardtack. She had come to heartily loathe trout and ptarmigan, the principal meats. But she hadn't told Charlie that, any more than she'd told him how she loathed his fumbling hands on her breasts. Or how she hated bobbing her head up and down his limp cock, pretending it might be some use to a female. Or how much she wanted a real man with a stiff cock and the skill to use it for a woman's pleasure. It was an art that Morgan Evans had undoubtedly mastered, judging by that woman's contented, cowlike demeanor that afternoon.

She cursed under her breath. Goddamn bitch. The nerve of Jessamyn Evans, offering tea and cheese crackers in the middle of the wilderness, as if she were sitting at a shabby-genteel Memphis tea party! Maggie desperately wanted to be back at her own house in Denver, with the fine dining room copied from that castle in France. There she would show Mrs. High-and-Mighty Evans just who had true money and style!

Charlie tossed his fish bones into the stream. "Listen to me, men."

There was a rustle of wary interest. Maggie cocked an eye and started nibbling on a piece of hardtack.

"My cousin Jessamyn stole a map from me, which showed where my uncle found gold in these mountains many years ago."

Maggie snickered at the image of Charlie's ladylike cousin stealing anything. Then the rest of his sentence hit her. He was confirming his men's hopes that they were searching for gold? But less money for her would be worthwhile if it meant Mrs. High-and-Mighty Evans rotted in her grave sooner.

She lowered the hardtack in her eagerness to listen.

"That's right, men—gold." Charlie smiled at his thugs, clearly enjoying their approval. "They told me they hadn't found it but I know they're lying. I'm a miner and, as God's my witness, there was never gold ore in the cave they showed me. So we're going back to take the real treasure from them—so much gold that a man can't wrap his arms around it."

Chapter Nineteen

The next morning, everything was quiet—far too quiet for Jessamyn's taste. High to the east, the distant peaks glowed golden, but here on the canyon floor, the ponderosa pines' elegant world enjoyed a beautiful summer morning. A chipmunk busily ate breakfast under a chokecherry bush and a mourning dove sauntered over to a pond to drink, while the horses and mules lazed in their corral.

Seven A.M. and not a sign of Charlie or his thugs in this valley.

The men had been rotating back to the campfire from their sentry posts since dawn for a hot breakfast. Morgan, Grainger, and Lowell were just finishing theirs, the last to dine.

Jessamyn sipped her tea, determined to project a semblance of calm. Given the day's uncertain agenda, she wore her American Ladies' Mountain Dress, composed of a long tailored jacket with pockets, a matching skirt that ended at mid-calf, and Turkish trousers gathered in a frill above her boots. It maintained ladylike decorum, while simultaneously allowing her the freedom to scramble like a boy up the canyon wall, should necessity demand. Her Sharps carbine leaned against her chair, well within her reach. In addition, she wore her Navy Colt and ammunition for all of her weapons.

Little rode into camp on his mustang, humming an old

German drinking song that Grainger promptly joined in. Jessamyn blinked, but Morgan simply raised an eyebrow. "Care for some coffee, Little?"

"No, thank you, sir." He swung down and handed his horse's reins to Daly with a quiet nod of thanks, clearly planning to change horses.

"Where's Jones now?"

"Still watching us from that rise over there." Little indicated it with a jerk of his head.

Jessamyn frowned. The rocky promontory must be a quarter-hour, maybe a half-hour's ride south. "Why are they staying so far away?"

Morgan shrugged. "Probably because we have more men, all veterans, and this is a natural fortress." He finished his biscuit and honey. "Time to look for the rest of the gold."

"How do we go there?" Jessamyn asked promptly.

He frowned. "You should stay here, where it's safer from Charlie."

"Don't be a fool."

"Jessamyn . . ." he warned.

"Morgan . . ." she mimicked his tone.

Grainger chuckled. They both glared at him. He flung up his hands in a gesture of self-defense.

Morgan harrumphed. "Very well, you're coming with me. Grainger, I need someone to stand watch."

"Anyone you like," Grainger answered promptly.

"Lowell then."

The young man brightened.

Morgan set down his coffee cup and began to double-check his Colts. He shot a hard look at Grainger. "I'll be taking two men out of the line, almost equalizing your chances against Jones."

Grainger snorted in derision. "Evans, everyone here is a combat veteran."

Jessamyn rose to inspect her own guns.

"Jones's men are paid killers, proven to stop at nothing—

especially when gold's involved. Don't underestimate them. They must have something planned to wipe us out." Morgan shouldered a pair of bandoliers.

Charlie refocused his field glasses very carefully. Cousin Jessamyn and Evans, with the young pup, had now climbed out of the canyon and onto the eastern ridge. They must be heading for that rocky gully, with the tumbled boulders.

Realization smashed into him, making him curse viciously. All those rocks were the perfect sign of a glory hole edged by pay dirt, where the Spaniards would have mined the gold. But where in that maze was the treasure itself? Those self-righteous fools, Evans and Jessamyn, must know.

All he had to do was follow them.

Thank God he'd waited until daylight to attack, figuring they'd be prepared if he came during the dark. If he'd come before dawn, he would never have seen them heading into there.

He'd tell his men to carry on without him; hurling dynamite at these damned teamsters should send them to perdition very quickly. The thunderstorm had left them with plenty of dynamite and other armaments, at least, kept in locked metal chests and thus safe from frantic hooves. Unlike the food, which had been scattered, soaked, and pounded into the ground, until most of it either vanished or was useless.

He closed his field glasses. "Maggie?" The hell he was leaving her out of his sight at any time.

She continued to watch the fools, no doubt ogling Evans. "What is it, Charlie?"

He managed not to hit her. "Plans have changed and you're coming with me. The rest of you, carry out my previous orders. Anything you find in the campsite is yours."

"Even the woman?" Donleavy asked.

He didn't hesitate. If Jessamyn turned back to the box canyon, then rape was fitting punishment for having caused him so much trouble. "Especially her. Come along, Maggie."

*   *   *

Sweating from the hard climb over the ridge, Jessamyn quietly followed Morgan and Lowell into the gully, using every trick she'd learned from Cyrus, Abraham, and Socrates. She didn't want to alert any possible watchers by setting off a rockslide. The gully was a rippling piece of ground, perhaps ten acres in size, covered with broken boulders, interspersed with rocks and gravel. It cut into the mountain on the northern and eastern edges, as if the little stream had once been a bigger river. But so irregular was its base and so frequent were the boulders that it was impossible to obtain a good idea of exactly where trails or water had once traveled. In some places, a man could jump from boulder to boulder. In other places, two or more men could hide behind a pair of boulders.

They threaded their way through the maze of boulders until they came to the gully's northern edge. Here, a large chunk of white quartz, almost as big as a man's head, blazed halfway up the ridge. The sight of such a clearly man-made object sent a frisson shooting down Jessamyn's spine. The quest's end was in sight.

Morgan's mouth curved mirthlessly at her reaction before he turned to Lowell. "You can take up watch anywhere along this hill."

Lowell's pale blue-gray eyes coolly assessed the gully before returning to Morgan. Given his easy grace with rifle and guns, he appeared every inch a warrior, not the coltish adolescent he'd occasionally seemed before. "Understood. Good luck, sir."

He shook hands with Morgan, then Jessamyn. "Ma'am."

"Good luck to you, too, Lowell." Forcing her uncertainties aside, she lit a lantern and followed Morgan between a pair of boulders.

*   *   *

Rifle at the ready, Lucas stood amid the pines north of the box canyon and listened hard for a bird. Any bird. Flocks of pine siskins should have been flittering through the trees, singing their delicate songs. Steller's jays should have been making a ruckus with their usual variety of calls, anything from a soft coo to a hawklike screech. Woodpeckers should have been drumming on the trees, like the percussion section of a great symphony orchestra.

A golden-mantled ground squirrel darted out from under a clump of fleabane and almost ran into his boot.

He froze, eyeing the little creature.

It stared at him for a moment, whiskers quivering, then dashed away into the grass.

He spun to the west, facing where it had come from, and listened. A moment later, the flat crack of a Spencer rifle sounded through the hills—and was followed by three more rounds in quick succession.

Lucas smiled faintly, the old battlefield calm wrapping him again. Rutledge had won the bet of who'd fire the first shot against Jones's thugs.

Another shot sounded, and another. Someone was shooting back at Rutledge with a Henry rifle.

Shots rang out to the south, from below the canyon, where Mitchell was stationed.

Lucas started edging back toward the canyon rim, where he'd be at the center, readily available no matter where the coming battle would rage hottest.

A sudden boom shook the earth to the west.

Dynamite? If Jones's thugs used dynamite, anything they tossed would cause massive damage—unlike firing a rifle, where a man could hope to only be grazed.

With the numbers in his favor, he'd hoped to come through this battle with only a few men wounded. Now he prayed at least one of his men would survive.

Wood cracked loudly then creaked and groaned. It fell,

making the ground shake as if giants walked again. A man's scream rose but was suddenly cut off.

Lucas hefted his rifle and began to run to the west, heading for a fight to the death.

Morgan and Jessamyn threaded their way through the maze of boulders toward the white quartz blaze. At the end of this rocky labyrinth, they found a cave large enough for two people to stand upright, although completely invisible to anyone in the gully.

The cave bent sharply, dropped, and quickly narrowed into a tunnel, barely high enough for Morgan to walk in and only wide enough for one person at a time. Its edges were very smooth, clearly worn down by water over centuries, although not a trace of damp could now be seen.

Jessamyn followed Morgan silently, the darkness weighing down on her until old nightmares reared up. She held on to her faith in Morgan like a lifeline.

But he wasn't the dashing young cavalier, slender and bold, she'd once fancied in Memphis. She'd grown to know this man on the long journey west, with his light-filled eyes that saw everything moving past, the crow's-feet from gazing at the far horizons, the laugh lines from chuckling at his men's jokes, the strong jaw that could stubbornly set—and not relax until a dozen men and their animals were safely across a raging torrent. This was Morgan, who'd sheltered her in his arms against thunderstorms and helped her cross mountains. Morgan, who'd expertly honed her sharpshooting skills. This was a man to ride the river with.

She bit her lip, the small pain shaking her into a different awareness, like the lantern Morgan carried. He'd always done what he promised on this journey, even when he didn't believe in the gold. Surely she could place her reliance on him. Surely.

Suddenly the tunnel widened out into a larger chamber,

which the lantern's beams didn't fully illuminate. The air was still and very dry, as if patiently waiting for something.

Morgan straightened and turned, swinging the lantern to see more fully. The walls and ceiling beyond the tunnel were rough-hewn, as if cut by stone axes, and sparkled, like a million tiny stars. His voice was rough when he spoke. "Light your lantern."

Jessamyn fumbled with the matches in her haste and her carbine bumped against her hip in its sling. Finally her lantern caught with a faint hiss, revealing the chamber's full dimensions.

A small dais lay at the light's edge. Nuggets of gold were piled on top of it, a yard tall and almost two yards wide. Dear God in heaven, it truly was more treasure than a man could put his arms around.

Morgan had brought her safely to it. The man who had slammed the greatest betrayal into her face had also brought her safely to her family's greatest treasure.

She took a step forward and another. "The gold," she breathed and sank to her knees. "How did it get here?"

Morgan came up behind her, like a column of protectiveness. "The boulders outside? They're water-worn, what you'd see in a placer mine. Ortiz must have noticed raw pieces of gold threaded between them, what miners call pay dirt. When he and his men mined them, they worked their way into the cave above us and down the tunnel very easily, still following the pay dirt."

"But this chamber?" Morgan was explaining mining techniques to her. Surely anyone planning to steal the gold from her wouldn't do that, lest she be able to poke holes in their scheme.

Complete trust built up with every word he uttered, as if welling up from the stone around them.

Morgan's hands rested on her shoulders. "This is a glory hole, a pocket of gold easily worked by a handful of miners.

When Ortiz found it, he hacked away at the rock until he took everything easy to find. See how rough the ceiling and walls are when you move away from the tunnel?"

A dull roar resonated through the very walls and floor around them. The ground trembled then shuddered under them. The nuggets rattled and dust sifted down from the ceiling. Jessamyn fell back against Morgan.

A cloud of gunsmoke rose over the hill, shutting off any view of the mountain and canyon beyond. Shots rang out almost continuously, especially from those two blazing Spencer repeaters. Maggie cringed, thinking of the time she'd seen a single Spencer shut down all traffic on an entire block.

But this was far more deadly. Where had Morgan come up with so many good fighters? Could Charlie's gang hold them off long enough for Charlie to snatch the gold?

Then dynamite roared again to the west, sending tree branches cracking. The guns fell silent for a moment, as if holding their breath, and one of Morgan's men shouted a warning.

She grinned. Good, Charlie's fellows were doing well.

Charlie growled from beside her. "Where the hell are they?" His field glasses bumped into her shoulder.

She rolled her eyes, certain for once that he couldn't see her—and punish her for impertinence. A hawk couldn't find a mouse amid these rocks—and one man couldn't find another here either.

"Do you think they are here?" she asked, careful to sound timid. Dammit, once they had Ortiz's gold, she was going to find herself a good-looking, stupid man who knew how to fuck and have him kill Charlie. Maybe she'd marry him afterward and maybe not. But at least then she'd have the gold and be free of this wretch.

He took the bait and launched into a display of his reasoning. "Of course they are, since their sentry was posted on that ridge. But there's no telling which godforsaken boulder hides their warren. We'll just have to wait and see where they emerge."

In the sun, with little food. Maggie blew out a breath and tried to find a comfortable position. At least they'd be close to the gold while they listened to Morgan's men being destroyed.

Jessamyn ducked instinctively, throwing her arms over her head. Morgan hauled her close against him and she leaned gratefully against his warm strength. "What is it?"

"Goddammit, Jones is using dynamite!" His mouth was set so hard, white grooves bracketed it.

The ground stopped shaking but dust continued to drift down. A few nuggets tumbled off the dais.

"We have to get out of here before the roof comes down." He released her and she turned toward the tunnel, refusing to look at the gold again, the treasure that could keep Somerset Hall free from greedy intruders.

"Put out your lantern and follow me closely, Jessamyn. We may be alone against whoever Jones has watching the gully."

They went silently back up the tunnel, slowly at first. But when another roar echoed through the stones and the ground heaved, Morgan fastened her hand onto his weapon belt. Her knuckles brushed against his back through his coat and shirt.

They ran up the tunnel in a cloud of dust, stopping only at the sharp bend for Morgan to put out his lantern. Dust sifted out of the walls and Jessamyn kept tight hold of Morgan.

"Ready? You'll have to be as quiet as possible," he whispered, chambering a round into his Spencer.

"Yes." She needed to talk to him about why he was behaving like this, and about Memphis nine years ago. She prayed they lived long enough to do so.

She choked back a cough and he patted her shoulder. "Good girl. Come on."

They crept up the last stretch as silently as they'd ever done on a childhood quest. It brightened at the top, showing the cave with the boulders along its entrance. Now they could hear muffled gunfire, making her reach for her Colt. The ground trembled slightly and a horse screamed in panic, echoing through the hills.

Jessamyn reluctantly stayed hidden in the tunnel, while Morgan scouted the cave. Her heart was pounding loudly enough in her chest that she couldn't hear the shooting clearly. If anything happened to him, she'd kill Charlie herself.

He touched her shoulder. Come on, he mouthed.

She nodded and followed him. He paused beside one boulder, farther north from where they'd entered.

A bullet suddenly pinged against the hillside just above the cave. Morgan immediately threw Jessamyn to the ground and covered her with his body. "Lucky shot," he hissed, almost silently. "He can't know exactly where we are."

"Evans!" Charlie shouted from a distance. "I know you're hiding in that hill. If you tell me where the gold is, I'll let you and my cousin live."

"Liar," she hissed bitterly. She wished she could savor the feel of Morgan's body this one last time. She'd far rather feel the pounding heat of carnal passion than the cold clarity that always possessed her when gunplay was needed.

"Agreed." He rolled off her slowly and came up into a crouch, rifle in hand. Horses bugled their alarm within the box canyon, their stampeding hooves a counterpoint to the gunfire.

She gathered her feet under her and matched his stance, eyeing the world beyond the cave. Her Sharps carbine threw a much heavier round than his Spencer repeater and could shoot farther and more accurately. On the other hand, he could fire thirty rounds per minute compared to her ten rounds. She was proud to be his gun partner. "I wonder if Maggie's with him."

"I hope not."

Something slithered and a few pebbles rattled. Both of their heads came up, then Morgan and Jessamyn heard Lowell gasp in pain. "Poor boy," she whispered. "Can we help him?"

He nodded, his mouth set, and crawled out, staying very low. Moments later, he returned, dragging a white-faced Lowell behind him. Lowell's right leg was broken, midway between his hip and knee, bending at a dreadful angle against his trousers. His face was white with pain. "Sorry," he whispered. "The dynamite rattled the ground and I fell between two boulders. After that, I could never get off a good shot at him."

Morgan started to lay his rifle down and Lowell jerked away. "Don't! There's no time to set it an' I can still shoot. You deal with them out there and I'll wait here. Okay?"

Jessamyn bit her lip at the young man's courage.

"Deal," Morgan said solemnly.

Another round burst against the hillside. "Evans! Do you want to live or die like a rabbit?"

Morgan's eyes met hers, brilliant with fury. "Jones must be on the other side of the gully on the little rise, the one place with some bare ground around it. He has us pinned down and there's only one way to stop him."

She waited for his orders, watching him steadily.

"It'll take a pincer movement. One of us has to draw his attention, while the other one goes up to the knob. I'll head for the knob."

"No! I love you, Morgan. You will not do anything stupid." Dear God in heaven, where had that announcement come from? But it was the truth.

He stared at her, a slow smile dawning on his face. "You surely know how to pick your moments to speak up, Jessamyn, when a man can't respond as he'd like."

She swallowed hard, torn between encouraging him and continuing to utter necessities. "You're too tall to hide behind many of these boulders. I, on the other hand, could do so easily."

"No!"

"Can you think of a better alternative?"

"No," he snarled, his fingers tight around his rifle. "No. Very well, I will distract him with my voice."

She relaxed slightly. "How do you want me to move?"

He frowned, agony showing briefly in his eyes. "Work your way around the gully to the north, until you reach that knob. From there, you can fire on Jones. He probably won't let you get in a good shot at him but you should be able to keep his head down. Once you're in position, I'll attack him from the other side."

She nodded, a warm glow growing in the pit of her stomach despite her nerves. It was the same precise instructions he'd give to his men, the same he'd given her as a childhood companion. They were placing full reliance on each other again. "Of course."

Suddenly he captured her chin with one hand and kissed her hard and fast. Startled, she barely managed to kiss him back before he lifted his head.

She kissed her fingers and laid them against his hard lips. His eyes closed, a silver tear touching one corner, and a muscle ticked hard in his jaw. Then she crept quickly to the cave's northern end before her courage failed.

Dynamite boomed again and gunfire continued to roll across the hills. Another bullet cracked into the hillside. "Evans!"

She eyed the closest boulder outside the cave, considered the sightline to Charlie's likeliest hiding place, and dashed for the rock.

"Jones, good fellow, why are we fighting?" Morgan called. He must have slipped out toward Charlie. He'd deepened and darkened his voice as well, until it seemed he spoke in a fine palace rather than a rocky gully. "Surely there's enough gold for all of us."

"Evans, just tell me where the gold is!" Charlie shouted.

"A partnership, cousin," Morgan purred, "A partnership."

Partnership? At least Charlie found the idea as astounding as she did, given his silence. Jessamyn ran for the next patch of shadow.

"With my Silver Queen mine in Arizona and your Firelight mine, we'd be the richest men west of the Mississippi."

"Charlie darling, Morgan's offer is intriguing," Maggie commented. The gunfire was quieter now and some trick of acoustics made her voice as clear as if they stood in the same drawing room.

"Perhaps . . ."

Jessamyn dived behind another boulder, panting.

"New York bankers would beg for our business. Evans & Jones," Morgan crooned.

"Jones & Evans!" Charlie snapped.

Jessamyn gathered herself for the next dash.

"We'd have to spend a large amount of time with Morgan," Maggie mused. "Dinners . . ."

Jessamyn rolled her eyes and ran.

"Why, we could build houses that would make Vanderbilt envious."

"A great house," Charlie mused.

Jessamyn squeezed between a boulder and a pine tree, grateful she wasn't wearing a habit.

"With immense bedrooms . . ."

Would the woman ever think of something else? Jessamyn considered how to reach a small clump of pines.

"We could take a tour of Europe together to shop for our houses," Morgan urged seductively. "Just the two of us, a partnership in action, traveling through France and Italy acquiring the best of everything . . ."

"Sharing the same hotels . . ." Maggie dreamed.

"You just want to sleep with Evans!" Charlie roared. He slapped her, the sound carrying clearly across the gully. Maggie screeched, a noise that sounded more like pain than fury.

Jessamyn looked across the gully but all she could see were

boulders and more boulders. If she headed directly for Charlie, he'd probably shoot her. She really shouldn't care if Maggie was hurt . . .

She cursed Charlie under her breath and picked up her pace, heedless of the risk to herself.

"Of course I do!" Maggie screamed. "He's more man than you'll ever be."

How stupid can you be, Maggie? What husband will tolerate that from his wife? Jessamyn dashed between three pairs of boulders without stopping.

"You think I'm not a man?" Another slap followed by another, this one a lighter weight than the first. Charlie yelped. "You bitch, you kicked me!"

"You're damn right I did, you Missouri ass!"

Charlie belted Maggie and she screamed long and loud. She fought back, though, in a contest as noisy as it was apparently bloody.

Jessamyn ran for the knob, heedless of discovery. She could not stand idly by and listen to a woman being threatened. In the distance, gunfire splattered from the box canyon.

She burst out onto the rocky overlook, gasping for breath, and immediately looked for Charlie. On the gully's western rim, she could see two people fighting hand-to-hand—Charlie and Maggie—their heads barely visible above rocks and sagebrush.

"This time, Maggie, I'll teach you to be quiet and stay with me," Charlie roared.

"Help me, please!" Maggie croaked.

Down below Jessamyn could see Morgan weaving through the gully. Suddenly he broke into the open and started running directly toward Charlie and Maggie.

Jessamyn was dumbfounded. Only a chivalrous idiot would risk his own life to save Maggie Jones. But, by God, if Morgan was going to be a fool, then she'd lay down some covering fire for him. Nobody would hurt her man, if she had anything to say about it.

She cursed the angle, which made it nearly impossible to hit Charlie. Perhaps if she blasted some stone chips at him, she could slow him down until Morgan arrived. Perhaps . . .

She settled the heavy Sharps into her shoulder and slowed her breathing, striving for greater accuracy. The front sight came into focus, and the top of Charlie's head in the far distance. She squeezed the trigger gently.

Missed! No time for regrets.

She fired again, throwing up stone chips from the rock in front of him. That made him flinch—excellent.

She fired rapidly, chipping away the boulders, and reloaded quickly, peering through the smoke. But Charlie was still alive and Morgan was still running, where her villainous cousin could shoot him. Why the hell did he have to be such a gentleman, as to risk his life for any female no matter how much of a slut?

Morgan vaulted onto Charlie's stone bulwark, just as Charlie whirled into the open, his rifle raised. Morgan fired once and Charlie dropped bonelessly into the dust. Then Morgan jumped down to where no sound had been heard from Maggie for far too long.

Jessamyn slung her carbine over her shoulder and ran down the gully, every sense focused on Morgan.

She stepped over Charlie's body without a second glance, barely conscious of a few spurts of gunfire near the box canyon. Behind the boulders was a trampled, sandy hollow, which had once been covered by grass, wildflowers, and sagebrush. Now it was bloody and flattened, with a woman's body lying far too neatly in the shade of one boulder. Morgan straightened to meet her, keeping her away from the tragedy.

Jessamyn flinched. "Is she still alive?"

Morgan shook his head. "No, he broke her neck." He wrapped his arm around Jessamyn and she laid her head against his shoulder. It was finally over. But she couldn't be glad Maggie had died in this way.

"Come, let's go back to Lowell," he said gently. She sighed

and matched step with him. All was quiet on the other side, even the horses.

When they were halfway across the gully, a shadow fell across the sunlight through the notch in the hill. Morgan and Jessamyn looked up quickly, their hands automatically going to their rifles.

Grainger stood there, a bloody rag tied around his head, and Little at his side. Mitchell, Rutledge, and Calhoun's heads and shoulders loomed against the sunset. They raised their rifles overhead in a roar of delight and ran forward, shouting "Donovan! Donovan! Donovan!"

Later that evening, there was little talk among the exhausted men gathered around the campfire, which now resembled a small hospital. Thankfully, none of their own were dead, although Taylor was very badly injured and most of them were wounded in one way or another. Lowell's broken leg had been set and Little was whittling him a set of crutches. Jessamyn's own badly bruised shoulder was now in a sling, thanks to long use of her Sharps.

She took a careful sip of her tea, eyeing the battered scenery. She was very tired after the long day but still fretting.

All of Charlie's men were dead, as befitted brutes who'd used dynamite as weapons. They'd even thrown explosives into the box canyon with the horses. Thank God Grainger and the men had pulled up camp that morning, packing all the gear under the overhang. They'd corralled the horses as thoroughly as possible behind the waterfall. By the time Charlie's men had finally managed to stampede the horses, they'd already thrown so much dynamite that they'd almost completely closed the narrow southern entrance where the Lizard flowed out and the horses and mules had simply run in circles around the canyon. Only two of the horses were dead and one of the mules, thanks to that. O'Callahan had spent much of the afternoon tending the others.

Mercifully, they'd have time to heal before the heavy snows came in September and closed the trails. They'd be well enough to take the gold with them by then. She didn't know how they'd fetch the horses out of Memphis any sooner.

Morgan touched Jessamyn's good shoulder. She glanced up at him and he inclined his head. She rose silently and followed, easily able to see him by the light of the full moon.

He led her to the lake's far shore, near the waterfall. It was a beautiful night, serene and peaceful with the moon gleaming on the lake and flowers shimmering amid the grass. Even the great ponderosa pines added their gentle mystery, rising tall but standing far enough apart so they appeared to be protective giants above a fairytale parkland. Water lapped against the lakeshore and the waterfall's roar was a muted hum, reminding her that tomorrow they'd begin working to bring the gold out of the cavern.

"You're probably worrying about Aristotle and Socrates," Morgan drawled, his normally melodious voice harsher than usual.

"Plus Cassiopeia and the horses," she agreed, studying him. She was glad he'd brought the subject up now; otherwise, she'd have worried about them all night. If they waited until all the men healed to leave, fever season would be over in Memphis and who knew if her friends would still be alive and the horses safe? Word had to go to them quickly—and money, if at all possible.

"I asked Grainger if his family's stud farm could move the Somerset Hall horses to safety."

"What?" A bubble of hope began to grow in her chest.

"He agreed with, I might add, a rather wicked amount of alacrity. So he and Little will make a fast run to Santa Fe, leaving tomorrow morning. Once there, he will order his family's stud farm to move the Somerset Hall horses to safety. We'll repay him when we bring the gold out. Aristotle, Socrates, and the rest will accompany the horses, of course."

"Thank God, thank God." Jessamyn leaned her head against his chest, almost sagging in relief. "I'll have to speak to them before they go, try to express my gratitude."

"Certainly you'll want to." He touched her cheek lightly and stepped away. "But there's more I need to say, Jessamyn."

He bowed his head, his fists clenching and unclenching at his side. She blinked, startled by his discomfort. What could make him so uncomfortable? Was he upset that she'd declared her love for him? She hadn't had time to be nervous before, thanks to the fight, but the delay seemed to triple her misgivings now. "Morgan?" she breathed. "Did I say something wrong?"

He shook his head fiercely, silencing her. She stared at him, unable to guess what he wished to discuss.

Then he blew out a long breath and lifted his face, gray eyes fixed on hers. "You accused me of avoiding my responsibilities by becoming a teamster, of never marrying and settling down. You said I was a rogue and a scoundrel without a care in the world for anyone but myself."

She reached out to him. "Oh, Morgan, I'm so sorry I ever thought such things! Can you forgive me?"

"Of course." He smiled at her, the moonlight making his face's harsh planes look like a statue of King Arthur's knights. "Because I roamed to avoid seeing you with Cyrus."

She couldn't believe her ears. She'd always thought he hated her so much, he wanted to have her far away from him. "What?"

"I never married because I never found anyone to look at me the way you looked at Cyrus. God knows I never looked at anyone else the way I've always regarded you, with love and passion—and yes, respect."

He lifted her hand to his lips. "Will you marry me, Jessamyn, and live with me forever?"

Joy ran through her veins, like liquid gold. "Oh yes, Morgan, I would be honored to be your wife."

He kissed her hand and gathered her up to him, his arms wrapping around her waist. "Dearest Jessamyn."

He tasted her lips gently at first, as if she were a delicate virgin who might shrink before a man's bold assault. She answered him sweetly, her tongue touching his delicately to explore his different textures. He groaned softly and pressed her closer. She murmured his name into his mouth. Her love.

He claimed her hungrily, pressing himself boldly against her. She threaded her fingers through his hair, enjoying the promise of his hot, hard cock against her hip.

"I have land in California that would make a perfect horse farm. We can take your horses there, the gold of Somerset Hall," he whispered against her throat, "and build a country estate for ourselves there."

She pulled back. "In California?"

"They'd be safe from yellow jack there."

Doctors' stories ran through her head, told by military doctors and riverboat captains. California, where her friends would be safe from yellow jack? Where the horses could run on broad fields of green grass below the tall Sierra Nevadas? She saw herself and Morgan, laughing as they galloped over their land toward their home, a white-columned building like Longacres. "Oh yes!"

His gray eyes were heavy-lidded with passion. "And save Somerset Hall for our children, for when someone knows how to cure yellow jack." His eyes flickered to where the pulse beat in her throat. He lowered his head again, his hand gently caressing her waist.

She fought to think against the rising carnal tide in her veins. She gently put her hand on his forehead, stopping him. "Where is your home?"

He shrugged, pulling her close enough to slide a leg between hers. She hadn't changed back into skirts. "I don't own one. I have apartments in Denver and San Francisco."

"Can I build one, besides the country estate?" He needed

something solid and impressive, as befitted his position in society. This conversation was sounding even more delightful.

He regarded her quizzically. "Is that something you'd like to do?"

"Oh yes," she cooed, considering the joys of finally setting down roots after nine years of living on either Army posts or charity.

"Then certainly you can build the town house of your dreams," he said gallantly. He nuzzled the back of her ear, sending a frisson down her spine.

"In San Francisco, I think," Jessamyn said emphatically, locking her knees against the urge to drag him down onto the grass in the moonlight.

Morgan chuckled softly, the sound rumbling through her bones. "Lordy, Jessamyn, how happy my father would be to hear you say that. He always wanted me to have a wife who valued life west of the Mississippi."

Chapter Twenty

Denver, October 1872

It was the very best of days. The weather was perfect, a brilliantly crisp autumn afternoon in late October. Inside the church, the organ was rippling through baroque preludes like waterfalls pouring down a mountainside, while the final guests were seated.

The wedding itself was to be everything Jessamyn's father and Morgan's parents had ever planned, as overseen by Cousin Sophonisba and Great-Aunt Eulalia. The largest church in Denver was barely enough to hold all of Jessamyn's Army friends, Morgan's business associates, and their families from Tennessee and Mississippi. A grand banquet would follow and dancing until dawn at the best hotel in Denver.

Jessamyn waited patiently in the church's anteroom, her heart soaring like a lark. Elizabeth Anne Spencer, Jessamyn's best friend as an Army wife, and her two daughters fussed over the yards-long train of Jessamyn's wedding dress. Michael Spencer warily watched the women from as far away as he could stand and still be ready to escort Jessamyn. She'd asked him to give her away to Morgan, since Cyrus and Michael had pledged to look after each other's families should the need arise. The curate stood next to him, casting an approving eye over them all.

A tree shifted in the breeze outside, opening a golden beam through the stained glass. Suddenly she could feel Cyrus, as if he'd touched her on the cheek with the sunbeam. She smiled and shaped a kiss. The tree shifted again and he was gone.

She brought herself back to the present and looked over her shoulder, sending her hat's trailing ribbons and her ringlets sliding forward. "Are you finished yet?"

"Not if you do that!" yelped Naomi, the youngest Spencer girl, and leaped up. "You must stand perfectly still."

Jessamyn rolled her eyes and met Michael's amused glance. Naomi quickly restored Jessamyn's coiffure to order and all three women stood back for a final inspection.

The wedding dress was a masterpiece of French craftsmanship, whose creation had dictated the wedding date. A princess tunic in Nile green silk, the season's most fashionable color, was swept back into a myriad of tiny flounces which extended into the train. The skirt was of the same Nile green silk, with matching flounces, while her small hat trailed green ribbons. Her eyes twinkled hopefully at Morgan's likely reaction to her undergarments.

Elizabeth Anne and her two daughters circled Jessamyn like Indian warriors eyeing a wagon train. Jessamyn grinned at her old friend, unable to contain her joy. "Will I do?"

"Oh, very much so!" They embraced, cheek to cheek, Elizabeth Anne careful to protect the wedding dress. "You are the most beautiful bride I've ever seen."

"The second most beautiful bride I've ever encountered," Michael said gallantly, coming forward at last, beside the curate.

His wife blushed and smiled at him. "Thank you, dear heart. Girls, you must find your seats now, quickly."

The two disappeared into the church rapidly, banging the side door in their haste. The organ inside started repeating arpeggios, stalling until it could announce Jessamyn's arrival.

Michael hastened to catch the door and ease it shut. "They'll probably dance the night away, with all the newfound handsome young men." He smiled ruefully. "Is it time to begin, sir?"

The curate expertly assessed their readiness and nodded his satisfaction. Permission thus granted to proceed, he flung open the doors to the church and the organ swung into "The Rejoicing" from Handel's *Music for the Royal Fireworks*. Elizabeth Anne started down the long aisle, carrying her bouquet of roses, and Jessamyn took one last sniff of her roses for courage. If it had been left to her, she'd have flown down the aisle on wings of joy.

She stepped into the church on Michael's arm, and looked for Morgan. He stood at the front, dressed in an impeccably tailored black frock coat and charcoal gray trousers, William Donovan at his side. She smiled at her future husband and lifted her bouquet slightly, with its white roses—and a single red rose in the center from his mother's favorite rosebush at Longacres.

Morgan inclined his head, tears gleaming in his eyes, and touched his boutonniere made of matching red and white roses.

Then Michael patted her arm and they started down the long aisle, past the remarkably clean teamsters wearing city clothes. Grainger and Little, Lowell, Mitchell, Rutledge and Calhoun, and all the others. Past Cassiopeia, Aristotle, and Socrates with their families, including Cassiopeia and Aristotle's daughter, who looked just like Cassiopeia. Past her friends from the Army, splendid in dress uniforms, and their wives and families. Past all of the relatives, who were nudging each other and grinning, especially George, who'd been telling everyone for months that he alone was responsible for this match. She thought she could even see Cyrus, her father, and Morgan's parents, smiling proudly beside the masses of flowers. Everyone, living or dead, was a blur, compared to Morgan's gray eyes drawing her closer.

She loved all of the guests but she had difficulties appreciating Michael because he insisted on keeping to the same steady pace, rather than letting her run to Morgan.

At last Morgan's hand closed over hers, a smile trembling on his dear mouth. "Dear love," she whispered, so overcome by emotion that those simple syllables were all she could utter.

Joy flashed in his eyes and he kissed her hand. They turned to face the minister and gilded light poured over them like wings.

The ceremony's beautiful words wrapped around her, and she couldn't stop smiling at Morgan. It was a mercy that the minister announced everything she needed to say, because she had a very hard time tearing her eyes away from Morgan. Her voice wavered slightly when she pledged her vows, but his beautiful voice was strong and clear when he gave his vows, weaving magic around her.

She sighed, gazing into his eyes. Dear heavens, all he ever had to do was speak and she'd do anything for him. He smiled back at her, equally passionate in his silent pledge.

Elizabeth Anne nudged her. The minister repeated himself, granting permission for the groom to salute his bride. Morgan blinked, grinned wickedly, and crushed her against him. She flung her arms around his neck and kissed him with enthusiasm.

Hours later, Morgan brushed a kiss over Jessamyn's knuckles. "My dear lady wife, do you feel properly married now?"

"Not really, dear husband." She glanced up at the enormous and very ugly brick mansion he'd rented, which was dark except for a few lights on the top floor. Still, she hadn't wanted to return to a hotel after the ceremony and he'd respected that wish.

He raised an eyebrow. He'd loosened his cravat and unbuttoned his collar as soon as they'd entered the carriage, so he now presented a most appealing picture of masculine dishevelment. She'd taken off her hat at the same time and she suspected at least one of her ringlets was sliding down, given his attentions in the carriage. "Is that a challenge, my dear?"

"Would I dare to challenge you?"

He hooted in derision and picked her up in his arms, tossing her train across her lap. From this close, he smelled of sweat from that last wild polka. And musk, too, both scents she was sure would grow stronger very soon.

"You will always ensure that I behave as you consider best," he retorted.

She smiled at him demurely and wrapped her arm around his neck. "As you will do for me."

"Always," he agreed, his eyes twinkling.

The great carved door swung open at the head of the stairs, revealing a liveried butler with a lantern. Morgan carried her up them effortlessly, his heart beating steadily against her cheek like the pledges they'd taken that afternoon. She kissed him on the cheek, wishing strongly that they were already upstairs. The butler, who was clearly startled at their behavior, stood aside for them when they entered and shut the door behind them.

But Morgan didn't stop: he continued up the great, massive staircase. Jessamyn squeaked, "Put me down!"

He ignored her.

She hit him on the chest. "Morgan, put me down. Dammit, Morgan, I want a wedding night, not a contest for who can pant loudest!"

"I'm stronger than that," he averred without breaking stride.

She thumped him again. "Are you? I have been planning a very long wedding night. What were you thinking of?"

He slowed down.

"We're at five thousand feet," she teased him and began to unbutton his shirt for additional emphasis. She wiggled two fingers inside and found his collarbone. So very close to his heartbeat, the sign of the lover's life she'd almost lost in the San Juan Mountains. She shivered at the memory and undid a few more buttons. "A very, very active wedding night."

He came to a stop on the landing. "We'd reach the bedroom faster if I carried you."

"We'll both be stronger if we run together." She traced his dear, stubborn jaw.

"You have a magical way of stating our partnership, Mrs. Evans." He kissed her fingers and set her on the ground, sliding her along his body so she felt the full force of his desire. "And I, too, would prefer a very long wedding night."

He caught her by the hand and began to run, barely giving her enough time to snatch her train up. She leapt up the stairs with him, delighted that he was holding back just enough to let her match her pace to his. They reached their suite together and he shouldered the doors open, swinging her up and over the threshold in a wild tumult of silken flounces and petticoats. "Morgan!"

He looked down at her, unrepentant and not quite laughing as much. "I want all the superstitions on our side tonight, Jessamyn."

She blinked back unexpected tears, standing before him in the great master suite. "We have them, dearest. We have all the love and the luck tonight as we never did before. Besides, who could want for anything in a room like this?" She gestured, indicating the entire space.

The master suite was an amazing cross between a medieval hunting lodge and a Gothic fantasy, with hanging tapestries, ornately carved beams and matching furniture, a fireplace large enough to roast a calf in, and oriental carpets on the floor. A bottle of champagne awaited them in a silver cooler, with frosty beads sliding down its sides, beside a great bowl of red and white roses. The immense four-poster bed was bedecked with still more tapestries, a silk coverlet and sheets. Furs were tossed across the coverlet and the carpets, while small golden lanterns hung from the ceilings and walls. A couple of small coal furnaces hid in the corners, keeping the temperature toasty enough for an Arabian prince.

They'd never slept in this room before, choosing to save it for the first night when their union would be blessed by the church. The first time when they hoped to make a child.

"A palace for my princess," Morgan said softly and cupped her cheek. "But we'll break ground on your San Francisco house next spring."

"A new beginning," she agreed, threading her fingers into his thick chestnut hair. It was warm and soft against her skin, as vibrant as he was.

Morgan kissed her hand, his gray eyes glinting at her wickedly. "Shall we drink a toast to that with iced champagne, my dear? Or are you perfectly comfortable buttoned up to the throat and down to the wrist?"

"Are *you* comfortable, my dear?" she teased. "Would you rather I insisted that you wear your long johns until dawn?"

She chuckled at his look of mock horror and caught his face between her hands. "You silly, silly husband. Of course I want to see you without clothing." She reached up to kiss him and found herself crushed in his arms.

He kissed her boldly, hungrily, claiming her as if they'd never tasted each other before. She responded eagerly, her lips parting for him and her tongue surging into his mouth. She moaned, sighing his name greedily. She needed Morgan the way she needed air to breathe.

But his damn starched collar was in the way and those pearl studs down the front of his shirt were ridiculous. Beautiful, but an intolerable imposition when a woman wanted to touch her husband. She pulled away and started unbuttoning him as rapidly as possible, her head down and her eyes focused on her task.

"Jessamyn," Morgan purred in that deep, dark voice of his that always made her knees turn weak and her heart melt, "why are you paying so much attention to my buttons and not my mouth?"

"Because they're stopping me from touching your chest," she snapped and yanked his coat off. She eyed his braces suspiciously, decided they just might be acceptable for the moment, and pulled his shirt open. Morgan stood with his fists on his hips, watching her, with a very promising bulge growing behind his trousers. She palmed it and closed her eyes, humming approvingly at its hot throb against her hand.

"Jessamyn." His voice was a trifle rough.

"Hmm?" She fanned her fingers over his cock and sighed. She could probably still wrap her hand around it so it wasn't fully erect. But it was already truly magnificent.

He coughed hard, several times before he spoke. "What about that long wedding night you wanted?"

"Hmmm . . ." She fondled him again and he jerked against her.

"Jessamyn," he growled warningly.

A small damp spot was starting to appear close to his waistband. She sniffed, regretting the necessity to remove her hand. But perhaps if they both undressed quickly . . .

She stepped away and unpinned her hat. "The first one undressed gets to tongue the other, agreed?"

"You must have fifty or more buttons, Jessamyn," Morgan pointed out, wrenching off his cuff links.

"Are you claiming an advantage?" Thankfully, she'd taken off her kid gloves in the carriage. She began to undo the tiny buttons on her cuffs. With luck, she'd have them out of the way and most of the ones on her tunic before he was undressed. Then she could have the fun of being pleasured and disrobed by him, without worrying about too much damage to her elegant dress.

"Not at all," he denied, dropping his pearl studs and cuff links into a tray. He pulled off his boots with more haste than style, a technique he employed on the rest of his clothing and which Jessamyn heartily approved of.

She was still unbuttoning her tunic when he faced her, gloriously nude and urgently erect. "How the devil can I claim my winnings, madame wife, when you're still so completely covered?"

She pouted at him and continued work on the recalcitrant buttons. He clucked, his eyes alight with laughter. "Dearest Jessamyn, you simply lack the proper education."

"Which you, no doubt, have as a thorough reprobate," she retorted.

"Exactly." He strolled over to the champagne cooler, providing an excellent view of his bobbing cock. She considered his dimensions, the potential of the beautiful branching vein as a roadmap to his most sensitive spots—and realized that she'd stopped moving. She cursed silently and went back to work, her fingers itching to wrap around his warm skin rather than lifeless buttons.

He opened the champagne expertly and filled a glittering crystal flute. Finally finished with the tunic, she glared at him.

"Allow me, madame," he bowed and handed her the champagne.

She accepted it suspiciously. He drew the tunic off her as efficiently and swiftly as any lady's maid, and tossed it into a corner.

"Morgan!" she objected.

He nibbled her bare shoulder in precisely the place where she was most sensitive, then licked it. She moaned, her eyelids drooping in anticipation. "You're wicked."

"Exactly," he agreed smugly and nibbled her again.

She opened one eye just enough to consider her champagne. This wedding night would definitely be extremely enjoyable. She took a long drink of the golden bubbles and tried not to contemplate leaping on him.

He ran his fingers up and down her spine. "Too many layers, I think," he remarked, slipping a single finger down the waistband of her overskirt. He wiggled it. Jessamyn moaned when it found the seam of her backside. How had the reprobate found the one place where he could touch bare skin by delving between layers?

It was all she could do not to whimper when he removed it to unbutton her overskirt. Or sob a plea for more when he teased her by drawing up her skirts over her flanks to remove her underskirt and petticoats, then stroking the delicate flesh of her inner thighs.

By the time Morgan had removed her petticoats, Jessamyn's heart was pounding loudly enough to be heard in Memphis. Her skin was flushed and tight, her nipples rasping eagerly against her fine silk chemise, desperate for his touch. All she wore now was her chemise, corset, and drawers. It was a wonder that her knees could still hold her up, yet somehow she eyed him seductively as he paced around her like a jungle cat. "Do you like what you see, husband?"

"Hell, yes," he growled and pulled her up to him by the shoulders. "You're mine now, Jessamyn, do you hear? Mine."

She threw back her head, her curls tumbling down her back. "Entirely yours, Morgan, as you are mine," she agreed huskily. Her core clenched and burned with longing for him.

His eyes roved over her desperately. "Dear God, how I have dreamed of you looking like this for me." He pulled her to him, crushing her against him, and her corset slipped open, his great strength having popped the steel busk's studs undone in front. Her breasts slipped free and rubbed against the wall of his chest. She gasped, shuddering as lust speared her from breast to groin. Morgan was her rock—yet all he had to do was touch her and he set her free to passion.

He flung her corset aside and stroked her back, his hips pushing against hers. Hunger rose higher in her, melting her senses until all she could feel or see was Morgan. Dearest Morgan, who'd risked his life for her dream.

She wrapped her leg around his and rubbed herself against him desperately. Her rhythm matched the one in her blood, in her hips, in his hands' hot caresses over her derrière, in his broken breathing. "Morgan, dearest Morgan . . ."

He ripped her chemise off, her fine Parisian chemise whose ribbons matched her wedding dress. Yet all she wondered was why it had taken him so long, and she clawed at him for more kisses.

He tossed her up on the bed, across the great bear skin, and ripped off her matching Parisian drawers. The fur was silky soft against her back, while the coverlet's embroidery rasped gently against her legs. She gasped in approval at finally being naked, her world narrowed to the big chestnut-haired man in the golden light above her. The only thoughts she had now were primal instinct, focused solely on completion in his arms.

He stared at her, panting, his cock richly crimson, swollen and dripping with his seed. For the first time, he made no effort to cover himself with a condom. Finally she'd feel the full glory of his skin and his seed. She smiled and held out her arms to him.

He came onto her in a rush that sent her sliding halfway across the bed. She locked her arms and legs around him, clinging to her lifeline where he held it in his heartbeat. His cock pulsed against her belly, his balls fat and heavy against her mound, swollen with seed for her womb. His rich musk scented the room, mixed with hers and their sweat. *Morgan, ah Morgan . . .*

He shifted, coming up onto his knees over her. His eyes met hers; hunger sparked and grew between them, as well as total understanding of the other's need. Hunger for the other, body and soul, plus the hope of a child rising in both of them.

His first thrusts were slow and careful. She objected strenuously with her voice and her arms and legs and her strong inner muscles. She wanted hard and fast. She wanted to see his eyes glaze over when he lost control in rapture.

"Jessamyn," he groaned, his neck muscles taut and his eyes closed. His hips pulsed against her.

She rippled her sheath around him, pulling him back in.

He snarled again, wordlessly, and plunged deep. She cried out in pleasure and clung to him, aiding him in every way she could. Her dearest, dearest husband.

He pulled out more slowly and drove in more quickly, grunting with effort. Wet slaps filled the room as their bodies worked together, striving for the pinnacle. Climax was close, so close, yet worth very little if not attained by both of them.

Morgan reached down between them and began to rub her pearl, using the stroke that always drove her wild. Jessamyn's vision blurred and her breath caught in her throat. Rapture surged higher and higher. The pulses in her womb built and tightened more and more around his cock until suddenly orgasm swept her over, crashing through her as if she'd fallen over a mountain waterfall.

Her climax irresistibly demanded Morgan's. He howled her name as he extravagantly jetted his seed into her over and over again, until it melted onto her thigh with her cream.

He fondled her pearl again, and to her shock, she climaxed again just as strongly, sobbing his name as stars spun through her head. She collapsed against him afterward, too exhausted to do more than try to catch her breath.

Morgan gathered her against him and eased them both under the covers. She buried her face against his shoulder as sleep warmed her bones. "Love you, husband."

"Love you, wife." He twined his legs between hers comfortably. "I'll be underfoot more than you expected in San Francisco."

She immediately opened her eyes. Her Southern devil had the most dreadful habit of raising important subjects exactly when anyone else would be asleep. "What do you mean?"

His eyes twinkled at her wickedly. "William has offered me a partnership. Grainger will be taking over my troubleshooter duties for Donovan & Sons so I won't be traveling as often."

She came up on her elbow to stare at him. "You'll be home?" Her voice rose to an embarrassing squeak but she ignored it. "Often?"

"As often as possible, madame wife." His gray eyes glinted at her. "I want that big family as much as you do."

She flung herself across him. "I love you, Morgan!"

He caught her to his heart. "And I'll always love you, Jessamyn dearest."

Author's Note

Beginning in 1867, Memphis, Tennessee, was decimated by a series of cholera and yellow fever epidemics (then known as yellow jack), which killed more than 5,000 residents and caused nearly half its population to flee. The city went bankrupt and surrendered its charter in 1879.

With the aid of Robert Church, a former slave and the nation's first African-American millionaire, Memphis was able to prevent future epidemics by drastic and farsighted sanitary reforms, and a new city charter was granted in 1893.

Today, Memphis thrives once again, highlighted by the status of its international airport as the world's largest cargo airport. It also still ranks among the nation's busiest inland river ports.

Don't miss this sneak peek at
Shannon McKenna's
HOT NIGHT.
Coming in October 2006 from Brava . . .

Abby was floating. The sensual heft of Zan's black leather jacket felt wonderful over her shoulders, even though it hung halfway down to her thighs.

They'd reached the end of the boardwalk, where the lights began to fade. Beyond the boardwalk, the warehouse district began. They'd walked the whole boardwalk, talking and laughing, and at some point, their hands had swung together and sort of just . . . stuck. Warmth seeking warmth. Her hand tingled joyfully in his grip.

The worst had happened. Aside from his sex appeal, she simply liked him. She liked the way he laughed, his turn of phrase, his ironic sense of humor. He was smart, honest, earthy, funny. Maybe, just maybe, she could trust herself this time.

Their strolling slowed to a stop at the end of the boardwalk.

"Should we, ah, walk back to your van?" she ventured.

"This is where I live," he told her.

She looked around. "Here? But this isn't a residential district."

"Not yet," he said. "It will be soon. See that building over there? It used to be a factory of some kind, in the twenties, I think. The top floor, with the big arched windows, that's my place."

There was just enough light to make out the silent question in his eyes. She exhaled slowly. "Are you going to invite me up, or what?"

"You know damn well that you're invited," he said. "More than invited. I'll get down on my knees and beg, if you want me to."

The full moon appeared in a window of scudding clouds, then disappeared again. "It wouldn't be smart," she said. "I don't know you."

"I'll teach you," he offered. "Crash course in Zan Duncan. What do you want to know? Hobbies, pet peeves, favorite leisure activities?"

She would put it to the test of her preliminary checklist, and make her decision based on that. "Don't tell me," she said. "Let me guess. You're a martial arts expert, right?"

"Uh, yeah. Aikido is my favorite discipline. I like kung fu, too."

She nodded, stomach clenching. There it was, the first black mark on the no-nos checklist. Though it was hardly fair to disqualify him for that, since he'd saved her butt with those skills the night before.

So that one didn't count. On to the next no-no. "Do you have a motorcycle?"

He looked puzzled. "Several of them. Why? Want to go for a ride?"

Abby's heart sank. "No. One last question. Do you own guns?"

Zan's face stiffened. "Wait. Are these trick questions?"

"You do, don't you?" she persisted.

"My late father was a cop." His voice had gone hard. "I have his service Beretta. And I have a hunting rifle. Why? Are you going to talk yourself out of being with me because of superficial shit like that?"

Abby's laugh felt brittle. "Superficial. That's Abby Mait-land."

"No, it is not," he said. "That's not Abby Maitland at all."

"You don't know the first thing about me, Zan."

"Yes, I do." His dimple quivered. "I know first things, second things, third things. You've got piss-poor taste in boyfriends, to start."

Abby was stung. "Those guys were not my boyfriends! I didn't even know them! I've just had a run of bad luck lately!"

"Your luck is about to change, Abby." His voice was low and velvety. "I know a lot about you. I know how to get into your apartment. How to turn your cat into a noodle. The magnets on your fridge, the view from your window. Your perfume. I could find you blindfolded in a room full of strangers." His fingers penetrated the veil of her hair, his forefinger stroking the back of her neck with controlled gentleness. "And I learn fast. Give me ten minutes, and I'd know lots more."

"Oh," she breathed. His hand slid through her hair, settled on her shoulder. The delicious heat burned her, right through his jacket.

"I know you've got at least two of those expensive dresses that drive guys nuts. And I bet you've got more than two. You've got a whole closet full of hot little outfits like that. Right?" He cupped her jaw, turning her head until she was looking into his fathomless eyes.

Her heart hammered. "I've got a . . . a pretty nice wardrobe, yes."

"I'd like to see them." His voice was sensual. "Someday maybe you can model them all for me. In the privacy of your bedroom."

"Zan—"

"I love it when you say my name," he said. "I love your

voice. Your accent. Based on your taste in dresses, I'm willing to bet that you like fancy, expensive lingerie, too. Am I right? Tell me I'm right."

"Time out," she said, breathless. "Let's not go there."

"Oh, but we've already arrived." His breath was warm against her throat. "Locksmiths are detail maniacs. Look at the palm of your hand, for instance. Here, let me see." He lifted her hand into the light from the nearest of the street-lamps. "Behold, your destiny."

It was silly and irrational, but it made her self-conscious to have him look at the lines on her hand. As if he actually could look right into her mind. Past, future, fears, mistakes, desires, all laid out for anyone smart and sensitive enough to decode it. "Zan. Give me my hand back."

"Not yet. Oh . . . wow. Check this out," he whispered.

"What?" she demanded.

He shook his head with mock gravity and pressed a kiss to her knuckles. "It's too soon to say what I see. I don't want to scare you off."

"Oh, please," she said unsteadily. "You are so full of it."

"And you're so scared. Why? I'm a righteous dude. Good as gold." He stroked her wrist. "Ever try cracking a safe without drilling it? It's a string of numbers that never ends. Hour after hour, detail after detail. That's concentration." He pressed his lips against her knuckles.

"What does concentration have to do with anything?"

"It has everything to do with everything. That's what I want to do to you, Abby. Concentrate, intensely, minutely. Hour after hour, detail after detail. Until I crack all the codes, find all the keys to all your secret places. Until I'm so deep inside you . . ." his lips kissed their way up her writst, ". . . that we're a single being."

She leaned against him and let him cradle her in his strong arms. His warm lips coaxed her into opening to the gentle, sensual exploration of his tongue. "Come up with me," he whispered. "Please."

She nodded. Zan's arm circled her waist, fitting her body against his. It felt so right. No awkardness, no stumbling, all smooth. Perfect.

Take a look at
OUT OF THIS WORLD
by Jill Shalvis.
Available now from Brava!

"What the hell happened?" he demanded. A few drops of water fell off the tip of his nose onto my face. "Why are you lying on the ground? *Are you okay?*"

Was I okay? Hmm, wasn't that the question of the hour? Trying to figure out that very thing, I looked back up into the sky, watching the raindrops coming down, one by one. Wow, it was really beautiful.

Every part of everything around me seemed deeper, more colorful, richer . . .

More intense.

"Rach?" Kellan tossed aside his glasses and leaned over me, protecting me with his body, stroking my hair from my face. "You're silent. You're never silent."

A bird flew overhead, and when I concentrated on its body, its wings flapping, I found I could see its heart pumping, beating . . .

Oh.

My.

God.

"*Rach.*"

"I think I broke a nail," I whispered.

He stared at me. "Tell me you're kidding."

"I'm kidding." I lifted my hand and studied my plain, trimmed-by-my-own-teeth nails.

"You're scaring me, Rach. Here, can you sit up?" He took my hand to pull me upright, then steadied me, his hands firm on my upper arms. "Are you all right?"

Without his lenses, his eyes were so clear and blue, I could have just looked at him all day long.

Wow. Gorgeous.

I wobbled, then set my head against his chest. Beneath the drenched shirt, his heart beat a bit fast but steadily, and he was warm, deliriously warm. Sturdy and solid and always-there Kel.

He extended his arms, pushing me back, so he could peer into my face. Man, he was cute. I smiled up at him dreamily, thinking I'd no idea just how cute . . . and while thinking it, a shiver wracked me. Probably it was the cold, but it might have been the totally and completely inappropriate surge of lust I was experiencing.

Kel kept his hands on me, drawing me back against his warm body, making me all the more aware of him, of his sweet but firm touch, of the strength that allowed him to easily take on my weight. I sighed in pleasure.

"You're scaring the shit out of me, Rach."

"Did you know you have the most amazing eyes?"

They narrowed on me. "Huh?"

"Seriously," I said, reaching up, touching his face, which was wet from the rain. "I could drown in 'em. Anyone ever told you that?"

"Uh, no. You're the first. Hold on there, champ," he said when I tried to get up, holding me down with a hand to the middle of my chest. "Don't move."

Good idea, since everything had begun to swim. I put my hands to my head. "What happened to me?"

"That's what I was going to ask you."

He was so cute with all his worry that it made me smile. "Kel? How come we've never gone out?"

"Out?"

"Hooked up."

He went still, then lifted two fingers. "Okay, how many?" he demanded.

"I'm fine," I insisted.

"I thought we were erasing that word from the English language."

I tried to stand up on my own. "Whoa." I reached for him, because maybe I wasn't so okay after all. "Hey, stop the world, would ya? I want to get off."

"You're dizzy?" He gripped my shoulders. "What the hell happened? Did you fall?"

I closed my eyes. But just like on the plane, that only made it worse, so I opened them again. I focused on a tree. Again, I saw right through the tree, as if I had X-ray vision, meaning I could still see the long line of carpenter ants making their way through the trunk. I followed their line down to the ground, where they emerged from a hole only a few inches from me.

One crawled out near my foot, and I would have sworn on my own grave that it craned its neck and glared at me for being in its way. I stared at it, stunned. "Uh . . . Kellan?"

"Jesus," he breathed, and for a minute my heart surged, thinking he could see through stuff, too, but he shook his head and pointed at my clothes.

They were smoking.

"You were hit by lightning," he said, and looked into my face. "My God. Are you okay?"

His eyes still seemed luminous, and filled with far more worry than before. I dropped my gaze from his, and then gasped.

Like with the moon, like with the tree, I could see through him. As in *beneath his clothes*.

Um, yeah, I was definitely different.

"I can't believe it," he said. "I mean, what are the chances?" Leaning in again, he began to run his hands over my limbs. Up my legs, over my hips, over my ribs—

"What are you doing?"

Take a look at Rosemary Laurey's
"In Bad With Someone" in
TEXAS BAD BOYS,
Available now from Brava . . .

Anger, shock and a touch of fury propelled Rod across the road with just a quick "Gotta go!" to his buddies. He pushed open the door and looked around *his* bar. What the hell was Mary-Beth playing at? The two suits were getting ready to leave. Maude Wilson and her cronies were playing rummy as they did most afternoons, practicing character assassination as they bet for nickel points. The only other occupant was the sharp-looking redhead he'd noticed earlier walking up Center Street.

Her perky little butt was poised on one of the counter stools while she ate . . . he walked closer . . . a burger and onion rings. A bacon burger with Swiss.

Cold rage at Pete's double-dealing clenched Rod's gut. Still not quite believing. Suspecting some twisted joke, Rod met Mary-Beth's eyes. She shifted them sideways to the redhead.

Shit!

Okay, deep breath here. He could hardly yank her lovely butt off the stool and slug her one. His mama had taught him better than that but dammit, what did she think she was doing claiming his bar as her own? Might as well find out.

Giving Mary-Beth a warning glance to stay cool, he took the stool nearest Madame Bar Snatcher. "Hey, there Mary-Beth. How about pulling me a nice, cold beer."

"I'm sorry. Excuse me," the redhead said and moved her pocketbook, giving him a glimpse of deep, green eyes before she turned back to her onion rings, cut one in four, stabbed it with the fork and chewed carefully.

Snob and prissy wasn't in it! Nice boobs though. Not that it was likely to do him any good. Her hair was something else though: the color of new pennies, and cut short in a mass of curls. He itched to reach out and let a strand of hair curl over his fingers. Pity it came with a bar snatcher attached.

"Here you are, Rod." Mary-Beth set his glass down with a thud . . . and a smirk. "Anything else I can get you?"

"Fine, thanks. This is just what I need."

She rolled her eyes and proceeded to refill Miss Prissy's ice water. What exactly Mary-Beth had done to earn that wide smile he'd like to know, but it did enable him to catch Miss Prissy's eye.

"Howdy!"

"Good afternoon," she replied, with a little nod.

"Enjoying Silver Gulch?" he asked before she had a chance to chop up another onion ring.

She paused as if weighing up whether to snub him or not. "It's interesting. Smaller than I imagined but . . ." She gave him the oddest look as her mouth twitched at the corner. "Definitely fascinating."

"Here on a visit or just passing through town?" He asked, nicely casual, as he lifted his glass and took a drink.

She smiled, almost chuckled. Her green eyes crinkling at the corners as she looked him in the eye. "I'll be staying, Mr. Carter."

Rod almost spluttered his Hefeweizen all over himself and the counter. He grabbed his handkerchief and wiped his mouth, thanking heaven he didn't have beer running out of his nose. Damn her! Damn the smug little smirk on her pretty face! And double damn Mary-Beth for setting him up like this!

"It wasn't Mary-Beth, so don't give her the evil eye like that."

Read minds could she? "How did you know who I was?"

"An educated guess, Mr. Carter. Gabe Rankin told me your name. Minutes after I identify myself to Mary-Beth you appear off the street where you were chatting. How many 'Rods' are there in a town this size?" While he digested that, she held out a slim, long-fingered hand. "I'm Juliet ffrench. My grandfather left me this building and the business."

"We'll see about that!"

He felt her green eyes watching him as he stormed out. Gabe Rankin had some explaining to do.

After twenty minutes cooling his heels to see Gabe and an acrimonious ten minutes face-to-face, Rod learned old man Maddock had done him dirty and given away the Rooster from under his feet.

"We had a deal!" Rod protested.

"I know you did," Gabe replied, shaking his head. "He knew it too. Said he had only three parcels of property and they had to go to his granddaughters. Said he'd make it right with you."

But the old codger had upended his fishing boat before he could. "So what now? I get kicked out after building up the business?"

"Now, calm down, Rod," Gabe went on. "It's not too bad. Part of the agreement was for Mizz ffrench to keep on all the employees." So he was an employee now, was he? "If you ask me, she'll not hang around long, whatever she's saying right now. You mark my words, give it a couple of months and she'll be back in London and you'll be running the Rooster just like always."

Not quite like always. He'd no longer be working for himself but prissy Mizz ffrench. "What if I just quit?" There was an idea!

Gabe waved his hands palms outermost and shook his head. "Now don't you start making hasty decisions, Rod. Why not bide your time and see how things go? The Rooster wouldn't be the same without you." It would be anything without him and Gabe damn well knew it. "You just hold on a week or two. See how things work out between you and Miss ffrench.

Fat lot of help Gabe was.

Rod was even more steamed when he walked back into the Rooster, ready to hash out a few details with the new owner.

Who wasn't there.

Neither was Mary-Beth. Lucas, the cook, was standing in at the bar. Where the hell were they? Off doing each other's hair? And he'd been stupid enough to think Mary-Beth was on his side.

"Don't look so sour, boss," Lucas said.

"Where the hell is Mary-Beth? She's got two more hours of her shift."

"She took the new owner on the tour. Say, is she really old man Maddock's granddaughter?"

"Yes, Rod, we were wondering that." Old Maude and her cronies swooped on him like the furies. "Is it true? And Pete left her the Rooster. How nice!"

It wasn't nice and it got worse. Two days later, Juliet ffrench had settled in. There was no stopping her.

She could have stayed in the comparative comfort of Sally Jones's B&B, or even the Hunting Lodge just outside town, Miss ffrench insisted in moving in. Since the other apartments were boarded up and uninhabitable, she moved into his. After a night on the lumpy sofa, she drove into Pebble Creek and the next morning, carpet and furniture were delivered and she spent the afternoon hanging drapes and unpacking as she staked her claim on one of the empty rooms. His final objection that there was only one functioning bathroom, was met with a bland smile and the unblinking assurance not to worry, she promised not to use his razor to shave her legs.

A weaker man would have given up.

Rod Carter braced for survival. He'd outlast Juliet ffrench and be a gentleman about it.

Please turn the page for a preview of the next book in
Jessica Inclán's marvelous, magical trilogy
REASON TO BELIEVE,
a Zebra trade paperback available next month.

Fabia opened her door, quickly running down the hall and stairs and then pushing out onto the street. The temperature had dropped even more than the report had predicted, Fabia's cheeks flushed from the slick slap of cold air. Rubbing her gloved hands together, she walked toward the man, slowing as she neared him.

"Hello," she said softly, blinking against the streetlight.

He stared at her—no, past her—his face expressionless. His face was smudged with dirt, a deep, dark red scratch running from temple to jaw, one eye blackened. Blood swelled the skin under his eye and hung in a painful purple moon over his cheek. As Fabia moved closer, she realized that his hair wasn't so much matted from the wet, dank air as from dried blood. There was a clear, perfect circle of reddish, broken skin around his neck, and she noticed now that the dirt she'd seen under his nails this morning was actually blood.

Whatever had happened, he'd fought back. Whoever he'd fought with probably looked as bad as he.

"Are you all right?"

The man turned to her, tried to look up, and then took a deep breath, his mouth trying to move. He was trembling, his arms tight against his body now, his black eyes filled with fog and sadness. Again, she tried to reach for his mind, but the iron wall was still there, planted solidly.

What do you think? Fabia asked Niall without even meaning to.

All that blood, Niall thought. *Maybe it's not his. Moyenne are messy murderers.*

He hardly looks capable of a right killing, Fabia thought.

True. He didn't do his level best, there. So he might be on the lam. Injured from the barbed wire he crawled under, Niall thought. *Just call the police.*

Fabia stared at the man, ignoring Niall for a moment. Maybe she couldn't read the man's mind, but there was something about him. Something kind even in his quiet, painful desperation.

Bloody bleeding heart, Niall thought. *But just be ready to escape. Be prepared to step into the gray, okay? Hop back to your flat.*

Yes, sir, Fabia thought, shaking her head. But Niall was right. It was easier to extend this kindness knowing that if the man grew strange or crazy or even dangerous, she could disappear in an instant, traveling through matter to the police station where she could report the crime she'd just escaped. The *Moyenne* she worked with at the clinic were always amazed that Fabia would go to flophouses and tenements and dark alleys looking for clients. What she couldn't tell them was that she was protecting them by doing so, keeping them away from danger from which they might not be able to escape.

Fabia bent down, trying to attract his gaze. But he wouldn't look at her, and she could feel the tension radiating from inside him.

"Hi, there," she said. My name's Fabia Fair. I live at the flat just down a bit."

He didn't move his eyes, but he blinked, once, twice.

"Would you like to come with me?" Fabia said, crouching down further and looking into the man's desperate, searching eyes. "How about a wee bit to eat?"

He licked his lips, breathing in, scanning the ground as if

he'd dropped some change. *Not drunk,* Fabia thought. *Schizo-phrenic.*

Perfect, Niall thought. *Go from Cadeyrn to just another crazy. Get yourself into another fankle.*

Haver on, man! Would you mind affording me some space here? she thought back. *Go watch your bleeding telly.*

Fabia closed her mind to her brother and moved closer to the man. He was shaking, his knees hitting together. Again, he moved his mouth, but then shook his head, tears streaming from the corners of his eyes.

Fabia watched him, trying everything she knew to get inside his mind, but there was no opening, as if the block was put there on purpose. And not by the man, who clearly was in no shape to create or even maintain a block, even if he were *Croyant,* magic, like her. And there was something about him, even with his quaking gaze and his long, thin, dirty body. Fabia couldn't read his mind, but she could feel . . . kindness.

"All right," Fabia said. "That's it. Please, come with me."

She stood up straight and held out her hand. The man breathed in, looking at her hand and then her face, her hand, her face, and then slowly, he lifted his dirty palm from his knee, studying his movements with surprise as if he'd never moved before. His fingers quivered, shook, and Fabia took them in her small gloved hand, feeling how cold he was even through the leather and wool.

Shit, she thought to herself, hating how *Moyenne* treated their castaways, knowing that in her world, the world of *Les Croyants des Trois,* this man would have food and a bath and a bed, no matter what was wrong with him. Adalbert Baird made sure of that, finding places for the damaged and weak—the only people who escaped his care were the ones who disdained it. Like Caderyn Macara. Like Quain Dalzeil. And what will happen if Quain wins, she thought.

We'll end up like this poor sod, Niall thought.

Shut it, Fabia thought and clutched the man's hand more tightly.

"Come on," she said. "Don't be scared."

But the man was scared. More than scared. She felt his fear in the energy coming off his body, in the sizzling whites of his distracted eyes, in his stiff, hesitant walk. Who had done this to him? What had happened?

"It's all right," Fabia said, her hand holding his as they walked slowly to the door of her building. "You'll be fine."

He turned to look at her, his black eyes so dark she couldn't see the irises. His forehead was creased with worry, his face gray with cold and hunger and fear. Despite the filth on his clothing, the blood on his head and body, and clearly distressed mind, Fabia wanted to stop, pull him to her, and comfort him.